The Forgery
Or, Best Intentions

by

G. P. R. James

Double 9
BOOKS

The Forgery
Or, Best Intentions
by G. P. R. James

ISBN: 978-93-61422-67-6

Published by

DOUBLE 9 BOOKS

2/13-B, Ansari Road
Daryaganj, New Delhi – 110002
info@double9books.com
www.double9books.com
Tel. 011-40042856

ABOUT THE AUTHOR

George Payne Rainsford James, a London-born novelist and historian, was born on August 9, 1799, and died on June 9, 1860. He served as the British Consul for a long time in a number of locations across the continent and in the United States. During the final years of William IV's reign, he was the honorary British Historiographer Royal. In 1799, George Payne Rainsford James was born in London's Hanover Square on St. George Street. His father was a doctor who had been in the navy and had fought alongside Benedict Arnold in the Battle of Groton Heights in America during the Revolutionary War. James went to the Putney school run by Reverend William Carmalt. He became passionate in learning new languages, such as Arabic, Persian, Greek, and Latin. When he was younger, he also studied medicine, but his preferences took him in a different way. His father, who had served in the navy himself, opposed his desire to enlist, which ultimately led to him being able to enlist in the army. James was injured in a minor battle after the Battle of Waterloo and remained in the army for a brief period of time during the Hundred Days as a lieutenant.

CONTENTS

CHAPTER I

INTRODUCTORY

One of the finest characters in the world was the old English merchant. We may and have improved upon many things, but not upon that. A different spirit reigns in commerce from that which ruled it long ago, and not a better one. We are more the shopkeeper, as a celebrated but not a great man called us, and less the merchant. As a people, our commerce is more extended, but the separate transactions are smaller; and minute dealings almost always produce paltry minds. Not at all do I mean to say that the old English merchant is without his representatives; but they are fewer than in other times, both with reference to our numbers and to our extended trade.

There are many still, however, whose notions are as vast and as just as those of any of our ancestors; and amongst them, not very long ago, was a gentleman of the name of Humphrey Scriven. He was a highly-educated and naturally-gifted man, the son of wealthy and respectable parents in a class of society peculiar to England--the untitled country gentry; and he had been originally intended for the church. Circumstances, however, are to most men fate. He became acquainted, by some mere accident, with the only daughter of a rich merchant--admired, loved her, and won her love in return. He was a younger son; but, nevertheless, her father was a kind and liberal man, and he consented to their marriage upon one condition: that Mr. Scriven should abandon his intention of entering the church, and become a merchant like himself. He fancied that he had perceived in the young man a peculiar aptitude for business, and he was not mistaken. Mr. Scriven became his son-in-law, his partner, and his successor; and well did he bear up the name and honour of the house.

It was a fine thing to see him, some twenty years after his marriage, when, with the business of the day over, he sat in his splendid house in St. James's Square, surrounded by his family, and often associated with the noblest and the proudest of the land. His wife was no longer living, but she had left him four very handsome children. She had herself been remarkably beautiful, and her husband was as fine a looking man as eye could see--tall, graceful, vigorous, and possessing that air of dignity which springs from dignity of mind. From the moment that five o'clock struck, Mr. Scriven cast off all thought and care of business; for, though there were, of course, with him as with other men engaged in similar pursuits, fluctuations and changes, bad speculations, failing debtors, and wrecked ships, still his transactions were too extensive for the loss of a few thousand pounds here or there to weigh upon his mind; and, being of a cheerful and happy disposition, he spread sunshine through his dwelling.

His family, at the time of which I speak, consisted of three daughters and one son, who was born some four or five years after the youngest sister. The daughters were all lovely, kind, affectionate, and gentle in disposition, very much alike in person, and so nearly of an age that it was difficult to tell which was the eldest. There was indeed some difference in character, in point of force and vigour of reason, but the spirit and the heart were the same. Maria, the eldest, was a girl of much good sense, but of a very humble appreciation of her own qualities and advantages. She thought little of her beauty and less of her wealth, and her humility mere worldly-minded people looked upon as weakness. Isabella, the second, though neither haughty nor presuming, was of a far more decided and independent nature; but Margaret, the third, was all gentle kindness, with much less mere intellect than either of her sisters. She had sense enough and principle enough never to do anything that was wrong, but not enough worldly wisdom to guard her own interests against her affections. The son was at this time a boy of fifteen--a sharp, clever lad, who had been a good deal petted by his mother, and had been taught by circumstances to attach more importance to the possession of wealth than it deserves.

In great things Mr. Scriven seldom made mistakes; in small ones he often did; and one of his mistakes was in not looking upon trifles in education as important. Perhaps it is there alone that they really are important; for every idea received in youth has a vast development in maturity. The seed may be small and insignificant in appearance; but, once sown, it is sure to grow, and may spread to a great tree.

The father destined his boy to succeed him in his counting-house. Though very wealthy, he had no inclination that his son should spend the fruit of his ancestors' labours in idleness. He had a great idea of the dignity of commerce; and Henry Scriven was taught from his earliest years that he was to be a merchant. He was educated with that view, and early initiated into business matters. Could Mr. Scriven himself have given up his time and attention to the lad, he might have acquired, with all the practical details, great views and noble purposes; but his father's time was necessarily greatly occupied, and he also felt some doubts as to his parental fondness leaving his judgment room to act in the case of his own child. At the age of fifteen, then, he sent him to receive the rudiments of a mercantile education with the correspondent of his house at Hamburg. This correspondent was known to be a good man of business, but he was no more than that; and pinning his pupil down to small details, and accustoming him to his own limited views of commerce, he narrowed all his habits of thought, while he gave vast development to certain germs of selfishness which were in the boy's own nature. His principles were always to gain something off every transaction; never to leave a penny unproductive; to buy in the cheapest and sell in the dearest market; to look to his pence, knowing that his pounds would take care of themselves; and, being a merchant, to regard everything with a mercantile eye. He held that no merchant should marry till he could retire from business. Indeed, he regarded marriage, like everything else, as "a transaction," and one quite incompatible with the conduct of a great commercial house. Such lessons always have their effect--the pupil sometimes going beyond, sometimes falling short of his master.

What were the impressions produced upon Henry Scriven will be seen very soon; but, in the mean time, his eldest sister, Maria, married. She made her own choice, and that without ambition having any share in it. The gentleman whom she selected was amiable, somewhat eccentric, but a man of high honour and much feeling. He was the second son of one of Mr. Scriven's oldest friends and fellow-merchants, and Maria's father had but one objection. It had been arranged that Mr. Henry Marston was to go out to India, with a sufficient capital to establish a house in relation with that of his father in London. Mr. Scriven did not like the idea of his daughter going to India at all; but he knew that people are the only judges of their own happiness; and, as Maria had made up her mind, he threw no impediment in the way. Shortly after Henry Scriven's return from Hamburg, where he staid two years, the marriage of his second sister, Isabella, took place. In this instance there could be no objection on any part, as the man she chose was just the sort of person whom such a girl might be expected to prefer. He was about ten years older than herself, good-tempered, but remarkably firm, cheerful without being merry, generous without being extravagant. His property was ample; for his father, the third baronet, had left him a large and unencumbered estate, and his mother a very considerable sum in the public funds. Thus Isabella became the wife of Sir Edward Monkton; but, as his property lay at no great distance from London, her separation from her family was not so complete as that of her sister Maria.

The youngest of the three sisters remained longer unmarried, although she was fully as attractive, both in person and manners, as her sisters. Nor was it that there was a lack of applicants for her hand; for some four or five unexceptionable men proposed to her, and were at once and steadily rejected, much to their own surprise and to that of the lookers-on. She was so gentle, so affectionate, so easily led, so over-anxious for the happiness and welfare of others, that everybody had supposed her heart would be carried at the first assault. Perhaps, indeed, it was, and this might be the cause of her remaining single to the age of twenty-four.

There was at that time moving in the highest ranks of English society a Sir John Fleetwood, who realized completely the idea of "a man of wit and pleasure about town." He had served with some distinction in the army, though he had not seen more than thirty summers; was very handsome, very lively, with a smart repartee always ready, a slightly supercilious air towards all men but his own choice companions, and a manner most engaging to all women whom he thought it worth his while to please. He had towards them an easy familiarity which did not in the least savour of vulgar impertinence--a constant display of little attentions, which seemed to show that the person who received them was occupying all his thoughts--a protecting kindness of tone, with a musical voice, and a habit of speaking low. He danced with Margaret the first time she ever appeared at a large party; he danced with her again, and then he obtained an introduction to her father. Mr. Scriven received him coldly, much to the poor girl's mortification--it might almost, indeed, be called repulsively; and as he saw that Margaret was not only surprised by his unusual demeanour to her handsome partner, but more vexed than he could have desired, her father judged it best to explain his motives at once.

"You were astonished, my love," he said, as they were driving home, "at my coolness towards Sir John Fleetwood; but I do not wish to encourage any intimacy between him and any of my family, and I wish to make him feel at once that it cannot be. I know him, Margaret, to be a bad man, as well as an imprudent man; and I should be incurring too great a responsibility were I to suffer him to visit at my house. He has had every advantage in life--family, fortune, education--and he has misused them all."

Margaret was silent for a moment or two; but then she said--

"How do you wish me then to behave to him when we meet, as must often be the case, I suppose? He will certainly ask me to dance, and then I shall not know how to act after what you have said."

"The customs of society, my dear child, will prevent your refusing to dance with him, unless engaged to another," her father replied; "but I should wish you to be as often engaged as possible, and not to suffer any approach to intimacy that you can avoid."

Margaret to the best of her abilities followed the directions of her father; but she met Sir John Fleetwood often--she danced with him often; and, with the best intentions in the world, what between nervous doubts as to how she should behave on her part, and skill, boldness, and experience upon his, he did not want opportunities of making progress in her regard. Margaret therefore remained unmarried, and reached her twenty-fourth year single, but less blessed than she might well have expected to be.

Two days after her birthday, her father went out to ride in Hyde Park; his horse took fright, ran away, and threw him. Mr. Scriven was brought home little more than an hour after he had set out, with a compound fracture of the thigh. The surgeons said that, with his strong constitution and equable temper, there was no danger; and Mr. Scriven's spirits did not in the least give way. Three or four days after, however, mortification appeared; and he then with perfect calmness informed the medical men that he felt his life was drawing to a close. They endeavoured to persuade him that such was not the case, but there are internal sensations not to be mistaken; and Mr. Scriven sent for his lawyer, and a young gentleman of the name of Hayley, who had been placed in his counting-house some seven or eight years before, by highly respectable but not wealthy relations. Mr. Hayley had conducted himself remarkably well, and had risen to be the chief clerk of Mr. Scriven's house.

He approached the great merchant's bedside with looks of sorrowful concern; and Mr. Scriven, after shaking hands with him kindly, said--

"I have sent for you, my young friend, to give you a little testimony both of my gratitude for various services, and of my confidence in your character. I am dying, Hayley, though the surgeons say not; and if I die at present, Henry, my son, is not yet old enough to manage entirely such large concerns as must fall into his hands. You are acquainted with all the details. I owe you a good deal for your care, attention, and zeal in my service; and I do not think I can either recompense you better, or do my son a greater service, than by leaving you an eighth share of the business, which was that portion bestowed upon me at my marriage. There is only one observation I have to make, and do not suppose it to imply censure, but merely warning. Though born of a race of gentlemen, it is very necessary for you to remember that you are especially a merchant. To that consideration you should sacrifice much, and it you should sacrifice to nothing. Your education at a public school has given you several acquaintances of a higher class of society than our own, and some of very expensive habits, I am told. Friendships are too valuable to be given up; but no examples are worthy of being followed but those of honour, virtue, and truth."

"I can assure you, sir," replied Hayley, "I have preserved none of my school acquaintances of a higher rank than my own, except that of Lord

Mellent, son of the Earl of Milford. We were first at a private school together, then at Eton, in the same form; and it would, I acknowledge, be a most painful sacrifice to give up his friendship. With greater means than myself, he is of course able to maintain a much more expensive style of living; but I trust you have never observed anything in me which should induce you to suppose I affect to rival him, or even to join him, in any extravagance. However, I feel as deeply indebted to you for your advice as even for your kind intentions towards me. The one shall be remembered as a guide to my conduct; and I do still hope and pray that it may be long, very long, before the latter receives execution."

Perhaps, had Mr. Scriven been at all a suspicious man, he might have thought his *protégé's* reply too neat and rounded; but ill as he was, and by nature generous in his appreciation of other men's motives, he was well satisfied. His anticipations, however, regarding his own fate, were but too surely realized. Three days after this conversation his eyes were closed for ever; and his son succeeded to a large property, and found himself at the head of a firm hardly rivalled by any in the world. With the habits of thought which he had acquired, the possession of so much wealth, and of such vast means of increasing it, served to close rather than open the heart.

He felt an awful responsibility of getting money upon him, and of preserving what he had got; and all his first acts indicated sufficiently what would be his future course. Those who were observers of human nature remarked, "If young Scriven is so close and grasping as a mere lad, what will he be as age creeps upon him?" And those who had perhaps calculated upon gaining some advantages over the son which they had not been able to obtain over the father, soon gave up the attempt and regretted the change.

Henry Scriven's first step was to discharge all his father's old servants, and to pay all legacies, though he did not scruple to say that he thought his sisters had been somewhat too liberally provided for. He then sold the house in St. James's Square, as requiring a larger establishment than was necessary for a young man; and he retired to a lodging in Brook Street, comfortable enough, but greatly within his means. He was much annoyed at the bequest of an eighth share of his father's business to Mr. Hayley; but he took advantage of all that gentleman's knowledge; and Hayley, soon by mild, almost timid manners, and active services, contrived to ingratiate himself as far as possible with a not very generous person.

In the mean time Margaret, viewing with wonder and disapproval all her brother's conduct, retired for three months to the house of her sister Isabella, and then went for some time on a visit to a friend. Before she returned, a letter announced to Mr. Scriven and Lady Monkton, that their sister was about to bestow her hand upon Sir John Fleetwood; and as soon as she came back to London, the baronet pressed eagerly for the consummation of his happiness. Isabella, with knowledge of the world and strong good sense, saw, as her father had seen, unanswerable objections to the marriage, and she urged them strongly, though kindly, upon her sister's attention; but she soon found that to urge them was labour in vain. Margaret admitted that she knew her lover had been what was then, and still is, called a gay man, and, moreover, an extravagant one; but she assured her friends that he was reformed in both respects and that she looked upon it as a duty to aid as far as was in her power to complete the happy change. Lady Monkton wisely abandoned the task of opposition, and hoped, but did not believe, that the reformation would last. Mr. Scriven attached himself to one object: to ensure that his sister's large fortune should be settled upon herself; and in this he would probably have succeeded, if Margaret would have consented even for a few short days not to see her lover, or would have steadily referred all matters of business to her brother. Unfortunately, however, Margaret had lost confidence in him who was now really striving for her good; and she would not trust to his generosity, while she was inclined to place the fullest reliance on one whose selfishness was only of a more sparkling kind. All that Mr. Scriven could accomplish was to have seven hundred a-year and a house settled upon his sister, though she brought her husband three thousand per annum; but that small sum he took care so to tie up, that no after weakness on her own part could deprive her of at least a moderate independence. Sir John Fleetwood, after the deed was signed, laughed with a gay companion, and observed, that Harry Scriven was the best man of business in England; and on the following day Margaret became his wife. The after fate of all the family shall be briefly told in the succeeding chapter.

CHAPTER II

Where is the family in which the retrospect of ten years will not present a sad and chilling record--with the open tomb, around whose verge we play, and the yawning gulf of fate, which stands ever ready to swallow up the bright hopes and joys of early life? Maturity and decay shake hands.

In the family of Mr. Scriven many changes had taken place during that space of time: flowers had blossomed and been blighted; expectations had passed away which were once fair; sorrow had shadowed some happy faces; death had not spared them any more than others. But I must trace the history of each, though it shall be very briefly.

The only one of the four children of the merchant who had undergone few vicissitudes, who had known but little change, and that merely progressive, was the son. Mr. Henry Scriven was the same man, ten years older. He laid himself open to few of the attacks of fate; he had neither wife nor children. His fortress was small, and therefore easily defended. He had made money, and therefore he loved it all the better; he had lost money, and therefore he was more careful both in getting and keeping it. The circles round his heart went on concentrating, not expanding, and were well-nigh narrowed to a point.

Even in business this was discovered by those who had to deal with him. People said that the house of "Scriven and Co." was a hard house; but still everyone pronounced Mr. Scriven "a very honourable man," though he did sundry very dirty tricks. But he was known to be a rich man, and his business most extensive. Did you never remark, reader, that a wealthy man or a wealthy firm is always "very honourable," in the world's opinion? I have known a body of rich men do things that would have branded an inferior establishment with everlasting disgrace, or have sent an unfriended and unpursed vagabond across the seas; and yet I have been boldly told, "It is a highly honourable house."

So it was in a degree with Mr. Scriven, but still he was careful of his character. He never did anything very gross--anything that could be detected; and though all admitted that he was very close and somewhat grasping, people found excuses for him. Some thought he would build hospitals. Even his very nearest and his dearest knew him not fully, and did not perceive what were the real bonds which kept his actions in an even and respectable course. It is wonderful how many persons, women and men, are restrained by fear!

Maria Scriven had accompanied, as I have said, her husband, Mr. Marston, to India; and there, as far as worldly matters went, they were very prosperous. Still they had their griefs. Who has not? Their eldest child was a boy, whom they named Charles; and a stronger, finer little fellow never was seen. Her letters were full of him. But the second child was lost when a few months old, and the third did not survive its birth a year. Maria's own health also suffered from the climate, and with much pain it was resolved that she should return to Europe with her boy. Mr. Marston was to rejoin them at the end of three years. But human calculations are vain. When Maria reached England she was carried from the ship to the shore, and thence by slow journeys to London, for she was very ill. She revived a little in her native air; but the improvement was not permanent, and she died about two months after her arrival.

Her husband's great inducement for revisiting the land of his birth was gone; and leaving his son to the care of his brother-in-law, he remained plodding on in India.

Lady Monkton had her share of sorrows, too. Her first three children died in infancy. They were all bright, blooming, beautiful. Health and long life seemed written on their fair faces; but the battle is not to the strong, nor the race to the swift; and one or other of those maladies of childhood which often make a cheerful household desolate, had swept away the whole successively. Isabella, gay, happy, strong-minded as she was, quailed under these repeated blows. She was too firm and sensible to yield entirely; but a shade of sadness came over her once clear brow, and when a fourth child appeared, it was with some awe she watched its infancy. This child was a daughter, more delicate to all appearance than the others; but when illness fell upon her it was comparatively light, and with years health and strength seemed to increase. The fair, fragile form developed itself with a thousand graces; the bloom came upon the cheek, the soft, languid eyes grew bright and gay, and hour by hour hope and confidence returned. There was still a terrible shock in store, however. One day Sir Edward Monkton returned from a ride, very wet, was detained by a person he found waiting for him on business, was seized with shivering during the night, and inflammation of the lungs succeeded. Five days of watching and terror left her a widow, with a heart, the very firmness of which rendered its affections the more enduring. Mr. Scriven's character had not fully displayed itself to the eyes of Sir Edward Monkton. He knew him to be a good man of business, and believed him to be an honourable and upright man. Even Lady Monkton did not know her brother thoroughly; and she was glad to have him joined with herself as the executor of her husband's will and the guardian of her daughter. She soon found cause for some regret that it was so; for his arrangements did not altogether please her; but still there was not much to complain of; and at the end of the ten years which followed her father's death, she was living peacefully at her house in Hertfordshire, about fifteen miles from London, occupied with the education of her daughter Maria, seeing very little society, dwelling calmly, though gravely, upon the past, and looking forward with hope and consolation to the future.

One of the greatest anxieties which Lady Monkton felt at this time-- and they were anxieties which amounted to grief--proceeded from the circumstances of her sister Margaret. Sir John Fleetwood had turned out all that Mr. Scriven had anticipated--reckless, extravagant, licentious. His whole thought and occupation seemed to be, how he might soon run through his own property and that part of his wife's fortune over which he had control. He was very successful in his endeavours. What bad associates, male and female, did not contrive to dissipate soon enough, cards, dice, and horses succeeded in losing; and at length he endeavoured to get rid of his wife's settlement. She would willingly have given it up to please him; for though he had been a negligent and offending husband, yet so long as money lasted he had always been gay and good-humoured with her, treating her more as an innocent and unsuspecting child than as a companion. But Mr. Scriven had taken care of his sister's income. It could not be touched even with her own consent. No creditor had power over it; her own receipt was necessary for every penny of the income, and being settled upon her children, though she had none, it was inviolable.

Sir John had not clearly perceived these stringent conditions when he signed the deed; and some sharp discussions took place between him and his brother-in-law. He became gloomy, morose, fretful; and still he would appear at Ascot or at the gambling-table, though he could no longer maintain the appearance which he had once displayed. It was at the former of these places that a dispute took place between himself and another gentleman *of the turf*. It matters not much to this work which was wrong or which was right, and indeed I do not know. Hard epithets were exchanged, and Sir John employed a horsewhip, not for its most legitimate purpose. Two mornings after he was brought home in a dying state, with a pistol-shot through his lungs, and never uttered a word during the half-hour he continued to exist. It must have been an awful half-hour, for it was clear that his senses and his memory were all still perfect; and what a picture memory must have shown him! Poor Lady Fleetwood was in despair. Her love had never failed, nor even diminished. She had never admitted his faults even to herself; or, at all events, had found excuses for them in her kind and affectionate heart. Now that he was gone she was still less likely to discover them; for bitter sorrow drew a veil between her eyes and all that might have shocked her in the conduct of the dead. It is true, there was one thing could not be concealed from her: that he had wasted every penny of his own property, and of hers, too, as far as it was in his power to do so. But then she fancied that he had been only unfortunate, and doubted not that, had he lived, all would have been set right. Her brother, Mr. Scriven, tried hard in his cold, dry way to open her eyes, but he only wrung her heart without convincing her; and though she both feared and respected him, he could never induce her to admit that her husband had acted ill.

Lady Monkton, with tenderer feelings, never attempted to undeceive her, but brought her at once to Bolton Park, and there tried to soothe and comfort her. Nor was she unsuccessful. Her own calm and quiet demeanour, somewhat touched with grief, but yet not melancholy, the gay and cheerful company of her little girl Maria, and the occasional society of her next neighbours, Lord Mellent and his wife, a somewhat indolent but amiable and lively woman, gradually restored Lady Fleetwood to composure and resignation. Her greatest solace, indeed, was her niece Maria; for, though enthusiastically fond of children, she had had none herself; and now, the gay, happy girl, about ten years old, addressed herself, with more thought and feeling than might have been expected of a child, to amuse her widowed aunt and win her mind from sad thoughts and memories. Maria's young companion, too, Anne Mellent, the daughter of their neighbours, though of a different character from Maria--quick, decided, independent in her ways--was always exceedingly tender and gentle to Lady Fleetwood, and from time to time another was added to their society, whom they all knew and all loved, though he was at this time not above thirteen years of age. But of him and his family I must speak apart, as, although it was intimately connected by circumstances with that of Mr. Scriven, it was not allied to it either by blood or marriage.

CHAPTER III

In mentioning the circumstances which attended the death of the great merchant, I have spoken of a young gentleman of the name of Hayley, who, when his family fell into adverse circumstances, had been placed in Mr. Scriven's house as a clerk, and had risen by good conduct and attention to be the chief clerk in the counting-house. He was still under thirty when his friend and patron died, and, as I have said, received, as a recompense for his services, an eighth share in the house. Perhaps enough has been displayed of his character to enable the reader to estimate it justly; and I will only add, that he was of a gentle, yielding, almost timid disposition, although it might perhaps have been somewhat fiery and eager--as indeed it had seemed at school--had not early misfortunes and long drudgery broken his spirit and cowed the stronger passions within him. It is not an uncommon case.

During the time that he remained a clerk, and for a year after he became a partner in the house, Mr. Hayley lived as a single man with an unmarried sister, somewhat older than himself, in a small house in one of those suburban quarters of the town where people fancy they get country air. But at the end of that time he one day brought home with him a fine little boy of two years old, very much indeed to the surprise of his sister. Some explanation was of course necessary, as well as many new arrangements; but, for the first time in his life, a strange degree of reserve seemed to have fallen over Mr. Hayley. He would tell his sister part, but not the whole, he said, in answer to her anxious inquiries. He did not affect to deny that the child was his son; but he desired that he might not be questioned at all about the boy's mother, and seemed annoyed at the least allusion to the circumstance of birth.

Now, Miss Hayley was as affectionate a creature as ever drank in the milk of human kindness from the gentle air of heaven, and she was devotedly attached to her brother. But she was proud of him, too; and she had very strong peculiarities, and also a strong and quick temper, which is not unfrequently joined to a heart soft even to weakness. She was not satisfied with the information she had received; she thought her brother did not place sufficient confidence in her; and, after considering the matter for some hours, she took her resolution, and with an air of grave dignity went down to the room where Mr. Hayley was seated looking over some papers.

"Stephen," she said, "I want to speak with you for a moment."

"Well, my dear Rebecca, what is it?" asked her brother, hardly looking up.

"I must know more about this little boy," said his sister.

"I must indeed request you not to trouble me or yourself," said Mr. Hayley, with unwonted sharpness, "about what does not concern you."

Miss Hayley fired up instantly. She insisted that it did concern her very much, and the sharpest dispute took place between herself and her brother that had ever occurred in their lives. It ended by her declaring, that if he did not satisfy her at least upon one point, she would leave his house, and by his telling her that she was at liberty to do so--very well assured, be it remarked, that she would not. She turned to the door, however, with such a look of determination that Mr. Hayley became a little alarmed, and he called her back.

"Now, what is it you want to know, Rebecca?" he asked. "You say one point. That must, of course, be a point of consequence; for I think you would not quarrel with me for a trifle, or for anything that does not actually concern you. What is it?"

Miss Hayley paused for a moment, for she had come with an intention of making him tell all, and when driven from the broader ground by his resolute resistance, had not exactly the point on which to make her last stand.

"Is the child legitimate or illegitimate?" she asked at length.

"He was born in lawful wedlock," answered her brother.

"And the mother?" inquired his sister.

"That is not fair, Rebecca," said Mr. Hayley: "you declared that you would be satisfied with explanation on one point; now you require more. However, I will satisfy you on this head also, upon the clear understanding that I hear not one word more upon the subject, now or ever. Do you agree?"

"Yes, then I shall be content," answered she; "but on these two matters I have a right to information, for I am not going to----"

"There, there!--I want not your reasons," exclaimed her brother, interrupting her. "Upon that understanding, then, I tell you, his mother is dead, poor little fellow--has been dead for some months; and I should have brought him home before, if it had not been for the anticipation of all this fuss and explanation. You may therefore tell any impertinent person who inquires, that Henry is my son by a private marriage, and that his mother is dead.

"Very well," replied Miss Hayley with an offended air; for she was not at all pleased with the half-confidence she had received, when she thought that she had a right to the whole story, and she walked dignifiedly out of the room.

When she got up to the drawing-room, she found the boy playing about upon the floor under the charge of one of the maids; and she had a strong inclination to sulk a little, even with the child. She found it impossible, however. He would not let her; her own heart would not let her; and in three days she was doing her best to spoil him completely. She tried to draw from him--for he could speak very nicely--some of those facts which her brother had withheld, or at least a clue to them. She questioned him regarding his "mamma;" but the little fellow stoutly maintained he had never had a mamma, asserting that "Nurse Johnston" was the only mamma he had ever had, and she was not his mamma either, for his papa had told him so. The next thing was to ascertain, if possible, where he had previously lived; but of that the boy could tell her nothing but that it was a great, great way off, had taken a long time to travel thence (which was afterwards reduced to two or three hours), and that the house had a garden and was opposite to a toll-gate. All that she could arrive at was, that the boy's first recollections were of being dressed in a white frock with black ribbons, and sometimes having on a frock altogether of the same sombre colour.

In time curiosity died away, and simple love for the dear boy succeeded. Proper arrangements for his careful education were made; a nurse was hired; his letters were learnt; Mr. Hayley seemed to dote upon him, and Miss Hayley actually did so; for a more engaging child never was seen-- kind, gentle, docile, yet playful, bold, and frank.

In the mean while a house had been hired in a more fashionable situation, the number of servants was increased, a better style of living assumed; and even Mr. Scriven admitted that Hayley was a very prudent man, who had waited to see the extent of his means before he at all increased his expenditure.

Mr. Scriven was not an inquisitive man. He was accustomed to say that he had too many affairs of his own to allow him to mind other people's, and he saw the little addition to Mr. Hayley's family without much comment or inquiry. He was well satisfied with the assurance which his partner gave him, in answer to the only questions he did put, that he never intended to marry again; and he even seemed pleased with and fond of the little boy, whom he frequently saw--as pleased with and as fond of him as he could be of anything but money. When little Charles Marston was left under his charge, indeed, by his sister's death and her husband's absence, he naturally became more attached to his young relation. Nevertheless, he often had little Henry Hayley to play with his nephew, and the two boys became inseparable as they grew up. Henry's manners and disposition won his way everywhere, and he was looked upon almost as one of the family by Lady Fleetwood and Lady Monkton. At Bolton Park he was always a most welcome guest; and a fondness, which might have alarmed some mothers who had ambitious views for their daughters, arose and increased from day to day between him and Maria Monkton, who was but a few years younger.

In the mean time Mr. Hayley's style of living became gradually a good deal more expensive; and that taste for high society which the elder Mr. Scriven had remarked showed itself more strongly with his altered circumstances. The names of several noblemen were added to that of Lord Mellent on his list of friends; and rumour said that he occasionally lent money to the more needy of his fashionable acquaintances. Still his intimacy with his former friend and schoolfellow continued unabated. Lady Mellent, who was herself the daughter of a banker, readily adopted her husband's feelings towards him, and Mr. Hayley was generally a guest at their house on the Saturday and Sunday.

After having seen their friend's little boy once or twice at Lady Monkton's house, the noble lord and his lady were as fascinated with him as others had been; and the next time Mr. Hayley came down to Harley Lodge, he was asked to bring his son with him. The invitation was repeated till it became customary; and till he was ten years of age, each Saturday saw Henry a guest at Lord Mellent's house, and the companion of his daughter.

Nothing to please or to instruct was spared upon the boy by Mr. Hayley. He was determined, he said, not to send him to a private school, and consequently masters were engaged to teach all sorts of rudimental knowledge at home. He had his pony, too, and a groom was generally ready to go out with him; but it was remarked that, whenever he got away from his lessons early, he was soon on the road to Bolton Park, and roaming about with Maria in her play-hours. At length the period arrived for sending him to Eton; and now of course he was only seen during the holidays by his young companions, except by Charles Marston, who followed him six months after. Both boys distinguished themselves a good deal at school; but Henry's abilities were decidedly higher, or his application greater. Nor was this produced by any want of those inducements to inattention which rich and fond parents often supply to their children; for Mr. Hayley was a very indulgent father, and the allowance that he made to his son was more than ample, at least during the first three years of Henry's stay. Indulgence did not seem to spoil him. On only two occasions--and they were both honourable to him--did he go beyond the strict limit of what was allowed him; and his attachment and devotion to a father who showed him such tender kindness were unbounded. The course pursued, however, was undoubtedly foolish. Mr. Hayley had not made a fortune: it was still to make; and his over-liberality towards his son in matters of expense generated habits which could only be kept up in after life by a very wealthy man.

During the period of the holidays the gay, happy lad was still a frequent guest at Bolton Park and Harley Lodge. He was very tall, finely formed, and of a remarkably handsome and expressive countenance, older both in look and in manner than his years, and yet with all the grace and frankness of boyhood unimpaired. There was something noble and even proud about his look, too, although he was as gentle as the spring; and if, considering his youth, his habits were expensive, he could hardly be blamed, seeing that Mr. Hayley did nothing to restrain them; and his aunt, whose fondness for him had now grown to a pitch of extravagance, did everything that excessive indulgence could do to encourage them. He had but to ask and to have; and as he had never been taught the value of money, of course it had no value in his eyes.

The period at which youth puts on manhood varies very much in different individuals, and Henry Hayley looked and was two years nearer maturity at fourteen than his young companion, Charles Marston, who was not quite a year younger. Nevertheless, Lady Monkton always saw him the companion of her daughter with pleasure. She let things take their course, and did not even think fit to foresee a time when the intimacy must receive a check. This very unworldly view depended upon her own character. Though a sensible girl and a very sensible woman, she had never had the slightest share of ambition. She considered that happiness consists of happiness; which, simple as the conclusion may seem, is a view that very few people indeed take. She did not believe that she would have been in the slightest degree happier with her own husband if he had been a peer: she was sure she should not have been less happy if he had been a merchant; and she left Maria to choose for herself, without the slightest precaution as to how she might choose, except inasmuch as she resolved that she should never have the opportunity, if she could prevent it, of choosing a Sir John Fleetwood.

Not so, however, Lady Mellent, who became somewhat uneasy at young Henry Hayley's constant association with her daughter. It is true that she was only ten years of age; it is true that the lad's boyish prepossessions were evidently in favour of Maria Monkton; but still she thought it right to represent to Lord Mellent that "Henry was really growing quite a young man;" that "boyish intimacies often ripened into more tender feelings;" that "as Anne grew up, it would not do to have such a thing as an attachment even reported between her and young Hayley;" with a number of the usual etceteras.

But her representations had not the least effect upon Lord Mellent. Henry was now his great favourite. He took him out to shoot with him; he mounted him; he took him out to hunt; and he never was happier than when the lad was with him. His society also was of great advantage to Henry Hayley; for, though Lord Mellent had in his young days been both an extravagant and a somewhat dissipated man, yet there was at bottom a fund of strong good sense and high principle in his character, which had shown itself in a complete change of habits and pursuits after his marriage--in the casting off of all dissolute associates, and the abandonment of all evil or dangerous customs. Lady Mellent felt a little piqued perhaps at her husband's great fondness for the handsome boy. She felt sure, and perhaps not unreasonably, that Lord Mellent regretted he had not a son such as Henry Hayley; but she was too good-humoured and too indolent to press her opinions after they had once been expressed, and everything went on as before.

Thus all matters proceeded till Henry returned from Eton for the summer holidays, when he was somewhat more than fifteen years of age; but on his arrival at his father's house he found a great change had worked itself during his last absence. Mr. Hayley was gloomy and depressed; Miss Hayley was evidently uneasy, though a fitful and excessive cheerfulness was assumed to cover care and thought. No explanation was given him; and on the second day after his arrival, finding that even his presence, which usually spread sunshine around, and all his efforts to please and amuse, which never before had been unsuccessful, failed to cheer his home, he betook himself to call upon his young companion, Charles Marston.

Charles was out--he had gone down to his uncle's counting-house, the servant said; and thither Henry followed to ask him if he would ride to Bolton Park. He did not find him in the city; but he met with Mr. Scriven, who was particularly kind to him, asked after his progress in his studies, inquired especially into his knowledge of arithmetic, and questioned him as to how he should like to be a merchant. Nay, more: having a little time to spare, he gave him some of his own views of commercial matters, and seemed anxious to impress him favourably with the pursuits in which his own life was entirely spent. It was really kind--and he intended it to be so. The lady did not much like the subject; but with his usual sense of propriety he listened with attention, looked at some books which Mr. Scriven showed him, and though he did not express any great liking for a mercantile life, replied gaily that he doubted not he should soon bend himself to any course which his father thought fit for him to follow.

A certain feeling of shyness, he knew not well why, prevented him from turning his horse's head towards Bolton Park without Charles Marston; but he had no such feelings in riding to Harley Lodge. There, however, he learned that Lord Mellent had been for some weeks in the north of England, attending upon his father, who was dangerously ill; and after having lunched gaily with Lady Mellent and her daughter, he rode back to London, and went to call upon Lady Fleetwood, who had by this time taken up her abode in a small house in London.

Here, for the first time, Henry Hayley was informed of the real situation of his father. Lady Fleetwood was the best creature in the world, and the best creature in the world is always anxious to comfort everybody that requires comforting. It very often happens, indeed, that the objects of this kind influence do not know that they need it, and then the effect of the effort is generally the reverse of what was intended.

Lady Fleetwood, with the "best intentions," began the process by assuring her young friend that she was very sorry indeed for the differences between her brother and Mr. Hayley--the whole family were very sorry, and had long hoped that it might be made up; but that her brother had always been very firm--Lady Fleetwood would not call it obstinate, though that was what she meant to imply; but she was a woman of soft words, who never used a harsh expression in her life. However, her consolations showed Henry Hayley that there was something in his situation which needed consolation, and he proceeded to ascertain from Lady Fleetwood what it was. In regard to keeping a secret, it was a thing which Lady Fleetwood did not often succeed in effecting, though she sometimes attempted it; and Henry soon learned that Mr. Scriven, having heard, or discovered, or suspected, that Mr. Hayley occasionally frequented a fashionable gambling-house, had about two months before insisted upon an immediate dissolution of partnership. The accounts were even then in course of settlement, Lady Fleetwood told him; and she added, that she was very sorry to hear Mr. Hayley was likely to be greatly embarrassed by this business, as some speculations on his own private account had proved unsuccessful.

"She could not understand it," she said, "for she knew nothing of business; but she recollected quite well having heard her brother say, at the time of her father's death, that the eighth share of the business was worth more than thirty thousand pounds."

Henry Hayley left her with a heart terribly depressed. He felt himself compelled to think, and think deeply, for the first time in life; and that very fact proved depressing. When we first learn that the flowers of the garden, which this world generally is to youth, are doomed to wither, by seeing the fair, frail things fade and fall, the heart feels faint with apprehension lest they should never bloom again, nor others rise up in their places. But the mind of the lad was a powerful one, disposed for thought and apt for action.

"My father is ruined," he thought, "and perhaps his indulgence to me may have contributed to involve him. More than one-half of the *fellows* at Eton were not allowed to spend nearly as much as I was, and none more." Then came the thought, "What can I do to help him?"

It was a difficult question for a boy to answer, but Henry brooded over it. Everything he saw at home showed him that his conclusions in regard to Mr. Hayley's circumstances were but too just. All matters were going amiss, and his father's gloom was not to be mistaken. The young lad pondered and meditated in his own room for several hours each day, without arriving at any satisfactory result; but one morning he called to mind his interview with Mr. Scriven, and that gentleman's marked kindness towards him. He remembered the peculiar and unusual character of their conversation; and he could not help thinking that Mr. Scriven, in asking how he would like to be a merchant, had sought to point out to him the best course he could pursue.

"I will be a merchant," he said to himself; "I may help even as a clerk, and at all events relieve my father of the burden of supporting me."

The next step was to inquire how he was to proceed. He had a natural repugnance to going to Mr. Scriven again; yet, as Mr. Hayley had not mentioned to him his changed circumstances, he was anxious to keep his proceedings a secret at home till his arrangements were formed. Had not Lord Mellent been at a distance, Henry would have gone to him direct for counsel in his strait; for the frank kindness which that nobleman had ever shown him had won the boy's confidence entirely. But, cut off from that source of advice, he was obliged to act without consolation; and after long deliberation, he one morning put on his hat and issued forth to call upon Mr. Scriven.

When he was within a couple of hundred yards of the counting-house, he saw his father approaching with a quick and hurried step, his brow clouded and his eyes bent anxiously upon the ground. He was apparently coming from his late house of business, and was at some distance, when one of two merchants who were walking in the same direction as Henry, and close before him, observed to the other, "Ah! here comes poor Hayley. I am afraid the game's up with him."

"I cannot be sorry for him," replied the other, in a dry, harsh tone: "he has acted like a fool."

The next moment Mr. Hayley approached, still with the same thoughtful air; and probably in his reverie he would have passed even his son, had not the two men who had been speaking of him stopped him with the ordinary inquiries of the morning. He answered shortly, but on raising his eyes saw Henry before him, and inquired somewhat eagerly whither he was going.

"I am going to call on Mr. Scriven," replied the lad; "I have not seen him for several days, and he was very kind to me when last I was there."

"Stop, stop!" said Mr. Hayley; and then, after pausing for a few moments, and fixing his eye gloomily upon the pavement, he added, "Well--go," and hurried on.

The lad pursued his way to the counting-house and inquired for Mr. Scriven. He was asked to wait a few minutes, and then ushered into a large handsome room, where the head of the house usually sat.

"Ah, Henry!" he said, in a tone frank enough, "did you not meet your father?"

"Yes, sir," replied the youth; "I met him close to the door."

"Did he say anything particular to you?" demanded Mr. Scriven.

"No; he only asked where I was going," replied Henry, "and when I told him, he said 'Very well, go on.'"

"Humph!" said Mr. Scriven. "Have you any business to speak about, my young friend? or is this merely a call?"

"I can hardly call it business, sir," replied Henry, coming to the point at once; "but you were kind enough when last I saw you to talk about my becoming a merchant. I have been thinking over the matter since, and I have made up my mind to be one, if I can."

"Have you spoken to your father on the subject?" asked Mr. Scriven.

"No, sir," answered the lad in his usual candid manner; "I see he is very uneasy about something. I am afraid that I have been a great burden to him, and I want, if possible, to put myself in the way of relieving him rather than pressing upon him."

Mr. Scriven gazed upon him with a look of some surprise, and then said, "And have you not spoken with him upon the subject at all?"

"Not in the least," answered Henry: "I hope you do not think it wrong, for I wish only to do what is right. But as my father has not said a word to me about his affairs, and perhaps I may be found not to have abilities for what I desire to undertake, I thought it would be better not to say anything till I had tried, and then if I fail he would not be disappointed."

"You are a singular boy, upon my word," said Mr. Scriven; "Do you propose, then, to go as a clerk upon trial?"

"I do not know what steps I ought to take," replied Henry, "and that is the very subject upon which I came to ask your advice."

Mr. Scriven mused for a moment, and then called for his head clerk.

"Is young Hamilton likely to return to business soon?" he inquired, as soon as the clerk appeared.

"I am afraid not, sir," replied the other: "they tell me he is in a deep decline."

"Very well," said Mr. Scriven, and the clerk retired. An important conversation followed, though it was not a very long one; for all Mr. Scriven's ideas and expressions were so clear and precise that he got through much matter very rapidly. His counting-house was now without one of the usual clerks; and he proposed to Henry Hayley, as a favour to the young man-- though in fact it was some assistance to himself--to come to his house for three or four hours each day, and do part, at least, of the work of the sick lad who could not attend. He left him to tell his father or not as he pleased; but he made such arrangements as to hours that the communication need not be forced upon him. Henry accepted the offer joyfully, and returned home with a lightened heart. But in the mean time Mr. Scriven looked out for another clerk in the place of the one who was ill; for, though he had no objection to give the son of his late partner the opportunity of learning a little of mercantile affairs, and keeping some of his books for him at the same time, he had not the slightest intention of taking Henry Hayley into his counting-house.

"That would never do," he said: "the connection between his father and myself must be altogether broken off. It is lucky I discovered his habits so soon, before he had shaken my credit while he was ruining his own."

CHAPTER IV

Daily, to the tick of the clock, at the appointed hour Henry Hayley was at Mr. Scriven's counting-house, and earnestly and steadily did he apply. He became a great favourite with the head clerk and the cashier, whom he assisted alternately; and a quick and intelligent mind and retentive memory enabled him in ten days to master more than many other lads of his age would have acquired in as many months. Mr. Scriven himself he seldom saw; but that gentleman found that he was very useful, and likely to become more so; and he was inclined to regret that insuperable objections would prevent him from retaining him as a clerk. He suffered no hint of his intentions to escape to the youth himself, however, till he had found the sort of person he wanted for his office; and Henry was indulging sanguine hopes, and preparing to tell his father all that had occurred, when Mr. Scriven dashed his expectations to the ground at once by informing him, with all decent civility, that in a week a new clerk would come to fill the place he had lately been occupying.

"You have now seen enough of mercantile life, my young friend," he added, "to judge whether it is likely to suit your tastes or not. I think you seem well fitted for it; and if you decide upon such pursuits, I will do all I can to assist you."

With this promise Henry Hayley was obliged to content himself; but he returned home sad, and he soon had occasion for deeper anxiety.

Mr. Hayley, was out all the evening and a great part of the night. His sister was evidently in an agony of expectation; and from some casual words she dropped, as well as from almost instinctive suspicions in his own heart, the lad could not help fearing that his father had betaken himself to the gaming-table again. He sat up with Miss Hayley till her brother came home; but though Mr. Hayley's face was pale and his eye haggard with strong excitement, it was evident that he was elated, not depressed. The truth is, he had won a considerable sum of money, and, to use the idiot expression of persons of his habits, it seemed that the luck had turned in his favour. The next morning, just as he was going out, an execution was put into the house. It is true, the money was paid immediately; but it showed Henry clearly, for the first time, how low his father's means had been reduced.

He now resolved at once to tell Mr. Hayley what he had done, to explain to him his feelings and his wishes without reserve, and to beseech him in existing circumstances not to send him back to Eton, but to obtain for him the office of clerk in some mercantile house.

With a good deal of timidity, but with that grace which springs from the warmth of natural affection, he executed the task without giving himself time to shrink from it.

Mr. Hayley listened with utter astonishment, and for some moments seemed not to know what to reply. His first answer consisted of nothing but broken, incoherent fragments of sentences and exclamations. "You, Henry!--you!" he cried--"you acting as clerk to that fellow Scriven! The rascal! he has cheated me of thousands, and does not pay even what he acknowledges he owes me--forsooth, there may be other claims. To debase you to be his servant!"

After a moment or two he became more collected, however, though he remained greatly agitated through their whole conversation. "No, Henry," he continued, turning to the subject of his son's future prospects; "no--a mercantile life is not fitted for you, nor you for it. I cannot consent, neither do I think it will be needful. This pressure is but temporary, and I trust something will *turn up* to set things to rights."

He then paused, and walked up and down the room for several minutes in deep thought; and then turning again to Henry, he took his hand, saying with sorrowful gravity, "I must not conceal from you, my dear boy, that affairs are very bad with me at present. Mr. Scriven's unjust, tyrannical, and pitiful conduct has done all that he could do to ruin me; but he shall not succeed--by ----, he shall not succeed! This does not affect you, however. There is--there is a little something settled upon you, and no Scriven on earth can hurt you. There is quite enough to pay for your education at Eton, so do not let that trouble you. But I think you could do me a service, Henry, though you are very young, my dear boy, to trust with such things. Yet it is the only way. Still, I do not like to ask you."

"Oh, name it, my dear father! name it!" exclaimed Henry. "Do you not know that, if it were my life, I would willingly lay it down for you?"

"Oh, your life!" replied Mr. Hayley, smiling. "No, it is nothing so important as that. It is only to execute a task which I have a foolish reluctance to undertake myself. The fact is, this pressure is but temporary, and ten days will see it all at an end; yet in the course of those ten days I have several thousand pounds to pay, and look here, Henry--this is all I have in the world to pay it with;" and opening a drawer, he showed him about two hundred pounds in gold, adding, "There is not a sixpence at the bankers'."

"But what can I do?" demanded Henry Hayley, with youthful terror at the dark prospect so suddenly placed before him. "I have got ten pounds up-stairs, but that is nothing."

"Nothing, indeed," answered Mr. Hayley with a faint smile, "and there is only one person to whom I can apply for assistance; yet I have shrunk from telling him the whole, though I have written, giving him some notion of my state--I mean my friend Lord Mellent."

"But he is absent!" exclaimed Henry. "I went down to Harley Lodge, and found he was in the north."

"That is true," said Mr. Hayley, "and doubtless his close attendance on his father--a violent, harsh, and capricious man at all times, and now rendered probably more exacting by sickness--has prevented him from answering my letter. Now, Henry, what I wish you to do for me is this: go down to Lord Mellent in the north, see him, and tell him exactly the state of my affairs. I have not nerve for it myself; for I will be candid with you, Henry: driven almost to madness, I have done many things which I regret, and which I will never do again. Mellent would ask me many questions--he will ask you none. He is my oldest friend in the world, and has always, as you know, shown a very great fondness for yourself. He will not, I am sure, refuse you, if you ask him to lend me two thousand pounds for but one month. But press him warmly; tell him it must be done directly if he would save me from ruin. If he hesitates, make it your own request, and get him to give you a draft for it. Then hurry up as speedily as possible; for remember, if I have it not in seven days, I am lost."

"But if he has not got as much ready money as two thousand pounds?" said Henry.

"He has! he has!" exclaimed Mr. Hayley vehemently: "he had nine thousand pounds at his bankers' when he went away."

"Then I am sure he will lend it," replied Henry in a confident tone; "I am quite certain."

"I think so too," said Mr. Hayley; "I have no doubt you will succeed."

"Oh, yes, to a certainty," answered the inexperienced boy. "I will just write a note to Mr. Scriven, saying that I cannot attend any longer, and then I am ready to set out."

"You must travel by the mail, my dear boy," replied Mr. Hayley, "so you will have time enough. We cannot afford post-horses now, Henry. As to writing to Mr. Scriven, let me see--yes, you had better write, and I would moreover advise you to go there no more. He has used me shamefully, and he knows it. I must see him from time to time on business, but all friendship is at an end between us for ever."

"I shall certainly not go to one who has treated my father in such a manner," replied the lad, "and I will write to him directly, telling him merely that I do not intend to visit his counting-house any more."

Thus saying, he left the room, and Mr. Hayley continued for several minutes buried in deep thought. At length he said in a low tone, "He will lend it certainly--oh, yes, he will not refuse the boy. If he does send the money--and I think he will--he must--then I could take up the bill before it becomes due."

He then opened the drawer again, took out a small tin case, and from that drew forth a long slip of paper with a stamp at one end and a few brief lines written on the face. He gazed at it for a moment, and then thrust it back again, saying, "I won't till the last extremity. Yet I have a right: he owes me the money, and should have paid it without this quibbling evasion. I am a partner of the house, too, till it is paid; I have a right to consider myself so." But still he closed the drawer, and locked it, putting the key in his pocket.

About an hour after, a gentleman was admitted to Mr. Hayley--a stern-looking, business-like person, who remained with him for about half-an-hour; and their conversation was somewhat loud and stormy--so at least it seemed to the servants in the hall. When the visiter came forth his face was flushed; and holding the door in his hand, he said aloud, "Not another hour, sir!--not another hour! Twelve to-morrow, and if not, why----."

"My dear sir--" said the voice of Mr. Hayley imploringly.

"My dear sir! Stuff and nonsense!" cried the other. "I am not your dear sir," and he walked out of the house.

Mr. Hayley passed two or three hours alone. His sister Rebecca was very anxious, and made an excuse to go to his sitting-room; but she found the door locked and her brother from within begged not to be disturbed, as he was busy with accounts.

Henry walked away to the mail-office and took a place for the north; but he had no spirits to call on any one, and returning slowly, he did not reach home till about half-past three.

"Your papa has been asking for you, sir," said the servant who admitted him; and almost at the same moment Mr. Hayley opened his door, saying, "Henry, Henry! here!--I want you."

Henry entered the room, and Hayley put in his hands the slip of paper with the stamp upon it which he had been gazing at some hours before; but there was now something written across it.

"I wish you would take that, my dear boy, to my bankers', and ask to see Mr. Stolterforth, the head partner. You know Mr. Stolterforth, I think?"

"Oh, very well," replied the lad.

"Well, then, give him that, and say I should feel very much obliged to him if he will let me have a thousand pounds upon it. He will do it directly, I am sure, and perhaps may offer to discount it; for it is for eighteen hundred, and has only seven days to run; but you may tell him I do not want to put it into circulation--because, you see, it was given by Mr. Scriven in settlement of an account which is not yet finally made up, and there may be some difference, I do not know what--a few hundred pounds--you understand?"

Mr. Hayley's hand shook a good deal as he gave the lad the paper, and he seemed to think it needed some explanation; for, when Henry replied that he understood perfectly, his father added, "It annoys me very much to do this at all; for if Scriven were to know it, my credit would be seriously injured by it. You may tell Mr. Stolterforth that, and mind you let him know I do not want it to get into circulation."

Henry promised to do so, and putting on his hat again, he walked quietly away to the bankers'. Being well known there, he was admitted at once to the head partner, showed him the accepted bill, and delivered his message calmly and accurately. The banker at once agreed to do what was required; asked him several questions, indeed, which he could not answer, but showed no hesitation; and after one or two formalities, gave him the money, which he chose to have principally in gold, thinking it might be more convenient for his father's payments. Henry then got into a hackney-coach and drove away. Mr. Hayley was dreadfully pale when his son returned to him, but he seemed rejoiced to see the money, and immediately proceeded to speak of Henry's journey. He gave him twenty pounds in gold, and then added fifty pounds in five-pound notes, which Henry would fain have declined, saying he could have no use for them; but Mr. Hayley urged that accidents might occur, and impressed upon him strongly that he must be up before that day week, adding, "Should it be necessary, take a chaise, for time may be more valuable than money."

The lad's portmanteau was soon packed up, some dinner was provided for him, and at the proper hour he set out for the coach-office, took his seat, and was carried away from London.

Mail-coaches were then the quickest conveyances. The northern mail was supposed to travel at the rate of eight miles an hour, including stoppages; and on the young man was hurried from the capital towards Northumberland, squeezed up in a hot summer night with an enormously fat woman and a tolerably stout man. The distance he had to go was about three hundred and twenty miles, and the town where he was to get out was Belford, between which place and Wooler the mansion of the Earl of Milford was situated. Farther he knew nothing of his road, except that at Belford he should be able to obtain information. Night set in soon after he left London, and both his companions were speedily asleep; for they were of the taciturn breed, on which even the aspect of youth has no more effect than beauty upon a stone. They snored hard and sonorously, especially the man, woke up for a moment into half-slumbering consciousness while the horses were being changed, and then were as sound asleep as ever. Wherever provisions were to be had, indeed, the lady roused herself, and proceeded to the business of the hour with marvellous activity, considering her age and weight; but at most other times she was as silent as her companion, who seemed to consider that locomotion was the proper and natural stimulus to slumber.

The forty weary hours passed at length, very few words having been spoken; but the mail was not yet at Belford--indeed, it never was--and two more hours went by before the small town appeared. It was at that time very dull and dirty; and as he looked up at the sign of the "Old Bell," Henry felt the place had a sort of desolate aspect, which made the prospect of sleeping at Milford Castle very pleasant in comparison.

The landlord of the "Bell," however, had no intention of suffering him to depart so easily. Milford Castle, he assured him, was full sixteen miles to the westward; and when Henry replied that the distance did not matter, as he must go on that night, having business to transact, the worthy host discovered that all his horses were out, and would not return till two or three in the morning.

As there was no other house in the town which kept post-horses, Henry was obliged to be content, and ordering a light dinner, he determined to sit and doze by the fire till the horses returned. The landlord so contrived, however--what between the necessity of giving food and rest to cattle which were all the time in the stable, and the late hour at which they were reported to return from a journey they had never made--that the young traveller was obliged to remain all night and breakfast the next morning at the "Bell."

Still, little more than eight-and-forty hours had passed since he had left London when once more he was on the way again. He had been allowed six whole days to complete his task; and the coming time, to the mind of youth, is always long in proportion to the shortness of the past.

It was a bright morning when he set out again for Milford, and all looked gay and hopeful; but fatigue and impatience had done much to diminish confidence, and the way seemed interminably long, the postboy preternaturally slow. Half-way there, it was found necessary to stop and feed the horses; and although Henry endeavoured, with a look of importance, to enforce the necessity of great speed, he was too young for his commands to be received with any great deference.

At about nine o'clock, however, a little village between bare, high banks presented itself--a mere hamlet, with a chandler's shop and a public-house--and shortly after were seen large gates and a lodge. The gates were opened by an old woman, who seemed, like the few stunted trees around, to have been bent by the prevailing wind; but a drive of two miles through the large, wild park was still before the young traveller. The scenery certainly improved, and gave him some objects of interest to look at; the trees became large and fine; pleasantly-varied hill and dale succeeded to round-backed rises; and occasional glimpses of an old grey mansion-house caught his eyes as he strained his sight out of the front windows of the chaise. The house disappeared again in thick plantations as he got nearer, and it was with surprise that he found himself suddenly driving up to the doors. He was too much accustomed to good society to feel anything like shyness, but yet he was somewhat anxious; and, advancing his head as near the window as possible without putting it out, he looked up over the house with some curiosity as the postboy rang the great bell.

To his consternation he perceived that all the windows were closed, and bidding the driver open the door, he jumped out.

No one answered the summons of the bell, and he rang it again after waiting several minutes. It required a third application to bring any one out, and then it was merely a slipshod country servant, who came round from the back of the house without condescending to open the great doors.

Her first salutation was, "What d'ye want, man? Don't you know that the old lord is dead, and they are gone to take the corpse over to Wales, to the place where they're all booried?"

Henry professed his ignorance of all this, and anxiously desired to know where the young lord was to be found. The girl, however, could give him no information, but referred him to the steward, who lived across the park--only adding, "It's a pity ye didn't come this time yestermorn, for then ye'd have found the young lord and the old lord too--only he was dead, poor body."

To the steward's house Henry then betook himself; but the steward himself was out, and his wife could only tell the visiter that he was likely to find the present earl at Caermarthen, as he was to meet the body of his father there, the family vault being in that neighbourhood. An Eton boy's knowledge of geography, at the age of fifteen or sixteen, is not usually very great, for the most important objects of education are generally those the most neglected in this happy country; but still Henry was aware that he would be nearer Caermarthen at Wooler than at Belford. The driver was indeed unwilling to go that road, and his reluctance was only overcome by a promise of good payment. The greater part of the day, however, was wasted by all the delays he had encountered; and although he was resolved to go on under any circumstances and find his father's friend, yet the journey was a long one, and he felt puzzled and apprehensive.

Luckily, at Wooler he found an intelligent landlord, who gave him some serviceable information regarding the line of his journey; and after writing a brief note to Mr. Hayley, informing him of what had occurred, he resumed his expedition, resolved to travel night and day. This was not so easily achieved as determined; but I need not follow him through all the difficulties that beset him. Suffice it, that at Preston his gold fell short, and he was obliged to change one of the notes which had been given him by Mr. Hayley. This occurred again before he reached Caermarthen; for, though he was anxious to pursue his course as economically as possible, stage-coaches were scanty, their hours were often inconvenient, and he recollected with a feeling of apprehension the last expression of his father, "Time is more valuable than money." Eagerly--I might say vehemently--he hurried on; but still the long, long journey from one side of the island to the other occupied far more time than he had expected. Sometimes horses could not be had; at others a whole hour was wasted rousing ostlers and postboys; then came slow drivers and hilly countries, bad roads and worse horses.

The fifth day from that of his departure was drawing towards its close when he at length reached Caermarthen, weary, exhausted, and feeling ill. Still, before he took any refreshment at the inn, he inquired for the family seat of the Earl of Milford. The waiter could tell him nothing about it; the landlord was sent for, and proved more communicative. It lay at twelve or thirteen miles' distance, he said. "But if you have come for the funeral, sir," he added, looking at the lad with a good deal of interest, "you are too late. It took place early this morning; and the new lord--that is, Lord Mellent as was--passed through about four hours ago, on his way back to London."

"I must follow him directly," said Henry, almost wildly. "I have business of the greatest importance with him."

"Then you had better take a place in the mail, sir," said the landlord: "it starts from this house, and you will save more time by it than by posting. It starts at two, and it's now nine; but between this and town you'd lose more than five hours by getting out horses and slow going."

Henry's experience showed him that what the good man said was true. The mail must bring him into London just at the beginning of the fatal seventh day; by posting he might delay his arrival; and he thought, if he reached his father's house by five in the morning, there would still be time enough, before business hours began, for Mr. Hayley to see the earl and obtain his assistance.

His course therefore was soon determined, his place in the mail secured, and during the time he had to stay, he endeavoured to refresh and strengthen himself for his onward journey. Even in the gay and bounding days of youth, the mind is in sad slavery to the body. Fatigue and exhaustion will make the aspect of all things gloomy, and rest and food will restore their brightness. The landlady at Caermarthen was a good, kind, motherly woman; and taking the weary young traveller into her parlour, she soon provided him with a light supper, and a few glasses of wine added revived the lad's spirits greatly. He eased the aching of his limbs by walking up and down the room, and when the mail was ready to start felt quite equal to the fatigue. There was no other passenger in the inside, and he amused himself as best he could, sometimes by sleeping, sometimes after daybreak by gazing out at the prospect. At length night began to fall again, and Henry fell asleep once more. He was awakened by the coach stopping to change horses. All was ready, and in haste the beasts were put to; but while he was looking out of the window there was a good deal of bustle at the inn door, and he saw something carried in by three or four men. He had no time, however, to make inquiries, for the coachman was mounting his box, and the next moment the mail dashed off.

Two stages farther on, it was announced to him that a quarter of an hour was allowed for supper; and as he got out he inquired of the guard what was the matter a couple of stages behind.

"Why, the gentleman's carriage had been overturned at the bridge, sir," replied the guard, "and he had been stunned, with what they call a concussion of the brain, Mrs. White said; so they were carrying him in. That was what you saw, I dare say."

"Do you know who he was?" demanded Henry, with feelings of unaccountable alarm.

"Oh, yes, sir," replied the man: "I saw him at Caermarthen yesterday. It's the young lord whose father's just dead and buried. He's like enough to be soon dead and buried too, for he's badly hurt, and his carriage all dashed to smash."

A moment of bewildering uncertainty succeeded. Henry asked himself first, should he go back? then, for what purpose? But he soon saw that to do so would serve none. He could not see and speak to Lord Mellent in such a state; and he resolved to hurry on, though to be the bearer of such disastrous tidings to his father made his heart sink. He ate no supper; he slept no more; and driver and horses being good, he arrived at the General Post-office a little after four. A hackney-coach was soon obtained, the guard and coachman were feed, and before five he was at his father's house.

The instant the coach stopped, the door was opened by Mr. Hayley himself, and Henry sprang out to meet him.

"Put the portmanteau in the hall, and wait," said Mr. Hayley to the coachman; and holding Henry's hand, he led him towards his own sitting-room. The lad saw that his father was pale and haggard, and he dreaded the effect of what he had to tell; but still he would not delay, and even as they went to the room the main facts were poured forth. To his surprise, Mr. Hayley seemed hardly to listen; and when they were in the study, he locked the door and gazed earnestly at the boy.

His words were short, sharp, and to the lad seemed wild. "Henry," he said, "you love me, I think--do you not?"

Henry gazed in his face, utterly astounded.

"I know you do," his father added; "I am sure you do. Now, my dear boy, you can prove it. You can save my life--my honour."

"How?--how?" cried the boy. "I will do all--anything you please, my dear father; only tell me what.

"It is, Henry, to get into that coach again and drive down to Blackwall. You will there find a steamer ready to start for Rotterdam at six in the morning. Embark in her; from Rotterdam go up the Rhine, through Germany to Italy, and stay at Ancona till you hear from me. Here are money and a passport."

"But why?--why?" asked the boy earnestly. "Oh, tell me all, for fear I make any mistake."

Mr. Hayley grasped his arm very tight, and bending down his head, whispered in a voice hardly audible, yet stern too--"Henry, that bill which you took to the bankers' was forged--*I* forged it! If you stay, you must stay to be a witness against me and condemn me to death."

The young man sank down in a chair, with a face so pale that his father thought he was going to faint. "Here, take some wine," he said, pouring him out a tumbler-full from a decanter that stood on the table, and Henry drank it all.

The father gazed upon his face with a look of agonised expectation, while the lad put his hand to his head, as if to recover his scattered thoughts.

"But they will say I did it," he murmured at length. "I shall be an exile for ever, and never see you more."

"They will say you did it," replied Mr. Hayley; "they think, even now, you did it. I was obliged to deny I sent you, even to gain time; for it was discovered last night, and an officer set off into Northumberland immediately to seek you. Do as you will, Henry. You now know all; but it you stay, I will go and give myself up directly. You shall see me again if you go, for as soon as the inquiry is over I will come and join you. But no time is to be lost--your resolution must be taken in five minutes."

"I will go!--I will go!" said the lad faintly; "but, oh, my father! give me means of proving my innocence hereafter."

"I have it ready," said Mr. Hayley; "I have thought of all--prepared all. Look here," and taking up a paper he read--"'I, Stephen Hayley, acknowledge that the acceptance of Mr. Henry Scriven to a bill'" (I need not read all that) "'was forged by me, and that my son took it to Messrs. Stolterforth's by my orders, without knowing it to be forged.' Then further I state, as you may see, that you go abroad to save me. Now, Henry, my life is in your hands--act as you like." And sinking down into a chair, he covered his eyes with his hands.

The next instant Henry's hand was laid upon his arm. "I am going," he said: "farewell, my father! farewell!"

"Stay! stay!" said Mr. Hayley, starting up: "remember the passport-- and the money, too. Here are two hundred napoleons--they go everywhere. Ah, Henry! dear, good lad!--your consolation must be that you have saved your father's life."

Henry made no reply, but the tears fell over his cheeks. Mr. Hayley pressed him to his heart; it was a selfish one, but still gratitude did mingle with rejoicing for his own safety. In five minutes more he was in the coach, with another portmanteau which had been prepared for him the night before by his father, bearing marked upon it, "Henry Calvert, Esq. passenger by

'City of Antwerp.'" On looking at the passport he found the same name therein, and saw (for that Mr. Hayley had forgotten to explain) that he was to take that name during his flight.

In about three-quarters of an hour he stood upon the deck of the vessel, and in ten minutes after his embarkation she was going quickly down the river.

The same morning, on the arrival of the Newcastle mail, two officers in plain clothes had walked up to the side, and examined every passenger both inside and outside. There were in all three men and two women; but neither of the men bore the least resemblance to Henry Hayley, and the officers turned their attention to the coach-offices. The Caermarthen mail escaped unexplored.

An examination into the affair took place that day at Bow Street; but it was proved that Henry had, unknown to Mr. Hayley, frequented the counting-house of Mr. Scriven for more than a fortnight; that he was anxious to conceal his doing so from his father; that, on the very morning of his departure for Northumberland, he had written to Mr. Scriven to say he should come no more; that at four o'clock that day he had obtained money upon the forged bill, and then gone, no one rightly knew whither, further than that his journey was towards Northumberland; for Mr. Hayley took care to give no explanations on that head.

A thousand little circumstances of no real value, such as some small bills at Eton left unpaid, tended to make up a mass of evidence against him; and thus the guilty escaped--if not without doubts, yet without any charge against him--while the whole weight of suspicion fell upon the innocent boy, who was sailing away over the sea to Rotterdam.

CHAPTER V

The curious state of society in which we exist, and the complex causes and effects which it comprises--the fictitious, the factitious, the unreal, the unnatural relations which it establishes between man and man--are always producing unexpected results and events which no one can rightly account for, because no one can trace all the fine lines which connect one piece of the complicated machinery with another. It must have often struck every thinker who gathers up the passing events, and marks the impression which they produce upon the world at large, that matters, often of great moment, will excite little or no attention--will be slurred over in newspapers, pass without comment in society, be hardly heard of beyond the narrowest possible circle round the point at which they take place--while mere trifles will set Rumour's thousand tongues a-going, men and women will interest themselves with eager anxiety about things that do not affect them in the least, and half the world will be on fire as to whether a feather was blown to the right or the left. The basest political scheme that ever was practised for depriving a queen of hope, happiness, and power, and a great country of its independence, will excite far less attention and curiosity than the disappointment of one priest's ambition and the compensation of another priest's unmerited persecution.

When first my attention was directed to this subject, I said, "A cannon fired in an open country cannot by any chance produce such terrible results as a spark in a powder-mill. It is not the event itself that is important, but the things with which it is connected that make it so." But I soon became convinced that this explanation, though specious, was not true--at least, that there was something more; that whenever anything made a great noise, it must connect itself by some of the many hooks and pulleys of society with some of the loud tongues in high places. By high places I do not mean elevated stations, but positions in which men can make themselves heard: some newspaper scribe--one of the things in parliament assembled--a popular preacher--a mob-orator--is either interested in the matter directly or indirectly, immediately or remotely, or else has nothing else to do and wants a hobby, and the whole affair is made the talk of the town.

In short, it were endless to search out, arrange, and classify the infinite variety of causes which may render any event notorious, or consign it to speedy oblivion, though it may rend the hearts, ruin the fortunes, desolate the prospects, and destroy the peace of all within a certain little circle.

The forgery upon Mr. Scriven made little or no noise in the great world. The first investigation at Bow Street was fully reported in one or two of the morning newspapers. Some others, which had no reporters of their own, abridged it from their "esteemed contemporaries." Others declared there were no matters of public interest at Bow Street that day, because they had not room to report more than the donations of five-pound notes to the poor-box, the receipt of which had been requested to be acknowledged.

But the event was a terrible one in the midst of those more immediately interested. Mr. Scriven pursued the inquiry into the facts with a fierceness and a virulence which had not before appeared in his nature; and undoubtedly Mr. Hayley himself might have fallen into danger, had not many little circumstances, some accidental, some skilfully prepared, combined to fix the guilt upon the innocent.

As an instance of one of those accidents which served to shelter him, I may mention, that upon the examination of his servants, one of the footmen deposed, and deposed truly, that three or four days before Henry's disappearance, Mr. Hayley had been eagerly inquiring if any one had found a piece of stamped paper--a draft, in short--and seemed very uneasy about it. Mr. Scriven admitted that Hayley had told him he had drawn upon him, and that he had refused to accept the draft. Thus, the body of the document being evidently in Mr. Hayley's handwriting, and the acceptance, which constituted the forgery, being in a feigned hand very like that of Mr. Scriven, the inference was established by the servant's evidence, that Henry had found the draft and used it for his own purposes.

The fact was, that Mr. Hayley had mislaid the document for some time, at the period when he first contemplated the forgery, and had inquired for it anxiously till he found it in the place where he had concealed it. But many other things occurred in the course of a few days to confirm the suspicions against the poor boy. Three five-pound notes, which Henry had changed in his long travelling across England, found their way to the Bank of England, where the numbers and dates of those given upon the forged draft had been notified. They were traced back from hand to hand, till the chain ended with Henry Hayley.

The whole of his wandering course, with a very few intervals, was tracked by the officer sent in pursuit of him to Northumberland. He was found to have been at Belford, at Wooler, at Caermarthen, and then to have come to London in the mail. With the instinct of bloodhounds the officers pursued their inquiries; got a clue, at the office of the Dutch consul, to his further course; and, furnished with the necessary authority, set out for Rotterdam.

Now Mr. Hayley began to tremble, and Mr. Scriven to rejoice.

"We shall soon have him now!" said the latter to Lady Fleetwood, rubbing his hands; "we shall soon have him now! P---- is not a man to give up the chase till he has run down his game."

"Why, I am sure, Henry, you do not think him guilty," said Lady Fleetwood; "nobody that knew him can think so; and even if you did, you would never wish to destroy the poor lad."

Her brother gazed at her in utter astonishment.

"Do you wish me to think you a fool, Margaret?" he said. "Nobody but one totally destitute of common sense can doubt his guilt."

"Well, I do, Mr. Scriven," replied Lady Fleetwood, a little nettled. "I never pretended to any great sense, and I dare say you have a great deal more; but he was all his life a fine, frank, honourable boy, and it is not into such a heart as his that a crime enters easily. However, even if he had done it, I do not think you would be cruel enough to punish with death a mere boy like that, who could not know all the criminality of the act."

"I have nothing to do with it," said Mr. Scriven. "It is the law will punish him, and that soon, I hope, else there will not be a clerk in all London who will not be forging his master's name, and then pleading his youth."

"Then I trust, with all my heart, the law won't catch him," said Lady Fleetwood. "What are a thousand pounds to you, Henry? It would have been much kinder of you to have paid the money and said nothing about it."

Mr. Scriven gave her a look of unutterable scorn, and buttoning up his coat to keep out such ridiculous notions, quitted the house.

He was a good deal surprised, however, to find that even his clearer-sighted sister, Lady Monkton, in some degree shared the views of Lady Fleetwood. She expressed herself somewhat more cautiously, perhaps, but not less firmly, and gave him to understand that, judging from long observation of Henry's character, nothing would persuade her that he had been guilty of the act imputed to him.

"Then pray who was it, Lady Monkton?" asked Mr. Scriven sharply.

"That is quite another question, and one that I will not take upon me to answer," replied Isabella; "but let us drop the subject, for it is a very, very painful one. We all loved him as if he had been one of our own relations; and he could not have made himself so loved by people who saw his whole conduct, if there had been anything dishonourable or disingenuous in his nature."

"Your love blinds you," replied Mr. Scriven; and Maria Monkton, who had been drawing at the other end of the room, rose with tears in her eyes, and went out.

Those who did love the poor lad--and they were many--had soon fresh cause for grief.

Six weeks passed without anything being heard of the officer who had gone to seek for the young fugitive. Not a doubt existed in his mind that the Henry Calvert of the Dutch passport-office was identical with the Henry Hayley of Bow Street; and, having got a full account of his person and general appearance, this conviction was strengthened at Rotterdam, where he traced him to the Bath-house Inn. He thence pursued him up the Rhine to Cologne, where for two days he could discover no further track, from his assumed name having been terribly mutilated in the books.

Stage by stage he pursued him still; sometimes, indeed, almost giving up the undertaking in despair, but always, by perseverance, gaining some new clue. Thus, to Munich, Innspruck, Trieste, and Venice, he was lured on; and there for five days remained baffled, till it struck the consul that it might be as well to inquire of a celebrated *vetturino* at Mestre. When they went over, the man was absent with his horses, and the officer had to wait another day for his return. The subsequent morning, however, he was more fortunate.

His questions were answered at once. Ten days before, the *vetturino* said he had carried a young English lad, answering exactly the description given, to Ancona. Instead of being fresh-coloured, he stated that the young man was very pale; but then he was ill when he quitted Mestre, and got worse every day till they reached Ancona. There the people of the inn would not take him in, for by that time the youth could not hold up his head at all; and not knowing what to do with him, nor how to make him understand--for he spoke little Italian--he had applied at the house of the Franciscan friars, where he knew there were some Irish monks, and they had charitably received him. There the officer would find him, he said; and that personage without pause set out at once for Ancona.

It was night when he reached the city; but he delayed not an instant, and finding that he could not get aid from the police of the place before morning, he went at once with a guide to the monastery, to give notice of his errand, and ensure that the culprit was not suffered to escape. He had some hopes, indeed, that the monks would give him up at once; but nothing was opened in answer to the great bell except the small shutter over a grate in the door. The porter who appeared behind was an Italian; but the guide could speak a little English, and served as interpreter.

To the first question, whether a young Englishman of the name of Henry Calvert was there, the monk replied; he did not know, and to the officer's demand of admittance returned a direct refusal. The other explained his errand, but it was of no avail. It was contrary to the rule, the good brother said; and, whatever was the officer's business, he could not have admission at that hour.

The latter next demanded to speak with some of the English or Irish brethren, and after some hesitation the old man went away to bring one to the gate.

The officer had to wait fully half-an-hour; but at length a lantern was seen coming across the court, and the shaven head of an elderly man appeared behind the grating.

"What is it you want, my son?" he asked in English, after gazing at the officer attentively as he came up.

"I understand, and that upon sufficient evidence," replied the other, "that within this monastery you have a person named Henry Calvert, otherwise Hayley, charged with forgery to a large amount. I am the bearer of a warrant for his apprehension, which I can show you, and I demand that you deliver up his body to my custody."

"We know nothing of English warrants here," replied the monk, "and the gates of this convent are opened after nine to no one, either to admit or to send forth. Go your way, my son, and return to-morrow if needs must be; but come not without the authority of the state in which you are, otherwise you will come in vain."

The monk was retiring, but the officer called after him, in somewhat civiller tones than perhaps his heart dictated, saying--

"Tell me, at least, sir, if the young man is here."

"Perhaps I should be wise to refuse an answer," said the monk, "seeing that I know you not, neither what right you have to inquire; but as there are plenty ready to defend any of our just privileges, I will venture to say that a lad--a mere boy--calling himself Henry Calvert, is here; but he is, I tell you, at the point of death, having been brought in sick of the malignant fever which is now raging so fiercely in those parts of Italy."

"I must see him notwithstanding," said the officer, doggedly; but the monk waited no further conference, and retired from the gate.

The Londoner and his guide walked back to the inn; and as they went along through the dark and gloomy streets, a slow and solemn sound, the tolling of a heavy bell, burst upon the ear.

The next morning, at the earliest possible hour, the officer's application was made to the police of Ancona. Assistance was immediately given him, and with his guide and a commissary of the government he returned to the monastery. The outer gates were now wide open, and a number of people, monks and others, were passing in and out. At a small door of the principal building stood the old man he had seen on the preceding night, and to him the commissary of police at once led the way. Some conversation took place between them in Italian, and then the monk turned to the officer, saying--

"This good man, my son, tells me you are duly authorised to take into your custody the lad named Henry Calvert--otherwise, you say, Hayley. We do not resist the laws, and he shall be given up to you. Follow me."

The three men followed across the court to a low wing of the building, the monk preceding them with a slow and heavy step. They then walked along a sort of cloister, dry and shady, and at the fifth door on the right the old man stopped and turned a key.

"There he is!" he said throwing open the door; and the officer entered.

Upon a low pallet, stripped of its usual coverings, lay a corpse, with a few flowers strewed upon the bosom. The waxy hue of the face, the plain ravages of illness, the closed eyes, the emaciated features, might make a great difference; but still the colour of the hair, the age, the height, and the general lines of the features, showed the officer that there indeed before him lay all that remained of the gay, frank, happy boy.

He gazed on him for a moment or two, and even ne was moved in some degree.

"When did he die?" he asked in a low tone.

"Last night, five minutes before ten," answered the monk: "when I returned to him, after seeing you, he was in the agony."

Another pause succeeded; and then the monk, pointing to an English portmanteau, which stood in the corner of the cell, said--

"I am ordered to give that and its contents into your custody. There are, besides, this pocket-book, containing the passport with which he travelled, and some bank-notes. He had also a small sum in gold and silver with him, for which the convent will account to the police, and the police to your own consul, after the expenses of the funeral are paid. Can you tell me whether he was a Catholic or not?--we are troubled about the burial."

"I don't know, I am sure," replied the officer; but he then added, with a desire to avoid any unpleasant proceeding, "I dare say he was a Catholic--I think I have heard so."

"Then he shall have Catholic interment," replied the monk, and after a few more questions the officer withdrew.

The portmanteau was put into a hired carriage and conveyed to the inn; the notes were compared with a list which the officer carried, and found to correspond with seven of the numbers there inscribed; and after a conference with the British consul, the Bow Street runner took his departure from Ancona, saying--

"The old monk declared there was only a small sum in gold. I know there must have been a good lot, if the lad did not lead a terribly riotous life as he came, and of that I heard nothing."

There were many who wept for poor Henry Hayley; but there was one who felt that he had more cause to weep than all, though he could not shed a tear. Mr. Hayley fell into profound melancholy, from which nothing could rouse him. His affairs righted themselves, in a very great degree, without his making an effort; several of the speculations in which he had engaged proved eminently successful, but they brought no comfort. He walked about his house and the town like a ghost, never speaking to any one but those who spoke to him; and it was observed that he often talked to himself, but no one heard anything escape his lips save the one solitary word, "murder," murmured in the accents of horror and despair.

CHAPTER IV

This shall be an exceedingly short chapter, merely destined to wind up that preliminary matter with which it was absolutely necessary for the reader to be made acquainted before perusing the real business of the tale. Another long lapse of nearly ten years must intervene before we take up any of the characters afresh; and the reader will soon see now the preceding events connect themselves with those that follow. The characters, indeed, were sadly diminished in number between the time at which the story opens and that to which I have now to proceed.

Of the four children of the elder Mr. Scriven, only two survived--Lady Fleetwood and Mr. Scriven. Lady Monkton survived her husband just ten years, and then died very suddenly, leaving her daughter Maria the heiress of great wealth at the age of about twenty. She was, indeed, a few months more when her mother was taken from her, and Mr. Scriven's guardianship had not long to run--a fact with which that gentleman was not well pleased; for, besides the authority which the guardianship conferred--and all men like authority--the whole of the fortune which his sister Isabella had received, and the accumulated surplus of the rents of Sir Edward Monkton's estates, making together a very large sum, remained in his hands, and he found them exceedingly convenient; nay, more--somewhat lucrative. He clearly accounted for the interest upon every penny at a moderate rate; but he did not think it at all necessary to state to Maria, or to calculate in any way, except for his own private satisfaction--and I do not know that he even did that--all that he gained by turning and returning the funds of hers at his disposal. That went under the general head of "profits of business."

I am not aware whether this would be considered right, fair, and honourable, in the mercantile world or not. There is a good deal to be said on both sides of the question; but certainly, while he allowed, as I have stated, interest upon every penny that he received, at the exact rate which that penny would have produced if invested in the public funds on the day that he received it, he made sometimes twice, sometimes three times, that amount by the use of the money.

Maria, however, knew nothing about this. When she did come of age, she passed the accounts as a matter of course, and begged her uncle to continue to manage her affairs for her as he had been accustomed to do. But when this source of anxiety had gone by, Mr. Scriven had another. Maria inherited all her mother's beauty: she was a gay, gentle girl, with a natural cheerfulness of character generally predominating over and subduing occasional clouds of melancholy, which might well be produced by the early death of parents deeply beloved. Lovely, wealthy, graceful, engaging, with a heart full of warm affections, and a kind disposition, it was more than probable that she would marry early--indeed, only wonderful that she had not already married. Then, again, she chose to reside during a great part of the year with her aunt, Lady Fleetwood. In London her aunt's house was the only proper place for her, but still it made Mr. Scriven somewhat uneasy; for Lady Fleetwood was the kindest and best intentioned woman in the world, and though by no means what is called a matchmaker, she had a very strong conviction--which her own experience had not shaken in the least--that marriage was the only state in which a woman could be really happy.

On this point Mr. Scriven differed with her entirely; and it was not at all pleasant to him to know that she was continually dinning her own system into Maria's ears. However, there was no help for it; and his only consolation was, that his niece was fond of going down alone from time to time to Bolton Park, which was kept up exactly in the same state as at Lady Monkton's death. It was generally, too, at the time when London was fullest and gayest that Maria chose to make her retreat; and at Bolton she saw no one but her neighbour, Lady Anne Mellent, the similarity of whose situation to her own drew closer the bonds of early affection, though their characters were very different. It may be said in passing, that Lady Anne had been longer an orphan at this time than Maria; for Lord Milford had not survived the death of his father many years, and Lady Milford had died the Christmas before her husband.

Lady Anne, gay, lively, and decided in character, had been left to the guardianship of mere men of business, and soon set at defiance the trammels they endeavoured to impose upon her. At eighteen she was as much mistress of her own house as if she had been eight-and-forty; and although her old governess continued to live with her, at the earnest request rather than the positive command of her guardians, yet the very idea of governing anything never seemed to enter into the good lady's head. Yet, whether in resistance or compliance, in the display of her independence or the exercise of her strong good sense, there was so much good humour and even fun in Lady Anne Mellent's manner, that neither guardians nor relations could be angry. There was one, indeed, of the former--an old gentleman with a pigtail and powdered poll--who would sit and laugh at her till the tears ran over his cheeks--ever and anon putting on a grave face, and proposing something to which he knew she would never consent, merely to excite her resistance, and always beginning--

"Now, my dear young lady, you really ought--" &c.

But, whether serious or in jest, Lady Anne always had her own way; and her guardians often came to the conclusion, that her own way was generally the right one.

There was an old maiden aunt of her mother's--the only near female relative she had, whom one of her father's executors thought fit to propose as a suitable person to live with her and keep up her establishment. But Lady Anne at once replied--

"Indeed she shall not. In the first place, all the wine in the cellar would be turned sour in a fortnight. In the next place, she would spoil all my prospects of 'establishing myself for life,' as she herself calls it; for by her own account she is a most dangerous rival, and has had more proposals than ever I hope to have; and in the next place she would attempt to control me, which neither she nor any other person ever shall do--except my lord and master, if I should some day happen to have such a thing."

In short, Lady Anne Mellent was a very pretty, nice, clever, independent girl, whom many people considered completely spoiled by fate, fortune, and her relations, and who might have been so, if a high and noble heart, a kind and generous spirit, and a clear and rapid intellect would have permitted it. She loved and respected Maria Monkton, who was a little older--would often take her advice when she would take that of no other person--frequently in conversation with others set her immeasurably above herself--and yet often would call her to her face a dear, gentle, loveable, poor-spirited little thing. Her last vagary before she came of age was to take a tour upon the Continent with her old governess, a maid, and three men-servants. Her guardians would here certainly have interfered, had she ever condescended to make them acquainted with her intentions; but the expedition was plotted, all her arrangements were made, and she herself was in the heart of Paris, before they knew anything of the matter. In writing to the old gentleman with the pigtail, she said--

"You will not be at all surprised to learn that I am here on my way to Rome and Naples; and I think, as I have nobody with me but Mrs. Hughes and my maid and the other servants, I shall enjoy my tour very much. Charles Marston, my old playfellow, was here the other day, and very delightful--nearly as mad as myself. He intends to go heaven knows where, but first to Damascus, because it is the only place where one can eat plums.

If anybody asks you where I am, you can say that I have run away with him, and that you have my own authority for it. Then none will believe a word of it, which they otherwise might. Send me plenty of money to Milan, for I intend to buy all Rome, and set it up in the great drawing-room at Harley Lodge, as a specimen of the true antique."

Enough, however, of the gay girl, and almost enough of the chapter. There is only one person, I believe, whom I have not mentioned sufficiently. Mr. Hayley's fate was sad, but not undeserved. In vain Fortune made a perverse effort to befriend him; in vain matters turned out favourable which had once looked very dark. The worm that perisheth not was in his heart, and it consumed him. He strove to establish a prosperous business for himself, separated from Mr. Scriven, and he succeeded to a certain extent; but he had no spirit to attend to anything long. He neglected everything-- himself, his affairs, the affairs of others, his friends, acquaintances, his own person. He became slovenly in habits and appearance; people said he drank; business fell off; correspondents would not trust him; and after a struggle of eight years, he retired upon a pittance, gave himself up to intemperance, went mad--died.

Such was the end of one to whom, not twenty-four years before, had been opened a brighter career than his hopes had ever pictured.

The reader may not exactly see how several of the characters and events which have passed across the stage in this phantasmagoria can have any influence upon the story that is to follow; but let him wait patiently, and he will see that not one word which has been written could have been properly omitted; and for the present let him remember that just four-and-twenty years and a few months had passed since the death of the elder Mr. Scriven, so that his son was now a man of middle age, and his only surviving daughter approaching her grand climacteric; that his grandson Charles Marston was now twenty-four, and his grand-daughter Maria Monkton not quite twenty-two.

CHAPTER VII

A fine but yet a solemn evening trod upon the steps of a May day. There was a red light in the west under deep purple clouds. Overhead, all was blue, intense, and unbroken even by a feathery vapour. A star, a planet, faint from the sun's rays still unrecalled, was seen struggling to shine; and a lingering chillness came upon the breeze as it swept over a wide heath. The road from London to Southampton might be traced from the top of one of the abrupt knolls into thousands of which the heath was broken, winding on for four or five miles on either side, and dim plantations bounded the prospect. Between, nothing caught the eye but the desert-looking, wavy expanse of uncultivated ground, except where, in a little sandy dell through which poured a small white line of water, appeared a low thatch and four ruinous walls. At first one thought it a cowshed or a pigsty, but a filmy wave of smoke showed it to be a human habitation. The nest of the wild bird, the hole of the fox, the lair of the deer, is more warm, and sheltered, and secure than it was.

A carriage came in sight from the side of Southampton, dashing along with four horses. At first it looked in the distance like a husk of hempseed drawn by four fleas; but as it came rattling on, it turned out a handsome vehicle and a good team. The top was loaded with boxes, imperials, and all sorts of leathern contrivances for holding superfluities, towering to the skies. Underneath was a long, square, flat basket of wicker, likewise loaded heavily.

The carriage dashed on over one slope, down another, across a sharp channel left by a stream of water which had flowed down two or three days before after heavy rains, up part of a hill, and there it suddenly stopped, toppled, and went over. The axle had broken, and a hind wheel had come off. The servant flew out of his leathern cage behind, lighted in a huge tuft of heath somewhat like his own whiskers, and then got up and rubbed his shoulder.

Then a gay, joyous, mellow voice was heard calling out from the inside, "Spilt, upon my life! What a crash! Are you hurt, Mr. Winkworth? Venus and all the Graces smashed to pieces, for a thousand pounds! Ha! ha! ha!

Well, this is a consummation--Here, boy! open the door and let us out. I always lie on my right side--I think, Winkworth, you'll be glad to get rid of me."

"Uncommonly!" said a voice from below. "I thought you light-headed and light-hearted; but something about you, boy, is heavy enough."

By this time the postboys were out of their saddles and the servant was hobbling up. The door was opened, and forth came a tall, good-looking young man, dressed in gay travelling costume, who instantly turned round to assist somebody else out of the broken vehicle.

The next person who appeared upon the stage was a man of sixty or more, spare, wrinkled, yellow, with very white hair and a face close shaved. If he were ugly, it was from age, and perhaps bad health, the colour of his skin being certainly somewhat sickly; but his features were good, and his eye was clear, and even merry, though a few testy lines appeared round the lips. He stooped a good deal, which made him look short, though he had once been tall; but in no other respect did bodily strength seem decayed, for he was as active as a bird. No sooner was his younger companion out of the chaise than he was seen issuing forth, all legs and arms together, in the most extraordinary manner possible, and the whole process was accomplished in a moment.

"Pish!" cried the elderly man, peevishly: "pretty reception to one's native land after seven-and-twenty years' absence."

"It has had time to forget you," said the younger, laughing.

"To break down on the first road I come to!" went on the other. "It is all because you overloaded the carriage so. I should have done better to have travelled by the stage, or any other conveyance, instead of taking a seat in your mud-loving vehicle."

"The stage might have been overloaded and broken too," rejoined the other. "Take all the rubs of life quietly, Mr. Winkworth. Something must be done, however. One of you fellows, ride on, and get the first blacksmith you can find. Send a chaise, too, to meet us; we'll walk on. You, Jerry, stay with the carriage, and when it is mended bring it on. You're not hurt, are you?"

"My shoulder, sir, has suffered from too close an intimacy with mother earth," replied the servant in an affected tone, "and my leg, I take it, is of a different figure from the ordinary run; but I dare say all will come straight with time."

"Puppy!" grumbled the old gentleman, and began walking on as fast as his legs would carry him. He was soon overtaken by his young companion, and as they walked on together the postboy overtook and passed them. They said little; but Mr. Winkworth looked about him and seemed to enjoy the prospect, notwithstanding the accident which had forced it upon his contemplation.

The postboy trotted on, and the two gentlemen walked forward; night was falling fast; and just when the messenger sent for the chaise had disappeared on one side, and the carriage with its accompaniments on the other, a bifurcation of the road, without a finger-post, presented itself.

"Now, Mr. Charles Lovel Marston, what is to be done?" said the old gentleman. "You and I are two fools, my dear sir, or we should have mounted the two posters, and let the postboys get themselves out of the scrape they had got themselves into."

"It is just as bad to gallop along a wrong road as to walk along one," replied his young companion with a laugh--"only one goes farther, and faster to the devil."

The Old gentleman laughed heartily. "There is something on there which looks like fellow-humanity," he said: "it may be a stunted tree or a milestone, but we may as well ask it the way;" and putting on his spectacles, he walked forward with his head raised to see the better.

Charles Marston followed; and for a minute or two both were inclined to think the form they saw would turn out a mere stump after all, so motionless did it appear. On a nearer approach, however, a human figure became more distinct. It was that of a woman, old, and evidently very poor, sitting motionless on the top of a little hillock, her hand supporting her chin, and her eyes bent upon the ground. The short-cut grey hair escaped from under the torn cap; the face was broad, especially about the forehead; the eyes were large and black; the skin, naturally brown, was now yellow and wrinkled; and the hand which supported the head, while the other lay languidly on the lap, was covered with a soiled and tattered kid glove. Round her shoulders was an old dirty shawl, mended and patched; and the rest of her garmenture was in as dilapidated a state.

She took not the least notice of the two travellers, though they stood and gazed at her for a full minute ere they spoke. At length Mr. Winkworth raised his voice and asked, "Can you tell us which is the London road, my good woman?"

The poor creature lifted her eyes, and looked at them with a scared, wandering expression. "They shaved his head," she said, in the most melancholy tone in the world, "indeed they did. They thought he was mad;

but it was only remorse--remorse. He never held up his head after he was quite sure the poor boy was dead--he whom he had wronged, and blighted, and killed."

She paused and began to weep.

"She's mad, poor thing!" said Mr. Winkworth: "she should not be left on this common alone."

"He saved his own life at the boy's expense," said the woman again; "but what a heart he had ever after! Wine would not quiet it--spirits would not keep it up. But when he found the boy was dead, then was the time of suffering. And they thought he was mad when he raved about it, but remorse will rave as well as madness; and they shaved his head and put a strait waistcoat on him; and one of the keepers knocked him down when he struggled; and he died in the night, you know. It was no fault of mine," she added, looking straight at the old man, as if he had accused her. "I could not leave him in his misery because he was sinful. He was my own brother, you know. No, no; I could not do that."

"Of whom are you speaking, my good woman?" asked the younger gentleman in a commonplace tone. "Why, my brother, to be sure," said the poor woman, looking at him with an expression of bewildered surprise--"whom else should I be talking of?--Ay, ay; he was a rich man once, till he took to gambling."

"Stay! here is some one coming," said the old gentleman; "this is a sad sight, Charles Marston. This poor woman has seen better days. This is a bit of a real cashmere shawl she has over her shoulders; I should know one when I see it, I think. We cannot leave her here alone. We'll ask this boy, who comes trudging along, if he has ever seen her before or knows anything about her."

"Come, Bessy--come in. I have got one-and-ninepence for the eggs, so I bought a loaf and an ounce of tea. Don't sit moping there--it's cold, Bessy."

His tone was very kind and affectionate, and the two gentlemen examined him as well as they could by the failing light. He was a lad of fourteen or fifteen years of age, short, but seemingly strong and well-made; and his countenance, as far as they could see, was frank and intelligent. His clothing was both scanty and poor, but it was well patched and mended, and he had a pair of stout shoes on his feet.

"I'm coming, Jim; I'm coming, my dear!" replied the old woman, in quite a different tone from that in which she had been speaking to the strangers. "I just went out to get a little fresh air; and I found another nest, and put all the eggs on the shelf, my man."

The two gentlemen called the boy to them, and in a low tone asked several questions about the poor creature whom he called Bessy--especially the younger one, who seemed a good deal interested. The elder inquired whether she was his mother or any relation. The boy replied that she was not, and his little history was soon told. She had come about their cottage, he said, three or four years before, and had slept one night upon the heath. His mother, who was then living, had been kind to her, and had taken her in.

"We had two cows then," said the boy, "and used to feed them on the common; and it was a good year, and poor Bessy used to do what she could to help. She's a famous hand with her needle, and mended all the clothes; my mother had a little washing, and we got on well enough, what between the butter and the washing, and a few vegetables out of the garden. But, a year ago last Christmas, mother died, and I and Bessy have lived here alone as well as we can. She is not at all dangerous, and at times quite right; and she helps me to find plovers' eggs, and to watch wheat-ears, and all that she can; she mends the clothes, and does many little things; and she has taught me to read and write in her well times. When she's at the worst, she can always read the Bible of a night. I'm sure I don't know what I should have done without her since mother died."

"Was she better dressed when she first came to your cottage?" asked Charles Marston.

"Oh! to be sure," replied the boy; "but her clothes are worn out now, poor thing!"

"Well, we'll come and rest at your cottage," said Mr. Winkworth; "our carriage has broken down on the common, and we've sent for a chaise."

The boy seemed to hesitate for a moment, and then said--

"It is a poor place."

The gentlemen, however, persisted; and again rousing the poor old woman, who had once more fallen into a fit of gloomy thought, the lad led them to the hut of which mention has been made in the beginning of this chapter.

It was a poor place, as he had said--as poor as it could be. The unmended windows, in spite of rags and paper, let in the winds of night; the door leaned back upon its heels, like a drunken man trying to stand soberly; the thatch was worn through in many places; and it was a happy time when it did not rain. In short, it had been originally but a hovel of clay of the poorest kind. Now it was still poorer; and when the boy and the old woman together--for she helped him--had lighted a fire with some bundles of dry heath, and the flame rose high and flickered round the broken walls, the two men, accustomed to luxury and ease, and comfort of every kind, felt a shuddering impression of the evils to which their fellow-creatures are often subject, which was likely to do both their hearts no harm. The boy was communicative enough, and told all that he knew with quiet intelligence; but they could get the old woman to speak no more. She answered every question with a monosyllable, and then fell into silence again.

They did not leave the hovel as destitute as they found it. They had with them neither provisions, nor furniture, nor suitable clothing to give; but they had that most malleable of metals, which, when properly hammered out, spreads into meat, drink, and clothing.

Nor were they satisfied with this. When they reached a little town, the old gentleman with the yellow face sent for a bricklayer, gave him some orders in a low tone, and wrote down an address upon a piece of paper. The younger one talked for half-an-hour with the landlady in the bar, and next morning paid her four pounds nine shillings more than his own bill. That was a happy day for the poor people of the cottage on which Charles Marston and his old companion broke down upon the heath.

CHAPTER VIII

There is a small house in the purlieus of fashion, surrounded on every side by mansions five times as big as itself. You know it quite well, dear reader--you have passed it a dozen times or more, and looked up and wondered what it did there, surrounded as it is by the mansions of ancient aristocracy; for the part of the town in which it is situated is not one of the new rookeries of new people which have risen up to the south-west and north-west of the capital, upon spots that were fields within these thirty years.

It is tall, and thin, and brown, like a spinster of a certain age at a county ball, amongst a row of bland and brilliant dowagers--quite the sort of house, in short, which the wonderful George Robins would have advertised for sale as "a unique bachelor's residence, situate in the very heart of the fashionable world, commanding advantages rarely met with singly, but never, perhaps, united, except in this most charming abode."

Nevertheless, it was not the residence of a bachelor at all, nor of a married man, nor of a spinster, old or young. It was the town house (and indeed the only house) of a very excellent and respectable widow lady, with a moderate income and the best intentions in the world, but not the best wits to guide them.

Having spoken of her income, I must make that matter quite clear. She had just seven hundred a-year, and would not, indeed, have had that, had it not been for the care and circumspection of a very prudent brother, who had interfered to see the affairs of her marriage settlement properly conducted.

I need not add, after this, that there dwelt Lady Fleetwood. When she was alone, her household consisted of a footman, well powdered and laced, a cook, a housemaid, and her own maid--a somewhat extravagant establishment, considering her income; but in all other things she was very economical--at least she thought so, and Maria Monkton fully agreed in her opinion. She did not pamper any of the appetites, nor indeed any of the vanities, of the flesh, except in the instance of the powdered footman. Her table was always regulated with great exactness, and her certain number of glasses of wine was never exceeded. Her dresses, by the skill of her maid, appeared in various forms, with very great success; and when Maria was with her there was always a carriage at her command. Nor, in truth, when Maria was at Bolton Park, did Lady Fleetwood go without; for a chariot and a pair of horses were always left at the stables, with a particular request from the niece that her aunt would use them every day, lest the horses should grow frisky for want of exercise.

When Maria was in town, however, the case was different. Three or four servants were always in the hall; the whole establishment was increased; the little house had more occupants than it seemed capable of containing--more, indeed, than it really did contain at night; and then, as this was all for Maria Monkton's convenience, Maria Monkton insisted upon paying the whole expenses. Now, as, upon an average, Maria was eight months out of the twelve with her aunt and two or three of the remaining four Lady Fleetwood passed at Bolton Park, the fact of her income fully meeting her expenditure, and leaving her a little surplus at the end of the year, may be accounted for. Lady Fleetwood, it is true, did not understand it altogether, and would sometimes run up her accounts with a somewhat bewildered air, and in the end give up the task, acknowledging that she never had a head for figures.

It might be a little wrong of Maria thus to mystify her aunt; but she was a dear, good girl, notwithstanding; and, accustomed to pet Lady Fleetwood from her own childhood, she well knew there was only one way of managing her, and what that way was. She even went farther than saving her good aunt's income for her by taking the greater share of all her expenses upon herself: she calculated that one of two events--one very common, and one universal--might occur to herself: that she might die, or that she might marry; and, to put it out of the power of any one to leave her aunt in embarrassed circumstances, her first act on coming of age was to settle upon her, without her knowing a word of the matter, a sufficient sum to make her income a very comfortable one.

In the month of May, then, about the middle of the day, Lady Fleetwood was seated in her drawing-room, writing little notes--an occupation of which she was rather fond. Maria was out of town, but expected to return on that day or the following morning, and all was duly prepared for her reception. The curtains of the room were partly drawn, to keep out too much light, for the house was on the sunny side of the square; and in the mitigated glow Lady Fleetwood, though her hair was now very grey, and the wrinkled impress of Time's claw was on her fair skin, showed many traces of that great beauty which had once distinguished her.

She had just sealed one small billet and begun a second, when she heard the near rush of wheels through the roll of many others more distant, and a carriage stopped at her own door.

It was too early for ordinary visitors, who, with a due economy of time, always choose the hour to call when they are likely to find their dear friends absent.

"It is Maria," said Lady Fleetwood to herself. "She has come up early."

The next instant the door was flung open, but not by a servant; and without announcement a young and good-looking man entered with a light and gay step, and threw wide open his arms before the good lady.

"Here I am, my dear aunt! here I am!" cried Charles Marston; "safe and sound from perils by land and perils by water, perils by robbers, perils by cooks, and perils by chambermaids. Come to the nepotal arms, and banish all anxieties upon the bosom of kindred love!"

"Charles, Charles!--you mad boy!" cried Lady Fleetwood, embracing him tenderly; "how can you startle me so?--you know how nervous I am. Why, you have come back six months before you intended."

"And three days," answered Charles, laughing; "which means to say, my dear aunt Flee, that you think I have come back six months too soon. I'll be affronted--I'll pout. Really!--'well, I never!' as the Kellnerin at Brixen said when I kissed her before company. This is the coolest reception of a returned prodigal that ever I heard of."

"How can you be so absurd, Charles?" exclaimed his aunt. "What is a Kellnerin? Where is Brixen? Do you mean Brixton?"

Charles burst into a shout of laughter, patted his aunt's cheek in the most paternal manner, and led her back to her seat by the tips of her fingers.

"Haven't time, my dear aunt--haven't time," he said. "I'll tell you all about Kellnerins and Brixens by-and-by, if you're a good girl. Just now, I've got a particular friend and travelling companion in the carriage with me--Mr. Winkworth--the most extraordinary piece of yellow skin and dry bones you ever saw. He comes from Egypt; and I have brought him over, intending to present him to the British Museum or the Zoological Society, either as an extraordinary and almost unique specimen of the fossil man, or the only instance in Europe of the living mummy. I must bring him up-stairs and introduce him to you, and you must ask him to dinner. I've invited him already in your name: was not that a kind, considerate nephew?"

"Impossible, my dear Charles!" exclaimed Lady Fleetwood, in a great flutter. "I am really not prepared--you forget, my dear boy, my small means. I am not always ready to receive people at dinner: a stranger, too! There is no turbot--nothing but some slices of cod and----"

"Never mind, never mind, my dear aunt. It will do quite well. Cod is excellent," exclaimed Charles Marston. "I have not tasted cod for a year and a half, and I'll answer for it my mummy has not seen such a thing since he was cook to one of the Ptolemies--I forget which, but he'll tell you all about it. I'll go and bring him.--Heaven and earth! I do believe the carriage is driving off."

And down-stairs he ran as fast as possible, but only to see his carriage-and-four driving round the square at a very rapid rate.

"Why, where are they gone? What the devil's the matter with them?" cried Charles.

"The gentleman inside told the boys to drive him to Lloyd's Hotel, sir," said Lady Fleetwood's servant--"just on the opposite side, sir. The carriage will be back in a minute."

"Well, the old gentleman must have his own way, I suppose," said Charles Marston; "and so I'll go up to my dear aunt again."

"Well, now, my dear aunt, he's gone," continued the nephew, in a mock reproachful tone. "I am quite sure he heard all you said, and thought it very inhospitable."

"Nonsense, Charles! he could not hear, I am sure," replied Lady Fleetwood, going to the window to see if it were open. "Is that your carriage? Why, it is loaded like a wagon."

"Well it may be," answered her nephew, "or more like a stage-coach licensed to carry twelve outside, for there are the nine Muses and the three Graces. I am afraid it would come under the penalties of the act, however; for there are moreover two or three Apollos, half-a-dozen Venuses, to say nothing of Seneca and Aristides, Osiris, and Acis and Galatea. I intend, my dear aunt, to have them all arranged here in this very drawing-room. Your room will look like a Walhalla, or a studio, or a Greek temple, or Spode's manufactory, or a stone-mason's shop; and you shall have a helmet, and a shield, and an owl, and pass for Minerva."

"Indeed, Charles, you are mad, I think," said Lady Fleetwood: "the room is small enough as it is, without being loaded with Graces and Muses, and all sorts of things."

"Tell my servant to open the cases when he comes back," cried unpitying Charles Marston, as Lady Fleetwood's footman entered with a note; "and bid him get seven men to help him, and bring up the statues--I always have my own way, my dear aunt. I will see your room classically decorated; and then, if you do not like your marble palace, you can throw the statues out of the window, or get in a number of porters to do it for you. They will be capital metal for macadamising the roads. Then the people will say you have been playing at marbles, you know, and it will all pass off as a joke."

"Charles, Charles! do let me have one moment's peace to read what Maria says," exclaimed Lady Fleetwood: "really, I had forgotten what a wild creature you are, or else you are worse than ever."

"Mere exuberance of spirits, my dear aunt, at seeing you and England once more," replied Charles Marston; "but I'll be serious--nay, I am quite serious. What does Maria say? Where is she? When shall I have the pleasure of giving her a kiss? It is not every man who has the privilege of kissing such a lovely girl gratis. I long for it, I assure you. Nay, I am quite serious; I have several very serious things to talk to you about--most profound. But somehow, my dear aunt Flee, when I see you, I get quite boyish again--you are so charming. It's a pity the prayer-book says we must not marry our mother's sister. You are the only woman who would suit me in the whole world--indeed you are.--There, I'm as grave as a judge! Read your note, read your note, and tell me all about Maria afterwards."

And sitting down, Charles bent his head, gazed at his clasped hands, and fell into a fit of thought, to all appearance much more deep than his rattling manner would have led one to suppose his mind capable of sustaining for two minutes.

"There! Maria does not return till to-morrow," said Lady Fleetwood, finishing the reading of her note.

"Then I shall have you and the cod all to myself," replied Charles Marston, looking up with one of his gay laughs; but, instantly resuming a more serious tone, he said, "And now, my dear aunt, I have three very grave subjects to talk to you about."

"Indeed!" exclaimed Lady Fleetwood, putting on an important look: "what may they be, Charles? I am sure I am ready to give you any advice in my power."

"Dear creature!" cried Charles Marston--"as if she thought I ever took anybody's advice! But to the point. Has a gentleman of the name of Frank Middleton called to inquire for me within the last week or two."

"Oh, dear, yes!" exclaimed Lady Fleetwood; "he called yesterday. I forgot to tell you."

"As if she had had time to tell me anything!" said Charles.

"His card is in the dish," continued Lady Fleetwood. "There is no address on it, or I would have written to him to say you were not expected for some months."

"That would have been kind," said her nephew; "now, how the deuce am I to find him out?"

"Oh! he will call again--he said he would call in a day or two," replied his aunt.

"Wise Frank Middleton!" exclaimed Charles; "he seems to have divined you, my dear aunt."

Lady Fleetwood looked bewildered.

"And now," continued her nephew, "can you tell me what my mysterious uncle, Scriven, wrote to me for, to come back directly, as he wanted to see me on particular business? I always like to meet my excellent uncle prepared--with full forethought of what is to come next; and he was as dark in his communication as the Sphinx's mouth."

"No! did he send for you?" exclaimed Lady Fleetwood. "He did not tell me a word about it--how strange! I saw him only yesterday, and was talking about you, but he did not say a word. He was always very close and discreet, you know, Charles."

"Wise man!" said Charles Marston; and he fell into thought again for a moment or two. "Pray, my dear aunt, what was he saying about me?" he inquired after this pause.

"Oh, I don't recollect--nothing particular, I believe," replied Lady Fleetwood, the colour growing a little deeper in her cheek.

"Ho, ho! a secret!" said Charles to himself, and then continued aloud, "Well, my dear aunt, I know you have a short memory, and I know my uncle never tells you anything of importance, for he says you forget it as soon as you hear it."

"He is very wrong there," said Lady Fleetwood, who rather piqued herself upon her powers of recollection, "for I never forget anything----"

"Then what was it he said?" inquired Charles, abruptly.

"Oh! I do not know it was intended for your ears," replied Lady Fleetwood, "or that Maria would like such a thing to be talked about."

"Then it was about Maria too?" said Charles with a laugh: "now I know all about it. It was that Maria was dying with love for me, and that I was wandering all over the world, flirting with every pretty woman I met. Well, I dare say she will not be much obliged to him for saying that."

"He did not say that at all, my dear Charles," replied Lady Fleetwood in a little alarm: "he only said what a good thing it would be if you and Maria were to marry; and I thought so too, for you are very fond of each other, and you are both only-children, and----"

"Poor orphans!" exclaimed Charles Marston, laughing heartily. "Well, matrimony is as good as any other orphan asylum. I don't think it will do, my dear aunt. We are more like brother and sister than lovers. However, to my third profound problem. Now, tell me, dear lady mine, do you recollect a certain Mr. Hayley, who was once my uncle's partner?"

"To be sure!" answered Lady Fleetwood: "don't you, Charles? Why, his son, poor Henry----"

"I recollect him perfectly, dear aunt," replied Charles, gravely: "my head is not such a colander, nor my heart either, that people can slip out of either one or the other even in ten years. But what I want to know is this: had not Mr. Hayley a sister?"

"Yes, to be sure he had," replied Lady Fleetwood--"a nice, quiet, good sort of creature, devoted to her brother and the poor boy. She used to play beautifully upon the piano and sing----"

"I don't care a pin about that," said Charles. "I never saw her more than two or three times; but what I wish to know is, what was her name?"

"Her name--her name," said Lady Fleetwood, "her name was Rebecca, I think----"

"Which in the Hebrew means 'plump,'" said Charles Marston. "Well, when I last saw her she was thin enough."

"No, indeed, Charles; she was quite the contrary," said Lady Fleetwood. "I do not mean to say that she was fat; but----"

"Oh, say she was fat if you like, dear aunt," replied Charles Marston, laughing: "she is not here to listen, and I won't betray you, so it will not pain her."

"I would not pain a fly willingly, Charles," answered his relation.

"I am sure you would not," said her nephew, laying his hand upon hers affectionately; "but now the case is, my dear aunt, how we can rescue this poor thing from a situation of great misery. You must know that I should have been in town last night, but that my carriage broke down on a miserable wild common. It had to be mended; and while a blacksmith was being sent for, Winkworth and I wandered on and met with a poor crazy woman, in rags and wretchedness, who, we found, had been living there in a dilapidated hovel for some years, with an orphan boy, whose mother had been very kind to her as long as the poor thing lived herself. As soon as I saw her, I thought that her face was not unknown to me: you remember Miss Hayley had very peculiar large black eyes; but six or seven years have passed since Hayley gave up business altogether and went to live over at Highgate, and I have not seen his sister since. Some words that she dropped, however, led my mind back to the past, though all she said was rambling and incoherent; and the more I think of this, the more I am convinced that it is poor Henry Hayley's aunt."

"Good gracious!" cried Lady Fleetwood--"that is very sad indeed. I am so sorry that I did not go again to see them at Highgate! I went twice, but never found her, and she did not return my call; and your uncle was so angry I had been at all, that I did not go back. I heard that Hayley himself was dead some time ago, and I always intended to inquire for his sister; but just then came poor Isabella's death, you know."

"Nobody who knows you, my dear aunt, can suppose you would be unkind to any one," replied Charles Marston; "but something must be done for this poor thing."

"Certainly, certainly!" replied Lady Fleetwood. "I will talk to your uncle about it, and I am sure he will----"

"Do nothing at all," said Charles, almost sharply, "or at best put her into a cheap madhouse, where she will be dieted upon gruel and maltreated by keepers--worse off than she is now. I will go down to-morrow or the next day, and see about the matter myself. In the mean time, both Winkworth and I have done something to make her and the boy more comfortable."

"And who is this Mr. Winkworth?" asked Lady Fleetwood, whose mind was of that peculiar species which may be called the collateral--one of those minds that are always carried away to one side by the slightest possible circumstance--to which a word, or a sound, or a look is ever one of Hippomene's apples, and sets the wits running after it with all the speed of an Atalanta--"who is Mr. Winkworth? He seems to have become a great favourite of yours, Charles."

"He has laid me under the greatest possible obligation," replied her nephew, smiling.

"Indeed! How was that?" inquired his aunt.

"Why, he was kind enough to permit me to save his life," answered Charles. "You must know, as I was riding along, not a hundred miles from a place called Antioch, which I dare say you never heard of----"

"Oh, dear, yes!" said Lady Fleet wood. "It's in the Bible."

"Yes, and in Syria, into the bargain," continued Charles. "But, as I was saying, as I was riding along, not a hundred miles from Antioch, with servants, and Arabs, and all manner of people with me, I came to a place under the high rocks, when I suddenly heard half-a-dozen shots fired. My guides thought it would be better to wait a little till the firing was over, but I judged it proper to ride on and see what it was about. So, when we turned the corner of a great, black, overhanging rock, like Westminster Abbey turned topsy-turvy, I saw two or three unfortunate servants upon the ground, rather silent, and quite still, with about a dozen other fellows with blackish faces, long guns, and a great deal of white cotton about them, two of whom were taking aim at the only one of the travellers left alive--in other words, Mr. Winkworth, who for his part was trying to cover his angles-- which are many, by-the-way--with his horse. He had got a long pistol in his hand; but that was nothing against guns, you know, my dear aunt; and, besides, twelve to one is not fair play. So I spurred on, and my fellows being obliged to spur after, though a little unwillingly, did very well when it came to fighting; and we drove the banditti up into the hills, shooting one or two of them. We then came back, and found my poor countryman mourning over his dead. He was wounded himself, so I was obliged to stay and nurse him, and we have travelled together ever since."

"But who is he?--what is he?" demanded Lady Fleetwood, after she had exclaimed upon her nephew's peril, and praised heaven for his escape.

"Well, my dear aunt, as to who he is, I never thought of inquiring," answered Charles; "and as to what he is, I can but answer, he is certainly a gentleman--a very well-informed, amiable, clever person--a little testy, very eccentric and old bachelorish, but kind-hearted, generous, and benevolent, and moreover evidently very rich, though he has his own particular ways, out of which he does not choose to be put."

"Well, if he is rich, that does not signify," said Lady Fleetwood.

"Now, would not any one who heard that think you the most mercenary old creature in the world?" exclaimed Charles--"you, who would give away your last nightcap to a beggar!"

"But, my dear, you know there are so many impostors," said his aunt, with a very sagacious air.

"Every one of whom would take you in in a moment," replied her nephew. "However, to set your mind at rest, Mr. Winkworth would not consent even to take a place in my carriage till he had stipulated that he was to pay one-half of all the expenses."

This satisfied Lady Fleetwood's first doubts--doubts which she entertained merely upon abstract theory; for she was, or chose to be supposed, the most suspicious person in the world at a distance, but at close quarters she was soon overcome.

Charles Marston's carriage had by this time returned, and an hour was spent in unpacking an imperial; the nephew assuring his aunt that in ten minutes her drawing-room would be full of statues, and she, poor lady, begging pitifully, but in vain, to be excused from receiving the three Graces and the nine Muses. Merciless Charles Marston would not relieve her mind in the least, till at length twelve beautiful small alabaster figures, none of them a foot high, were brought in, and found easy accommodation upon consoles and cheffoniers, much to the delight of the good lady, who declared that they were the most exquisite things ever seen, and thanked him over and over again for the gift.

When all this was done, Lady Fleetwood pressed her nephew to go at once and see his uncle; but Charles had a fit of restiveness upon him.

"No, my dear aunt, I won't," he said: "my uncle has something disagreeable to tell me, or he would not have sent such a way; and I am resolved to stay one day at peace in the midst of the great capital. So here I remain, unless you absolutely want to get rid of me."

"Not at all, Charles, of course," replied Lady Fleetwood; "but only I think it would be a great pity for you to offend your uncle. You know that he has no other male relation, and he must be enormously rich."

"I really do not care whether he is rich or poor," answered Charles. "I am as rich as--or indeed richer than--he is; for, thanks to my father's generosity, I have as much as I want; and I am quite sure my uncle Scriven could not say that."

So there he sat, discussing many things with his aunt, telling her strange stories of his adventures in foreign lands--all true, indeed, but tinged in the telling with a gleam of the marvellous, for the purpose of exciting Lady Fleetwood's astonishment. In that endeavour he was very successful, for the organ of wonder was quite sufficiently developed in her head; and the day passed over very pleasantly, till it was time for Charles to seek a lodging for the night, which he easily found at the hotel opposite, where his friend Mr. Winkworth had already taken up his quarters.

Before he bade his aunt farewell, however, he gave directions to her footman, if Mr. Middleton called, to inquire particularly where he was to be found in London, and to let him know that his two friends, Mr. Winkworth and Mr. Marston, were at the hotel; and then came inquiries from Lady Fleetwood as to who this other crony of her nephew's could be.

"I will not stop to tell you all, my dear aunt," replied Charles, who by this time had his hat in his hand: "suffice it that he is the most charming man you ever saw--take care you do not find him too charming. He is quite a Don Alonzo-ish sort of man--pale, dark, wonderfully handsome, more than six feet high, with a sabre-cut across his face, sufficient to win the hearts of all the women in London. He is a colonel in the Spanish service, and has all sorts of orders and chains, though he is not above seven or eight-and-twenty. I believe his mother was a Spanish lady--I think, indeed, somebody told me so; but at all events he is quite the person to fall in love with, if you are inclined, my dear aunt."

"My dear Charles, how can you be so absurd?" exclaimed his aunt; "but now you have not told me how you met with him."

"I'll keep that for a *bonne bouche*," replied Charles, and walked away to his hotel.

CHAPTER IX

It is my full and firm belief, that if, on any given day of any given year, you were, dear reader, to take the accurate history of any five square miles, not exactly a desert, upon the solid surface of the earth, and examine with a microscope the acts and deeds, the circumstances, the accidents, and the fate of the people upon it, you would find strange romances enough going on to stock a library. Look into a cottage--what will you find? Perhaps a romance of love and tenderness struggling with sorrows, difficulties, and penury; perhaps a broad farce of a quarrelsome wife and a drunken husband; perhaps a tragedy of sin, crime, and misery. Look into that stately mansion, the house of a great merchant--what is there? It may be the comedy of purse-proud affectation; it may be the tale of the tenderest affections and highest qualities; or it may show that agonizing struggle which the falling man makes to sustain himself upon the edge of the precipice at the foot of which he is soon to lie, dashed to pieces. A romance is but a microscopic view of some half-dozen human hearts.

The above observations may apparently be wide of the subject; but still there must be some link of association between them and what is to follow, as they naturally occurred to my mind when considering how I could best tell the events which are about to be related. Perhaps it was that I thought it somewhat strange that, at the very moment when the conversation took place which has been detailed in the last chapter, one of the personages therein mentioned was up to the neck, if I may so express it, in an adventure which, though trifling in itself, was destined, like many another trifle, to work a great effect on the destinies of many.

It was a beautiful evening, then, about the twenty-seventh of May. The spring had been somewhat rainy and boisterous, and the few preceding days, though clear, had been cold, especially towards the afternoon; but it would seem that Winter had puffed forth his last blast, for the summer had got full possession of the day, and held it to the end. The birds, which had been nearly silent on the twenty-sixth, were now in full song; the wild-flowers starred the wood-walks and the banks; and if a cloud came over the blue sky, it was as soft and fleecy as a lamb's first coat. Under this summer heaven there was a very beautiful lane--an English country road--running between two banks, on the top of each of which, keeping parallel with the road, was a paling, above which again spread the arms of tall trees, holding their broad leafy fans over the head of the traveller below. By the distance of the bolls of the old elms and beeches from the fence which guarded them, it appeared as if there was a good broad walk within the boundary; and when the banks, at the end of a quarter of a mile, slanted down so as to bring the paling nearly on a level with the lane, that walk might be seen, together with a view over the well-rolled gravel, to a green and shady park dotted with fallow deer. Coming down the lane was a carrier's cart with the drag on, for there was a somewhat steep descent, and the road was as smooth as a ball-room floor; and at the bottom of the hill where the carrier stopped to remove the shoe was a gentleman, who also paused, and asked him some questions.

In the mean time, somewhat higher up, and within the enclosure, as if taking an evening walk, was a lady--a young and very beautiful lady, with some traces of mourning about her apparel, although its general hue was light. There was a certain harmony between her dress and her air and expression; for, though the dark hazel eyes and the rich, glossy brown hair, the warm, healthy cheek, and the arched lips of the small mouth, had altogether a cheerful look, yet there was a shade of melancholy thought in Maria Monkton's fair face as she walked through the scenes where every object that she saw, every step that she took, was full of memories of early days, and childhood's joys, and friends departed. They are always melancholy pleasures, those of memory, for they are the rays of a star that has set.

With her eyes bent down, then, and a slow step, she walked on, took a little path to the left through the trees till it led her to the more open part of the park, and then stopped to gaze over the scene. The broad lands which she saw were all her own; the herds of deer were hers; that was her mansion, an angle of which peeped over the old oaks; but yet the sight and the knowledge were not altogether pleasurable, though it might seem that they ought to have been so. There was a feeling of loneliness in it all--of the heart's loneliness. It was quite a woman's sensation. She would rather have had all she saw another's, and herself too. Yet it was by no means that craving after marriage which some women feel, for she certainly had not been without many an opportunity of gratifying it had she been so inclined; but she wished that all she saw had been a father's still--a mother's--anybody's but her own, and that she had not been a solitary being on the earth, with so much wealth, such great responsibilities, and so little kindred sympathy. Her thoughts were of her father and her mother, of the companions and friends of her childhood, and of every one who had shared those happy hours which, like the flowers of spring, are far more beautiful than the fruits of summer; and in the scenes where she had known so much happiness, the very memory of those whom she had loved seemed dearer to her than the presence of any whom she still knew.

She felt that her mood was not for the wider scene; and she turned back into the narrower paths, the green soft shades of which suited better with the humour of the moment. She had gone on for about a quarter of a mile, still buried in thought, when she heard a step and looked up. The path wound a good deal in its course, so that, seeing no one upon it, and being within ten or twelve yards of the lane, she fancied that the footfall must have been upon the road. The next instant, however, just at the turn, within a few feet of her, she beheld a stranger. Maria was not by nature cowardly, nor what is vulgarly called nervous; she had no bad habit of screaming at trifles or jumping at the banging of a door; but she certainly did start at this sudden apparition, and for a moment hesitated whether she should go on or turn back. An instant's consideration, however, was sufficient to make her resolve to follow the former course.

"It is ridiculous to be frightened," she thought, remembering that there were a stile and one or two gates into the lane: "he has probably come to see the steward or some of the people at the house."

And after a just perceptible pause she walked on, merely glancing her eye over the stranger's form as she did so. That glance showed her nothing to be frightened at; for there is certainly something in air and mien, and general appearance, which, although devils will take angels' forms at times, has a powerful effect upon that very unreasonable thing, human reason. Briefly as her eyes were turned towards the person before her, they had no time to scan him very accurately; but still she saw at once three very important facts: that he was very well dressed, that he had the bearing and look of a gentleman, and that he was a remarkably handsome man, though very dark.

In the mean time, what was the stranger about? He too had suddenly paused, and he looked for a moment irresolute. The next instant, however, he advanced straight towards the beautiful girl before him, and, raising his hat with a graceful inclination of the head, he said--

"I fear I am trespassing. May I ask if these are the grounds of the Earl of Milford?"

All Maria's little tremor was at an end, and she looked up frankly, replying--

"No; these are mine. Harley Lodge is on the other side of the road; but----"

And she stopped and hesitated, not knowing whether to tell the stranger abruptly of Lord Milford's death or not.

"You were going to add something," said the stranger, after having waited a moment for the conclusion of the sentence.

"I was merely about to ask who it is you wish to see," replied Maria; "for I fear you will find nobody there but servants----" And she blushed a little as she spoke.

"It is-strange!" said the gentleman: "a carrier I met just now told me that on this side was Harley Lodge, and that the opposite property belonged to Miss Monkton."

"He was mistaken, I assure you," answered Maria, with a smile at the doubt he seemed to entertain. "I am Miss Monkton. This is Bolton Park."

"I did not doubt you, of course," said the stranger: "the man was very stupid so to mislead me. But, to answer your question--it was the earl I wished to see, and if not himself, Lady Milford or Lady Anne."

Maria's brow grew dark.

"It is long, I imagine," she said, raising her eyes to the stranger's very handsome face--"it is long, I imagine, since you have seen any of the family, sir; and many sad changes take place in a few years----"

The stranger started, evidently alarmed.

"The earl----" he asked--"is the earl----"

"I am sorry to pain you," said Maria, much struck by the agitation he displayed, "but he has been dead some years, and Lady Milford also."

"How they go out!" said the stranger with a deep sigh; "how they go out!"

"What go out?" asked Maria, in some surprise.

"Hopes!" said the other, in a tone of such deep melancholy that she felt there must be some very painful feelings awakened by the words she had spoken; and she gazed at her companion's face attentively, as he remained with his eyes bent upon the ground. A sudden fit of trembling seized her; but the next moment he looked up, and their eyes met.

"I beg your pardon, Miss Monkton," he said: "I will not detain you longer, if you will merely tell me which is my best way to reach Harley Lodge, for I must go up to the house, at all events."

"I will show you if you come with me," said Maria in an agitated tone; "but there is no one there. Lady Anne is in London."

The Forgery | 71

"I should like to go, at all events," said the other, turning to walk on by her side.

"I suppose you were well acquainted with the late earl," said Maria, after a pause, "and I am afraid the news I have had to give you is very painful."

"I knew him well," replied the stranger, "and have met with many acts of kindness at his hands. I should be most ungrateful were I not deeply grieved at hearing of his death. But let me speak of a pleasanter subject, Miss Monkton. In a few days I shall have the honour of claiming your acquaintance upon a better foundation than at present--at least, if I am not mistaken," he added hurriedly, "in supposing you the daughter of the late Sir Edward Monkton. I have a letter for you from my friend Charles Marston, and one also for Lady Fleetwood. Am I right?"

"Oh, yes!" replied Maria. "I shall be very happy to hear from my cousin. It is seldom he does any one the favour of writing. Have you seen him lately?"

"About six months ago," answered her companion; "but I must explain the cause of my long delay in delivering his letters. I then intended to visit England directly, but other affairs intervened which called me back to Spain, and I only arrived in this country the day before yesterday."

"Have you resided long in Spain?" asked Maria.

"Very many years," was the reply, "ever since I came from Mexico, when I was a mere boy."

Maria looked down upon the path, and fell into deep thought, while the stranger went on to say--

"I have travelled in other countries, it is true; but Spain I look upon almost as my native land."

She made no answer, but still walked with her eyes bent down; and the stranger gazed at her unobserved, with evident admiration; and well indeed he might, for in whatever lands he had rambled he could not have seen anything more lovely. After a brief pause, however, as she still remained silent, he said--

"By-the-way, I have Marston's letter in my pocket-book, and may as well deliver it at once, to prove to you that your kind courtesy, Miss Monkton, is shown to a gentleman."

"Oh! I do not doubt it in the least," replied Maria, looking up brightly; and then she added in a very marked tone, "I never doubt--I never have doubted or suspected in my life."

The stranger looked full into her eyes, and then he in turn fell into a fit of thought. An instant after, he roused himself with a start, and taking out his pocket-book produced the letter he had mentioned.

Maria took it, and read merely the address--"Miss Monkton, by the hands of Colonel Francis Middleton."

"I will read his epistle by-and-by, Colonel Middleton," said Maria, stumbling a little at the name. "Have you known my cousin Charles long?"

"Yes," he answered at once, and then, correcting himself, added, "that is to say, eighteen months or more; but there are some men easily known, and Marston is so frank and open that we became intimate from a very early period of our acquaintance."

"I wonder," said Maria, "that he did not tell you the history of your friends here, which would have spared me the pain of giving you evil tidings."

There was again something peculiar in her tone; and her companion's cheek grew somewhat red, showing more distinctly a scar across his cheek, which was visible, but that was all, while his face retained its ordinary dark brown hue.

"It did not occur to me to ask him," he replied, with some degree of embarrassment; and both he and Maria fell into silence again for a few minutes.

At length Maria asked--

"Do you intend to visit London soon? I return to town to-morrow, and I am sure Lady Fleetwood will be most happy to see you."

"I go to-night," replied Frank Middleton; and Maria fell into a reverie once more.

A minute or two after, they reached a little summer-house at the top of the bank overhanging the fence. Beside it was a small gate in the park paling, with stone steps descending to the road; and Maria laid her hand upon the latch, but paused ere she raised it, as if irresolute. The next moment, however, she opened the gate and pointed up the road, saying--

"About a hundred yards farther on, you will find a stile which will lead you by a little path straight to Harley Lodge. You cannot mistake the way."

Her companion gazed at her earnestly while she spoke, and for a moment or two after; and then, thanking her for her kindness and apologizing for his intrusion, in words of course, but with tones that spoke much more, passed out of the gate, drew it after him, gave her one more look, as if he would fain have impressed her features on his mind for ever, and descended the steps.

Maria stood like marble where he had left her, and her cheek had become like marble too. She trembled, and her eye was strained eagerly, but sightless, upon the ground. She raised her hand to her head, as if to still the agitated thoughts within; and then, the next instant, she stretched out her hand to the gate, and threw it open, exclaiming, "Henry! Henry!"

The other turned, gazed at her, sprang up the steps, and taking both her hands in his, replied by the one word, "Maria!"

"Oh, Henry!" sobbed Maria Monkton, overcome by agitation, "I must speak to you--I must talk to you before--before you act so rashly. For your own sake--for heaven's sake--think of what you are doing!"

"Angel!" said her companion, gazing at her with deep tenderness; "and do you still remember me? Do you still take an interest in me--in me, the outcast, the exile, the friendless, the forlorn--in me, whom you must, whom you do, believe criminal?"

"No, Henry! no!" exclaimed Maria, a generous glow spreading over her face. "I do not believe you criminal--I never did--neither did my dear mother--we knew you better. I am sure you are as innocent as I am."

"Thank God for that!" said Henry Hayley; "there were then some who did me justice, and they the noblest and the best. Oh, Maria! the most painful part of a terrible situation has been to think that those whom I loved and esteemed the most would cast me from their affection, and look upon me as criminal and dishonoured."

"Oh, no!" cried Maria; "few did, of those who knew you. But I must do an imprudent thing, Henry, and ask you to go back to the house--for I am too much agitated to talk to you calmly here; and yet, indeed, I must reason with you as to what you are going to do."

Henry looked at her with a smile; but he accompanied her without reply, for it was an invitation that he would not refuse. And yet he knew that her arguments in regard to his future conduct would be in vain; for he had made up his mind, and was not one likely to change.

Through the fair scenery amidst which they had so often walked and played in childhood those two took their way, some object at every step awakening memories of the hours when they were the happiest; and more than once Maria looked up to her companion's face and asked, "Do you remember this?" or, "Do you remember that?" And he ever did remember right well, and added some incident which showed how clearly the whole was in his recollection.

Oh! it is very pleasant, when two old and dear friends, long parted, are reunited, to talk over old times and scenes, and let butterfly memory flit from flower to flower in the past; but doubly sweet when the recollections are those of happy childhood, without a stain upon their white garments which regret might vainly wish to clear away.

Soothing and cheering are such themes; and by the time they reached the house, Maria felt that she could talk to her companion of almost anything, without fearing that agitation which had made her seek the shelter of her own dwelling.

Nevertheless, she thought it better to follow her first plan; and, though the door was not locked, she rang the bell, and led the way for her visiter into the library.

The first object which struck his sight was a large picture of Lady Monkton; and, walking up to it, he gazed at it earnestly for a minute or two. When he turned round, there was a tear in his fine dark eye, and, taking Maria's hand, he kissed it, saying--

"She was ever kind to me."

"And to all, Henry," said Maria, her own eyes running over.

"But to me especially," he replied.

"She loved you very much," answered Maria, with a sigh. "But now tell me," she continued, seating herself, "what you are going to do; for indeed I feel so terrified at seeing you in this country, that I could not let you go away without expressing my fears for your safety. At first I felt so bewildered at finding one living whom I had long believed dead, that I did not know how to act."

"I do not think any one but you will recognise me," said Henry Hayley. "How you came to do so I cannot conceive, for your cousin Charles has associated with me for months without showing the slightest remembrance of me."

"That is strange!" replied Maria: "he was your schoolfellow and friend, too."

"It is true, yet I was much more frequently here, or at the lodge, than with him," said her companion. "We were in different forms at school; and, moreover, I believe women's eyes are quicker, and their memory of friends better than men's."

"Would you not have remembered me?" asked Maria, a little unfairly, perhaps.

"Anywhere--instantly!" replied Henry, eagerly; "but you are very little changed, comparatively. This gash upon my cheek, those large whiskers, and this tanned skin, I thought, would have concealed me fully."

Maria shook her head, and he went on to ask if she had recognised him directly.

"No," she answered, "but very soon. Your height and figure being so much changed, together with the other circumstances you have mentioned, as well as the conviction that you had been long dead, blinded me at first; but after a few words, you looked at me as you sometimes used to do when we were boy and girl; and then a sudden feeling--for I cannot call it anything else--came over me, that it must be Henry. For a little time I dared not look at you again; but when I told you of Lord Milford's death, and you stood gazing on the ground, with the eyelids drooping over the eyes, I became quite sure, and trembled so that I could hardly support myself."

They were pleasant words to the ear of Henry Hayley--they were indeed very sweet. To any man, and under almost any circumstances, they might well be so; for the deep interest of a beautiful and amiable being like that could surely never be a matter of indifference, and such emotions as those words betrayed could not exist without a deep interest. But in Henry they excited very peculiar feelings. In long, homeless wanderings--in strange turns of fate and struggles with the world--in sorrows and reverses, in prosperity and distress--he had still asked himself, "Do those loved so dearly still remember me with affection? or do they hate and contemn me? or have they forgotten me, as amongst the dead?" Amongst those he thought of, when he put such questions to his own heart, certainly Maria Monkton had ever been prominent.

As I have shown, when he fled from England, though not yet sixteen, he was much more manly in thought and feeling than most boys of his age. He had loved Maria almost as a brother might love: he had thought her the most beautiful as well as the most amiable of creatures, it is true; and perhaps he might have gone on only loving her with brotherly love, if he had never been separated from her. When, however, in after years he had suffered his mind to rest upon the past--when he had asked himself, "Does Maria remember me still?" and when he had wondered what she was like then--there had mingled with such thoughts tenderer and more imaginative feelings. He had thought, "Perhaps, if I had remained and all gone well, Maria might have become my wife;" and then the beautiful eyes that he remembered, and the sweet smile, and the many affectionate looks of the past would return to the sight, almost as distinct and clear as if her face were still before him. He knew not--when to save a father he abandoned his country, and encountered danger, sorrow, and despair--how much he really loved the girl who now sat beside him again; but he had discovered it afterwards; and now, how sweet--how very sweet it was to find that her bosom could thrill with such emotions on his account.

He gazed on her face while she spoke; but when she paused, he bent down his eyes again, and let the mind plunge into a sea of memories.

Maria suffered him to think for a few minutes, believing that his mind was busy with the circumstances of his present situation and future fate.

She had none of that grasping vanity which makes many a woman believe that each male companion must be thinking only of her. She had never asked herself one question as to what might have been Henry's feelings to her, or hers to him, had he remained in England. She had only thought of him during his long absence as the dear companion of her childhood and her early youth--as one excellent, amiable, and noble, who by some strange, mysterious fate, which she did not try to scan, had been destined to sorrow, undeserved disgrace, and early death. A whole crowd of tender regrets, it is true, had gathered round his memory, like flowers showered upon a tomb; and it is likewise true that the character of Henry Hayley, as she had conceived it and decorated it with her own fancies, had served her as a touchstone to try that of other men; but still she never fancied that she had loved him otherwise than merely as a brother.

She let him think, then, for a short time; but at length she said--

"Well, Henry, what do you intend to do? Is not your presence in this country dangerous to you? for you must now see that many may recognise you."

"None but you," said Henry: "no, none but you."

"Oh, yes, indeed!" replied his companion: "there is at least one who will do so, I am sure. I mean Lady Anne. We have often talked of you together, and I am quite sure she will at once remember you. Perhaps, indeed, you intended to tell her, as you were going to her house."

"No, certainly not," answered Henry. "There were only two to whom I proposed to acknowledge my own name, unless I acknowledged it at once to all the world--her father and yourself: to her father because, as the kindest friend I ever had, I intended to ask and follow his advice as to my conduct; to you, Maria, because I would not have quitted England again without telling you how I have thought of you, how I have remembered you, how I have blessed you for all the kindness you once showed me--for all the happiness you poured upon my happiest days."

Maria's cheek turned somewhat pale; and after pausing for a moment, Henry went on, saying--

"Lady Anne Mellent will not remember me, depend upon it."

Maria shook her head.

"You are mistaken," she said: "I am quite sure she will. She has your portrait, and it is still very like."

"My portrait!" exclaimed Henry Hayley: "impossible, dear Maria! I only sat for my portrait once, and that was to Saunders--for a miniature for my poor father."

"She has it, at all events," replied Maria, with something like a sigh. "Perhaps she bought it at poor Mr. Hayley's sale."

"That is very odd," said Henry. "Under such circumstances, I had better not call at all. Yet, even if she did recognise me, it could do no harm. No one now living, dear Maria, knows who I really am but yourself--no one can prove it but you, to whom I have acknowledged the fact; and with you," he added, laying his hand gently upon hers, "I know I am as safe as if the secret still rested in my own breast. People might suspect--people might feel sure; but yet no one, I repeat, could prove that I am any but Frank Middleton, an officer in the service of Spain; and I can prove that I am what I am not, beyond all possibility of refutation--the son of an English gentleman and a Spanish lady, brought up in Italy, and serving long in the Spanish army."

Maria looked bewildered.

"This is very strange," she said; "I do not comprehend it. Every one here certainly thinks you dead; and indeed I now remember the officer saw you lying apparently a corpse, and a certificate of your death was sent over by the consul. I do not wish, Henry, to inquire into anything that you may wish to conceal; but still----"

"Still, I can have nothing to conceal from you," he answered. "The strange part of my history is very soon told and explained. First, as to my innocence, Maria: a few words will clear that up at once;" and he lowered his voice to a sad tone. "My father forged your uncle's name--in a moment, I believe--I trust--of madness. He sent me to get the money for the draft, without my knowing anything of the deed. He then despatched me on a long journey to seek the means of paying the sum he had so wrongfully obtained before the draft came due, furnishing me with several of the notes which had been given him for the draft, and which were, doubtless, used to prove my guilt. On my return from the north he told me all, and left me the choice of seeing him executed as a felon, or flying from the country and bearing the load of suspicion myself. I hastened on to Ancona; but, having caught a fever by the way, I was carried, almost insensible, not to the hospital, but to the Franciscan monastery in the town. There were several Irish monks in the brotherhood, and one of them nursed me with the utmost tenderness. I told him all, under a solemn promise of secresy, and proved to him my innocence. When the officer arrived in search of me, I was rapidly recovering; but in the same monastery was the son of a Spanish lady, the wife of a Mr. Middleton, who had separated from her husband, and who, fearing on her deathbed that her son would be brought up as a Protestant, had placed him in concealment with the monks. He had caught the same fever, for it was then raging in that part of Italy; and on the very night the officer first applied at the gates, in order to have me delivered up, the poor boy died. The monks consulted together, and agreed to shelter me against pursuit, in the hope, I believe, of ultimately converting me. They removed me from the cell where I had been placed, carried the dead body of the poor lad thither, and passed it for mine, both upon the officer and the consul. Thus I escaped pursuit; and in the cemetery at Ancona stands a little tomb, inscribed with the name of 'Henry Hayley.'"

"Ah! but tell me more, Henry," exclaimed Maria--"what became of you then?"

"Does it interest you?" he asked, with a sad smile. "Well, then, I will sketch out all. I remained in that monastery three months longer--the good monks instructing me diligently in the Roman Catholic faith."

Maria's countenance fell, but Henry went on:--"At length there came a letter from the uncle of Mrs. Middleton, in Spain, demanding his niece's child should be sent to him, with a promise that he would provide for it. The monks accordingly sent me, with instructions to personate the poor boy; but I had resolved what to do; for, although their ideas did not permit them to see any evil in the deceit, which, they said, would confer much happiness on the uncle, as well as ensure my own safety, yet I could not make up my mind to benefit by a cheat. The old man received me most kindly, but was surprised to find how little Spanish I knew, for I had only learned the mere rudiments in the convent; and, as he could speak no other tongue, I was obliged to wait for more than six months ere I could tell him the whole, as I had resolved to do. During that time he conceived the greatest affection for me, sent me to a college, treated me as his heir, and lavished every sort of kindness upon me. It was all terribly painful; but, at length finding myself sufficiently master of the language to tell my tale, I took an opportunity when he was alone, brought him every present he had made me--money, jewels, trinkets, all--and then informed him of the facts. He was struck, and very much affected, and for some minutes seemed not to know how to act;

but at length he threw his arms round me and said, 'Dear boy: you shall not suffer for your honesty. Say not a word of this to any one, and be still to me a son.'"

"And did you become a Roman Catholic?" asked Maria, somewhat sadly.

Henry gazed at her for a moment with a look which she found difficult to interpret. There was something almost reproachful in the expression, and yet something joyful, too. It might perhaps have been interpreted, "Do you doubt me? and yet your very doubt shows that you do take a deep interest in my fate."

"No, Maria--no!" he answered; "had I done so, I might have been now one of the wealthiest men in Spain. Almost the first question asked me was regarding my faith. You are not perhaps aware that no very strict religious notions of any kind had prevailed in my poor father's house, and I had obtained but little religious instruction there. Neither was my new, my adopted father a bigot; but still he was a Roman Catholic; and when I told him that I had been brought up as a Protestant, he, like the good monks, insisted that I should receive instruction in his own faith. Of course, to that I could not object; but the instruction was interrupted. He was obliged to go to Mexico, and took me with him; but I had learned to inquire for myself, and my inquiries left no doubt. I had at first a difficulty in obtaining books on any side but one; but at Lima, whither we afterwards went, I found several Englishmen, from whom I got all that was needful. I took the Bible and common sense, and I could not be a Papist. South America was at that time in a state of great confusion, and we returned to Spain when I was about eighteen years old, or a little more. My adopted father reached his native land, but with shattered health, and a few months after he felt that he was dying. At that last solemn moment, he required me to tell him whether, in sincerity and truth, I could now embrace and keep the Roman Catholic faith. I answered him sincerely; and, though grieved, he was not offended. He pointed out to me, however, that he could not leave the bulk of his fortune to a heretic; in fact, that his doing so might prove dangerous to myself, by calling attention to facts, regarding my opinions, which had hitherto passed unnoticed. He made his will the same night. Great wealth thereby passed to very distant relations, who had every right to it, and a more humble, but still an ample, share of his fortune came to me. Why, he did not explain; but, probably, in order to gain me good repute amongst the ecclesiastics of his own church, he left several large sums to be distributed by me to religious establishments in Madrid and Toledo; and, as I took care to comply with his instructions in a liberal spirit after his death, no inquiries were made at the time as to my religious views, nor any observations upon my neglect of the forms of the Romish religion. I had entered the Spanish army before my kind friend's death, and ever since have been actively employed, till political changes and some rumours respecting my creed, which might have become dangerous, induced me to go to Italy, where my first visit was to the monks of Ancona. I found that the good brother John, who had been so kind to me, was dead; but he had left with another of my countrymen in the monastery the papers necessary to prove my real name and birth, should it be necessary. I have them safe; but there is no copy of them, and thus there is no one living but yourself who can prove that Frank Middleton is Henry Hayley."

"I suppose that my fears proceed from inexperience," said Maria thoughtfully; "but yet I cannot feel so well assured as you seem to be, Henry; and, oh! how I wish that you could boldly proclaim and clearly prove your innocence, and take once more your place amongst us all, free from even a suspicion!"

"I have had thoughts of attempting it," he replied; "and upon that very subject it was that I intended to consult the Earl of Milford. My poor father, before I went, furnished me with a paper in case I should be captured, which he believed would be sufficient to exculpate me fully. But I have looked at it often since, and doubt that it would have the effect. He therein takes the guilt upon himself, and solemnly declares that I was perfectly ignorant of the whole transaction; but the paper wants form, and, drawn up at a moment of terrible agitation, the handwriting has little resemblance to his usual, clear and business-like hand. Will you be my adviser, Maria, as I cannot obtain counsel of the earl?"

"Willingly, willingly would I," she replied, "if I had judgment and knowledge enough to render my advice worth having. But I shall see you again soon in London, I suppose."

"There we may have no sweet private moments, such as we have here," he answered, with a voice shaken by some strong emotions. "In the record of ten long years, I have much, very much, to tell to the only one in all the world to whom the thoughts, and feelings, and actions--ay, and fancies, and dreams--of all that period can be told. Oh, Maria! you can form no idea of what has been the solitude of my heart during those long, long ten years. I have mingled with the world, I have taken an active part therein, I have associated with many, had acquaintances and friends, such as the world gives; but in my own breast I have been lonely. With all around me there has been no one link of sweet association, no memory in common, no interchange of early sympathy. I could never refer to the sweet hours gone by. I could never talk of those I had loved. It was as if I were a creature of two existences--one for the world in which I moved--active, eager, bustling, full of enterprise, and danger, and adventure, but cold, hard, inanimate; the other for myself alone--still, silent, motionless, confined to my own bosom, but full of memories and visions, kindly sympathies, aspirations, hopes, loves--all still living, but entombed."

Maria was very pale, and her bright eyes were cast down; but over her cheek, as he ended, a drop like a diamond rolled slowly. She would not wipe it away; she hoped he did not see it; but he did, and it was hard to restrain himself from kissing it off that fair cheek.

"Hark!" cried Maria, starting up--"there is a carriage coming. Who can it be?"

"Compose yourself, dear girl," he answered; "be calm, Maria--be calm! Remember, I have brought you a letter from your cousin; and, oh, Maria! remember also that you have given me an hour of the purest happiness my chequered life has ever known. Let that tranquillize the sad feelings which the sight of Henry Hayley has awakened."

"Ah! but," she said, holding out her hand to him, "they are not all sad, Henry."

He pressed his lips upon the hand she gave; and then she hurriedly opened Charles Marston's letter, and wiped the tear from her cheek.

The next moment the door was opened, and Lady Anne Mellent announced.

CHAPTER X

Time, the great wonder-worker, had done much in his own particular way with Lady Anne Mellent during the last ten years. When Henry Hayley had quitted England she was a gay, decided, clever little girl, somewhat spoiled by her mother, but more reasonably treated by her father, for whom she had a deep and devoted affection, and much respect. She had then been very small for her age, and, being a year or more younger than Maria Monkton, had looked at least four or five years her junior, for Maria at thirteen had been not much less in height than she was at two or three-and-twenty. Lady Anne, indeed, had not at that time taken her start. Everything has its start in the world, and very few things go on with quiet progression; but especially in boys and girls there is generally a period at which they make a great and sudden rush towards manhood or womanhood, and that period is often preceded by one of great inactivity of development. Much greater, then, was the difference in Henry's eyes between the Lady Anne of the present and the past than between the Maria of the present and the past; and when the former entered, as he sat beside Miss Monkton, he was surprised to find so little that had any hold of memory in the young and graceful woman who appeared.

Lady Anne Mellent was not very tall, indeed, but still she was somewhat above the middle height of woman. She might be five feet four, or perhaps a little more; but, formed with great delicacy, small in the bones, and slight rather than thin, she seemed less in height than she really was. Nevertheless, her figure was of course greatly changed since Henry had last seen her; the child had become a woman, and the features, then round and barely developed, were greatly altered; for, though still delicate and beautiful, they were now clearly defined and chiselled. Her dress was somewhat peculiar; for over the ordinary morning habit of the time she wore a light silk tunic bordered with rich and beautiful fur, and on her head, instead of a bonnet, was a sort of Polish cap trimmed with the same skin. On her hands were thick doeskin gloves or gauntlets, with flaps almost to her elbows, and her tiny foot was lost in a furred shoe.

Ushered in at once, she paused the moment after she had crossed the threshold, in surprise at the sight of a gentleman seated *tête-à-tête* with her fair friend; but the next moment she advanced to Maria and kissed her with sisterly affection.

Maria was somewhat embarrassed, and the trace of tears was still upon her cheek; but she gracefully introduced Colonel Middleton to her fair visiter, and Lady Anne turning towards him, surveyed him with a rapid glance from head to heel, bowing her head as she did so, and merely saying "Oh!"

There was something rather *brusque* in the tone, which did not altogether please Henry, and served further to embarrass Maria, whose bosom was too full of emotions to suffer her to exert that command over her demeanour which she usually possessed; and in order to carry off the appearance of agitation, and to account for the presence of a stranger, she proceeded to explain to Lady Anne, that Colonel Middleton had brought her a letter from her cousin Charles.

"And none for me!" exclaimed the fair lady, in a gay and jesting tone. "On my word, that is too bad! But Charles Marston and I are certainly the two rudest people in the world: do you not think so, Colonel Middleton, now that you know us both?"

"No, indeed," replied Henry; "I do not think the term applicable in either case. Marston is certainly not a man of ceremonies, and I have not yet----"

"Oh! fine speeches! fine speeches!" exclaimed Lady Anne; "when will men have done with fine speeches? But, to fix you to the point, first, do you not think, when a gentleman has promised to a lady to write to her every month, giving her the whole account of his travels, and does not write, that it is very rude? Well, Charles Marston promised me to do so when we parted in Rome, and I have not heard a word of him since."

"You never told me you had seen him in Rome," said Maria, with some surprise.

A slight blush fluttered over Lady Anne's cheek as she answered--

"Did I not? Well, love, I dare say something prevented me; I do not know what, and shall not stop to inquire. Now for my second point, Colonel Middleton: do you not think it very rude for a lady--and a young lady, too, who should, of course, be full of prim propriety--to stare at a gentleman for full two minutes, when she is first introduced to him? Maria, dear, will you order me a cup of coffee, or a glass of wine, or something? for I am either quite mad, or very ill, or very happy, or very something."

And she sank quietly and gracefully into a large armchair near, and covered her eyes with her gloved hands.

"You are indeed very wild," said Maria, ringing the bell.

But Lady Anne did not answer till the servant had come and gone, while Henry and Maria exchanged looks of doubt and surprise. Some wine and some biscuits were brought, and the servant again retired; but Lady Anne did not rise, speak, or uncover her eyes, till Maria, really alarmed lest she should be ill, touched her gently on the arm, saying--

"Dear Anne, here is the wine; pray take some. Are you ill?"

"No, no, no!" said Lady Anne; "I will not have any--I will do better."

She withdrew her hands from her eyes as she spoke, and there were evident marks of tears upon her cheek.

"You have not answered me, Colonel Middleton," she said, "and I will answer for you. It was very rude--or rather it would have been very rude had there not been a cause. But do you know, sir, you are so very like a dear friend whom I have lost--a friend of childhood and of early days--a friend of all who were most dear to me--one whom I loved as a brother, though I often used to tease him sadly, and who loved me in the same way, too, though he used to love this dear beautiful girl here better--that in a moment, when I saw you, the brightest and the sweetest part of life came back; and then I remembered his hard fate and shameful treatment, and I thought I should have gone mad."

She paused for a moment, and gazed at him earnestly again; and then, starting up, she cried--

"But what is the use of all this?--Do you not know me? Do you pretend to have forgotten me? I am Anne Mellent. Henry! Henry! did you think you could hide yourself from me or her?"

And she held out her hand to him, warmly.

Henry Hayley took it and pressed it in his own, saying--

"I cannot and will not attempt to deceive you, dear Lady Anne; but yet I must beg you to keep my secret faithfully, for some time at least, till I have resolved upon my course."

"Be sure of that, Henry," replied Lady Anne, thoughtfully: "your course must be well thought of, but I will be one of the council, as well as Maria--nay, more," she added, with a sparkling look: "as she has had one long conference with you, all alone, I will have one also. It shall be this very night, too, in my own house here. There--do not look surprised, Maria. You know my reputation is not made of very brittle materials, or it would have been broken to pieces long ago. Yours is a very different sort of thing; you have spoiled it by over tenderness, like a child, and made it so delicate that it will not bear rough handling. I was resolved that mine should be more robust, and therefore set out with accustoming it to everything. I do believe that half the mad-headed things I have done in life were merely performed to establish a character for doing anything I pleased. They could but say that Anne Mellent was mad--and I took care not to go the length that is shut-up-able."

What were Maria Monkton's sensations it would be hardly fair to inquire. She had often talked with Lady Anne of Henry Hayley, and had often heard her express the same feelings towards him which were now so openly displayed; but perhaps she had listened with more pleasure, while they both thought him dead, than she did now. I do not say that she was in love with him. That would be a very serious assertion, not to be made without proof. The little prince of gods and men does not always wing his way in a direct course, and, if he was at all busy with fair Maria's heart, she was quite ignorant of the fact. She had thought all her life a good deal about Henry Hayley, it is true; she had liked him better, remembered him with fonder regard, than any one whom she had ever known; she had pitied him, wept for him; and within the last hour she had felt more and stronger emotions on his account than she had ever felt for any one on earth. But still all this might be without love. The sensations the most decidedly like that passion which she experienced were certainly those which Lady Anne Mellent's affectionate greeting and frank, unfearing invitation called up in her bosom. She felt inclined to think her friend odder than ever--to wish that she was not quite so odd. But Maria was a frank and generous character; and although she could not banish some of woman's weaknesses entirely, yet whenever she found them out she felt ashamed of them, and tried to repress them.

"Why should I be vexed with her conduct just now?" she asked herself; "is she not always the same? and are not all her eccentricities amiable?"

Whether Lady Anne perceived what was passing in her friend's bosom, from the varied expressions which flitted over her countenance, or whether she only suspected it from the intuitive knowledge which almost every woman has of woman's heart, I cannot tell; but after an instant's pause she went on, with a slight toss of her head, saying--

"After all, you know, Maria, at the worst, they could but say I was in love with him, and he with me; and, besides knowing ourselves that it is no such thing, we could soon prove to them that there was not a word of truth in it. So now, Henry, you will come to the Lodge, will you not--after dinner I mean--about nine o'clock?"

"I had intended to return to London to-night," replied Henry, hesitating.

"Without seeing me at all!" exclaimed Lady Anne--"that is unpardonable! I could punish you if I would, Henry--I could punish you if I would; but I will be generous----"

"You are mistaken, indeed," answered Henry, eagerly: "I intended to see you, as Miss Monkton can tell you--indeed, my first visit was destined to Harley Lodge; but she thought I should find no one there but servants."

"Miss Monkton!" exclaimed Lady Anne, with a gay laugh, "do you intend to let him go on calling you that name, Maria? Oh, those prim proprieties!--how I hate them! That ten years should make such a difference between people who have been like brothers and sisters all their lives! But I suppose that the human heart is like that stone which is soft enough and easily formed when first dug, but hardens by exposure to the air."

"He was indeed going to the Lodge when I met him accidentally," said Maria; "and I did tell him, that he would find no one there, for I thought you were in London."

"Whether you were right or wrong depends upon how long he has been with you," answered Lady Anne, with a malicious twinkle of the eyes. "The truth is, I drove down with my beautiful ponies about an hour ago; lodged my dear old governess at the rectory, where she is going to dine; stopped at the Lodge for two minutes to tell them to get something ready, and then came on here, with a sort of second sight, I suppose; and now I will return, insisting upon your coming at the time stated, and giving me a full account of yourself, Henry. I cannot ask you to dinner--not because it would be improper--for that I should like beyond everything, but because there is nothing in the house, I believe, but three or four eggs. I must go, however, for it is growing dusk, and those wild young things of mine are as fresh as if they had come out of the stable a minute ago."

Henry rose to conduct her to her carriage; but before they reached the door of the hall, Lady Anne stopped, saying--

"Go on, Colonel Middleton; I want to speak one word more to Maria;" and running back into the library, she threw her arms round her beautiful friend, saying, "Oh! is not this joyful, Maria?"

"I trust it may prove so for him, poor fellow," replied Maria, with a sigh; "but I have many fears."

"And I none," said Lady Anne; "but you have thought me stranger than ever, dear girl. I have seen it all the time; but, never fear, it will all come right. I love him very much, Maria, but I am not in love with him. I care not what the world says, for the world will find itself a fool, as it so often does, when it sees me his wife's bridesmaid, as I intend to be. But mind, I warn you I intend to do everything that is odd in the mean time; so that every one will think, but you, Maria--but you--that I am making love to him in open day. *You* will not mistake me, I think."

And away she went again, with a gay, light step, leaving Maria Monkton with her eyes ready to run over under the influence of emotions strange and new.

"What am I feeling? what am I doing?" were questions that flashed through her mind with the rapidity of lightning; but, before she could answer them, Henry was again by her side. There was a look of hope and light in his eyes which agitated her more than before; and she was about to sit down, to hide, as far as possible, her emotion; but Henry took her hand, saying--

"Dear Maria, it is growing dark, and I do not think you would wish me to stay longer with you at present; but yet, before I go--for we may not easily, perhaps, find such a moment of happy privacy for a long time--let me say that, which some words which have been spoken to-day induce me to say sooner than I otherwise would have done----"

"Oh! we shall easily find moments to converse," replied Maria, catching at the first pause, and making a great effort to delay what she was sure would overcome her.

"Nay, not so," answered Henry; "I must not leave you now doubtful as to any part of my conduct."

He gazed at her for a moment, earnestly, tenderly; and as by the faint light he saw her eyes cast down, her glowing cheek and trembling form, he went on rapidly.

"You know me too well, Maria--you judge me, and have ever judged me, too nobly--to suppose that I would seek to bind you to the fate of an exile, an outcast, or even a suspected man. I ask you not to tell me any of your own feelings towards me--I ask you not even to say one word of your own situation. Your heart--your hand even--may be engaged to some happier man----"

"Oh, no! no!" she cried; "no!"

The words rushed from her heart, burst from her lips, without the act of her will; but she felt that she had never loved till then, and they would be spoken.

"Thank God!" said Henry, in a low voice, and then added, "well, then, dearest Maria, my mind is made up. I will cast this load from me--I will clear myself of all doubt, if it be in human power to do so; and if it be done-

-if I stand before the whole world exculpated from all charges but of deep, perhaps too deep, devotion to a father, then I will tell you how Henry Hayley has loved and thought of you from boyhood till now; how he loves you still--how he will love you till his last hour. You will find that his course has not been dishonourable or inglorious, and you shall decide whether he is to be as happy as his boyish dreams once pictured. And now, farewell for the present."

He pressed his lips upon her hand, and was departing; but a soft, low, musical voice caught his ear ere he reached the door.

"Henry," it said, "oh, not yet, Henry! do not leave me yet."

Henry Hayley turned at once, and seated himself beside her; he took her hand, and it remained in his, and when he at length departed, the sky was quite dark, but his heart had daylight in itself.

CHAPTER XI

Three chapters to one group of people is almost more than it is fair to allow; and yet the fact of there being three in the group, as well as a strong predilection on my own part for chronological progression, must excuse my remaining attached to Henry Hayley and his fair companions, at least till that day had reached its close. Now the period of a day's close may be differently estimated, according as a man is astronomical, Judaical, ecclesiastical, or chronological. Some will have it that sunset closes the day; some say midnight is the day's end--which, of course, is a contradiction in terms; some one hour, some another; but as men have never been agreed upon the subject since the beginning of the world, and I am decidedly fond of paradoxes, I prefer midnight, and therefore declare that, when I say "the close of the day," I mean neither more nor less than twelve o'clock at night.

With a light and joyful step Henry Hayley took his way through the park where he had so often played in infancy and boyhood, towards one of the two lodges, selecting that one, the gates of which opened upon the road, near a little village, at which he had left the post-chaise that brought him from London. The moon, just risen and not far from the full, showed him many an old familiar sight; and the happiness of his own heart harmonized so well with the pleasant memories of the past that he almost fancied himself a boy again, and all the terrible realities of the last ten years nothing but a painful dream. There was one thing, indeed, which might have proved to him that it was not so--that there was a wide interval between the past and the present, and that was the sensation of passion. Yes, there was now passion in his bosom--passion which had not been there before--passion which even at the dawn of morning he had not felt.

Let not the reader marvel. There are certainly such things occasionally as love at first sight, but with him it was very different. If the eye which runs over these lines saw the sun rise as often as mine does--I see him open the curtains of the night, I believe, more frequently than any man in England, more frequently even than the matutinal labourer of the fields--if any reader, I say, saw the sun rise as often as I do, he would understand the whole process of Henry's love in a moment. Not that it had anything to do with sunrise, or with sunset, or with the rising, southing, and setting of the moon; but there is a certain comfortable arrangement which every early riser practises, or should practise, in the winter, and which perfectly explains Henry Hayley's case. You direct the housemaid to take a bundle of dry sticks--called in some places a fagot, in other parts of the country a bavin: in London men use square bits of deal--and, laying them artistically, with sufficient spaces between them to allow the air to pass, to place over them a mass or quantity of paper: such a manuscript as this would do very well, but a newspaper is better, for a thousand to one it contains more inflammable materials. Over all you superinduce a thin and pervious stratum of bituminous coal; and then in the morning, when you rise, you put a candle (lighted) to the paper, and the whole mass is in a blaze in a moment. Now, in Henry Hayley's case, Fate had been the housemaid; the friendships and affections of youth, piled one above the other, had been the wood nicely laid. The paper might perhaps be represented by all the longing, eager memories and fancies of and regarding the fair companion of his youth during the last long ten years; a warm, earnest, ardent heart was the inflammable coal at the top; and the sudden sight, and tender interest, and kindly affection of Maria were the light which kindled the flame in a moment.

He had, in short, met her that night, loving her very much; and he left her, loving her as much as it is possible for man to love.

He went through the park, then, with the spirit of the past and the present on either hand, leading him through paths of fairy flowers to scenes of imaginary happiness. Ah! that quarter of an hour was well worth the ten years of suffering.

He could hardly make up his mind to pass the gates; but there was no use in lingering, and he sped on. Such a frugal dinner as he wanted was easily obtained at the little public-house--for it did not deserve the name of an inn; and when it was over, he still sat for a time and thought of Maria--not of Lady Anne--till his watch, which he had laid on the table, showed him that it was time to depart for his next visit. Then, indeed, he turned his mind to her whom he was so soon to see; but still Henry Hayley was a gentleman--not in manners alone, but in heart and mind--and a gentleman never misunderstands a woman.

There was not one thought in his bosom which could have pained or offended Lady Anne, if she had seen them all.

"She is a dear, kind, good girl," he said to himself as he walked on, "and still so like what she was as a child. Happy state!--happy character!--which changes not with the hard world's experience--which has no need to change. Mistress of herself, her actions, and her fortune--armed in honesty of purpose and purity of heart--why should she bend the finest feelings and the noblest principles to the cold rules of the world?"

The lodge-gate was soon reached; the grounds were soon passed through; and when he stood under the portico and stretched out his hand to the bell, the village clock, clear and musical, struck nine.

"I am to the moment," he thought, "and I am glad of it. I would not repay such regard with the slightest appearance of neglect."

The servant who opened the door showed no wonder at the sight of a young and very handsome stranger asking to see Lady Anne at that hour of the night. All her servants had given up wondering at Lady Arnie long ago. Giving his name as Colonel Middleton, Henry was at once led to the drawing-room where she was sitting; and as soon as he had entered, the door was closed. She at once rose from the book she had been reading, and advanced to meet him with both her hands stretched out. He took them affectionately, and to his surprise she raised her face to his and kissed his check.

"There, Henry!" she said--"now that I have astonished you enough, I will try and be reasonable; and, first, that you may not think me anything but very mad, I will tell you something--but first sit down by me here. Well, I was going to say I have made up my mind that you are to marry Maria Monkton--I am quite sure of it. There were tears upon her cheek when I came in, and love enough in your eyes to show me the whole. Then, again, as I have told Charles Marston, if he asks me some day when I am in a good humour, I may marry him--it is all arranged. And now you think me odder, stranger, wilder than ever; and I believe it is so, for the very great joy of seeing you again, when every one but myself believed you dead, has carried me quite away."

"And did you not, then, believe me dead, Lady Anne?" asked Henry.

"Do not call me that odious name!" she answered, and then added, "Only half. I doubted, and so did my poor father till his last hour. Little reason had we to doubt, it is true; but still, you know, Henry, doubt is a very clinging plant. Look here!" she continued, raising a light from the table, and leading the way through chairs and sofas, and various sorts of furniture, to the other side of the large room: "look here! Do you know whose picture this is?"

"Mine," answered Henry, with a smile; "what could tempt you to buy it?"

"I did not buy it," she said: "it was given to me, and I have always hoped--faintly, fearfully, but still hoped to see that face again--the face of the brother of my girlhood. I one time thought of giving it to Maria, for I knew it would be a comfort and a consolation to her, but I had not the heart; and now, of course, you will have another painted for her, which will please her better, as it will be more like the present. That will do well for me: it is the Henry, of my remembrance."

It must be owned that Henry Hayley was puzzled. He had seen and observed many women acting in many circumstances; but he had never yet seen sisterly affection so warmly, so plainly, displayed towards any one not actually akin to her who felt it. Yet, let there be no mistake: he did not misunderstand Lady Anne Mellent for an instant. He did not suppose that she was moved towards him by any feelings but those which she acknowledged; but he thought, and thought with a sigh, that those feelings might be misunderstood by others; for the world rarely, if ever, as he well knew, understands perfect sincerity of character.

He saw, however, that his love for Maria was not to be concealed from her, and therefore that there was no use in attempting to hide it, and he answered--

"You must not suppose, dear lady, that all my hopes and wishes are so near attainment as to justify me in even dreaming of painted pictures. There is much to be thought of, much to be considered first. You must be aware that I am even now in a very dangerous situation; and, although I need not tell you I am innocent of all that was ever laid to my charge--though I think I can prove my innocence, and am resolved to attempt it--yet there is peril even in the attempt."

Lady Anne smiled gaily. "I do indeed know you are innocent," she said, "and my dear father knew you were innocent. He told me so himself, upon the bed of death," she added, a grave shade spreading over her fair face. "He saw Mr. Hayley for some hours, as soon as he had recovered from a terrible accident he met with, and from his lips he heard and knew the whole. But now, Henry, sit down and tell me all your history; for, satisfied that you are here, living and well, I have hitherto asked you no questions. But still there must be a strange tale to be told; for even Mr. Hayley himself was fully convinced of your death till his own last hour. After you have done, I have something to give you which my father left you, if ever you should appear again. He gave me other directions also, which I ought to have acted upon before; but which--whether fortunately or not, I cannot say--I have not acted upon, in my thoughtless levity, as yet. They were to make public what I knew of your innocence, and of the circumstances which cast suspicion upon you, as soon as Mr. Hayley was dead. But I have been absent from England, roaming about, and since my return I forgot it all."

"I am glad you have not as yet said anything upon the subject," replied Henry, thoughtfully. "Your unsupported testimony of what your kind and excellent father believed would do little legally to establish my innocence; and I should wish to make every preparation before I discover myself. At present I am so far safe. Although I now see that those who knew me well may recognise me more easily than I had imagined, no one can prove my identity with Henry Hayley, while I can establish, by proofs which cannot be controverted, that I am Frank Middleton, the son of an English gentleman and a Spanish lady. Step by step, from infancy to manhood, I can show my identity with that person, without, by one word from my own mouth, violating truth in the slightest degree. The Spanish consul-general, now in London, would at any time swear that I am the son of Mrs. Middleton, having seen me many times at the house of her uncle, recognised as her son by all the family. This character I shall certainly keep up for some time, till I have carefully sought for and arranged all the evidence that is yet to be found regarding that transaction which condemned me to ten years of exile and disgrace. Nay, listen; for depend upon it such things are not so easily proved, to the satisfaction of a court of law, as kind and inexperienced hearts, like yours and dear Maria's, are willing to believe. Nevertheless, I do think my innocence can be established; for, in corroboration of a paper which my father gave me, acknowledging the act as his, and exculpating me, some of the innkeepers at whose houses I staid, while seeking your father in Northumberland and in Wales, must still be living, and can show that I was not, as has been asserted, flying from justice with the money obtained by forgery, but eagerly following a nobleman of unimpeached honour, upon business of importance. I think it will not be difficult, in short, to prove every step of my course, so as to bear out fact after fact of the plain and simple tale I have to tell. I must also seek and find my poor aunt as soon as possible; not only for affection's sake, but because I feel almost certain that sooner or later my father must have told her the truth. I will therefore beseech you, dear Lady Anne, to keep my secret with the utmost care for some weeks to come, and not to betray any recognition of me as Henry Hayley, by a word, a look, or a sign."

"That I will promise, and faithfully perform, Henry," replied Lady Anne, with a smile; "but still we have much to talk of--and first, tell me all your history, and then I will tell mine in return."

The same tale was told by Henry to his present auditor as had been told to Maria Monkton, though not exactly in the same words. Though somewhat drier in the details, and though more a relation of mere facts than of facts and feelings mingled, as it had been to Maria, yet it took long in telling, and before it was concluded the sound of a carriage driving up hurried him to the end.

"That is Mrs. Brice, my old governess, who lives with me still," said Lady Anne. "Henry, there is much more to be said. You must come to me to-morrow evening, in London; I will contrive to get rid of her there. Here, perhaps, I could not manage it without paining the good creature, and awakening her attention too closely to yourself. Come and dine with me *tête-à-tête* at seven, and tell Maria not to be jealous."

Henry promised, and the next moment Mrs. Brice entered the room.

After an introduction to that lady by Lady Anne, delivered in an easy, commonplace tone, the visitor took his leave, and in half-an-hour after was on his way back to London.

CHAPTER XII

It was about eleven o'clock in the day. The London thunder had not begun. There might be a few carts creeping about the streets, but they crept lazily and almost silently; the rattle of a hackney-coach might be heard here and there, but still it was but a temporary rattle; and the comparative stillness of the whole town gave a dreamy sort of quietude to the air, which was pleasant and full of repose. It harmonized well with the character of the day, too, for it was quite a summer morning.

The sun was streaming into Lady Fleetwood's drawing-room, sending oblique rays over the corner of the houses of a neighbouring street, and the motes were dancing drowsily in the long pencils of light. A droning fly, which had somehow or other got into a long-necked, deep blue carnation-glass, and could not get out again, was buzzing as if it had nearly tired itself to sleep; and the waving of the plants at the open windows, stirred by a light air, had a slumberous sound with it.

"Really, this is very pleasant!" thought Lady Fleetwood, as she sat, after breakfast, enjoying the delicious sensation of life which a fine summer day gives; "it is all so calm and tranquil that one could almost go to sleep."

Strange, strange life!--that one of thy best blessings should be to lose the consciousness of thine existence!

She soon found, however, that to go to sleep was not for her. Hardly had the thought passed through her brain when a sharp double knock at the door dispelled the stillness, and the next moment Charles Marston, the incarnation of mobility, entered.

"Well, my dear aunt," he said, "I have determined upon my course for the day; laid out everything in the most methodical and scientific manner; and having just half-an-hour to spare, came to bestow it upon you."

"You should really go and see your uncle, my dear Charles," replied Lady Fleetwood. "It would have been much better to have given it to him instead of to me; for he may well be offended if he hears you have been here twice without going near him."

"You are wrong, dearest of aunts!--you are wrong," answered Charles: "you always are sweetly wrong, you know, most excellent of women. I sent half-an-hour ago, to ask if he was at home; for, although one may have to swallow a bitter pill now and then, there is no reason why one should needlessly walk a mile and a half to take it. But he was out; and so, when I go hence, I shall diligently pursue him to his dingy hole in the city, where pray heaven there may be plenty of business stirring to cut our conference short! I am now only waiting for Winkworth, who is going to the city too."

"I cannot think, Charles, why you should feel such a distaste to your uncle's conversation," said Lady Fleetwood, meditating upon the problem; "everybody admits he is a clever man."

"Undoubtedly, my dear aunt," replied Charles; "but I will tell you why I am not very fond of his conversation. It is because that same conversation of his transforms everything into arithmetic. Now, I never had an arithmetical head in my life: I know that two and two make four, but it has not been the study of my life to discover how many blue beans make five. I cannot calculate friendships by the rules of profit and loss, nor look on love upon the principles of tare and tret, nor subject every feeling of the heart to the computations of the interest-table, nor measure poetry by the square foot, nor extract the cube root of an acquaintance's purse, in order to estimate how intimate I should become with him, nor regulate my own thoughts and wishes by quadratic equations, nor always keep my own conduct and purposes within an exact parallelogram. The sages of Laputa must have been great bores, my dear aunt; but they were nothing, depend upon it, to the men of the present day, who subject not only their understandings, but their very emotions, to the stiffest rules of calculation. Besides, the sight of poor Miss Hayley has not altogether taught me to like my uncle better--nor has what you said about him, it *à propos* to her."

Lady Fleetwood looked scared, and in a moment her mind ran back to all that had passed during the preceding evening, to ascertain if she could possibly by any blunder have said aught to produce mischief between uncle and nephew.

"Why, my dear Charles," she exclaimed, "I am very sure that I never uttered one word to make you believe that your uncle is at all aware of the poor thing's condition. He would be the first, I am sure----"

"I never said you did, my dear aunt," he replied, interrupting her; "but you told me he had been angry because you went to see them in their distress at Highgate. I have a strong notion he did not behave well to poor Hayley. I remember something of an unsettled account."

"Oh! but poor uncle always said, that as soon as Mr. Hayley produced certain papers he would go into that," exclaimed Lady Fleetwood. "I remember quite well that Hayley always declared there was a large sum due to him--fifteen or twenty thousand pounds; and he declared once that he would put it into chancery or some law court; but he lost heart, poor man, after the sad business of Henry's death; and, though he talked a great deal, he never did anything. But now I recollect--that was what made your uncle so angry, Charles. He said Hayley had defamed him; and you know your uncle is always reckoned a highly honourable man, though a little too fond of money, perhaps."

"Rich men are always honourable men," replied Charles, in a graver tone than was customary with him, "and poor and unfortunate men are great rascals--in the world's opinion, my dear aunt. In this good country of ours, wealth does find ways, if not to corrupt justice, at least to fix the balance and the sword immoveable. Law is too expensive a luxury for poor men to treat themselves to much of it; and many an honest cause is lost for fear of the inseparable punishment, in this land, of seeking right by law--I mean expense, if not ruin. I remember hearing a clerk give a message to Hayley, exactly to the purport you mention: that Mr. Scriven had no time to write, but that he would go into the account whenever Mr. Hayley was prepared to produce the papers. Do you know what Hayley replied, my dear aunt? He was then in a shabby black coat, and his face looked as if he had been drinking, I must confess; but he spoke distinctly and bitterly. 'Be so good as to ask Mr. Scriven,' he said, 'how I am to do that, when all those papers were left here, and I have never been able to get them out of this house?'--and with a fierce imprecation upon my uncle's head, he walked away without waiting for an answer. I was witness to the whole, and a sad scene it was?"

"Oh, dear! that is very terrible!" said Lady Fleetwood; "but do you think it could be true, Charles?"

"I really do not know, my dear aunt," answered her nephew; "but I have a sort of feeling that the Hayleys have suffered by our family; and consequently, as I am quite sure this poor thing whom I saw upon Frimley Common is one of them, I have resolved to go down again this very day and see what can be done for her. Winkworth will go with me, and as he is one upon whose advice I can fully rely, I shall consult him in regard to all I do for her."--"But, dear me, then you will not see Maria to-day!" said Lady Fleetwood: "she will be here by two o'clock."

"Oh, yes, I shall," answered Charles; "we do not set out till three, and I shall be back from the city by two."

Lady Fleetwood's arrangements were all deranged. She had planned a pleasant little dinner-party for Charles, Mr. Winkworth, and Maria, at which she proposed to engage Mr. Winkworth in conversation with herself, while Charles and Maria would be thrown upon each other's hands entirely; and she did not in the least doubt--being a fine politician in her way--that what between Maria's natural charms, a sudden meeting after a long absence, and a great many other advantages of the same kind, love and matrimony would as naturally rise up as the flame of a spirit-lamp when a match is applied to it. We must remark that Lady Fleetwood never doubted for a moment that any of her plans would succeed; nor did the experience of more than twenty years, during which period every one that she had ever formed had broken to pieces, convince her that there was always, somehow or another, some element wanting in her calculations which ensured their failure. She laid defeat upon the back of accident--one of the three or four broad-shouldered accessories to human infirmities which bear all the sins and misadventures of the world--the scapegoats of conscience and self-reproach. Accident, ill-luck, the devil, and adverse circumstances, are the favourite deputies to whom we transfer the burden of our faults in the present day, since Zeus and his Olympian household are no longer chargeable, as in the days of Homer.

> Perverse mankind! whose wills, created free,
> Charge all their woes on absolute decree;
> All to the dooming gods their guilt translate,
> And follies are miscalled the crimes of Fate.

Accident was Lady Fleetwood's pack-horse; and she thought it a most unfortunate accident indeed that Charles had arranged to go with Mr. Winkworth into the country that evening, rather than stay and fall in love with his cousin upon her plan.

While she was thinking, however, of how she could induce him to give up his journey for the day, and balancing with nice casuistry whether she ought or ought not to try, kindly feeling for poor Miss Hayley pulling her one way, and a natural hankering for her own schemes tugging her the other, the knocker was again heard doing its function; and her servant, a moment after, announced that Mr. Winkworth was below, waiting for Mr. Marston.

"Oh! ask him up, by all means," said Lady Fleetwood; "I shall be delighted to see him."

"I asked him, my lady," replied the man: "but he said he had no time at the present moment."

Lady Fleetwood would have pressed the point; but Charles represented that, if they did not set out for the city at once, he should not be back in time to see his cousin, and ran down-stairs without delay.

Under any ordinary circumstances, the solitary meditations of a lady on the sear side of fifty can be of no great interest to the general reader. There is something in youth--in its freshness, its vigour, its excitability, its world of emotions--which renders the young mind, as well as the young frame, in its bloom and perfection, a pleasant object of contemplation; but with age, alas! it is seldom so. I will, therefore, only say that good Lady Fleetwood sat and thought, for full five minutes, of how unfortunate it was that Charles should have spoiled her evening plan for his benefit; and having no other scheme for making people happy in her own way ready-made at the moment, she might have gone on for five, or even ten minutes more, had she not been interrupted by a visit from her brother.

"Well, that is the most unfortunate thing in the world!" exclaimed the poor lady, as soon as she saw Mr. Scriven's face. "Charles has just this moment gone into the city to call upon you."

"Humph!" said Mr. Scriven; "I wonder he did not call upon me last night."

"I dare say he was tired, poor fellow," replied Lady Fleetwood, who had almost always an excuse ready for everybody; "but he sent, the first thing this morning, to see if you were at home."

"It would have been better to have come himself," rejoined Mr. Scriven, drily; "then he might have discovered that I was not ten doors off, and would return directly. Now, I suppose, he will call at the counting-house, and, finding I have not arrived, walk away again. I must see him to-day, Margaret: I have some important matters to tell him. If he comes back, then, keep him to dinner, and I will come in and join you."

"I cannot do that," answered Lady Fleetwood; "for he has just told me that he is going down to Frimley Common at three o'clock."

"What for?" asked Mr. Scriven with a look of surprise.

Lady Fleetwood hesitated, and her brother's face assumed a stern look.

"Is he going to fight a duel?" asked Mr. Scriven.

And his poor sister, in a fright lest she should produce a wrong impression, poured forth the whole story of Miss Hayley, and Charles Marston's intentions, and Mr. Winkworth's kindness in going with him.

Moreover, one part of the tale requiring, in her estimation, explanation by another, she went on to give sundry portions of her conversation with her nephew, to account for his determination to take care of poor Miss Hayley, which she well knew, in its bald state, Mr. Scriven would think very absurd, romantic, and extravagant; and she added various hints with regard to what she and Charles judged he, Mr. Scriven, ought to do for the poor lady; adding that some people thought the Hayleys had not been altogether well treated.

There was a sort of consciousness in her heart all the time that she was blundering, which only made her flounder more and more amongst the shallows into which she had plunged; and the deep, imperturbable silence with which her brother sat and listened to a long story--a thing he was rarely inclined to do--only added to her embarrassment.

When she had done, he asked no questions, but only raised his eyes to the timepiece; and with a last convulsion to get right again, or at least to cast the weight from her own shoulders, she added--

"Well, Henry--I do not understand all these matters, as you well know."

"Perfectly well," rejoined Mr. Scriven.

"And so," she continued, "you had better talk with Charles about them yourself."

"I will," said Mr. Scriven.

"He will be back from the city before two," added Lady Fleetwood, "and he sets out for Frimley at three."

"Ha!" said Mr. Scriven. "And now, Margaret, I will go; for I do not see anything further that can be gained by staying here."

Now, Lady Fleetwood would have given a great deal to have unloosed his taciturn tongue and discovered what he was going to do next; but Mr. Scriven was not inclined that it should be so, and took his departure.

He had a brown cabriolet at the door--that was an age of cabriolets; and when he had got into the vehicle, he first turned his horse's head, as if he would have driven, as usual, to his house of business in the city; but by the time he had got to the other side of the square he had altered his mind, and sweeping round with a whirl, he directed his course back to his private residence.

It was very strange that he should do so, for Mr. Scriven was the most methodical of men. He arranged in the morning all that he intended to do during the day, and on all ordinary occasions he did it. But there was something stranger still; for, notwithstanding his having told Lady Fleetwood that he must and would see his nephew Charles that day, he took a very good way of preventing himself from so doing.

He first looked into a posting-hook, then ordered one of his servants to go to the counting-house and say that he should not be there till the next morning, and then directed another servant to order a pair of post-horses.

As soon as they arrived he went out of town.

CHAPTER XIII

With his arm linked in that of Charles Marston, Mr. Winkworth, such as I have described him, walked on towards the city; and much did he seem to marvel at all he saw by the way. It was not, indeed, that he was unacquainted with London; but cities as well as people change their dress, only with this difference, that they very often grow smarter as they grow older. The new garb of his old friend, however, was apparently not at all to Mr. Winkworth's taste. He commented on all he saw with splenetic causticity, declaring that the good old brick houses of Swallow Street, with their plain brown faces, were infinitely preferable to the lath-and-plaster edifices of Regent Street and Waterloo Place, which he pronounced an insult to architecture, and a hodge-podge of every sort of enormity. Then, again, the macadamised streets excited his indignation: they had not yet been paved with wood, or heaven knows what he would have said of them; but as they were, he declared that their sole object must be to wet the feet and splash the apparel of the lieges of the land.

"My dear sir," he said, "this is true modern reform and improvement. It is a good specimen of the customs and legislation of the age. Everything that the wisdom of ten or twelve centuries, and the experience of whole races of men, have devised and pronounced good, is swept away, knocked down, chopped up, simply for the sake of change, and to show that we are wiser than our ancestors. In my young days, these good streets of London were paved with large, firm, solid lumps of granite; you could step across from stone to stone quietly, easily, and drily. They wanted little or no repair, except when some villanous water company chose to pick up the stones in order either to carry a pipe to, or cut it off from, some of the adjacent houses."

"If you ever come to drive a cab or a curricle through the streets, Winkworth," said Charles Marston, "you will find it much more pleasant to roll over Mr. Macadam than over those same jolting blocks of granite you talk of."

"Heaven forbid that I ever should commit such a mad action!" replied the old gentleman, still striding on with his long legs and his somewhat rounded body and shoulders, not at all unlike a hen-turkey in the moulting season; "but that which strikes me as the most curious part of the whole process is, that you people of the present day think you are advancing all the time, and call your operations progress, when, in fact, like the crab, you are going backwards. Here you have very nearly reduced the streets of London to the same state in which they were left by King Lud, whose name very appropriately rhymes to mud."

"I suppose all things do go in a circle," answered Charles Marston, "like that wheel which you see turning round; yet the wheel in turning round rolls the carriage forward; and so, I suppose, the gyrations of society help on the great machine."

"As bad an illustration as ever was given!" exclaimed Mr. Winkworth--"one which would break down at the first turn. Good heaven! what a quantity of plate-glass!"

"You must admit that that is, at all events, a great improvement," rejoined the younger gentleman, "compared with the small dingy panes, which even I can recollect. You can have nothing to say against the plate-glass, I think."

"A whole volume!" said Mr. Winkworth. "In the first place, the shops and houses must be as hot as cucumber-beds. This window lets the whole sun in."

"You forget you are not in India, in Arabia, or on the shores of the Red Sea," replied his companion; "but what more?"

"In the next place," continued Mr. Winkworth, "every stone-throwing urchin, discontented snob, or butcher's boy with a tray on his shoulder, has two or three hundred pounds at his mercy. A chimney-pot falling, a flower-pot overturning, or almost any other accident you please, can pick your pocket of much more than it may be convenient to lose, in the shape of glass. Then look at that jeweller's shop. Think what a temptation it must be to a poor rogue to pop his hand through and seize all those diamonds and pearls. Upon my life! it is worth the risk of transportation. Then, again, as a matter of calculation, my dear lad--I don't know what is the price of plate-glass now, but I am very sure that three or four thousand pounds would not buy the shop-front of that mercer. Who pays for it, sir?--who pays for it? Why, you, and I, and everybody who wants a silk handkerchief, a dozen of gloves, or a pair of silk stockings. Now, what I want is a silk handkerchief, not plate-glass; and I do not see why I should be obliged to contribute my quota to enable Harry Thompson, or John Jenkins, or any one else, to cover his wares with a plate of stuff only fit for a looking-glass, as dear as gold and as frail as a dancing girl."

Charles Marston laughed outright. "That last part of your speech, my dear Winkworth," he said, "is worthy of my uncle Scriven."

"Then he must be a wiser man than you seem to think him," rejoined Mr. Winkworth, with a smile.

"I never said he was not wise," replied Charles Marston. "Oh, no! he is a very wise man in his generation. Neither do I think he would carry the matter as far as you do, nor object to any one but himself buying as much plate-glass as he pleases, perfectly certain that if he, Mr. Scriven, is obliged to pay something additional in his bill on account of that commodity, he will find means to make the possessor pay him back with interest, if they have any further dealings together."

"Loving nephew!" said Mr. Winkworth, drily; "pray, are you as affectionately fond of all your other relations?"

"Nay, that is hardly fair," replied Charles Marston: "you know quite well, Winkworth, how dearly I love my good aunt Fleetwood, and my noble, generous-hearted father. But I will tell you one thing: that it is the contrast between his conduct, feelings, and thoughts, and those of my good calculating uncle, which makes the society of the latter so very unpleasant to me."

"It is all prejudice, I dare say," answered Mr. Winkworth, in a morose tone. "You love your father, doubtless, because it is customary. Piety, piety, you know, Marston--it would never do, not to love one's father; and then you hate your uncle because he has got the whip-hand of you."

"You are very much mistaken," replied Charles Marston sharply: "my uncle has not the whip-hand of me in any way. Thanks to my father's generosity and confidence, I am as independent of him as of that chimney-sweeper."

"Humph!" said the old man, "but what has your uncle done?"

"Why, nothing, perhaps, that the world would blame," answered Charles, "but nothing that I ever heard of that any man of heart and mind would praise. In that very business of the poor Hayleys, which I was telling you about last night, he persecuted Henry in the most relentless manner. The bankers who lost the money, and were the real parties interested, did not show half the eagerness after the poor fellow's blood."

"That might proceed, in your uncle, from a natural love of justice," said Mr. Winkworth.

"Pooh!" exclaimed Charles Marston, with an impatient look.

"Did he pay the bankers the money?" demanded his companion.

"Not one penny," rejoined Charles. "But let us get into some sort of vehicle, or we shall never arrive at the city;" and calling one of the street conveyances, they proceeded on their way.

As the reader is already aware, Charles Marston did not find his uncle at his counting-house; and having nothing further to detain him in a place which he abhorred, he drove back again at once to his aunt's house, leaving Mr. Winkworth to finish his business in the great centre of the world's commerce, and rejoin him as soon as it was possible.

Charles Marston found Lady Fleetwood's drawing-room already well tenanted. His cousin Maria had arrived earlier than she had been expected; not ten minutes after her appearance, Lady Anne Mellent had presented herself; and she was followed closely by Colonel Middleton.

A crowd of gratulations and welcomes poured warmly upon Charles.

It is at such first meetings after long absence that, to the eyes of the observant and experienced in human character, the deeply-concealed feelings of the heart peep out in little traits.

Had the eyes of Lady Fleetwood been of any great use to her, she would have seen the ruin and destruction of one of her favourite schemes upon the cheek of Maria Monkton, and in the eyes of Lady Anne Mellent.

The former was nearest to the door by which Charles entered. She received him with every appearance of affection, returned his embrace warmly, and expressed, with no lack of tenderness, the pleasure she felt at seeing him again; but not the slightest change of colour in the cheek betrayed any deeper emotion: no quivering of the lip, no trembling of the frame, showed the agitation inseparable from love.

Not so Lady Anne Mellent: she sat still as stone while Charles was welcomed by his cousin; but a ray of joyful light, bright, and pure, and radiant, poured forth from her eyes, while her cheek became very pale, and her lips parted with a sigh that would not be suppressed.

She was evidently a great deal agitated; but, with a degree of command over herself, which circumstances rendered more habitual with her than people generally believed, she overcame the emotion in a moment; and by the time the greeting of Maria was over, she was quite prepared to resume the gay and sparkling levity with which she often covered deeper feelings.

"Do not come near me, Charles Marston," she said, as the young traveller approached; "I am determined not to speak to you. I cast you off--I abandon you! If I were a rich grandfather, I would cut you off with a shilling;" but at the same time she held out her hand to him, and it trembled as he took it. "Did you not promise to write to me continually," she asked, "and to tell me all your adventures? for I was quite sure you would get into all sorts of scrapes, and be delightfully near losing your life a hundred times. And now tell me, sir, have you written me a single word for six months?"

"I wrote you two long letters--the last not three months ago," replied Charles Marston; "and you never condescended to answer either."

"Because I never received them," replied Lady Anne; "but you will lay it all upon postmasters, of course."

"You shall see the record and the dates in my journal, little infidel!" said Charles Marston in a low tone, and then added aloud, "but I did even more than all this. I was impudent enough to write to your merry old guardian, Sir Thomas Wickham, to ask him for your address."

"And what did he say? what did he say?" exclaimed Lady Anne, laughing: "something very funny, I am sure."

"He told me that he was not an astronomer," replied Charles Marston, "and could not at all calculate the transit of Venus; adding, in less figurative language, that he could not tell where you might happen to be, as he had never known for two hours consecutively in his life; but that, if he might venture a supposition, your ladyship was probably looking for me somewhere in Palestine or Crim Tartary."

"My ladyship was doing nothing of the kind," answered Lady Anne. "But there is Colonel Middleton, exceedingly anxious to say civil things to you, while I should say nothing but what is uncivil--at least, till you have done penance; so go and speak to him."

The greeting between the two friends was very warm, and while it took place, Lady Anne's eyes were fixed upon Charles Marston's countenance with a keen and scrutinizing glance.

As the secrets of all hearts are, of course, in the bosom of him who writes their history, I may very well aver that Lady Anne was anxious to discover whether Charles Marston was really as unconscious of the identity of Colonel Middleton and Henry Hayley as he appeared to be; but there was nothing in any part of his demeanour which could induce her to suppose that he entertained even a suspicion of the truth.

"These men are strange beings!" she said to herself as she gazed. "Here are two girls who discover a fact at once, and an old woman who becomes very much puzzled, and very doubtful, evidently--for beloved aunt Fleetwood is clearly on thorns at this very moment with doubt and curiosity; and yet, quick, too rapid Charles Marston jumps over the truth, and lights a hundred yards beyond. Upon my life, I think women are creatures of instinct more than anything else!--although I do not know that it is a compliment to their understanding to suppose they share a gift peculiarly characteristic of beasts."

The welcome was succeeded by general conversation; and, general conversation being the most tedious thing upon the face of the earth to all but the persons engaged in it, and very often to them likewise, there can be no necessity for repeating it here.

Though the sweetest tempered woman in the world, Lady Fleetwood was in a mood for fretting herself; and, to say the truth, circumstances wonderfully assisted her. In the first place, she was evidently one too many. The party divided itself, naturally, into a quadrille without her; but it divided itself not according to her taste.

Had Charles Marston attached himself to the side of his cousin, and his friend Colonel Middleton devoted all his attention to Lady Anne, she would have borne the awkward fact of her own superfluity with the utmost meekness and patience; but, very perversely, they chose to do quite the reverse of all this. Charles, in the window, carried on with Lady Anne Mellent what seemed to his good aunt a regular flirtation, while Maria was left entirely to the attentions of Colonel Middleton.

Still, as the reader may suppose, no four persons could have been more perfectly contented with their position than these four, could Lady Fleetwood have been contented to let them alone, and not tried to arrange matters better; but she first joined in the conversation of one party, and then interrupted that of another, taking care to choose the exact moment when something of importance was to be said, or some word of affection to be spoken, which was most willing to hide itself from listening ears.

At length, however, Mr. Winkworth was announced, and the arrival of a stranger put out all the former combinations. Advancing into the room, with one hand behind his back and his hat in the other, he made a formal sliding bow all round, till his eye rested upon Charles Marston at the end of the line, and the latter advanced to introduce him to the rest.

Though gay, frank, and bluff, as we have seen, where he was intimate, Mr. Winkworth was clearly very formal and ceremonial amongst strangers; but yet there was a certain degree of old-fashioned courteousness in his manner which perfectly suited the notions of Lady Fleetwood. The very scrape of his left foot upon the carpet, as he made his exceedingly decided bow, and the little expletives with which he seasoned his replies, savoured of that dignified stateliness which, even within her own memory, was the distinctive quality of the old court.

"You have been a long time in India, I think, Mr. Winkworth," she said, looking rather too curiously at his sallow complexion.

"Madam, I fear it is written on my countenance," he replied, with another low bow; "but I have, as you say, been a good deal in India; and I learn from your nephew that my old friend Marston is your brother-in-law."

Lady Fleetwood was delighted to hear that Mr. Winkworth was an old friend of her sister Maria's husband; and she soon engaged her visiter in giving her a full statement of all he knew concerning Mr. Marston in India, which was certainly well calculated to be gratifying to her ears. It proved also a seasonable diversion in favour of the lovers in the other part of the room; for it occupied all the excellent lady's attention, and prevented her from attempting to make them comfortable.

The announcement that Charles Marston's carriage was at the door, about ten minutes after his companion's first appearance, put an end to the explanations he was giving to Lady Anne; and the two gentlemen departed upon their charitable expedition, leaving Henry still by Maria's side.

One gentleman amongst three ladies is but small provision; but Colonel Middleton seemed in no degree inclined to depart, and for a minute or two Lady Anne was kind enough to make a diversion in his favour, by going over and occupying the attention of Lady Fleetwood. How Maria and he took advantage of this movement, it is not for me to say. Certain it is they talked in a very low voice for some minutes, till Lady Anne suddenly rose as if to depart, and then Maria took a liberty with her aunt's house, which she would have done without the slightest hesitation where no deep feelings were concerned, but which now, from some cause or another, called the colour somewhat warmly into her cheek; saying aloud--

"Will you not dine with us to-day, Colonel Middleton? My aunt, I am sure, will be very happy to see you."

Before Henry could answer, or the little sort of agitated consideration of *pros* and *cons* which seized upon Lady Fleetwood could resolve itself into anything like form and shape, Lady Anne held up her finger, exclaiming--

"Remember, you are engaged to me, sir, for to-night at least. To-morrow I will give you up to Lady Fleetwood with all my heart."

Maria certainly did think her young friend very strange, and perhaps felt a little mortified. It was but a transitory emotion, however, but it was sufficiently strong to cause Henry's answer to escape her; and the next moment, while he had turned to Lady Fleetwood, to answer with thanks the invitation, which she cordially seconded the moment it was declined, Lady Anne, crossing the room, laid her hand upon Maria's arm, saying in a whisper--

"Trust me, dear girl! trust me! I am neither a flirt nor a coquette, whatever you may think."

"Indeed, I think you neither, Anne, though perhaps a little strange," Maria Monkton replied; and with a gay laugh and a nod of her head Lady Anne Mellent ran out of the room, leaving Henry with Maria and Lady Fleetwood.

There we also must leave him, dear reader, for the time, to follow Charles down to Frimley; and though the journey was not a very long one and the stages were short and easy, even in those days--merely from London to Hounslow, from Hounslow to Egham, from Egham to Bagshot, and from Bagshot to Frimley, passing by the "Golden Farmer" and stopping at the "White Hart"--I should undoubtedly abridge the way by stepping over the whole country, after the fashion of the pair of compasses with which one measures distances on a map, were it not for one peculiarity which must be pointed out. The old road to Southampton and a great many other places, for some distance beyond Frimley, runs only through two counties, and those metropolitan counties, too: first Middlesex, and then Surrey; and yet, perhaps, were you to look for any thirty miles throughout all England which comprise more waste land than any other thirty miles, you would have to pitch upon these in the immediate vicinity of the capital. Only take the names I have given above, and add the word heath or common to them, and you have at least fifteen miles of waste out of the thirty.

Hounslow Heath, Egham Heath, Bagshot Heath, Frimley Common-- over all these they rolled as fast as two good horses and a gay postilion could manage to make them; and about half-past six o'clock they reached the spot where they had seen poor Rebecca Hayley two nights before.

The carriage was stopped, and out they got, as near the hovel as possible; and then, wandering down the little path by the side of the swampy stream smothered with moss, they made their way to the door. It was closed, but not locked; and Charles Marston, without the ceremony of knocking, lifted the latch and went in. There was but one tenant in the place, and that was the boy Jim; but the poor fellow's face and manner no more displayed that calm, good-humoured, patient, steadfast opposition to adversity and sorrow which they had so lately shown. He sat by the fireless hearth and wept.

"Why, what is the matter, my lad?" asked Charles, "and where is your old friend Bessy?"

"They have taken her away," replied the boy, "and I am left here alone."

"Taken her away? taken her away?" said Mr. Winkworth, following his young friend. "Who took her away? If your story, Charles, be quite correct, I do not see who can have any right to take her away. Who was it took her away, Jim?"

"Oh! he had right enough, I dare say," answered the boy: "at least, he seemed to have, for he ordered about him quite free, and the people did just what he liked; and when I asked him what was to become of me, he said, 'Whatever might happen. He had nothing to do with that.' He would have been more civil, I think, if he had had no right."

"I can't tell that," replied Mr. Winkworth, who was occasionally given to moralise, as the reader may have perceived: "wrong is often a very uncivil thing; but what was he like? Was he an old man or a young one?"

"Younger than you are, a good bit," replied the boy; "but older than he is, a good bit;" and he pointed to Charles Marston.

Further questions elicited that the person who had carried away poor Miss Hayley was a gentleman between forty and fifty years of age, tall and thin, with grey hair but no whiskers. He had come down in a carriage, the boy said, having a servant with him, and together they had put poor Bessy into the vehicle, whether she would or not.

"She seemed to know him, however," he added, "and called him by his name, and was very much afraid of him. She cried and sobbed very much, too."

In answer to another question, the lad stated that he had forgotten the name which his poor old friend had given to the gentleman.

"The description is uncommonly like my uncle Scriven," said Charles Marston.

"That's it! that's it!" cried the boy, eagerly. "That is what she called him--I remember now."

"I'll swear that my dearly-beloved aunt Fleetwood has been at the bottom of this," said Charles, "with her excellent intentions. I'll answer for it she has told my uncle all about our having found the poor old lady here, and tried to persuade him to do something for her. Thus he has learnt all about it, and for some reason of his own has come and carried her away. But I will have this affair investigated to the bottom."

"Quite right, my dear boy--if you do not run your head against sundry stone walls in so doing," replied Mr. Winkworth; "but you should always remember, Charles Marston, that you have got brains, and that stone walls have none, so that it is not a fair fight between you and them. However, now let us think of the boy."

"Oh, I will take him into my service," replied the younger man, "and put him under my fellow, to teach him----"

"All manner of wickedness," said Mr. Winkworth, "and therefore you shall do no such thing. I will take him into mine, where there's no blackguard with long whiskers to corrupt him. I'll drill him into all the precise notions of an old bachelor's service, and when he's fit for that, he's fit for anything. Would you like to come and live with me, my good boy, and be my servant?" and the old gentleman's yellow countenance lighted up with a benevolent smile, which made it look quite handsome.

"I should like it very much," said the boy, eagerly: "and then, perhaps, I can sometimes see Bessy."

"I dare say you can, though I know not why you call her Bessy," answered Mr. Winkworth: "at all events, I will not prevent you. Good heaven, my dear Charles! how much happier, and brighter, and better a world it would be, if we all continued to love our Bessies through life as this poor boy seems to love his! There--do not stare so. I mean by Bessies, the best friends of our youth--not, perhaps, the mere corporeal flesh-and-blood friends, but the pure, ingenuous, open-hearted candour of early years, which would be a better friend to man, if he did but cling to it with affection through life, than all the worldly friends we gain in passing through existence--shrewdness, caution, prudence, selfishness, wit, or even wisdom. But it is no use in trying to indoctrinate you, I see: you only laugh at all my most beautiful illustrations, and think me the most foolish old man in the world."

"Not I, indeed, my dear sir," replied Charles Marston. "I should only like some day to put your sarcasms when your spleen is moved, and your fine sentiments when your enthusiasm is excited, side by side, in double columns as they print books, and see how they would look when compared."

"They would mutually balance each other, and so come to nothing," said the old gentleman. "But now, my good boy, Jim--what is your name besides Jim?"

"Brown," replied the boy.

"I thought so," exclaimed Mr. Winkworth; "I could have sworn it! Jim always precedes Brown, and Brown always follows Jim--it is a natural collocation. How strange it is, Charles Marston, that particular names have such strange affinities for each other, so that they appear to unite by the mere attraction of cohesion! How extraordinary that this boy's godfathers and godmothers, without any preconcerted consideration of the subject, were driven by a sort of inevitable necessity to call him Jim! They had, indeed, but one alternative, and that was Tom. However, Tom is less dignified, being frequently attached to cat. And now, Jim Brown, to proceed to business: you shall either have your choice of getting into the dickey of that carriage, and coming up with me to town to be fed, lodged, receive twenty pounds a-year, and wait upon an old gentleman with a yellow face, or you shall stay here for a day or two longer, to put your little affairs in order, and follow me up to town for the same purposes."

The boy had listened with profound attention to Mr. Winkworth's comments on his name, though with a slight expression of wonder on his face, but not of stupid wonder. To his proposal he gave not less attention, and then thought for a moment before he answered. Poor boy! he had been early taught to think; for circumstance is a hard master, and often teaches severe lessons to youth, only fitted for age.

"I think I would rather stay for a day," he replied at length; "for there are some things of my poor mother's which I should like to pack up and not have wasted."

"Well, then, there is a guinea for you to pay your journey up on the top of the coach," said Mr. Winkworth; "and now, have you got such a thing as a pen, that I may write down my address in London?"

"Here's poor Bessy's pen," said the boy, "which she used to teach me to write with."

While with the well-worn stump, a drop of ink in a little phial, and a scrap of somewhat dirty paper, Mr. Winkworth wrote down his address in London, Charles Marston gazed out of the cottage-door upon the heath, over which the purple shades of evening were falling fast.

"Who are all those people passing across the common?" asked Charles Marston, turning to the boy: "is there any great work going on here?"

"Oh, no, sir," replied Jim: "those are people, I dare say, from the great meeting to petition for a reform in parliament, which was to be held farther up on the common to-day. The men were coming down all the morning, and a bad set they were, too; for they walked straight through William Small's garden, trampled down all his beds, and gathered all the flowers. He said they were nothing but a set of thieves and pickpockets from London, and they have done him damage for twenty pounds or more."

"Ha! Charles, that's bad," said Mr. Winkworth, rising, and folding up the paper on which he had written the address: "we had better get away before the shades of night are upon us. I hope your Whiskerandos has got the pistols with him."

"I dare say he has," replied Charles Marston; and after a few words more exchanged with the boy, they left the cottage and got into their carriage again. Mr. Winkworth, however, seemed to have thought better of his plan of operations, especially when they got into the midst of a noisy and somewhat turbulent crowd, one worthy member of which amused himself by throwing a stone at the head of the servant.

"After all," said the old gentleman, "I think it will be better to stop and dine, and let these admirable reformers disperse."

Charles Marston was very willing to do anything that he liked; for, to say the truth, his mind was very busy, and wanted to be busy; and, as the reader is well aware, when such is the case the spiritual part cares very little what the corporeal is about, provided there be no interruption to its own operations. They consequently drove to the inn where they had already stopped on their way to town, ordered dinner, and, according to the usual process, waited for it and ate it--not exactly in silence; for, notwithstanding all that philosophers can say, either mind or body will often carry on two operations at once, and Charles talked of indifferent subjects while his mind was occupied with one particular theme: that is to say, he talked mechanically; for conversation is much more the effect of mere machinery than we think. Now, internally he was occupied in considering what could be the motives of his uncle in the act he had just performed; and he mingled therewith sundry doubts, hesitations, and inquiries, with which it is needless to trouble the reader. In a word, Thought, mounted upon Imagination, went galloping away hither and thither, while the mechanical part of mind remained at home, taking care of the house.

In the mean time there was a good deal of noise and bustle in the inn, which on their first visit had seemed as quiet a little place as any at which hungry travellers ever ate new-killed chickens or tough beefsteaks; and the landlord thought fit to inform his respected guests, in an apologetic tone, that there were several of the orators of the great meeting just dispersed-- the spirit-shakers of that day--then dining in the house, and several of their admirers waiting in the yard to cheer them as they went home. Now, it is very natural for orators to be noisy--first, because the unruly member is their spoilt child, and next, because--at least I never yet saw, met with, or heard of one of them with whom such was not the case--they never consider any others than themselves.

Mr. Winkworth and Charles Marston, then, were not the least surprised at the inn being noisy under such circumstances; and the only effect was, that they hurried their dinner in order to get out of it as soon as possible. Whenever the meal was concluded, the horses were put to, the lamps lighted, for it was now quite dark; crack went the whip, round went the wheels, and off went the carriage. Through the little town they drove quietly and easily enough, and for some distance beyond it; but at length awful Bagshot Heath spread around them. True, it might have been any other place on the earth for aught they knew. The night was cloudy; the stars were all in bed and fast asleep; the moon would have nothing to do with Bagshot Heath that night; and neither Charles nor his companion had the least idea that they were in the midst of a place notorious for robbery some ten years before, when a loud voice cried "Stop!" and the carriage was brought to a sudden halt. It is probable that some of the gentlemen who, anxious for an extension of the franchise, had attended the meeting in the morning, seeing a carriage indicative of wealth in the court-yard of the inn, had thought that they might make their day's expedition serve two purposes, and tend first to the expansion of their rights and liberties, and secondly to a more equal distribution of property. At all events, some persons, animated by the latter object, appealed to the travellers, pistol in hand, to convey a portion of their superfluity to their more needy fellow-countrymen. The servant at the back of the carriage, however, produced a pair of tubes very similar to those in the hands of the applicants, and without much ceremony fired.

The shot was instantly returned, but with what effect Charles Marston did not wait to see; for, seated on the right hand side of the carriage, which was opposite to that where the attack was made, he put forth his hand, the window on that side being down, opened the door, jumped out, and applied a thick stick which he had with him to the head of a gentleman who was holding the horses.

The head was a hard one, and probably not unaccustomed to such calls to forbearance; but the blow was sufficiently well directed and forcibly applied to stretch him for one moment flat upon his back. The next instant he was upon his feet again; but, not willing to take a second dose of the same rude medicine, and totally forgetful of his hat, which, to say truth, was not worthy of great solicitude, he ran off across the heath as fast as he could go. Now, running is the most infectious of all diseases; and the two other gentlemen who were with him were seized almost simultaneously with the same malady.

Charles Marston did not think fit to pursue the fugitives, but merely inquired of the servant, who had by this time descended from his leathern box, whether the shot the fellows had fired had hit him.

"No, sir," replied the man, in his peculiar affected tone; "the gentlemen's line of fire was not well directed. It merely damaged the crystal of the carriage, I think."

And Charles Marston, calling him a puppy in his own mind, went round to the other side, got in, and ordered the postboy to drive on.

For a moment or two Mr. Winkworth was completely silent; but at length he remarked, in a low, quiet tone--

"Well, I do think, Master Charles Marston, that I am a very unfortunate man, and that my left shoulder is a very unfortunate shoulder, both being subject to suffer by encounters with highwaymen, whether Syrian or English, Mahommedan or Christian."

"Why, my dear sir--you don't mean to say you are wounded?" exclaimed Charles Marston.

"I do indeed," replied Mr. Winkworth, "and within one inch of the spot where I was wounded before. Luckily, it is lower down, and on the outside, so it is only in the flesh, I fancy; but I am not obliged to them, nevertheless. I was just stooping a little, forward to see what was going on, when the ball came crashing through the glass and into my shoulder."

Charles Marston was now, as may well be supposed, under a good deal of anxiety for his friend; but Mr. Winkworth would not consent to stop at the next inn longer than was necessary to ascertain that the bleeding was not great. Charles insisted upon putting on another pair of horses to the carriage to accelerate their progress, and in about two two hours and a half they reached the door of their hotel. There a surgeon was immediately sent for; and after what seemed to Charles a very long delay, the man of healing entered the room.

CHAPTER XIV

Human life is a strange thing, consider it in what way we will. Strip it of all factitious adjuncts, and leave it bare and bald, as a mere lease for sixty or seventy years of sensations, feelings, thoughts, hopes, expectations, still it is strange--very strange; but man has made it stranger. Society has put so many clauses into the lease that the covenants are not always easily fulfilled, and the tenancy occasionally becomes troublesome.

I do not mean to say that this was altogether the case with worthy Mr. Winkworth. That he was rich was evident; that, notwithstanding his meagre body, stooping shoulders, and yellow face, he was strong and in good health, his capability of enduring long fatigue, and the rapidity with which he had recovered from his former wounds in Syria, proved sufficiently. But still he seemed very indifferent to life; and when the surgeon, as surgeons often will upon very slight occasions, thought fit to look grave and solemn while examining his wound, the old gentleman turned laughing to Charles Marston, and said, with a nod of his head--

"I'll remember you in my will.--My dear sir," he continued, addressing the surgeon, "do not look so serious. You cannot frighten me, I assure you. Life in its very best and palmiest state, with all its joys and pleasures unimpaired, is not so valuable a commodity in my eyes as to cost me two thoughts about losing it. There is no great chance of that, however, this time; and, even if there were, this old, crazy, worn-out body--of which, as of a house long in chancery, there is little more than the framework left--may just as well go down to mother earth to-day or to-morrow as after a few score more morrows, which will very soon be passed."

The ball, however, was soon extracted; and the old gentleman retired to bed, treating the whole matter somewhat lightly.

The next morning, when Charles Marston went to visit him, some degree of inflammation had naturally come on, rendering him rather irritable, of which he was conscious.

"Go away, Charles! go away!" he said: "go and see your uncle, as you ought to have done before now. I am cross, and if you stay, you will find me as bitter as a black dose."

"Well, I shall tell my servant, at all events, to be in readiness to attend upon you in case you ring," replied Charles Marston.

"Tell him to go to the devil!" exclaimed Mr. Winkworth: "the whiskered coxcomb, with his airs and graces, would drive me mad in a minute. No, no; go away and see your uncle, and leave me to myself. You may come in about one or two o'clock; but mind how you open that door, for it makes such a villanous squeaking that one would suppose it had not moved on its hinges for half-a-century."

There was a house which Charles Marston would undoubtedly have much preferred to visit, if he had followed his own inclination; but, nevertheless, with a strong resolution, he turned his steps towards his uncle's dwelling, feeling conscious that he had certainly made no great exertions to see him since his return. He was immediately admitted, for Mr. Scriven seldom betook himself to his counting-house before eleven or twelve o'clock; and being a man of very regular habits, the ordinary process was to read three or four articles in the morning papers before he set out, partly during breakfast, and partly during the first steps of digestion afterwards. I have said three or four articles, because in reading newspapers, as in everything else, Mr. Scriven went upon a system. He was one of those men who always have a motive, and his motive was usually one and indivisible.

There was no such thing as an impulse in his nature; he did not recollect ever having had an impulse. He was Babbage's calculating machine, in flesh and blood.

His sister, Lady Fleetwood, had told her nephew, as we have seen, that Mr. Scriven had been "very angry" upon one occasion; but Lady Fleetwood made a mistake. Mr. Scriven was never very angry; it did not come within his calculations to be so. He could be exceedingly severe, bitter, caustic, and coolly regardless of other people's feelings; but he was not the least angry, all the while. He either wanted to prevent them from doing a thing he did not desire to be done, or to stop them from ever doing it again. It was still upon a motive.

Thus, in reading the newspaper, he read those articles alone which were likely to affect himself personally, either immediately or remotely. He cared nothing about politics, except as the price of the funds, the value of merchandise, the risks of speculation, or the amounts of taxation, were concerned. Highway robberies, murders, suits in chancery, police reports, trials at bar or in the Arches' Court, interested him not in the least, except as excepted. They were all about other people; and he would have considered it a want of due economy to give them the least attention. Births, deaths, and marriages, in the abstract, he cared nothing about; and the whole world might have been born, wedded, or buried, without producing one sensation in his bosom, provided he could have carried on his transactions without them.

The "Gazette," the shipping list, the money article, the commercial statement, a few trials for swindling, forgery, and breach of contract, together with reports of the budget, the estimates, and any debates in parliament referring to commercial matters, were all that he ever thought of reading; and the lucubrations of editors, in what are called leading articles, he passed over with utter contempt, saying that he trusted he could form as good an opinion himself on matters of fact as any they could give him.

The reader must pardon me for dwelling so long on Mr. Scriven's character; and I do so, not because it is at all a singular one, for it is as common as the air, under different modifications, but because there are very few men who, possessing the jewel of perfect selfishness, are bold enough to display it openly and without disguise to the eyes of all men. But Mr. Scriven was at the acme of his class. He was, as a naturalist would say, the most perfect specimen ever found; and it requires to be so before selfishness can be considered a virtue and a matter of pride.

When Charles Marston was ushered up to his uncle, he found him busily reading an account of the barque "Louisa" having been spoken with by the "Arcadia" mail-packet, in latitude so-and-so, longitude so-and-so. Neither the latitude nor longitude signifies a pin to you or me, reader, though it did to him.

Mr. Scriven looked up over the top of the paper as his nephew was announced, dropped it a little lower when he saw him, and said--

"How do you do, Charles?--how do you do, Charles? I will speak to you in a moment."

And he read out the ship-news without moving a muscle.

Charles Marston had a great inclination to put on his hat and walk away; for it must be recollected that eighteen months had passed since Mr. Scriven had last seen his nephew; and Charles, without being angry at the coolness of his reception, argued in this manner:--

"He does not care to see me; I certainly do not care to see him: why should I be bored by stopping while he reads the paper?"

There were two or three other little *pros* and *cons* in Charles Marston's mind; but they were brought to an end by Mr. Scriven finishing the subject which he was reading, and turning to his nephew with his usual dry air.

"Well, Charles," he said, "here is the third day since you arrived in London, and I have the honour of seeing you at last."

Charles Marston did not think fit to make the slightest excuse or apology, contenting himself with the simple facts of having sent to his uncle's house to inquire if he were at home, and having afterwards called upon him in the city.

"If you had come yourself, Charles," said his uncle, "the servant would have told you that I was near at hand, and would be home directly; and if you had thought fit to remain in London till you saw me yesterday, you might have met me at your aunt's house last night, I having gone there in the hope of seeing you."

"This seems to me something like an accusation," answered Charles, a little nettled; "and in regard to the first count of the indictment, I must plead that I could not divine that your servants would tell lies. They assured mine that they did not know where you were or when you would return. In regard to the second count, I had business, which I judged of importance, to take me out of town; and, as you knew I was gone from dear aunt Fleetwood, and was aware also of the business that took me, I could not suppose that the expectation of meeting me among the number of her ladyship's guests would take you to her house. Had I known it, I might have hurried my return to London."

"Then Lady Fleetwood told you that she had informed me of your expedition?" said Mr. Scriven in an inquiring tone, but with such perfect composure that it provoked his nephew.

"Not so," replied Charles: "I divined it from her usual conduct, and felt sure of it when I found that you had forestalled me in my object."

Mr. Scriven remained silent for a moment, but then he replied, quite unmoved--

"Your combinations are good, Charles, but sometimes may be mistaken, and are always rather too hasty."

"The simple question is this, my dear uncle," said Charles: "did Lady Fleetwood inform you or not that I had discovered poor Miss Hayley in very great misery not far from Frimley, and that I intended to go down yesterday, have her brought to town, and see that she was properly taken care of? and did you not set off immediately and carry her away to a madhouse?"

"Who puts the question?" asked Mr. Scriven, with his usual equable manner.

"I do," answered Charles.

"Rather respectful from a nephew to an uncle," replied Mr. Scriven, drily; "and now, my dear Charles, to more serious matters. I wrote to you to come over immediately, as I wanted to see you----"

Charles was angry at the somewhat contemptuous brevity with which his uncle dismissed the subject.

"You will excuse me, sir," he said; "but I wish for an answer to my question before we enter upon any other matter."

"You shall have an answer before you leave the room," replied Mr. Scriven; "but I think it necessary to proceed in order; for you know, my good nephew, that I am very methodical, and as my letter to you is the first incident, chronologically speaking, I wish to deal with that first."

"Very well, sir," replied Charles: "what might be the occasion of your wishing my immediate return?"

"One of some importance," answered Mr. Scriven. "You and your cousin Maria have been brought up in habits of great affection for each other. She is exceedingly beautiful, and her fortune, very large at her father and mother's death, has not, as you may well suppose, diminished under my management. Although she does not go so much into the world as most young women at her time of life, yet there is every day a probability of some proposal being made to her which she may think fit to accept. Now, my dear Charles, I would not have you go on wasting your time in wandering about upon the Continent, and throw away an opportunity which may never occur again."

Charles Marston smiled.

"Dear aunt Fleetwood has bit you, sir, I think," he replied. "Maria and I have a great deal of affection for each other, but it is quite brotherly and sisterly, I can assure you, and will remain so till the end of our days, whether I am at Babylon or her next-door neighbour in London."

"I advise you for what I think the best, Charles," replied his uncle. "You are too wise, and have too much knowledge of the world, I am sure, to sacrifice all the important objects of life for romance."

"Decidedly," answered Charles Marston: "you must be very well aware that I have not a particle of romance in my disposition--plenty of fun, my dear uncle, and a great deal of nonsense of different kinds, but none of the kind called romance. Nevertheless, setting aside all objections to marrying at all, which I suppose you are the last man on earth to undervalue, I have an immense number of sufficient objections to the important act and deed of proposing to my cousin Maria."

"Pray, what may they be?" asked Mr. Scriven, drily.

"In the first place," answered his nephew, "it would take her quite by surprise, and I do not wish to surprise her; in the second place, she would to a certainty refuse me, and I do not want to be refused; in the third place, if she did by some miracle accept me, which nothing but a miracle could produce, we should find out in three weeks that we were not suited to each other: and in the----"

"But why not suited to each other?" demanded Mr. Scriven, interrupting him, after listening to his objections with marvellous patience. "You have no vices that I know of, though a great many follies, and Maria is the sweetest tempered girl in the world."

"You have touched the exact points of difficulty, most excellent uncle," replied Charles Marston. "Maria is not fond of follies, and I am not fond of sweets; I never was: even from childhood, I always preferred a little sour in my sweetmeats--and, in short, Maria and I would never do together. She would always let me have my own way, and say, 'Do just as you like, my dear Charles.' Now, what I want is a wife who would say, 'You shan't do anything of the kind, you mad-headed fellow!'"

"You were going to state a fourth objection, I think, when I interrupted you," said Mr. Scriven, with the utmost composure: "the first three I do not judge very sound."

"I do," answered Charles, "and the fourth is still sounder. Fourthly, and lastly, then--I intend to marry somebody else."

"Whom?" asked Mr. Scriven.

"There, my dear uncle, you will excuse me," replied Charles. "I will beg to keep my own secret till I am formally accepted; and I only mention the fact to you to show you that the idea of a marriage between Maria and myself is a horse without legs--it won't go, my dear uncle."

"Very well," said Mr. Scriven, gravely; "and now there is another subject upon which I want to speak to you. You have been a very long time doing nothing but amusing yourself: you have arrived at an age when many men are making fortunes, or laying the foundations of honourable distinction and a great name. Worldly prosperity is too insecure a thing for any man to rest contented with that which fate or fortune has chosen to bestow, without further exertions of his own. A man must labour to gain, if he would wish to maintain; and I think it high time that you should adopt some steady pursuit, and give up this reckless roaming about the world. You have passed the time at which those professions usually selected by young men of gay dispositions, idle habits, and small brains, are open to aspiring youths like yourself: I mean the army and navy. For law, physic, or divinity, you are not fitted either by intellect, study, or character. Mercantile pursuits, however, may be embraced at a later period of life, and with less preparation. To them I should advise you strongly and urge you warmly to apply yourself, and that at once."

Charles Marston was a good deal annoyed by his uncle's lecture--not so much at the matter (for he could not help acknowledging that there was a great deal of good sense in what Mr. Scriven said) as at the manner, which was dictatorial, cold, and a little contemptuous. He replied, therefore--

"I am quite well aware, my dear uncle, that for the mercantile profession neither a large portion of intellect, a refined education, nor an amiable character is required. An instinct of gain supplies all deficiencies; and although higher qualities may, and often do, embellish the character of a merchant, many men do get on quite as well without. However, there is a good deal of justice in your observations; and although, as you know, I am not famous for thinking (Mr. Scriven nodded his head), I have thought of two or three of the topics which you have discussed; and, moreover, some time ago I wrote to my dear father, informing him of all my views, hopes, and wishes, without the slightest reserve. According to his directions and advice I shall act, as soon as I receive his answer; for I can perfectly trust to his kindness, to his liberality, and to his judgment."

"Very good," said Mr. Scriven. "I trust, and am even sure, that his views will be the same as my own; for, although your father is an exceedingly eccentric man, and never acts as any other man would act, yet he is in the main a man of good sense; and there are circumstances----"

Charles Marston did not at all like the tone in which Mr. Scriven was speaking of his father. He felt himself growing angry, and he knew that if he suffered the sensation to go on, receiving little additions every moment from his uncle's observations, his anger would explode. He therefore thought it better to cut the matter short, and interrupt Mr. Scriven's picture of his father's character.

"You pride yourself upon being a plain speaker, my dear sir," he said; "but observations upon my father's eccentricity, as you term it, are not pleasant to me. Having, therefore, listened attentively to your exhortations on marriage and commerce, I will revert, if you please, to the question I put regarding Miss Hayley."

"Will you propound it?" said Mr. Scriven: "I did not take a note of it."

"It was simply," answered Charles, "whether my aunt did not tell you that I intended to go down yesterday at three to bring Miss Hayley to town, for the purpose of having her properly taken care of, poor thing; and whether you did not immediately set out to forestal me, and carry her off to a madhouse?"

"One answer to the three clauses of your question will suffice," replied Mr. Scriven, perfectly unmoved: "yes."

"Then I must beg to know," said Charles, "where you have carried her; for I am determined, after the state in which I lately found her, to see with my own eyes that she is properly protected for the rest of her life, and to provide for it out of my own income."

"I promised to answer your question as first put," answered Mr. Scriven, coolly, "and I have done so, but I promised no more; and now I beg leave to say that I shall not tell you where I have placed Miss Hayley."

"And, pray, why not?" demanded Charles, in a sharp tone.

"Because I have more consideration for your income than you have yourself, young man," replied his uncle. "You will soon have need of it-- every penny of it, sir--and more important duties to perform with it."

"I do not understand your meaning, sir," rejoined Charles, a little surprised by a very meaning look upon Mr. Scriven's face, which was rarely suffered to convey anything more than his exact words implied.

"It is very simple," said Mr. Scriven, rising and pushing over to his nephew two papers, which he had held in his hand for the last five minutes. "By these two letters you will see what I mean. The one I received more than a month ago, when I wrote to you; the other yesterday morning. Your father is a bankrupt, Charles Marston--that is all. And now I must go to the counting-house, for it is past the hour."

CHAPTER XV

Lady Anne Mellent was seated alone in her drawing-room, in the large and handsome town-house which had been inhabited for many years by her father and grandfather. She looked less gay--more thoughtful than usual. Perhaps the weather might have some share in depressing; for most people born in England are more or less barometers, and subject to be raised or depressed by the state of the atmosphere.

Foreigners, I believe, generally imagine that the cause of two Englishmen, as soon as they meet, beginning to talk of the weather, is that they have nothing else to talk of; or that the variation of our changeable climate is the most prominent fact in the natural history of the land; or because the weather is the only open question, free from all tinge of the party spirit which affects all other things in our native country. But the real cause lies deeper. It is, that in almost all instances the fibres of an Englishman's body are affected by the changes of the weather, like the strings of a fine instrument--more or less, of course, according to the constitution of the individual. But still, as I have said, in most men it is so; and the mind, being in tune or out of tune in consequence, emits sounds accordingly.

Now, one of the strange vicissitudes of climate had taken place which are so common under our skies. A day or two of fine, clear summer weather had been succeeded by a morning covered with thick grey clouds, while the east wind hurried a sort of dim and filmy mist through the air, cutting to the marrow all who exposed themselves to its influence. It was the true picture of a reverse of fortune--the summer sun of prosperity clouded, dim uncertainty pervading the atmosphere, and the cold and cutting blast of ingratitude, and neglect, and contemptuous pity chilling the very soul.

Nevertheless, although I do not mean to say that Lady Anne Mellent was not at all affected by the weather, yet her grave and meditative mood had other, stronger causes. She had a great deal to think of just then; and she leaned her fair brow upon her hand, the thick glossy ringlets falling over her taper fingers, and her eyes fixed upon a sheet of writing-paper, whereon her other hand was fancifully sketching all sorts of strange figures. Her mind had nothing to do with what her hand was about or what her eye was fixed upon. I do not know what part or portion of the strange mixed whole, expressed by the little monosyllable man, it is that occupies itself with trifles, while the high spirits, the sensitive soul, and the intellectual mind are engaged in reasonings deep of other, mightier things; but so it often is, that when the brain and heart are most busy with strong thoughts, something--I know not what--gives employment to the corporeal faculties: just as a nurse amuses a sick child with playthings while two learned doctors are consulting of its state.

Thus it was now with Lady Anne. Her mind saw not the things she was drawing--the dancing men and women, the flowers, the fruits, the trees, the wild and graceful arabesques, the ruined towns and castles, the volutes, the capitals, the columns: she had not an idea of what she was about; but, deep in some little chamber of the brain, with the doors and windows closed, while Imagination held a taper and Memory spread out a map before her, the mind sat and studied the chart of the past, trying to lay out plans for carrying on into the unexplored future the roads along which her destiny had hitherto run.

She was startled from her reverie by a servant opening the drawing-room door and announcing Mr. Charles Marston; and, raising her head, with a slight glow upon her cheek, she held out her hand to him with frank and kindly greeting.

"Well, you have come to see me at length," she said, "and I suppose I must take your yesterday's apologies in good part, especially as I find that one of the two letters did arrive; and I have been reading this morning all the nonsense it contains, with a great deal of interest and satisfaction. There is nothing in the world like nonsense, either for pleasure or amusement. Sense is so hard, so square, and so sharp in the points, that it is always scratching one somewhere. I am sure Adam and Eve must have been talking nonsense to each other all day long in paradise, otherwise it would not have been half so pleasant a place as it is represented."

Charles Marston took a seat by her side, with a very faint smile, saying--

"I am afraid, dear Lady Anne, that I must give up nonsense for the future, and devote myself to dull, hard, dry sense."

"Stir the fire, Charles Marston," replied his fair companion: "the cold east wind has made you melancholy. Now, for the last three-quarters of an hour I have myself been much more sober and reflective than is at all proper and right, and I do not choose to be encouraged in such bad habits by the seriousness of anybody else."

"What can have made *you* serious?" asked Charles Marston, in a tone of doubt, his eyes fixed upon the paper on which Lady Anne had been sketching. "Your gravity must have been somewhat frolicsome."

"Good heaven! did I draw all that?" she exclaimed, looking down at the paper to which he pointed. "I was not in the least aware of it."

"Nay, then you must have been serious indeed," replied Charles Marston, with a tone both of surprise and sympathy. "What can have happened to oppress your light heart?"

"What can have happened to oppress yours, Charles?" rejoined Lady Anne. "Something must have occurred, I am sure; for, though I have known you from childhood, I never saw you in such a mood till now. What is it?"

"A change of fortune, dear Lady Anne," he said, "implying the relinquishment of the dearest and fondest hopes my heart ever entertained--hopes and wishes which, though treated gaily, lightly perhaps, were not the less deeply rooted, the less profoundly felt."

He paused for a moment, as if summoning strength to go on with a task that nearly overpowered him, and she sat gazing on his face with a look of anxious alarm. At length he proceeded--

"I have loved you, Lady Anne, deeply, sincerely, well, I can assure you----"

"I know all that," she exclaimed, resuming for a moment her gay and sparkling manner: "you told me so twelve months ago, in Rome; you told me so years ago, when I was a foolish girl of thirteen; and I believed you both times. What have I done that you should cease to love me now?"

"Cease to love you!" exclaimed Charles Marston. "I love you better--more dearly than ever: just as one prizes a jewel, the last possession that one has, which he knows must be parted with soon."

"No, you do not love me," she said, "or you would not keep me in suspense. What has happened, Charles?--tell me at once what has happened."

"It can be done in very few words," he replied. "When I told you in Rome how I loved you, I myself possessed a considerable fortune, settled upon me by my father at the time of my mother's death--what she inherited from her father. At that time I believed that, sooner or later, very considerable wealth in addition must be mine; and, although that fact could not change the difference between your rank and mine, yet it in some degree justified me in seeking your hand, and might have justified you in giving it to one who had known and loved you, as you say, from childhood. Well, well!" he continued, seeing her make an impatient gesture as if to hurry his tale; "the rest is soon told. This morning, my uncle, in the most unkind and indifferent manner, informed me that my father was a bankrupt. I need not tell you, Lady Anne, who I think know me well, that my first act must be to restore to my father the income he settled upon me. I will not, indeed, throw my mother's fortune into the hands of his creditors, for that I do not feel myself called upon to do; but the income of course is his for his life."

"Well?" said Lady Anne, as if she did not see the deduction which he would draw.

"I must, of course," continued Charles, "embrace some pursuit in order to raise the fallen fortunes of my family. That is painful enough, for one of my habits and character; but there remains the still more painful task of abandoning those hopes which you once permitted me to entertain, of giving you back every engagement and every promise you made me, and nerving my mind to all that must follow."

"Nonsense!" exclaimed Lady Anne: "how long is it since you heard this news?"

"Not an hour ago," he answered. "I determined to come hither at once, and do what was right by you, though I passed nearly an hour in the park, struggling with thoughts which well-nigh drove me mad."

"You should have come here directly," she answered, in a quiet tone, "and I would have taught you to overcome such thoughts, by showing you what weak and foolish thoughts they were. I was praising nonsense just now; but what I meant was merry, not sad nonsense. Now, this is very sad nonsense indeed. Do you pretend to know me?--do you pretend to love me?--do you pretend to esteem me, and yet suppose that any accidental change of circumstances, any mere pitiful reverse of fortune, would justify me in my own eyes for wishing to withdraw from engagements formed with as little consideration of wealth upon my part as upon yours? I do you full justice, Charles, and believe that you cared no more for my fortune when you asked my hand than I would do for the crown of England. I believed, and do believe, that you would have sought me for your wife, that you would still seek me for your wife, if I had little or nothing; and you have done very wrong, even for one moment to look upon this event except as a misfortune which affects us both. I cannot treat this subject so lightly as I might do most others, because I know what has occurred must be very painful to you on your good father's account; but, thank God, what I do possess, although not so large as is generally supposed, is still affluence--nay, wealth. Make over your income to your father as you propose. That will be abundant for him, and you will share mine."

Charles Marston laid his hand upon hers, and gazed at her with deep affection; but he still hesitated.

"Every one will say," he replied, "and your guardians above all, that you have thrown yourself away upon a fortune-hunter."

"I am my own guardian," she answered, with a gay laugh: "thank God, on the twenty-third of last month I arrived at the discreet age of one-and-twenty. So you have no excuse, sir. I see clearly that you do not wish to marry me; that you are fickle, faithless, and false to all your vows; that you have fallen in love with some Greek, or some Circassian, or some lady Turk. But I will have a distinct answer, Charles Marston, before you quit this room. You shall say 'yes' or 'no.' If you say 'yes,' well and good--there is peace between us; but if you say 'no,' I will prosecute you for a breach of promise of marriage, and produce all your letters in open court. I can establish a clear case against you; so think of the consequences before you decide."

She spoke gaily and cheerfully; but when Charles's arm glided round her waist, and he pressed his answer on her lips, Lady Anne's eyes overflowed with tears.

"You have treated me very ill, Charles," she said, "and I shall not forgive you for the next half-hour. How could you think so meanly and so basely of me? Did I ever talk to you about settlements, or stipulate for pin-money, or require that you should bring an equal share to the housekeeping with myself? or did I set others on to do that which I was ashamed to do? Fie, fie!--do not attempt to justify it, for it was unjustifiable. I am glad of it, for one thing," she added, dashing the tears from her eyes, and looking up with one of her sparkling laughs. "If ever I want to tease you, it will give me something to reproach you with. You shan't hear the last of it for some time, I can assure you; and I'll tell dear Lady Fleetwood how mercenary you are, and that you think marriage is merely a matter of property--that people should be perfectly equal in that respect at least. Then, how she will scold you! But now tell me all about it. Let me hear how your delightful uncle communicated this pleasant intelligence. He always puts me more in mind of the statue in 'Don Giovanni' than anything of flesh and blood I ever saw. I will answer for it, he told the whole as if he were an iceberg and every word were snow."

"Something like it, indeed," answered Charles; "but yet there was a keen, frosty wind coming from the iceberg, which was very cutting."

And he proceeded to give his fair companion a more detailed account of his conversation with his uncle, taking care to avoid that part of the discussion which had referred to Maria Monkton.

Women's eyes are very keen, however; and there is something approaching to instinct in the clearness of their perceptions with regard to everything where other women are concerned. It is only jealousy that ever blinds them, and there they are as blind as the rest of the world.

But Lady Anne was not jealous of Maria, and therefore she seemed to divine in a moment what had been Mr. Scriven's principal scheme. Charles had merely said, "He proposed to me several plans of action, none of which suited me."

"One of them, I am sure," said Lady Anne, "was to marry your cousin Maria. Dear Maria! how often people have settled that for her! But I could tell good Mr. Scriven, even if you had been willing, his scheme would not have succeeded. Maria is in love, Charles; Maria is in love!"

Charles Marston started and looked surprised.

"With whom?" he exclaimed.

"Nay, it is hardly fair to tell you," replied Lady Anne, "and I will keep you in suspense, as you kept me just now: moreover, I will tease you about it, ungrateful man! Watch me well, Charles, for the next two or three weeks; and if you see me flirt unconscionably with any man, while Maria stands calm and self-satisfied by, be you sure that man is her lover, and think that I am trying to win him from her, if you dare."

Charles laid his hand upon hers, and gazed confidently into her eyes.

"You cannot make me jealous if you would," he said; "I know you too well."

"And yet you would not condescend to give Colonel Middleton a letter to me," replied Lady Anne, with a meaning smile.

"Simply because I did not feel myself entitled to take such a liberty," replied Charles Marston, "without at least telling him our relative situation towards each other, which you forbade me to mention to any one till you were of age. So, so, then! Frank Middleton is the man of Maria's heart, is he? It must have been very rapid, or I must have misunderstood her; for I think she told me he had only delivered my letter the day before yesterday."

"Oh! he conquers exceedingly quickly," exclaimed his fair companion. "It is quite true he only delivered the letter the day before yesterday, and yet Maria is over head and ears in love with him, and will marry him, as you will see. I was introduced to him the same day; and, though not quite in love with him, do you know, my dear Charles, I was so smitten that I asked him to dine with me yesterday, which he accordingly did. We had the pleasantest evening possible, quite *tête-à-tête*; for, although good old Mrs.

Brice sat out the dinner very patiently, yet she went to her own room as usual immediately after, and left him to make me a proposal if he thought fit. He did not do it, which, after all the encouragement I gave him, was very singular; but you men are the most ungrateful creatures in the world--of that I am convinced. There, now--make the most of it, for you shall not have one word of explanation from me till I think fit; and you shall see me go on every day with this Colonel Middleton as wildly and as madly as I please, without being in the least jealous--unless I permit you."

Charles caught her in his arms, exclaiming in his old, gay, reckless tone, "I defy you, little tormentor! I have a great mind to punish you for your sauciness by kissing you till you carry the marks upon your lips and cheeks all over London." But then, gently relaxing his embrace, he added in a softer and sadder tone, "After the proofs of love you have given me, dear Anne, I could not doubt you, do what you would; and in despite of all you say, I know you would not pain me for a moment, even by a word or look."

"Be not pained then, dear Charles," she answered; "and be sure that for whatever you see I have a motive, and a strong one."

"I shall see very little, I fear," replied Charles Marston; "for, except during a short morning visit here, and an occasional party at dear aunt Fleetwood's, I shall seldom meet with you till I have forced my way into the gay world again, after an eighteen months' absence, which is quite sufficient to make all the affectionate people in London forget one."

"Come here and dine every day, if you will," replied Lady Anne, laughing. "I care not who knows it now, and only cared before, Charles, because I hate lectures, and dislike opposition when I am determined to have my own way. If you meet Frank Middleton here, you will, of course, be very civil to him; and if I want to speak to him alone, I can take him into another room, you know."

"Of course--of course," answered Charles, in the same tone of light *badinage*; "but I have another task upon my hands, which I must now run away to fulfil--that of nursing my poor friend Winkworth."

This announcement called forth questions, which again required replies; and after hearing the whole story, Lady Anne exclaimed--

"Get him well as soon as possible, for I intend to make you all come down and spend a happy week with me in the country--either at Harley, or Belford, or Caermarthen, or somewhere--Lady Fleetwood, and Maria, and you, and Middleton, and Mr. Winkworth, and all. I took a great liking to that old man, Charles, so you must engage him for me."

Charles Marston promised to obey; and after a few more words, with which, perhaps, the reader may have little to do, he was taking his departure, and had already reached the door of the drawing-room, when Lady Anne called him back.

"Charles! Charles!" she said, "I want to speak to you. And now, remember, I am talking seriously for once in my life: I am going to make a declaration, so remember it. It is somewhat unusual, and rather the reverse of what ordinarily takes place; but no matter. I love you truly and sincerely, and none but you;" and she laid her hand affectionately upon his arm, adding, "I never shall love any other; and I say this because your confidence, without any wish on my part to put it to the proof, may be tried somewhat severely."

"It will stand the test," answered Charles Marston. "I were unworthy of your love, dear Anne, if I could doubt you for a moment."

CHAPTER XVI

The day was near its close, and the keen, clear easterly wind had in the end swept all clouds and mist from the air, leaving the features of the landscape sharp and defined, in the peculiar purple light of the evening, when a man with a brass-bound mahogany box upon his back stopped at the door of the little hovel, on the wide, wild common to which I have so frequently had occasion to refer.

About three-quarters of an hour before, in trudging with his pack out of the neighbouring little town, he had been passed by a post-chaise coming from the side of London; and on turning his head he had seen that it contained only a single traveller--a handsome and fashionably-dressed young man, with a complexion considerably darker than is usually found amongst Englishmen. The pedlar very naturally concluded that the stranger was nothing to him, nor he to the stranger, and that he should never behold his face again; and trudging upon his way over the common, he turned a few steps aside, to see if the inhabitants of the hovel, who had more than once purchased bodkins and needles and such little articles of him, would now be tempted by any of his wares.

Pedlars--although by continual chaffering with every different variety of human beings they usually acquire a great deal of shrewdness, not to say cunning--may be deceived in their calculations as well as other people, and it proved so in the present case. He knocked at the door of the cottage, and then shook it, saying to himself, "The old woman's in one of her moping fits, I dare say." But still he received no answer; and then, going to the little window, he tried to look in. There was a board up in the inside, however, which effectually prevented him from seeing, and he was about to turn away, when he perceived a tall figure advancing towards him from the side of the high-road.

Now, the pedlar was a stout, broad-shouldered, clean-limbed man, of about fifty years of age; and having passed the greater part of his life in hardy excise, he was a match for most men in point of strength; but having had occasion, more than once, to fight for the worldly goods and chattels which he carried on his back, he always cast a suspicious eye towards any one who approached him hastily, which was the case with the stranger; and therefore, unslinging his pack, he put it down behind him, that he might have his right arm more at liberty for the exercise of the stout oaken staff with which it was armed.

At the moment when he first perceived the figure advancing towards him, it was coming up between the high sandy banks through which a little rivulet flowed, and the evening sun cast a deep shadow upon it. The instant after, however, it emerged into the broad light, and the whole dress and appearance removed at once anything like apprehension which he had previously felt. Another minute showed him the face which he had seen in the post-chaise; and touching his hat, he replaced his box upon his shoulders, in order to walk away with it, when he saw the stranger approach the door of the hovel and knock for admission.

"There's no one in there, sir," said the pedlar in a civil tone; "they are all gone, poor people, I suppose. Perhaps the old lady is dead, for she was in a failing sort of way when last I passed."

"No, she is not dead," replied the stranger; "but it is probable a friend of mine, who took an interest in her, has provided for her more comfortably than she could be here. I did not think he would have been so rapid in his proceedings, or I might have spared myself a journey. I wonder where the boy is who I hear was with her: are you sure he is not in the cottage?"

"He is not there, sir; the place is all shut up," replied the pedlar. "He's a good boy, and was very kind to the poor woman, though the people said they were not relations; and indeed I always thought she must have been a gentlewoman at one time."

"You were not far wrong," replied Henry Hayley--for he it was. "I suppose you are well acquainted with the country around?" he continued, turning away from the hovel and walking on by the pedlar's side towards the highroad.

"I know every inch of it," answered the man, "for fifty miles round and more, and many another part of the country besides. I have spent more than twenty years of my life in wandering about with my pack on my back, so that there is hardly a cottage in the counties I travel that I do not know."

"Perhaps, then, you can tell me my best way to the house of a farmer named Graves," said Henry Hayley; "I think it is some six or seven miles off."

"I can tell you the way well enough, sir," replied the man; "but I doubt, with all my telling, that you'll find it; for you see it lies on the other road, and the cross-country lanes are rather crooked."

"Can you show me the way?" asked Henry again; "I shall be inclined to pay you well for your trouble."

The man hesitated for a moment, but then replied--

"I may as well go that way as another, though it is out of my regular beat. But is it the old man or the young one you want to see, sir?"

"The old one, I think," replied Henry: "what is his age?"

"Oh, he is well-nigh upon seventy," answered the pedlar, "and a strange old man too. I don't know whether he'll be civil to you; but he's not to most people, though he's a kind old man at bottom, I hear. He had some troubles when he was younger, and that has made him very cross ever since. But we had better cut across the common here, for it lies away there to the westward."

"Henry turned according to his guide's directions, and followed him for some little way in silence; but at length he said--

"What troubles were they that you alluded to just now as having befallen the old man?"

"Troubles that the rich sometimes bring upon the poor, sir," answered the pedlar. "Just about the time when I first took to this trade, I remember him, as fine a looking man of forty-three or forty-four as any in the whole county, and as gay and light-hearted too. He had then two children, a girl of about seventeen or eighteen, and this young man who now holds the great farm: he was not above fourteen then, and the girl was the prettiest creature I ever saw in my life, and quite like a lady. Poor Mary Graves! I shan't forget her in a hurry. But she fell in love, one unlucky day, with a gentleman who came down into these parts from London--a rich merchant they said he was. He did not behave well by the old man, though not so bad as they said at first; but he coaxed the girl to go away with him, without her father's knowledge; and for a long time Farmer Graves thought he had seduced her, and it well-nigh broke his heart. In the end, however, he found that they were really married; but she died with her first child, poor thing, and the old man has never got over it."

"Poor man!" said Henry, in a very grave tone; "it is a sad tale indeed. Did his daughter's husband never do anything to compensate for the pain he had inflicted?"

"There are some things, sir," said the pedlar, "for which there is no compensation. He could not give him back his child again; he could not wipe out a long year of misery, during which the old man was ruined and dishonoured; he could never make his mind what it was before, nor take out of his heart all the bitterness he had planted there. I have heard, indeed, that he did offer to do a great deal which Farmer Graves would not accept of; and the people say that it was through him that the young man was enabled to take this great farm he now holds, and to stock it. They never knew rightly who he really was, for they say the name he was married under was a feigned one; and all they could find out was that he was a great merchant in London; for the child was put out to nurse for some time, and then the father came suddenly and took it away, and nothing more was ever heard of it, by the family at least."

Henry Hayley fell into deep thought, and the reader acquainted with the early part of his history may easily conceive the nature of his meditation. After a time, however, as they walked on, he resumed the conversation with his companion, but changed the subject entirely, talking of the state of the country and the condition of the country people, of the residents in the neighbourhood, and of the curious state of wandering commerce by which his companion gained his livelihood. He found him a shrewd, intelligent man, who was evidently accustomed, during the solitary hours he passed in proceeding from place to place, to think a great deal and deeply of the many different things that came to his knowledge in his travels over the face of the country. It seemed that while disposing of his wares he gained in exchange, not only money, but the history of those with whom he dealt; and that in journeying onwards he turned over and over in thought all the little facts he had acquired, or the scenes that he had witnessed, reasoning upon them with great acuteness and good sense, so that he was ever ready to comment with a degree of caustic precision unusual in the small trader of a town, who has little leisure for any thoughts unconnected with his business.

Curiosity, of course, was one trait in his character, and he did not fail to make sundry efforts to learn more of his companion, and to discover what could be his business with old Farmer Graves. Henry, however, set all questions at defiance; and in the end the pedlar, seeing that it was in vain to inquire, gave up his efforts in despair.

"That is a poor-looking house," said Henry, as they were approaching the opposite side of the common; "it, seems hardly fit for the habitation of a human being. Has it any occupants now?"

"No, sir; none at present," replied his companion. "It is a poor place surely; and yet it is better than it was twelve months ago, for, the gentleman who lives in the large house on the hill there--you cannot see it for the trees-- had the thatch mended. He does not think like a great many of the gentlemen about, and sets to work in a different way with the poor. It answers pretty well sometimes, and did in the instance of the lad who lived here."

"How was that?" asked the young wanderer. "I should like to have an example of his way of dealing with the poor: the subject is a very interesting one."

"Why, sir, the way was this," answered the pedlar; "I had it from the game-keeper who was with him when it all happened, and he's an honest fellow, so I'm sure the story's true:--Mr. Payne, the gentleman who lives up there, was coming home from shooting, one day last October--he's very fond of shooting; and as he was crossing this bit of the common about the time of sunset, with his two keepers, he saw this hut, and looked up at it. I must tell you, it was raining as hard as it could pour, and blowing fit to freeze one. So he said to the head keeper, 'I suppose nobody lives in that place?' 'I beg your pardon, sir,' said the keeper, 'but there does;' and then he told him all about it. There was a poor lad who had lived in the parish a good many years--an orphan--and as he had neither father nor mother to look after him, he had been badly enough brought up: that was Billy Small's first misfortune. The people pitied him a little, and some of the farmers gave him a bit of work to do, from time to time. But Bill was idle, and Bill was wild; and he got turned off here, and he got turned off there, and in the end everybody abused him, and would have nothing to do with him. Well, to make matters worse, when he was half starved himself, he must needs have some one to starve with him, and so he married a poor girl who had worked in the same fields with him; and you may guess what a to do there was in the parish. I believe they'd have hanged him for it, if they could but have proved that marriage was felony. He tried to get work, and his wife tried; but no one would have anything to say to him, though he promised hard to do better. They all said he was lazy and idle--which was true enough; and they said his wife was as bad, which might be true too, for aught I know; but, however, the two poor things went from bad to worse, till they took refuge in that hovel we passed just now. The boy said he would not go into 'the house,' to be separated from his wife; and there they lived--or, I should rather say, there they were dying--when Mr. Payne passed. The keeper told him how terribly they were off, and that they were both ill of pure starvation and want of covering. Well, the gentleman said he would go in and see with his own eyes; and he found them--the boy, and the girl, and their baby--all crouched up together on some straw, with nothing on earth to cover them during the night but the rags they had on during the day. As half the thatch was off, the rain was pouring in at the other end of the hut, and the wind blowing through at all quarters. The lad had just had a fit of some kind, brought on, the doctor afterwards said, by privation; and the girl was bathed in tears, thinking he was going to die. Well, Mr. Payne is not a bad-hearted man, as gentlemen go, and he was very sorry to see them in such a state; he had some sandwiches in his pocket, and some sherry-and-water in a bottle, and that made them the best meal they had had for many a day. He staid and talked with them, too, for an hour or more; and though he did not promise them much, yet he spoke to them kindly, and did not throw in the lad's teeth all the foolish things he had done, but asked him if he were well again, and work were given him, whether he would be steady and industrious. The lad looked at his little wife, and said with tears in his eyes that he would try; but that he was sure that nobody would take him, for he had asked for employment everywhere in vain. Then Mr. Payne told him not to be downhearted, for that when he was well enough to work he would give a stray job or two and try him, and in the mean time the girl might come down to the house for some soup and bread. Hope's a good medicine, sir, and that he left them, and as he went home, he thought how he might do them good; and that very night he sent for two of the farmers, who were guardians of the poor, and talked to them about the young man. At first they were very hard about it, and called William all sorts of names for marrying when he had no means of supporting himself, and worse still for not coming into the workhouse; and they declared that if people would but let him alone and not help him, he would soon be starved out of his obstinacy. Mr. Payne thought differently, however. He said he believed there were many people who would rather die of starvation than go in; and as to his marriage, he said, though it was certainly a very foolish thing, yet he had already been punished more than enough for what was no crime after all. And he told them, too, that he thought, from what he had seen of the lad, it would do him good rather than harm, for that he would work more steadily, now that he had somebody to work for, than he had ever done before. What he said made no impression upon one of the farmers; but the other seemed to think there might be some truth in it, and promised if the lad got well to give him a trial. Mr. Payne took care that he should get well, for all that he and the poor girl wanted was food and covering, and a very little medicine; and Mr. Payne sent his own doctor to him, and had the thatch mended, and sent them soup and bread every day, and now and then some meat--not much, indeed, for he afterwards told the keeper that the whole did not cost five pounds. Nevertheless, it was quite enough, for William got strong and hearty again, and so did his wife; and the baby, which was but a little bag of bones, throve wonderfully. It is strange what fine hardy babies starving people will have sometimes. A rich man's child would have been killed by one-half what that little thing went through. But, to cut my story short, sir, when they were all well again, and had some clothes given to them--flannel petticoats, and jackets, and things that Mrs. Payne keeps for the poor--they turned out very tidy, and Mr. Payne first tried the lad himself to work a bit in his garden, though he did not want him, but just for a trial, like; and when he had satisfied himself that the lad was inclined to do well, he put Farmer Slade in mind of his promise. The farmer was very willing when he found all had gone right, and took him upon the farm as a labourer. He has been well-nigh six months at it now, and every one says that there is not a more industrious, clever lad in all the place, and things have changed with him altogether; for he is gone down to live in one of the nice little cottages by the farm, for which he pays a shilling a-week quite regular, and they have contrived to pick up a good lot of furniture--part of which he made for himself, by-the-way, for he's not a bad hand at carpentering; and his wife's always neat and tidy, and so is the baby. The girl told me herself that she got all their clothes and such things by her own work in picking and hoeing, that Bill might be able to save a little out of his wages in case another rainy day should come; but I don't think it will, sir; for if they go on as they are going, they will make sunshine for themselves."

While the pedlar was telling his story, the truth of every word of which the author has had an opportunity of ascertaining, he had led the way up the slope of a little hill; and Henry Hayley turned round to take another look at the miserable hovel which had given rise to the narrative, and which was now about a quarter of a mile behind them.

"Either my eyes deceive me," he said, "or you are mistaken in saying that the place is uninhabited. There is smoke rising up out of it--don't you see?"

"So there is," said the pedlar, turning round and shading his eyes with his hand. "Ay, and there's a man down by the pond there: I wonder what he's about. There used to be good fish in that pond; it belongs to Mr. Payne."

As he spoke, the figure of another man appeared at the door of the hut; and they could hear a low whistle, which apparently caused the man at the pond to turn round and walk quickly towards the hut.

"We had better get on, sir," said the pedlar; "there are some bad sort of folks down here just now, and there's no knowing what they may do."

"What have they been doing?" asked Henry, walking on as he led.

"Oh! thieving, and sheep-stealing, and poaching, and all manner of things," replied the pedlar. "The people in London are at the bottom of it all; for these men would not dare to go on as they do if they could not easily and quickly dispose of what they steal. They were caught once by a cunning contrivance, and that stopped them for a long time."

"How was that effected?" asked Henry.

"Why, you see, sir," replied the man, "the way they carried on their trade was this: they went into a field, killed half-a-dozen sheep or so, skinned them upon the spot, and left the head, skin, and feet in the field. Then upon the commons, you know, there's a great number of donkeys. Well, they used to gather them all together, or as many as they wanted, put the mutton on their backs, and drive them away ten or twelve miles to market. They found plenty of butchers ready to buy the carcases, without asking where they came from--just as men buy game now-a-days. However, a man who had a donkey on the common found that every now and then he lost him for a whole day, and sometimes when he came home his back was bloody; and that roused suspicion as to how the stolen sheep were disposed of. For a long time they could not trap them; but at last a shrewd old fellow fell upon a plan, and getting the asses all together one night, they stuffed their hoofs with a compound of red ochre and something else to make it stiff, and then turned them loose, well knowing they would not go very far before morning. The next day, ten or twelve of the donkeys were missing, and a whole heap of people set out upon the track--for there were plenty of marks of red ochre near the field, where some sheep had been stolen the night before. They had no great difficulty now; for all along the road the thieves had taken, one stone had a mark, and another stone had a mark, for nine or ten miles or more, till they came to the place where the carcases had been carried; and there they found thieves, and sheep, and asses, and all. That stopped the business for some time; but now they have got another plan, which is safer. A man comes down from London in a light cart, and there are five or six different places, at each of which he stops, gets out, and goes into the next field. There he finds whatever has been stolen during the night; and whatever it may be, whether it be a dead sheep, fowls, or game, linen, clothes, or anything else, there is sure to be a ticket upon it with the price marked. If he likes the price, he takes the goods, and he almost always does, for they never put half the value upon them; and then he sends down the money every week to what they call their bankers, in some of the towns near; and they take the fellow-ticket to that which they left upon the goods, and get the money, giving the banker his share."

"Is it possible that such a system is tolerated in England?" exclaimed Henry. "Why, it could not be carried on even in Spain, where heaven knows, justice is lax enough."

"It's true notwithstanding," said the pedlar: "they would have been caught long ago by the old Bow Street runners, for they would have pounced upon the people in London; but you see, sir, we go on improving, this country of ours. We are always improving: that is to say, mending one thing and spoiling another. The streets of London are, I dare say, a great deal quieter and safer, though we hear of bad things enough still, considering how much is paid for keeping them quiet; but then, if a great crime is committed, or a gang of scoundrels formed for robbing and plundering honest men, months go by before these men in the blue coats find out anything about it."

As Henry Hayley knew very little of the affairs of the London police, he did not enter into the question of its efficiency with his worthy companion; and still conversing, though upon other subjects, they walked on more quickly after they had reached the summit of the rise, passed the lodge-gates of Mr. Payne, and soon after entered upon another heath, more wild and desolate-looking than the first. The sun had by this time set, but they had yet full half-an-hour of the long twilight of northern lands before them; and the rich purple tints of the whole landscape were a compensation, in the eyes of one at least of the two, for the brighter beams of the day. Passing onward across the heath, the grey shades of night gaining perceptibly upon the lingering light, they came suddenly upon the edge of a small sandpit, from which was rising up a glare that tinged with red the thick bushes of gorse near the edge. Both Henry and the pedlar stopped and looked over, when, certainly greatly to the surprise of the former, a group was seen seated round a good warm fire, engaged in an occupation perhaps the least to be expected in the world at such a spot and in such circumstances.

The party was composed of three: a man of fifty-four or fifty-five years of age, another of four or five-and-thirty, and a good-looking but rather robust young woman of six or seven-and-twenty. Some kettles and pots, a pair of bellows, and various other articles of the tinker's trade, with a bundle, apparently of clothes, sufficiently denoted the calling of the party; but that which was worthy of admiration and surprise was, as I have said, the occupation in which they were engaged. The young woman was seated by the side of the younger man, her head resting on his shoulder, and her arm thrown carelessly across his knee; but her eyes as well as his were fixed upon their elder companion, who, sitting with his back against the bank and his knees drawn up so as to form a sort of desk, was reading to them out of a large quarto volume, very neatly covered with green baize.

The clear, strong voice rose up distinctly, and Henry heard a part of the eighteenth chapter of St. Matthew. He would willingly have listened long, for there was something which seemed to him so fine and touching in the sounds of those holy words read by such a man, in such a situation, that the exquisite beauty and sublimity of the truths there written seemed to acquire, if possible, a deeper force than when read in the crowded church, or even in the solemn cathedral.

"For where two or three are gathered together in my name, there am I in the midst of them," read the poor man below; and Henry thought, "Surely it is so, even here;" but his companion, who did not understand the feelings which had been excited by the sounds, interrupted the reading with little reverence, saying aloud, "Ah, Master Barnes! is that you? How is it that you are not at Slade's to-night, and so near?"

"The barn is quite full," said the old man, as they all looked up, "and so we came here. We shall do very well; and Master Slade was very sorry he couldn't take us in, and gave us some milk to make up, so that's something."

"How do you do, James?" said the pedlar, nodding to the younger man. "I say--if any fellows should come and ask if you have seen us, and which way we have gone, tell them we have taken to the right. I don't half like the looks of things under Knight's-hill."

"Why, I saw two men go down through the gully there about five minutes ago," said the younger man. "I don't know who they were--strangers, I think. But I'll tell them what you say, if I see any one. Go on, father; I want to hear that out."

Henry Hayley and the pedlar walked on, and very naturally the former inquired into the history and character of the persons he had just seen.

"They are very good, respectable people," said the pedlar, who was more a man of thought than of feeling. "The father has travelled this country for a great many years, mending pots and kettles and all kinds of tinware. He always charges the same sum, which is moderate, bad times or good, and is supposed to be quite rich enough to lodge at a public-house if he liked it, but he never sets his foot in one of them; and the farmers are all generally well content to give him lodging in a barn or out-house, for they are certain that there will be no pilfering at the farm that night. When he can't get such accommodation, he passes the night anywhere--in a copse or in a sandpit, as you have seen just now. He always goes to church on a Sunday in a good clean suit, and the other tinkers and trampers call him. 'Gentleman Barnes.' The young man is his son-in-law, and I can assure you, sir, his daughter was as much courted as if she had been a great lady; but the old gentleman would not let her marry, if she had been inclined, which she did not seem to be, till he found a man to his mind; and I will say James Staples promises to be just such another as himself. We are not far from Mr. Graves's farm now. You can see the chimneys up there, just over the trees."

Imagination or memory must have helped the worthy pedlar, for Henry Hayley could see nothing at any distance, and it was in fact quite dark. The only objects visible were two rows of trees, one on either side of the lane they were entering, and some stars peeping out in the sky above. Once, through the trees, indeed, the young gentleman thought he caught the glimmer of a light, probably in a cottage window; and being somewhat impatient to arrive at least so far on the way as the house of Mr. Graves, Henry strode forward a little in advance of the pedlar, as in the lane there seemed no probability of missing the road.

They had proceeded thus for the distance of about a third of a mile when the young gentleman suddenly stopped and turned round, on hearing a sort of choking cry behind him; and he had just time, in the dim and obscure light of the night, to see two men pulling the pedlar backwards by the leathern strap which supported his pack, when he himself received a violent blow on the head from a thick stick, which made him stagger and fall against the bank. He had heard no one approach, for the lane was sandy, and the light sound of their own footfalls was all that met the ears of the travellers.

The fire flashed from Henry's eyes, and his brain reeled with the blow he had received; but he was accustomed to perils of all kinds; and while two of the assailants were engaged, apparently, in plundering the pedlar of his pack, he sprang upon the third as soon as he regained his feet, closed with him at once, and by an exertion of his great strength had mastered him and thrown him down, when a fourth man leaped from the bank above, and cast himself at once upon the young soldier.

The contest would not have been so unequal, even then, as it might have seemed, for Henry was a far more powerful man than either of his assailants; but one of the others, who had been engaged with the pedlar, left his companion to hold the wandering merchant down, and hastened to join the affray which was going on a few steps farther forward.

It still took the whole of their united efforts to master a man of great natural strength, rendered available in a moment by the habit of robust exercises; but he was at length brought to the ground by a tremendous blow of a stick, and for a moment or two lay unconscious of all that was passing around.

When Henry Hayley revived to a sense of what was going on about him, he found his head supported on somebody's knee, and a pair of hands at his throat, busily untying his black handkerchief.

Nature has an instinctive abhorrence of being meddled with in places whence the road to the life-blood is short, and especially about the throat; so that Henry's first impulse was to raise himself as well as he could, and thrust away the busy hands.

"It's all right," said the voice of the pedlar; "he's coming to. Thank you, James--thank you. If you had not taken it into your head to follow us, the blackguards would have done for us, that's clear enough. I feel the squeeze of that fellow's knee upon my breastbone now. But who is the other man who came with you, and who's gone to look after them?"

"It is John Wirling, one of Mr. Graves's men," said a voice which Henry remembered. And then it added, addressing him, "Well sir, how are you getting on now? You have spoiled one of the rogues anyhow, for he ran as if he could hardly get along. I should not wonder if John caught him."

"I hope he won't try," said the pedlar, "though they've got my pack; but they'll turn on him, to a certainty. No, no--here he comes."

With a giddy and aching head Henry Hayley now raised himself from the ground, and all that had happened after he was stunned was explained to him in a few moments.

Seeing some men walking rapidly after the travellers, and knowing that two others had gone on before, the younger of the two tinkers whom he had seen in the sandpit had followed as fast as possible, getting the assistance of a labouring man as he went. They had come up just as the villains were rifling Henry's pockets, and had scared them from their work before it was completed.

As the man who took upon himself the task of explanation concluded, Henry suddenly put his hand into his pocket, with an exclamation of alarm. The next moment he withdrew it, saying--

"They have stolen my pocket-book, full of valuable papers. I will give a hundred guineas to any one who recovers it. I would rather that they had taken all I have in the world than that."

"That is unlucky indeed, sir," exclaimed the pedlar; "but if it has got nothing but papers in it, perhaps we may get it back."

"It contains nothing but papers, and those only valuable to myself," replied Henry. "They have left my purse, which I should have cared little about, and taken that which it is impossible to replace."

"Well, sir, leave it to me," said the pedlar: "I marked one of the men well, and I'll see if we cannot get it; for I know somewhat of these people's ways, as you may have seen by what I told you. And now, sir, we had better trot on, if you are going to Mr. Graves's; for you've had a bad knock on the head, and may as well have something done for it."

"Whoever obtains that pocket-book for me with its contents shall have a hundred guineas for his pains, and all that he expends shall be paid," repeated Henry.

And after having given his address, at a hotel in London, to the two men who had come up to his assistance, and bestowed on them a considerable part of the money in his purse, he followed his guide, with a slow step and an anxious and thoughtful air.

CHAPTER XVII

An old brick house of a good size, with a little green court in front, stood before Henry Hayley and the pedlar at the end of the lane. Across the court, which was surrounded by low walls, was a narrow gravel path leading from a little gate in the wall to the door of the house; and on each side of this path was a range of yew-trees, which had formerly been cut into a thousand strange and fantastic shapes, according to the principles of the topiarian art--an art long now disused in this our land of England. For many years, it is true, the shears and the pruning-knife had not been used on the venerable yews; and the cocks and hens, and obelisks and pyramids, which they had once represented, had now burgeoned and sprouted, still leaving some fantastic degree of resemblance to the animal or thing first represented, in the midst of the efforts of nature to restore the native form of the tree.

By this time the pale edge of the moon was rising over the flat lines of the common, which lay below, and the gleam shone through the intervals between the trees, paving the little avenue with chequered light and shade.

Along this varied pathway Henry Hayley was pursuing his course when the pedlar touched his arm, saying--

"You had better let me go first, sir. Master Graves is a difficult man to deal with for a stranger; but I have known him for many years, and can manage him, I think."

Henry suffered him to lead the way; and advancing towards the door of the house, which was sheltered from the winds by a projecting porch with a peaked roof, the man struck a single blow with a large iron knocker, consisting of a single bar, thicker at one end than the other, somewhat like the pestle of a mortar.

They had not waited half-a-minute when the door was suddenly thrown open, and the master of the house himself appeared before them. He was a very tall man, perhaps six feet two or six feet three in height, with a forehead equally broad and high, rising from a pair of shaggy white eyebrows. The crown of his head was completely bald, and the hair upon the temples and at the back, though curling lightly, was as white as snow. His frame must once have been very powerful, and the broad shoulders and well-knit limbs seemed still not in the least affected by time, although he must have been very nearly seventy years of age; his hand was thin and bony, and his skin somewhat wrinkled. His teeth, however, were very fine, and his dark eyes as bright and clear as ever. Time had not, certainly, bent him with his iron hand, though it had thinned his flowing hair; for he stood straight and upright, rolling his eyes for a moment from the face of the pedlar to that of the stranger behind him, and then demanded, in a loud, stern tone--

"What do you want?"

"You forget me, Master Graves," said the pedlar, "though I have often sold you many a little thing, and you always owned that my wares proved good."

"I don't forget you, Joshua," answered the farmer, sharply; "I never forget. But what do you want at this time of night? and who is that?"

"He is a gentleman to whom I was showing his way, Mr. Graves," said the pedlar hastily, seeing that Henry was about to answer for himself. "We were attacked and robbed by four men, down at the end of the lane. They have taken my pack and the gentleman's pocket-book, and had very nearly killed him into the bargain; for he had to fight three of them, while one held me down. I thought he was dead, for that matter, for two or three minutes; but he was only stunned by the beating about the head, and so I brought him on here; for I was quite sure you would never refuse to let us rest a bit, after what has happened."

"You know, Joshua, I never receive visitors," replied the farmer, gazing first at one and then the other, with evident hesitation. "If men want to speak with me on business, they can find me at the market, in the fields, or in the farm-yard; if they want to speak of anything else but business, they had better not speak to me at all."

"Well, sir," said the pedlar, in a tone of grave reproach, "I did not think that of you; but we can go elsewhere."

Henry felt inclined to interpose, for he did not intend to go elsewhere if he could help it; but the farmer, who was better understood by his old acquaintance, replied more kindly to this appeal.

"No, no, Joshua," he answered; "I did not say that. I will not be wanting in hospitality. England was famous for it, when Englishmen were honest and man could trust man, and I will keep to it still, though those times have gone by. I must break through my rule. Come in--come in, sir; you shall be welcome, though there are few feet that have ever crossed that threshold for seven-and-twenty years."

Thus saying, and telling the pedlar to shut the door after him and bolt it, he led the way into a small sitting-room on the right hand side. Henry followed him, and when he entered the room, the farmer, still holding a candle in his hand, gazed at him gravely from head to foot, with a deliberate, meditating look. He seemed struck with his guest's appearance; but after a moment, as if conscious that his stare was rude, he said--

"I should think few men would like to deal with you single-handed, sir. You must be nearly as tall as I am, and a great deal stronger now."

"I am upwards of six feet," replied Henry, "and not easily overpowered. In the daylight I think I could have matched all three, but in the darkness I could not see whence the blows came."

"That's a bad knock upon your forehead there," said the farmer: "sit down, sir, and I'll make the old woman bring you some vinegar. You seem one who would not like to carry a great black lump on his forehead about the world."

"There's a worse wound on the back of my head," replied the young gentleman, seating himself. "I believe it would have fractured my skull, but fortunately my hair is very thick."

"Let me look at the wound," said the farmer. "I understand something about those things;" and holding down the candle, he parted the large curls of the young gentleman's hair, and as he did so, Henry heard him murmur, "I never saw any but one who had hair like that."

"Nor I either," said the pedlar, who was standing close at his elbow, and caught the sound of the words likewise.

"Ha!" exclaimed the former, starting up to his full height, and gazing at the man with a look of surprise. "Do you recollect her, then?"

"To be sure I do," replied the other, in a calm and quiet tone; "I shall never forget her as long as I live, nor her beautiful hair either--it was so thick, so soft, and so dark, except when the light fell upon it, and then it was like gold. I put it in a comb for her once--I recollect quite well."

The tears rolled from the old man's eyes, and going hurriedly to the door, he called aloud--

"Madge! Madge! bring some vinegar here, and some of the balsam."

He remained looking down the passage for about a minute, and when he returned the tears were gone.

When the vinegar and the balsam were brought, by a servant-woman apparently nearly as old as himself, he applied his remedies with his own hands; and often in doing so he muttered something to himself, but taking care that what he now said should not be heard.

When he had done, he sat down and gazed very earnestly at Henry's countenance, speaking, however, at the same time, as if to cover the scrutiny he was making.

"And so, sir, you have lost your pocket-book," he said; "was it very valuable?"

"It contained things to me of the utmost value," replied Henry: "a paper that can never be replaced, and a lock of my poor mother's hair, which I have carried over almost all the world with me."

"Is she living or dead?" asked the farmer, with a good deal of agitation in his tone.

"Dead," replied the young gentleman: "she died almost immediately after my birth, now six-and-twenty years ago."

Farmer Graves moved uneasily in his chair; but he answered, looking up towards the ceiling--

"It must be found, that pocket-book--it must be recovered."

"I have offered a reward of a hundred guineas to any one who will bring it to me," replied the young gentleman; "for one of your men and a man from the common came to help us, Mr. Graves, when we were attacked, otherwise I believe we should both have been murdered."

"I think I can get it back," said the pedlar: "my own pack is gone for ever, but that's a small matter."

"What will you take, sir?" said the farmer, abruptly, still looking at Henry. "I should think a little tea is the best thing for you."

"If you please," replied the young gentleman; "but I think I must soon go on."

"No, no," said the farmer warmly; "you had a great deal better stay here for to-night. There's the room my son sometimes has. It can be got ready for you in a minute, and I'll contrive to lodge friend Joshua here. I never thought to let two strange men into my house again, but now I am glad I did not shut you out."

"Why so?" demanded Henry with a grave smile.

"There--don't look so," cried the farmer, turning away his head; "you put me more and more in mind of her, every minute. Young gentleman," he continued, laying his large hand upon Henry's arm, "you think me very strange, I dare say; and I am strange--misfortunes have made me strange.

But I'll tell you why I've shut all men out, up to this day, and why I am glad I have not shut out you. I was once as glad to see my fellow-creatures as any one, and I let one man into my house--a stranger to me, as you may be--a gentleman, too, who paid me a high price for a horse I had to sell, and was rich and smart in his apparel. I let him in, I say, and he stole away the most precious thing I had. He well-nigh broke my heart, sir, and well-nigh turned my brain; and I have never let another in within these doors till now."

"But you know, Master Graves," said the pedlar, "that he did not do you the wrong that you once thought, so that should be some consolation to you."

"Yes, yes--I was wrong," said the old man, hastily; "I wronged him, and I wronged my poor girl too, by my suspicions; but yet what could I think? As she was his wife, why couldn't he acknowledge her as his wife? But she was his wife--I saw the certificate with my own eyes; she showed it me when she was dying."

"Have you got it?" inquired Henry Hayley, in as calm a tone as he could assume.

"No," replied the farmer; "I rushed out of the house like a madman, and came back here as soon as the last breath was drawn. I could not wait to put her in the earth--to see the dust shovelled upon the head of my poor, beautiful Mary. I came away at once; and when I came back, it was all over, the house empty, and the poor child, too, gone."

There was a dead silence for several minutes; and then Henry said, in a low tone--

"You should not think too hardly of her husband; there might be many most important motives to lead him to conceal his marriage: at all events, you should forgive, as you would be forgiven."

"I do forgive," answered the old man; "I have long forgiven; but there has been a bitter tree planted in my heart, which bears its fruit still. And now, young gentleman, let me ask your name; for you are so strangely like my own dear girl that I feel glad I have opened those long-closed doors to you. I have always had a notion that before I die I shall see my poor Mary's boy; and though I know that the name the man took was a false one, yet I caught a sight of the real one in the certificate, and I should recollect it if your name came somewhat near. I looked at it but little, it is true, in that terrible hour; but still I think I should remember."

Henry paused thoughtfully for a moment or two, and then replied--

"I am called Frank Middleton; but we will talk more about this, Mr. Graves, hereafter, tor there are some strange circumstances connected with my own birth, too--at present I feel rather giddy."

"I forgot--I forgot," said the old man. "We will have the tea, and talk more to-morrow. It is almost too much for my head, and must be too much for yours."

He rang the bell as he spoke; and then, returning to the subject, which he seemed to find a difficulty in leaving, he said--

"Where were you brought up, sir?"

"Principally upon the Continent," replied Henry; "in Italy and Spain, and for some time in Mexico."

"Ay, he was a merchant," said the old man, "and would have the means of sending the boy abroad. But Middleton--that was not the name."

"I have some reason to believe that my father's real name was not Middleton," replied Henry, "though that is the name I have gone by for many years, and perhaps by inquiring we could discover more. However, to-morrow morning will be time enough."

The last sentence was uttered as the old woman-servant came in with the tea, which, from her master's well-known habits, she judged was the object of his ringing the bell. She had brought but one cup, however; for, never having seen a human creature entertained in that room, she did not seem to grasp the possibility of two strangers being invited to share Farmer Graves's meal. His orders were given, however, to bring more cups and saucers, and more bread and butter, and prepare two rooms for the accommodation of his unexpected guests.

As soon as she was gone, Henry inquired, in the same quiet and low tone which he had studiously used, if Mr. Graves was acquainted with the name of the church at which his daughter had been married.

The old man shook his head.

"No, no," he replied; "no, I did not remark the name; but they were living then--at least, she had been living--at a small village in Hertfordshire, a little beyond Harrow, not much above ten miles from London; and I think I understood that they had been there ever since she left me. Ah, poor thing! poor thing!--she little knew what she was doing when she quitted her father's house. God help and forgive us all! But, as you say, we had better not talk more about it to-night; I feel the well of bitterness pouring forth all its waters again; and yet, when I look at your face, it seems to carry me back for nearly thirty years, and I can hardly think my child dead and gone, in the cold grave--she who was all life and brightness, while I am left here upon the sunny face of the earth, like a withered leaf in a summer's day. There--don't let us talk any more of it to-night."

Henry judged that it might be better not to press the conversation any farther; and indeed he wished in some degree to collect his own thoughts, and to determine fully upon his course of action, before he did so. That he was in the house of his mother's father he was well aware; but he had entertained no idea that his resemblance to his mother was so great as at once to awaken suspicion of the fact in the mind of the old man himself. He had consequently prepared in no degree for such a contingency; and he was well pleased to have time for consideration in regard to the next step which he should take. To avow his real name, and at once give Mr. Graves an explanation of all the circumstances, did not, as the reader may conceive, enter at all into his plans; but yet he feared that the discovery of so great a likeness would render the task of getting full information from the old man more difficult than he had at first imagined. He contented himself, therefore, during the evening, with studying his companion's character. It was not very difficult to comprehend, indeed. Frank, straightforward and decided, but yet kindly and affectionate, the apparent sternness proceeded more from rapidity of thought and feeling than from any real harshness.

"Perhaps, after all," thought Henry towards the close of the evening, "I have obtained as much information from the good old man as he is able to give; and although in the future I shall certainly tell him the whole, perhaps the best way at present may be to leave him ignorant of any further particulars till I can clear away all clouds at once."

The farmer seemed very willing to give him the opportunity of doing so, for till they retired to rest he studiously avoided all further reference to the subject which had already engrossed so much of their time. That he was thinking of it still was apparent, for he often fell into deep reveries; but he made an effort to find other topics of conversation; and Henry was surprised to find that in speaking of books or arts he was by no means an illiterate or ill-informed person. He seemed to have taken a delight in studying the older English poets; he had not only that general knowledge of English history which is sufficient to carry a man through ordinary conversation, or through the House of Commons, where facts mis-stated, or quotations garbled and perverted, are sufficient for the purposes of party, and very little likely to be exposed, especially if delivered with emphasis and the reputation of a good memory; but he had also that thorough and minute acquaintance with particular periods of history which very few men possess, but which is absolutely necessary to all who would view philosophically the motives, deeds, and results of past times, and see their bearings upon the state of society at present.

At a very early hour for one accustomed to courts and cities, Henry received an intimation from his host that the usual period of rest at his house was come. The old woman-servant, two or three other women, and several labouring men, were called in; and the good farmer, producing a small volume from a cupboard, read several short prayers to his household, and dismissed them to repose. He then led Henry to the room which had been prepared for him, provided him with whatever articles of apparel he might need, and when turning to leave him, held up his hand with the air and look of a patriarch, saying--

"God bless you, young man, and watch over you during the night! I do believe that my child's blood flows in your veins: if not, fortune has strangely sent you to renew, and yet to soften, the memories of the past."

CHAPTER XVIII

Love often keeps men awake: knocks on the head will have the same effect, if they be not too hard, when they sometimes prove very soporific; and agitating thoughts of any kind, with the generality of mortals, have the same tendency. It is not always so, indeed; for I know some people who, when they are very unhappy or very anxious, go sound to sleep. They are wise. It is the best thing they can do.

Nevertheless, although Henry Hayley was not one of the latter class, was in love, had received two severe blows on the head, and had had a great many strong emotions within him, he slept very soundly, for he was weary and exhausted.

There is something, too, in habit; for the mind is very much more like the body than we imagine, and either will learn to bear almost anything by custom, if it be not sufficiently strong to break down all powers of resistance at first.

Now, Henry had in the course of his life gone through so many agitating moments, and had so frequently encountered difficulty, danger, and distress, that he bore them now more lightly than most men, gave to thought the time due to thought, and to repose the time necessary for refreshment. Thus, as I have said, he slept soundly and well till daylight on the following morning; and he had just raised himself on his arm, and was looking at the sunshine playing with the white dimity curtains of the windows, when he heard a knock at the door.

"Come in," he said, and his friend the pedlar appeared.

"Good morning, sir," said the man. "I have just come up for a minute, while Farmer Graves is out, to have a chat with you upon what happened last night. I don't mean about the robbery, but about the marriage and all that."

Now, Joshua Brown was somewhat forcibly in possession of a portion of Henry Hayley's confidence: I say forcibly, because our young friend was not a man to entrust his affairs to the discretion of a wandering pedlar, whom he had only known for a few hours, although all that he had seen of him was favourable. But the pedlar, having been present when so much had passed regarding his early history, had that degree of command of the story which rendered it a nice point of discretion whether he should be told more or not. Henry resolved to see farther, however, before he decided, and to allow the man to take the lead, maintaining, for his own part, what may be called the defensive in the conversation.

"Well, my good friend," he said, in reply, "it is a very curious circumstance that this good farmer should see so strong a likeness between myself and his daughter."

"I don't know, sir," said the pedlar; "that is as it may be. That you are very like her is certain, for I remember her well; and if you do not know who your mother was, it is just as likely that she was your mother as any other woman."

This proposition Henry did not think fit to contradict; and the next moment the pedlar went a step farther, saying--

"Besides, sir, I rather think that you must yourself have some cause to believe that you are this poor young lady's child, because, although Farmer Graves, from the way I took with him, does not know anything about it, I know that you came over seeking him."

"I might have a thousand other things to talk to him about," replied Henry, although he could not help feeling that this was a home-thrust.

"Well, sir," answered the pedlar, "I do not want to pry into your affairs: it is not curiosity or anything of that kind that makes me speak; but I think I can perhaps help you in what you want--that is to say, if I am right in believing I know what you do want."

"If you will tell me what you suppose me to want," replied Henry Hayley, "I will at once answer you, yes or no, and will moreover ask you a few questions in return, your answers to which will soon satisfy us both as to whether you can afford me the assistance I require, and for the wish to render which I am very much obliged."

"Why, you see, sir," rejoined the man, "last night you asked Mr. Graves, quite quietly, whether he had got the certificate, and some time after, whether he knew at what church the marriage took place. Now, I fancy that your object is to prove that you are legitimate, whether you may think fit to acknowledge your mother's family or not; for I can see clearly that you have been bred up as a very high gentleman."

Henry Hayley smiled.

"My good friend," he said, "let me assure you, in whatsoever rank I may have been brought up, I would never disclaim as relations good and honourable men, to whom I am really tied by kindred blood. A much higher rank than ever I shall attain to would not at all justify such evil pride. I will acknowledge, however, that my object is that which you state, and I will reward any one very handsomely who will enable me to prove the marriage of Miss Graves."

"I think I can do it, sir," said the pedlar, rubbing his hands slowly one over the other; "I don't doubt it. This wandering trade of mine is one of the best and most interesting in the world; we see all that happens round about us in every part of the country, hear a great number of curious stories, and as we go very quickly from one place to another, we often get the two ends of a history which itself takes a very long turn between them, and learn more about it than people who have more to do with it."

"But how do you intend to act in this instance?" demanded Henry: "have you any particular information?"

"Not much, sir," replied the man; "but I will work it out, not with standing."

"I should like to hear how," said the young gentleman; raising himself higher in bed. "When we were talking with Mr. Graves, you seemed to have no further information than that which you had previously given to me, and I should be very glad to hear what more you know."

"That is hardly fair, sir," said the pedlar with a smile.

"I can assure you," replied Henry, "that whatever you tell me will make no difference whatever as to the recompense I shall give, if by your means I can prove the fact of the marriage."

"That is not the point at all, sir," answered Joshua Brown. "I am quite sure you would behave like a gentleman. I should know a gentleman when I see him, I think, or I have walked the world for well-nigh thirty years to no purpose. But you see, sir, there's a pleasure in working a thing of this kind out by one's self. It's a thing I'm very fond of, and often, when I see something happen that I don't understand, I set to work to make it out; and I get a little bit of information here, and a little bit there, till the whole thing is as clear as possible. I don't mind telling you this much, however, if you'll just let me follow the string my own way:--Some seven-and-twenty years ago--it was in the month of August--as I was trudging along with my box on my shoulders, down in Hertfordshire, just about the place where Farmer Graves told us last night he was sent for to his daughter, a post-chaise passed me, and I saw in it a face I thought I knew. It was a woman's face, and one not likely to be forgotten; but she had on a white bonnet with a white feather in it, and a white lace veil partly hanging down; and as I had never seen the young lady so dressed, I was puzzled for a long time to think who it could be. I went along saying, 'It is surely pretty Mary Graves;' but I was not quite certain. About a mile farther on I came to a church, and looking over the wall of the church-yard I saw the clerk, or the sexton, or somebody, shutting the vestry-door. So I hallooed out to him, 'Master Clerk, do you want anything in my way?' He was a sulky old fellow, and he said 'No.' Then I answered, 'Come, come--you want a ribbon for a wedding favour for the two young people who have just passed, who have been tying the knot with their tongue they can never untie with their teeth.' So he laughed a little at that, but he said, 'No, I don't. If they had wanted me to wear a favour, they might have given me one.' Then speaking quietly, just as you did last night when asking about the certificate, I said, 'Pray who are they, Master Clerk?' But he answered quite short, 'What's that to you?' and I couldn't get another word out of him, for he walked away. Some nine or ten months after that, I came down here--I always take these parts about the end of May or the beginning of June--and I began to ask the people questions. I soon found that Mary Graves had gone away with a rich young merchant, was married to him, and was dead: in short, I heard the whole story that I told you. It was two years after that before I saw her father again, but then I found him quite heart-broken still."

"Do you know the name of the church?" asked Henry eagerly.

"No, I do not, sir," replied the man; "but I'll find it out, and see the register for that year--only I don't know what name to look for."

"Mary Graves, of course," replied Henry; adding, the moment after, "bring me a certificate of her having been married in that year, and I will make you a rich man for the rest of your life. But, my good friend, it may be months before you trace the whole of this business; and from particular circumstances it is necessary for me to ascertain the facts immediately."

"It shan't be long, sir," said the pedlar. "I must go back to London, for I have no pack now, and so I travel light."

"What might be the value of your pack, my good friend?" asked the young gentleman.

"Oh, not very much, sir," answered the man, "for I had sold a good deal out of it. There were ten pair of spectacles, some gold pins, and two or three wedding rings; but the whole wasn't worth more than nine pounds, I think, and the box wasn't worth a pound more, for it was an old one."

"Do you think you can get me a pen and ink and a sheet of paper?"

"Oh, certainly," said the pedlar, walking away; and when he returned he found the young gentleman up and partly dressed.

"I will pay you for your pack, my good friend," he said, "as it was lost in consequence of your guiding me here. I have not got money enough about me, for I gave the greater part of what I had to the men who came to help us; but a cheque upon my banker, I dare say, will do as well."

"I'm very much obliged to you indeed, sir," replied the pedlar, "though it is scarcely fair to take it, I think."

Henry, however, drew the cheque and gave it to the pedlar, whose eyes instantly fixed upon the words "Frank Middleton," written at the bottom. A look of some surprise came upon his face, evidently showing he had not quite believed that the name which had been given to the farmer was the real one. Nevertheless, he made no comment, but only said--

"Now, sir, will you let me have your address in London? I think in three or four days you shall hear something more of me."

Henry gave his address accordingly, at the hotel where he was lodging; and merely reading the words "Colonel Middleton," the pedlar seemed about to retire, when the young gentleman stopped him, saying--

"There is another thing we have to consider, my good friend--namely, the recovery of my pocket-book; for there are some papers in it of the utmost importance."

"I will put that in train, sir, before I go," replied the man; "and I don't mind telling you how, for you must give me authority. As to trying to catch these men and get it from them by force, that is out of the question. The only way to do is, to apply to some of what they call their bankers. They call them 'blinds' in London, I believe. Now, I have heard the names of two or three of these scoundrels, in the different towns round about; and I'll go to them, and tell them that you will give a hundred pounds to get the book back again with all it contains."

"You may say I will give that to the people who have got it," replied Henry, "and fifty pounds more to whichever of these so-called bankers gets it for me."

"And no inquiries made," said the pedlar: "that will soon settle the matter, I think. But now I'll go, sir, for there I see Farmer Graves coming up the walk, and it's as well he shouldn't know that we've been talking over these matters."

"I have not the slightest objection to his knowing," replied the young gentleman; "for it is my intention to tell him this morning a great deal more concerning myself than I did last night, as I think he will now be able to talk over the matter more calmly."

"He will like your telling him, and his telling you, much better than my having anything to do with it," said the pedlar, "and therefore I had better go. Good-bye, sir: a week shan't pass without your hearing from me."

Thus saying, he quitted the room, leaving Henry to finish his toilet; and Henry dressed, and descended the large, wide staircase, which, to say the truth, occupied nearly a third of the whole house. He entered the room where he had taken tea the night before; and seeing that, although it was untenanted, the table was laid for breakfast, he sat down and gazed out of the window, obtaining a view to the left of the double row of yew-trees, over the top of the neighbouring copses, to the wide-extended heath of which he had traversed a part during the preceding evening. The country lay soft and fair in the hazy morning light; but, though Henry's eyes were fixed upon it, he saw little, except that a sweet picture was hung up before him; for his mind was occupied with thoughts too eager and too active to suffer the volatile part of the mind to stray after the ordinary sources of enjoyment. He had not much faith in the success of good Joshua Brown's efforts to recover his lost pocket-book; and when he came to consider all that it contained, the necessity of regaining it became every moment more and more evident to his eyes. There was in it, first, the paper given to him by his father, immediately before he started for the Continent. Besides this, there was his passport under the name of Frank Middleton; and there were documents of various kinds, which went a great way to establish the identity of the person so named with the Henry Hayley who had fled from England more than ten years before. Whether the possession of these papers would ever be of any great service to himself, he might doubt, in the undecided state of his mind as to the course he should pursue; but yet he saw clearly that they might be very dangerous in the hands of another, if ever the person who had possessed himself of them should obtain a clue to the history of the real owner. Yet, however much he thought over the circumstances, he could see no better plan for recovering his property than that which had been proposed. To employ an officer of police would have been more dangerous than to leave it where it was. To search for it in person offered very small prospect of success, as he was but little aware of the haunts and habits of the persons by whom he had been assailed.

He resolved, however, to consult the good old fanner as to the best means of proceeding; and the opportunity was not long wanting, for in about ten minutes Mr. Graves entered the room. He advanced towards

Henry with an outstretched hand, and with his eye fixed--I must call it anxiously--upon his guest's countenance; he asked how he was, how he had slept, how his head felt; and he then told him that his guide of the night before had just departed.

"He's an honest fellow, Joshua Brown," said the old man. "I have dealt with him in small things for many years, and never found him deceive me. I would willingly have kept him to breakfast; but he would take nothing but a slice of bread and a cup of beer, and then posted off upon his way."

"I must go very soon likewise," replied Henry; "but before I go, and before breakfast is served, let me say one word to you, my dear sir. I have many reasons to believe that we are very near akin to each other. My early history is still a mystery, in some degree, to myself; but I will now tell you fairly, which I did not choose to do last night, that the name of Mary Graves has been mentioned to me, once in my life, as that of my mother."

The old man threw his arms round him, pressed him to his heart, and Henry clasped his hand warmly; but he said--

"Do not let us yet feel too sure, Mr. Graves. I have determined to investigate the whole matter to the bottom, and to discover all the facts; nor will I delay at all in so doing. My father has been dead some years, otherwise the whole would have been made perfectly clear before now; for many circumstances, which I cannot well explain at present, prevented him during a long period from holding any communication with me regarding my birth. Of this, however, be assured, Mr. Graves--that as soon as ever all the facts are in my possession, I will see you again; and, if it be as I think, will gladly claim that connection with you which my father did not acknowledge--not from any feeling of pride on his part, but from motives so powerful that you yourself, when you hear them, will admit their force."

The old man mused, with tears in his bright dark eyes.

"They should be powerful indeed," he said, "to justify--nay, to palliate--such conduct as his. But perhaps, after all, he knew not how I loved her; perhaps he knew not the full bitterness of the cup he forced me to drink. Often have I cursed him, but I curse him not now: I have learned to forgive, and I pray that God may forgive him."

"Amen!" said Henry. "Every man needs forgiveness; and he who has caused another pain and grief, however it may have happened, requires it much."

As he ended, the woman-servant came in with the materials for breakfast; and he and the old man sat down together, avoiding, as if by mutual consent, any reference to the subject of their previous conversation. Henry spoke at large, however, with regard to his pocket-book, and explained to Mr. Graves as well as he could, without describing the contents, how important it was for him to recover it.

"I could wish," he added, "though I don't know if it be possible, that it should be restored to me without being opened."

"I would not look into the inside for the world," replied the old man; "but if it be still within ten miles of this place, I think I will have it before night; for immediately after breakfast I will mount my horse, and I will get all my own men and my son's together, and will sweep the whole country between this and Frimley, without leaving a hole unsearched in which any one of the villains could harbour. But where are you going to now? Cannot you stay and help us?"

"I am afraid not," replied Henry: "I have promised to be in London to-night; but I will write down my address, and hope to hear from you."

"Don't write; tell me," said the farmer: "that is as good as writing. I never forget: since that terrible day, it seems as if everything that happens to me is dug into my memory as if with a penknife. Like names that boys carve on the bark of trees, the marks grow larger and stronger as time passes. These things touch different men in different ways. I have heard of some men who have quite lost their memory under misfortunes--with me the effect has been the reverse. What is the address?"

When Henry told him, he murmured--

"Colonel Middleton!--that is not the name."

"I do not believe it is," replied Henry; "I do not believe it is my own name; but that will be all explained to you hereafter. And now, is it possible to get a chaise to Hartford Bridge? I left my portmanteau there last night, and must go back for it."

"You can go in my gig," said the old man: "tell the people at the 'White Lion' to send it back. I will order it directly; then go you on your way while I go on mine--and success attend us both!"

CHAPTER XIX

Maria Monkton was dressing for dinner when she heard a loud double knock at the door of her aunt's house. It wanted fully half-an-hour of the time at which any guest but a lover could be reasonably expected; and while she herself hurried her toilet, she bade the maid look out and see who was the visiter.

"It is only your uncle, ma'am," said the abigail; "it is his cab and servant."

"Is Lady Fleetwood dressed?" demanded Maria, rather anxiously.

"Oh, dear, yes, ma'am! She has been down these ten minutes," replied the maid, setting hard to work again upon her lady's hair.

Now, if Maria had been anxious to hasten all her proceedings when she thought that the early guest was Henry Hayley, she was even more desirous of getting down soon when she found that it was her uncle who had arrived: not that her love for Mr. Scriven was at all eager; for heaven knows that, however affectionate a heart might be, it would have found it a hard task to love him very warmly. Green ivy and blushing honeysuckle will twine, it is true, round a cold, stiff post; but it would have required a still more clinging passion than even love to make any heart attach itself to Mr. Scriven. Avarice perhaps might do.

No: Maria's haste proceeded from other causes. There was never any telling what Lady Fleetwood might say or what Lady Fleetwood might do; and her niece very much wished to prevent her from saying or doing much with Mr. Scriven that day. Indeed, had she been at all aware that her aunt had asked him to dinner, Maria would have prepared accordingly, and gone to dress earlier; but dear Lady Fleetwood had always her own little secrets; and, as she fully concurred in her brother's desire that Maria should marry Charles Marston, she had resolved to invite Mr. Scriven without letting her niece know anything of the fact, in order that her own efforts, both offensive and defensive, might be well seconded; for Charles, who she was afraid would *not* fall in love with Maria, and Colonel Middleton, who she was afraid *would* fall in love with Maria, were both to be there at dinner.

Perhaps this does not explain very clearly why she kept the invitation secret from her niece; but the truth is, Lady Fleetwood was afraid Maria would dissuade her from sending it. Now, Lady Fleetwood, as the reader knows, was the most persuadable woman in the world; and she had an internal consciousness of this sort of *persuadability*--I may as well manufacture another word while I am about it--which made her reluctant to expose that particular side of her character to the assault of an antagonist.

As she wished very much to have Mr. Scriven there, and had determined that it would be quite right and proper so to do; and, moreover, as she knew that Maria could persuade her not to ask him, and thought it very likely she would do so, Lady Fleetwood, with a little *ruse* upon herself, quietly wrote a note to her brother, sent it off in secret, and then was afraid to tell her niece what she had done, till Mr. Scriven was actually in the house.

As I have said, Maria dressed herself with the utmost expedition, and descended as fast as possible to the drawing-room. She found her aunt and uncle full tilt, however, in what seemed a very interesting conversation, for Maria had rarely beheld Mr. Scriven's face so full of expression before. Her entrance took place with ladylike grace, just as Lady Fleetwood was finishing a sentence.

"As like as it is possible to conceive," quoth Lady Fleetwood; "exactly the same person, only taller and older."

Maria saw it all in a moment; and, though she was a good deal agitated and somewhat alarmed by what she did see, she composed herself as best she might, and gallantly hurried forward to the scene of combat.

"Ah, Maria! good evening," said her uncle. "Your aunt has just been telling me who are to be her guests to-night. Amongst them is a Colonel Middleton, I find--a friend of yours."

"He brought me a letter from Charles," replied Maria, struggling desperately against emotion. "Do you know him, sir?"

That would have been scarcely fair of Maria, if it had not been that Mr. Scriven had spoken in a tone which might very fairly be interpreted to imply that he had some acquaintance with the gentleman of whom he spoke.

"No, I don't know him at all," replied Mr. Scriven. "Pray, do you see this extraordinary likeness between him and young Henry Hayley?--though perhaps you do not recollect the lad, for you were but a child when he ran away."

"Oh, yes! I remember him perfectly," replied Maria, in as indifferent a tone as she could assume. "You forget, my dear uncle, I was between thirteen and fourteen when he went. There is a likeness certainly, though Colonel Middleton is darker in complexion, and has darker hair. There are various other differences, too; but still I can see the likeness which my aunt has discovered."

"I always doubted the story of that boy's death," said Mr. Scriven, drily, looking first at his niece and then at his sister.

"Oh, dear me! how can you fancy such a thing?" exclaimed Lady Fleetwood. "Why, the officer saw him lying dead."

"The officer never saw him alive," said Mr. Scriven.

"But you don't suppose that Colonel Middleton is the same?" exclaimed his sister, who saw that she had excited suspicions which she had not the slightest wish in the world to arouse. "Why, this gentleman has been all his life in Spain and Mexico, and his mother, I hear, was a Spanish lady."

"I suppose nothing at all," replied Mr. Scriven; "I never suppose anything. But if it were Henry Hayley, he would of course take a different name and fabricate some history for himself: such a one as you have just told is as likely as any other. We will soon find out, however; for if he be a Spaniard, or half a Spaniard, he must be known to Spaniards."

Maria smiled, for there she felt herself upon strong ground, in consequence of what Henry had told her.

"You seem pleased or amused, Maria," said her uncle.

"A little amused," she answered; "for poor Henry Hayley seems to be what the French would call your *bête noire*, my dear uncle. You see him in every bush. However, Colonel Middleton, in conversation the other day, mentioned the names of a great number of Spanish gentlemen with whom he is acquainted, and amongst the rest that of the Conde de Fraga, the secretary of the Duke of San Carlos, the ambassador. As my aunt knows the young conde, she has invited him here to-night to meet Colonel Middleton, so you will soon see if they are acquainted."

Mr. Scriven had just time to say "Humph!" before Charles Marston was announced. Then came Lady Anne Mellent, and she was succeeded by Colonel Middleton himself. Henry's eye, as he entered the room, fell at once upon Mr. Scriven; but he took not the slightest notice, and betrayed no knowledge of him even by a change of expression. He paid his compliments to Lady Fleetwood gracefully and easily spoke for a moment to Lady Anne in a gay and laughing tone, and then took a chair by Maria, who, though standing before he entered, had seated herself immediately, feeling her heart beat so violently that she feared she should fall.

During the whole of this time, and while Charles Marston crossed over and shook hands with his friend, Mr. Scriven continued to examine his sister's guest with a keen, scrutinizing stare. There he was before him--tall, handsome, commanding, graceful, dressed with the most perfect taste, and having a star and a smaller order on his left breast, but still very, very like what he should have expected to see in Henry Hayley, had there not been good reason for believing him dead. Still there was some slight difference; and perhaps a discoloured mark upon the forehead, left by the blow he had so lately received, made him less like his former self than he otherwise would have been.

The young officer did not seem to perceive the rude examination he was undergoing, and was giving a sketch of the attack which had been made upon him the night before to Charles and Maria, when Mr. Scriven touched his nephew's arm, saying--

"Charles, you have not introduced me to your friend."

With perfect ease, which showed that he at least was unconscious of even a likeness between Colonel Middleton and Henry Hayley, Charles Marston presented his uncle to his aunt's guest. Henry rose and bowed, looking slightly at Mr. Scriven, without even a glance of recognition, and then proceeded with his tale.

Mr. Scriven stood by and listened; but it was less the words than the tones he attended to, and they produced a very strong effect. Henry's voice, as I have said, was very peculiar--rich, full, and exceedingly melodious; and the merchant felt almost sure that he had heard those sounds before.

"Upon my word, Marston," said Henry, in conclusion, "you, who boast yourselves to be, and probably are, the most civilized people in the world, should look a little better to your police. In my country such things are expected, torn and divided as it has been by factions; but in England they should not take place."

"I am very sorry to find you do not count yourself an Englishman, Colonel Middleton," said Mr. Scriven; "and yet you speak our language with a purity, both in accent and grammar, which I never yet heard in a foreigner."

Henry made him a low bow, as if he supposed that a compliment was intended. He replied, however, at the same time--

"My father's language was the first I learnt; and I have always taken care to keep it up by seeking the society and conversation of Englishmen, of whom plenty are to be found both in Spain and Mexico."

"Oh! you have been in Mexico?" said Mr. Scriven. "Pray, did you ever meet with my friend Mr. Odel there?"

"Yes," replied Henry: "he was a great friend of my uncle's, Don Balthazar Xamorça; but he has been dead for many years."

Now, Mr. Odel had been dead so long that Mr. Scriven had great difficulty in reconciling his suspicion that Henry Hayley and Colonel Middleton were the same person, with the knowledge which the latter seemed to have had of him. He resolved to inquire further.

"Poor Odel had a very beautiful place, I believe, in the city of Mexico," he said; "quite a palace, I have been told."

"Not exactly in the city," replied Henry: "he had only a counting-house in the town. But about three miles in the country, towards the foot of the mountains, he had one of the most beautiful villas I ever saw, with magnificent gardens, quite in your English style. It was called Casilla, and was in fact a palace. His hospitality was unbounded; I have passed many a pleasant day there."

Now, the assertion was perfectly true, for the Casilla had for some years belonged to Mr. Odel's son, after his father's death; and during Henry's stay in Mexico, the greater part of the young gentleman's time had been spent there.

Mr. Scriven was becoming more and more puzzled; but further questions were prevented by the entrance of the Conde de Fraga and his young countess. His compliments were first, of course, paid to Lady Fleetwood, who proceeded to introduce him and his wife, who could speak but very, few words of English, to the rest of her guests; and this operation was proceeding when the young lady's eyes lighted upon Henry, and her whole face beamed with pleasure at seeing one whom she knew well, and who could converse with her in her own language. The warm and friendly recognition which then took place between the young Spanish nobleman and the object of suspicion did not escape the eyes of Mr. Scriven; and it would undoubtedly have removed all his prepossessions, had it been possible ever perfectly to eradicate an idea which had once taken possession of his mind.

The expected guests had now all arrived, and Lady Fleetwood had ordered dinner to be served; but before it was announced, Mr. Scriven, who was slightly acquainted with the conde, took an opportunity of drawing him aside and questioning him in regard to Colonel Middleton. Henry saw the man[oe]uvre; and it must be acknowledged that, even while carrying on a gay conversation with the young countess, he listened to what was passing behind him with a good deal of interest. He could not exactly catch

Mr. Scriven's first question; but he heard the young count reply, in very tolerable English--

"Oh! a most respectable person, of a very high family in my country-- by the mother's side, related to all the Xamorças, and grand-nephew to Don Balthazar, who left him a very handsome fortune."

"Have you known him long?" asked Mr. Scriven.

"Yes," answered the count--"from my boyhood; we were at school together, and in the same regiment afterwards: indeed, we are distantly related, for my grandmother's niece married Don Balthazar's brother's son, who likewise inherited a part of his large fortune."

Mr. Scriven seemed satisfied, but he was not; and very shortly after the whole party went down to the dinner-room.

Now, in her arrangements in regard to that very difficult but yet important process, the pairing of her guests, Lady Fleetwood, with the strongest possible desire to make everybody happy, usually contrived, with that ill-luck which frequently attended her best efforts, to part all those who would have liked to be together, and to put those together who were least likely to suit each other. Thus, on the present occasion, there was only one person well satisfied.

The conde, of course, as highest in rank, took her down to dinner; but Maria was bestowed upon Charles Marston, Mr. Scriven gave his arm to Lady Anne, who hated him mortally, and Henry was put in charge of the young Spanish lady, with which part of the arrangement she was better contented than himself.

The dinner would, nevertheless, have passed off very quietly, notwithstanding the inconvenient manner in which the guests were planted; for there was only one person there who was not fully aware that in society, be it great or small--let it consist of two or of thousands--at a dinner-table or in the great scene of the world--every one must sacrifice something for the happiness of the whole, and that to make the best of our own position is the condition of our own felicity as well as that of all who surround us;--the dinner would have passed off very pleasantly, I say, if Mr. Scriven could have rested satisfied and left Henry at peace. He was certainly shaken in his belief that Colonel Middleton and Henry Hayley were one; but yet he was displeased with his great resemblance to the object of his persevering dislike. I do not call it hate, for hate almost implies emotions of a stronger kind than Mr. Scriven usually gave way to. He would have taken a great deal of trouble, he would have spent a considerable portion of time, he would even have devoted no inconsiderable sum of money, to prosecute Henry Hayley and to hang him; but yet he would have done it all coolly, deliberately, systematically, without any of the *fortes émotions*. I do not know that this can be called hate; but perhaps the secret of the passion, or whatever it was, being so perdurable, was the absence of all emotion. As machines which are much shaken in their operation wear out soon, so feelings accompanied by much agitation are generally of short duration.

On the present occasion, however, Mr. Scriven could not be content to let the young officer alone. He was not what can be called uncivil; for the words were all perfectly polite, and, as addressed to a perfect stranger, only gave the idea of his being what is called in England a *bore*. He asked him a multitude of questions about Spain, about his own private history, about things which had happened fourteen, fifteen, sixteen years before. He cut across his conversation with the fair Spaniard at his side some six or seven times; and though, as I have said, perfectly civil, there was a sort of cool superciliousness in his tone which annoyed Henry and aroused him to resist.

On the young officer's other side sat Lady Anne Mellent; and just at the period when the fish was being removed, she took advantage of the butler's body being thrust between her and Mr. Scriven to say a few words to Henry, in a low tone and a foreign language. They were only two or three, and what they were did not transpire, but they seemed to work a great change upon her left-hand companion; for from that moment his demeanour became more free and unconstrained; his manner, especially towards Mr. Scriven, not exactly supercilious, but ironical. There was a sort of playful, but yet rather bitter, mockery in his replies, which grew even more acerb as dinner went on.

"Pray, Colonel Middleton, were you at the taking of the Trocadero?" demanded Mr. Scriven, after a very brief pause.

"If I had been there at all," replied Henry, "I should have been at its defence; but I happened then to be at school. Boys are not admitted into the Spanish army, Mr. Scriven."

"I should suppose not," replied the merchant; "but boys do strange things sometimes."

"Very true, and men too," answered Henry, "otherwise the French would never have been there, and the English would never have let them;" and he resumed his conversation in Spanish with the lady by his side.

"I am afraid, from what I have heard," said Mr. Scriven, "that the improvements introduced by Florida Blanca into the commercial and financial regulations of Spain have not had any permanent effect."

"I am ashamed to say," replied Henry, "that I know as little of the subject, Mr. Scriven, as you would probably know of a regiment of dragoons."

"Perhaps I may know more of military matters than you suppose," answered Mr. Scriven.

"Of the city light-horse," replied the other, with a slight smile; "but I certainly shall not catechise you on the subject, and you must grant me the same indulgence with respect to commerce. I know nothing about it, though I have a very great respect for it in the abstract, as you probably have for the army."

"Oh, dear, no!" replied Mr. Scriven with the utmost coolness. "I have no respect at all for the army, I can assure you. I look upon it as a necessary evil, which should be diminished as soon as possible and as far as possible, and the navy too."

"You should have a little gratitude for the navy, at all events," said Henry, laughing, "as, if it had not been for the navy, many rich ships filled with English merchandise would have found their way into French and American ports during the late wars."

"Gratitude is altogether out of the question," answered Mr. Scriven; "in fact, it is a mere name. Soldiers fight and sailors fight because they are paid to fight. Why should I be grateful to them for doing what they receive my money to do? If they don't do their duty, they are broke or shot, as they ought to be; and if they do, they are paid for it. The account is balanced, and there is nothing more to be settled on either part."

"A very commercial view of the subject, indeed," replied Henry; "but I cannot help thinking, Mr. Scriven, that if soldiers and sailors fought upon such principles, neither merchants nor others would receive much effectual protection; and that if all British merchants acted upon such principles, they would find very few soldiers or sailors to fight for them. Silk, cotton, molasses, iron-ware, broadcloth, machinery, corn, wine, and oil, are not the only things to be considered in life, it seems to me; neither are gold and silver. We have heard of such things as honour and glory--which can only be worth having when obtained in a just cause--and generosity, and benevolence, and even gratitude; and if these things are all to be swept away as mere names, I see not why honesty and integrity should not go too. There are moral as well as material goods; and high principles of action, national honour and national glory, love, are in my mind not only compatible with, but inseparable from, a due consideration of the material interests of a country."

"Oh, doubtless," answered Mr. Scriven; "though the notions that we attach to such names are very vague and fallacious--derived from the rhodomontade ages of chivalry and feudality, and only serving to mislead imaginative boys."

"You are in no fear, then, of their influence," replied Henry. "Lady Anne, may I have the pleasure of taking wine with you?"

"With a great deal of pleasure," replied Lady Anne, "for the conversation has been so heavy that I certainly do want something to enliven me; and in pity, you two gentlemen, forbear, recollecting that I neither send forth ships nor command armies--am neither a merchant nor a field-marshal."

The conversation now took another turn. Lady Anne spoke in French to the fair Spaniard; Lady Fleetwood did her best to effect the same; Charles Marston talked to her in bad Spanish and good Italian; and till dinner was over and the ladies retired, all went on gaily and cheerfully.

The sole person left out was Mr. Scriven, who, though he wrote several languages with sufficient facility, was but little accustomed to speak any tongue but his own. He was not well pleased, indeed--not so much because he was excluded a good deal from the conversation, for he was usually as economical of his words as of his money, but because he clearly saw that those around him had recourse to another tongue in order to put an end to discussions which were pleasant to nobody but himself.

His first attack after dinner was upon his nephew, to whom he said, in a low tone--

"Why, Charles, you seem peculiarly lively to-night. How is that? I was afraid the news I gave you yesterday might have somewhat depressed your spirits."

"Not at all, dear sir--thank you for your good intentions," said Charles Marston. "I never was more cheerful in my life; and as to the 'How is that?' I have many reasons for being cheerful. A little misfortune sometimes, rightly viewed, changes to a benefit. In the first place, I have an opportunity of proving to my dear father how grateful I am for all his past kindnesses, which I never should have had if he had gone on in perfect prosperity; and then, again, I have had proofs of the sincerity and disinterestedness of several very dear friends, whose generosity I might never have known to its full extent had not this reverse occurred."

"A very philosophical view," said Mr. Scriven, between his teeth; "but, as I suppose you do not intend to live dependent upon these friends, let me ask if you have considered the hints I threw out with regard to your future course."

"I have not given them a thought," replied Charles. "I saw at once that they could be of no service to me, and therefore judged, my dear uncle, that it might be bad economy to waste much reflection upon them."

"You are as polite as wise, my good nephew," rejoined his uncle, drily.

"Oh, it is what you call due course of exchange," answered Charles. "You have told me a thousand times that you are fond of plain speaking, and have proved the fact to me in many instances. Middleton, you have not yet been to see our excellent friend Mr. Winkworth, and he is half angry with you."

"I was out of town all yesterday," replied Henry, "and did not arrive to-day till it was just time to dress. I was very sorry indeed to find, from your note, that he had met with such an unpleasant adventure. I hope he is better."

"Oh, going on quite well," said Charles, "and, though still obliged to keep his bed, will be very glad to see you."

"I will call early to-morrow," replied Henry; "and now, shall we not join the ladies? This sitting after dinner seems a very strange custom to our foreign eyes."

As he spoke, he rose, and the rest followed his example.

In the drawing-room the whole party were more at ease, for they divided themselves according to their several tastes, and Henry was by Maria's side during a great part of the evening. The moments flew happily with them; for, though she was a little anxious in regard to the keen and searching look with which her uncle observed the open attentions of her lover, yet there was a counterbalancing pleasure in his society and his conversation, which fully made up for the slight uneasiness she experienced.

She was too frank and straightforward in her nature to conceal altogether the happiness she felt, although she strove to do so as far as possible, and endeavoured to show every attention to her aunt's guests, who were soon increased by two or three visiters from the neighbourhood. She even fancied that she succeeded very well; but nevertheless there was hardly an eye in the room which did not remark certain small differences of manner when speaking with Colonel Middleton--a look of bright intelligence, a happy-hearted smile, which betrayed the secret to more than one talkative person, who was quite ready to carry the news over the whole town.

Henry, too, seemed either carried away by passion or perversely determined to display his love. When obliged to converse with others, although his conversation was very different from that of most men of the world in the great capital--deep, powerful, going to the very heart of the matter in question--yet withal there was a sparkling gaiety of manner, a laughing and almost ironical spirit, veiling the depths of the ideas. It was like one of those fine-toned and plaintive airs in the works of the Italian composers, to which is attached a gay and fluttering accompaniment, as if to bide under an airy mockery the strength of the feelings expressed. But when he conversed with her it was all very different: the language, though not the language of love, was all deep-toned, warm, and impassioned; and the manner, though it might not be sad, was in perfect harmony with the words.

Mr. Scriven marked the whole, very much displeased, and determined promptly to interfere, though he somewhat miscalculated the extent of his power. Excellent Lady Fleetwood, too, was very uneasy. Having made up her mind that Charles Marston ought somehow or other to marry his cousin, she saw all sorts of dangers and perplexities in the very marked attentions of Colonel Middleton, and the favourable manner in which Maria received them. She looked at Charles several times to see how he bore it, and was very willing, had it been possible, to have bestowed a good deal of unnecessary compassion upon her nephew. But Charles seemed obstinately resolved to show that he wanted no compassion at all. He talked a great deal to Lady Anne Mellent, and Lady Anne to him; and every now and then a quiet little ray of loving light stole out of her eyes as she lifted them to Charles Marston's, which might have undeceived any one but an aunt or a parent.

In the end, however, Lady Anne sent him away from her, saying in a low voice--

"There--go and talk to somebody else. We have flirted together enough to-night--perhaps too much, Charles; and now I am going to flirt with Colonel Middleton to make up for it;" and her ladyship kept her word, for she took an opportunity, very soon after, of calling Henry to her side, and to the eyes of most people in the room seemed to be coquetting with him in a very determined manner.

It were vain to deny that Charles Marston felt a little uncomfortable--I will not say exactly jealous, for that would imply more than he felt; but he wished that Lady Anne would be a little more cautious, and thought that she and Frank Middleton need not exactly talk in so low a tone, or with their heads quite so close together. He spoke worse Spanish than ever to the fair young countess, beside whom he had sat down; and he was going on step by step to make himself seriously uneasy, when Lady Anne's eyes were suddenly turned towards him, and found his fixed upon her face. A very grave look instantly came over it. It seemed to him like a look of reproach, and the words of warning which she had spoken to him the moment before instantly recurred to his mind.

"There is some secret here," he said to himself: "she warned me of the very course she is now pursuing, and told me she had a motive for it. It is difficult to conceive what it can be, and yet it is strange how I myself have always felt towards Middleton ever since I knew him. From the first moment he seemed like an old friend, and his face, too, was familiar to me. If I had not known that he had been brought up all his life in Spain, I should have fancied we had been at Eton together."

At that moment his uncle approached, and bending down his head, he said--

"I must have some conversation with you, Charles, about this friend of yours. Do you know much of his history?"

"Oh, dear, yes!" replied his nephew. "I heard the whole of it from the Spanish ambassador at Rome, who is a relation of his. He is the son of Dona Eleanora Xamorça, the niece of Don Balthazar, a rich old grandee who died some time ago. During some of the troubles in Spain she was sent into a convent for protection, and thence ran away with and married an English gentleman of the name of Middleton. They soon quarrelled, however, and separated; and the old gentleman took her boy and brought him up as his own son."

"Do you happen to recollect the face of your old schoolfellow Henry Hayley?" asked Mr. Scriven.

"Good heaven! so he is!--very like indeed," said Charles. "I have often been puzzling myself to think who it is to whom he bears so great a resemblance."

"Great indeed," said Mr. Scriven, drily; "so great that I do not understand it. It is impossible, I suppose, that they can be the same person?"

Charles Marston laughed.

"Utterly, my dear uncle," he said. "Here is Fraga, who has known him from his boyhood; and depend upon it, Spaniards are not such disinterested people as to suffer a stranger to deprive them of a large fortune, without being very sure that he had a right to it. Now, I know that Middleton came in for one-third of old Balthazar's riches. You may ask any one in Spanish society. The thing is perfectly well known."

"Humph!" said Mr. Scriven, and walked away.

He had suggested thoughts to his nephew's mind, however, which did not so speedily retire. The likeness, when it had been once pointed out, struck him more and more every moment. The strange intimacy which had arisen between the young officer and Lady Anne, to whom he was almost a stranger, and the evident regard which existed between him and Maria, whose heart was little likely to be captivated at first sight, were all extraordinary circumstances, which seemed to favour the suspicions that his uncle entertained, and were with difficulty accounted for on any other ground. But then, on the other hand, the information he had received, in regard to his friend's birth and history, was so precise, and had been given by persons necessarily so well informed, that it was impossible for him to doubt that the young officer was exactly what he represented himself to be. Charles was in a maze of perplexity, and remained so all the evening, till at length Lady Anne beckoned him to her side again, and playfully scolded him for his thoughts.

Charles laughingly evaded the attack, but she asked--

"Do you think I cannot read your looks? I will tell you one thing, Charles: if you could see what is going on in my heart, as well as I can see what is going on in yours, I should have no such looks to complain of. And now, for your pains, I will torment you for a week longer, the latter part of which you shall come and spend with me in Northumberland.--There! do not suppose I am going to insist upon your marrying me directly, for I do not intend any such thing; but I have engaged dear aunt Fleetwood and Maria, while you four gentlemen were down-stairs drinking too much wine, after the sottish custom of the land, and I asked Colonel Middleton just now, so you must come and be jealous."

"But Winkworth?" said Charles--"I do not like to leave him in his present state."

"He must come too," said the fair lady. "I will call and ask him to-morrow, so pray tell him that I never suffer myself to be contradicted by anybody."

"Can you not put it off for a week?" asked Charles. "I do not think Winkworth will be well enough to travel."

Lady Anne mused.

"No," she said, "I cannot, for I have determined to take Frank Middleton down there on Thursday next; and you know, Charles, it wouldn't do for him and me to go down and live together by ourselves till you and your friend were ready to come. Propriety--think of propriety!" and she looked up in his face with a gay and meaning laugh. "No, no; get your friend well as soon as you can. Maria and I and Lady Fleetwood will go down on Wednesday, Colonel Middleton will come down on Thursday, and you and Mr. Winkworth must join us afterwards. So now good-bye, for I am going home."

Charles saw her to her carriage, and then, without returning to his aunt's drawing-room, walked across to his own hotel; but during a great part of the night his thoughts were occupied with Henry Hayley and Colonel Middleton, and the same objects formed the subject of his dreams.

CHAPTER XX

To retrace one's steps is always a difficult, and very often a most unpleasant task, as every one must have felt who has left his note-book at home and had to go back for it. Imagination, however--kind, quick, ready Imagination--with one bound skips over the intervening space, and plants us on the wished-for spot without tracking back the weary footprints of our advance. She shall lend us her wings for a moment, to take us back to the spot where we left our worthy friend Joshua Brown, the pedlar.

From the door of Henry Hayley's room he walked down-stairs, spoke for a moment with Farmer Graves, took what little breakfast he would accept, and then departed, bending his steps towards the same common which he had passed during the preceding evening. He followed the same track exactly, and he had his reasons for so doing; for he very much desired to obtain some little information in regard to those rough friends who had become too familiar with his pack and his companion's pocket-book.

His first resting-place was at the sandpit where the tinker's family had taken up their abode, but there he only found the old man and his daughter; and sitting down with them, he chatted over the adventures of the preceding night, expressing his determination to try if he could not find out the men who had plundered him, and punish them as they deserved.

"You won't find them at the hovel under Knight's-hill," said the old tinker; "for James has been upon the lookout this morning with some of Mr. Payne's men, and the place is empty: they have gone farther off, because they know one trick of this kind is enough for the neighbourhood. They have left your box there, however, Joshua; and James would not bring it away, because he did not know you might come here, and thought it very likely you might get the people from the farm and go down to the hut yourself."

"I will go down alone, if you are sure there is nobody there--though I rather fancy the box is empty enough by this time, and it is not of much use when there is nothing in it."

"It's always worth something, though," answered the tinker. "I never saw anything that man made which might not be turned into something for a second turn after it had served a first. However, the hut's empty enough, and they'll not come back in a hurry--you may be sure of that."

After some further conversation of the same kind, the pedlar plodded on upon his way. He did not approach the hut without precaution, for the impression of the man's knee upon his chest was not as yet effaced from his memory; and being a peaceful personage, he was not at all inclined to encounter rough treatment himself or bestow it upon others.

He paused, then, upon the hill, from which a sight was obtained of the hovel, and watched with a keen eye for any indication of the place being inhabited.

Having satisfied himself so far, he descended the hill still farther, looking into every dell and hollow of the moor. Nothing was seen, however, that moved or had the breath of life, except a few lapwings hovering about, and every now and then resting upon the little knolls and mole-hills. Cautiously approaching the wretched hut, the pedlar looked through what had once been a glazed window, and then pushed open the crazy door and went in. On the floor lay his mahogany box, wide open, with all the contents taken out, while a little tray which it had contained had been thrown to some distance. Scattered round the hovel in every direction were small pieces of bright yellow carded cotton, on which his small articles of jewellery were usually displayed to attract the attention of admiring damsels; and numerous were the scraps of paper which had likewise been cast down. The worthy pedlar perhaps felt more vexed at the sight of the small reverence which had been shown to his cherished wares than he had even been to their loss at first.

"The rascals have taken them all out to carry them easily," he said, "and now they'll go and sell them all for ten shillings or a pound, I'll warrant."

With habitual care, however, he set to work, gathering up all the pieces of cotton and scraps of paper, and placed them hurriedly in the box. The lock had been dexterously picked with some instrument, showing that the gentry into whose hands it had fallen had come armed and well prepared for the various contingencies of their profession. The pedlar's own key easily locked it again; but the strap was gone, and he was obliged to take it under his arm, comforting himself by saying--

"It is light enough now, so it won't be heavy to carry."

This done, he trudged away, walking stoutly on over the three or four miles of common ground which lay between that hovel and the hut which had been lately inhabited by poor Rebecca Hayley. As he approached it, he was surprised to see the door and windows once more open; and he asked himself, not without some sort of apprehension, whether his assailants of the preceding night might not have migrated thither. He was relieved the moment after by seeing the apparition of the boy Jim at the door of the hut, and walking on confidently he said--

"Why, Jim, my man, I thought you were gone. I was here last night, and found a gentleman looking for you."

"Ay, I ought to have been in London," said the boy; "but I found a whole heap of things belonging to poor Bessy, whom they took away from me; and I didn't know what to do with them, so I packed them all up, and took them over to Mr. White, the parson, who was always so kind to us both; but he was away, so I was obliged to bring them back again. I am sure I don't know what to do with them."

"In London!" exclaimed the pedlar, seizing upon the only part of the boy's speech which surprised him: "what are you going to do in London, my lad? You'll never get on there."

"Oh, yes, I shall," replied the boy. "I've got a place there, and am going to be made a footman of."

"What! with the young gentleman I saw here last night, I suppose?" said the pedlar.

"No, not with the young one--with the old one," replied Jim; and then, following the train of his own ideas, he went on: "she had hid them away so cunningly under her bed that nobody saw them when they were taking her away."

"Saw what?" demanded the pedlar.

"Why, all manner of things," answered the boy: "bits of silk and shawls, and old gloves, and a quantity of paper and music, and a brass scent-box."

"Let me look at the scent-box," said the pedlar, "if you've got it here."

"Oh, yes, I've got it," replied Jim, "for I did not like to leave them with Mr. White's housekeeper. I put that in my pocket, too, for fear it should fall out of the bundle: here it is."

"Brass, you fool!" exclaimed the pedlar, examining a very large and richly-wrought vinaigrette. "Why, that is gold, and these are real stones, too, I do believe. Yes, they are, indeed," he continued, carrying the trinket to the door for better light. "That's worth more than a hundred guineas, or I'm no judge."

"All the worse for me," answered Jim in a desponding tone; "for what I am to do with these things I do not know."

"Why, the best thing you can do with them is to take them to the poor old woman herself," said the pedlar.

"But I don't know where she is," rejoined the boy. "I think I'll take them up with me to London, and give them into the charge of my master; for he's a very kind gentleman, and perhaps may find out where poor Bessy is."

"That's the best thing you can do," replied the pedlar; "but how are you to get them up?"

"I'm to go by the coach, which passes every day at three," was the boy's reply: "he gave me money, and told me how to come."

"Then I think I'll go by it too," observed the pedlar, thoughtfully, "if before it comes I can get to G---- and back;" and he named a town which I shall leave nameless, for fear any of the gentlemen of the place should judge what is to follow too personal.

"Why, it's only five miles there," answered the boy, "and the coach stops at the 'Tame Bear.' It can take you up there if you like to go, Joshua."

"Don't you show that gold box to any one, then," said the pedlar; "for there are a good many rascals about, as I know to my cost, and many a man would think it worth his while to give you a knock on the head just to get that box. But I'll tell you what will be better still, my lad," he added after a moment's thought:--"If you can get ready quick, you had better come along with me. I can carry something for you, for my pack's light enough now, and we shall be a sort of protection to each other by the way."

"Ay, there's been a sad heap of rascals down here lately," replied Jim; "but I'm quite ready this minute, Joshua. There's all I'm going to take: Mr. Galland, at the inn, has promised to send up some one to carry away the other things."

"Not much to take care of," answered the pedlar. "But come along; shut the door and windows close, and then give the key to Mr. Galland as we go."

The poor boy's arrangements were soon made; for whether, when justly weighed, the gifts of fortune be or be not more cumbersome than the cares of poverty, certain it is that little is more lightly looked after than much. Man is the most self-pampering creature upon earth; and he takes not into consideration whether in increasing his conveniences he does not increase his wants--whether in increasing his wants he does not increase his cares. He seeks that which is comfortable to him at the moment, without asking if it do not imply that he must seek for more, which may be more difficult to obtain; and the instinct of progress still carries him on, at once an evidence of his imperfection and his immortality. The instinct of beasts is wiser for this world. Offer a sheep, which stands half sheltered from the north-east wind under a leafless hedge, a coat, waistcoat, and breeches, and the beast will run away or butt you in disdain. Content with what he has, he looks not beyond the present hour, and shrinks from the luxury that may become a trammel, the comfort that must become a care. His life, his thought, his desire is for the present. But how different is man! His life is in the future; and every act, and thought, and aspiration, and custom, the history of the individual, the history of the species, the traditions of other years, the prophecies of time to come, the feelings of each moment, the deeds known or unchronicled--all show that there is a voice in the human heart crying ever, "On! on!--on to eternity!--on to progress, to improvement, to perfection!--on towards immortality and God!"

Happy, however, are those who have few cares--upon whose early years fortune, often called hard, has not showered desires, and tasks, and responsibilities. It cannot, indeed, be said of them, as it was sublimely said of the lily of the field, that "they toil not, neither do they spin;" yet the labour is light and has its reward--the privations are comparatively little felt, and the cares are few. The fruit of the tree of knowledge of good and evil contains in itself the seed of all desire and all regret; and those who eat the least of it retain, I do believe, the most of paradise, in paradise's best blessing--content.

The boy had little to care for, and his preparations were soon made. The barren spot on which his youth had passed was left with little regret, though perhaps regret might come afterwards. There was nothing to attach him to it firmly, for the only things which had given it sunshine had been taken away; and on he went, walking beside the pedlar, thinking and talking of what he was to do next.

His heart was a very open one: he had nothing to conceal; he had no motive whatsoever for keeping back, disguising, or adulterating one idea that rose in his mind, one fact that had occurred, one purpose for the future; and he naturally told the pedlar all the events of the last few days, and his great and strong anxiety again to see her whom he called Bessy. He could have opened his mind to no one better fitted to advise him than his accidental companion: and, to say truth, few were better fitted to understand his feelings and to take an interest in them.

"If you want to find out where she is, Jim," said Joshua Brown, "nothing can be easier. You say the driver was one of Mr. Galland's postboys. Well, they've each a line, and go to the same inns; we can easily get a posting-card, and trace them from one inn to another till we come to the last; and then a pot of beer to the boy who drove them on will make him tell you where he took the poor thing."

This hint of so simple a proceeding, which he had never thought of, was a ray of light to the poor lad, and he determined to act upon it without delay.

At Mr. Galland's he begged a card of the house, which, as was customary at those times of posting, had a list of the stages and inns on the road to London; and, satisfied thus far, he walked on more cheerfully with his companion till they came to the town, lying a little out of the direct road, at which Joshua Brown had some business to transact.

It was a large and populous place, with one broad street running up a hill, and several smaller ones deviating from the main road at right angles, with numerous lanes and alleys meandering at the back. Here Joshua Brown paused at the inn where the coach stopped, and at which he was well known and respected; and leaving the boy there, with a strong recommendation, he himself walked up the hill, stopping for a moment or two at one of those shops which, as is common in country towns, combined the sale of jewellery with that of pasteboard, stamps and books, soap, toys, and sealing-wax.

A few very significant words passed between him and the master of the shop; and then Joshua Brown sallied forth again, turned into one of the side streets, then down a narrow sort of lane, with small houses on either hand, and stopped opposite a portentous-looking black baby in a white cap and long-clothes, which hung suspended from an iron stanchion on the left hand side of the door. On the other side was a shop, with very small panes of glass in the window, over which was an inscription, purporting that Mingleton Bowes was a dealer in marine stores. Now, what anybody could want with marine stores in one of the most inland towns of all England, from which there was no communication whatever with the sea, except by wagon or stage-coach, the inscription did not set forth.

However, Joshua Brown entered the shop, and found it vacant of everything but rusty pieces of iron, coils of rope, rolls of lead, copper and iron weights, an immense variety of scales and balances, a great quantity of links and torches, the most complete assortment of candle-ends in Europe, large stone jars filled with dripping, two or three piles of rags, bundles of quills, packets of cocoa, numerous red-herrings, stock-fish, and kippered salmon, a jar of Russian cranberries, and an infinite variety of odoriferous articles, squalid to look upon, and not much more agreeable to the nose than to the eye. In short, it would seem the title of "dealer in marine stores" implies, that a man buys and sells everything under the sun.

As there was no human being in the shop, nor any other animate creature whatever except an enormous white cat sitting upon the counter, her hairy back resting upon the cut side of a single Gloucester cheese, Joshua first rubbed his feet upon the floor to call attention to his presence, and not finding that to succeed, he stamped once or twice. It is wonderful how indifferent the people of the house were to the chances of robbery; for, though he stamped, nobody came, and he might have carried off the large jar of cranberries itself without attracting any attention.

Now, whether it was that Joshua Brown thought it might be rude or dangerous to intrude upon the privacy of some persons who were talking together in the back shop with the door shut, or whether there was a touch of the fantastic in his disposition, I will not take upon myself to say; but certain it is that the method he took to bring the master of the house from his fit of absence was somewhat eccentric.

Having a good thick glove on his right hand, he approached it quietly to the tail of the large tom-cat, and getting the last joint between his finger and thumb, he said, in an authoritative tone, "Call your master!" adding at the same time an awful twisting pinch, which nearly wrenched the bone from its next neighbour.

A frightful squall was the first result, and then, with the rapidity of lightning, Tom's claws were applied to his assailant's hand and arm. The teeth would have followed; but at the same moment Joshua Brown shook the beast off, and a little white-faced man, with red eyelids and a rugged, pock-marked countenance, rushed in from the back shop, closing the door sharply behind him. He stared at the pedlar with his bleared eyes for an instant, and then, walking round behind the counter, asked in a very obsequious tone what he wanted.

Joshua put his head across, and whispered a few words in the man's ear.

The dealer in marine stores looked somewhat suspiciously at the stranger, and then shook his head, replying--

"I don't understand what you mean, sir."

The tone was the most innocent in the world, and the countenance expressed a dull surprise; but Joshua again advanced his head, and addressed a few more words in a whisper to the worthy shopkeeper, producing a slight smile upon the lips, which were very much like those of a toad, while a ray of intelligence shot from the dull eyes.

"All safe?" he said.

"Safe as a nut," replied the pedlar, "otherwise I shouldn't have pinched the cat's tail."

"I don't know anything about it at present," replied the man of marine stores; "but I dare say I can find out. Is it the box you want?"

"No, no," answered Joshua, impatiently; "I've been paid the full worth of the box already: I told you it is the pocket-book, and all that is in it."

"Where are you lodging?" said the shopkeeper. "I dare say I can find out something about it in a day or two."

"I am lodging nowhere," answered the pedlar, "for I'm only waiting for the coach to go to town; and as to staying a day or two, that's no go at all, Master Mingy Bowes; for if I don't take the book up with me, the whole business will be put in the hands of the Peelers, and then you know quite well I shall lose my share, you'll lose yours, and the gentlemen will lose theirs."

"Stay a minute," said the man; "I will just go and look in my books--I may have got it down, for aught I know. Two or three little matters have come in since the morning."

"Ay, do," said the pedlar; "and remember, we're all upon honour, and share according to rule."

The man retired into the back shop; and his books must have been somewhat difficult to read, though rather loquacious, for he remained a considerable time, during which there was a sort of buzz heard through the door, apparently proceeding from more tongues than one.

At length the shopkeeper put his head out and beckoned to the pedlar, saying--

"Just step in here for a minute."

Joshua Brown accepted the invitation, and walking round the end of the counter, entered the back shop. There, as he had expected, he found that the marine store dealer was not alone; for on one of the two chairs which were unencumbered by inanimate lumber sat a tall, powerful fellow, of no very prepossessing appearance, with a red and white handkerchief bound round his head, and a large, rough great-coat on. His chair was near the fire, his feet were upon the fender, and his back was towards the door; but he turned half round as he sat when the pedlar entered, and scowled at him with one eye--for the other was nearly closed, evidently from the effects of a blow.

With a quiet, deliberate step Joshua Brown walked straight to the other chair, and seated himself in silence, so that he had his face turned partly towards the grate on his right hand, partly towards the door of the shop and the preceding tenant of the room, while his back was exactly opposite to a window in a small paved court which ran at the rear of the house.

The position is in some degree important; and it may also be necessary to remark that the window was shaded by a wire blind, which prevented any one seeing distinctly into the room from without, while those who were inside could clearly perceive all that passed within certain limits in the lane.

Some men are born diplomatists; and, although I do not mean to say that this was the case with the pedlar, yet upon the present occasion he showed that he possessed one very important quality for skilful negociation--namely, that of holding his tongue. He had already taken the initiative in his communication with the master of the house; and that, he thought, was quite sufficient for the time.

This silence on his part seemed not at all satisfactory to the other parties present. The man by the fire glared at him with his one undimmed orb, but said nothing; and the first effort of the dealer in marine stores--who observed, as a sort of introduction to the conference, "This here is the gentleman, Sam"--produced no result, for both still sat perfectly silent.

He tried again, however, addressing himself now to the pedlar, saying--

"This here is the gentleman, sir. You must speak to him about what you were mentioning to me."

"What am I to say to him?" asked Joshua Brown. "I don't know who he is."

"Why, what the devil has that to do with it?" asked the man who had been denominated Sam. "You come here for something--don't you? Why don't you say what it is?"

"Because I don't like to talk of things to people who may have no concern with them," answered the pedlar. "However, as I suppose Master Mingy Bowes has told ye something of the business, all I mean to say is, that I know where a hundred pound is to be got for a certain pocket-book that was boned last night, about a mile and a half on t'other side of Knight's-hill."

"That won't do," muttered the other man to himself, in a tone which was perhaps not exactly intended to conceal the observation from the pedlar. "Those who have got it know well enough what it is worth, and it's worth more than that."

"I don't know," answered the pedlar, aloud: "all I know is what will be given; and I think, out of the hundred, I ought to have ten pounds for my share."

The man raised his eye to the pedlar's face, without, however, lifting his head, and muttered a low and very ferocious curse, condemning very grievously his own blood and eyes--though one of the latter seemed mortgaged to its full value--if any one got the pocket-book for that money.

"Well, I'm very sorry we can't make a deal, then," said the pedlar. "I always like to turn an honest penny when I can, and I thought this was a good chance; but if people won't be reasonable, I can't help it. I've a notion they won't get more, however, do what they may and think what they like."

"I know better," said the ruffian, lifting up his head; "and I tell you what, master: it shall cost him a cool two hundred, or he shan't have it. I don't care about any nonsense. There's that in this here," and he took the pocket-book out of his pocket, "which would hang a man or save a man. I've found that out, at all events; so you may go and tell him that if he doesn't choose, before to-morrow night at ten o'clock, to pay down two hundred pound in golden sovereigns, in this here parlour, I'll pitch the pocket-book and everything in it into that fire. Then he may find his neck twisted some day, before he knows what he's about; so he'd better mind what he's doing--that's all."

"I don't know anything of what's in the book," answered the pedlar, who was a little anxious to hear more. "I know there are things in it worth having, but that's all I've heard about it. I know, too, that if I go back without it, you will have the beaks put upon the scent, and they'll soon have it one way or another, as you know well. They'll think a hundred pound worth having, if you don't."

"Say that again!" said the man, with a threatening look, and holding the pocket-book between his finger and thumb, as if he were about to throw it into the fire. "You don't know but what's in this book might save the fellow from dancing a hornpipe upon nothing, and his neck's worth more than a couple of hundreds, I should think. If you like to promise upon your life and soul to go and get me a couple of hundred, I'll wait till to-morrow; if not, here goes!----"

"Come, come, Sam!" said the dealer in marine stores; "don't put yourself in a passion. I dare say the gentleman will do what's reasonable."

"Well, then, let him go and bring me the tin," cried the other, in a surly tone; but the moment after, with an eager gesture, he beckoned the master of the house to him, demanding in a low voice, "Who the devil's that, Mingy, walking up and down in the court? That's the third time he's passed."

The master of the house immediately turned his eyes to the window, and his cheek became a little whiter.

"Why--why," he said, in a faltering tone, "that's Jones, the constable! I say, Sam, you had better take the gentleman's offer. Come, come; let him have the book--you know worse may come of it."

"D--n me if he shall!" cried the ruffian, pitching the pocket-book at once into the midst of the fire. "He shall neither have it nor me. That's the only thing to show against me, and there it goes. D--n you, stand off!" he continued, snatching up the poker and planting himself in the way, as both the pedlar and Mingy Bowes were starting forward to snatch.the pocket-book from the fire: "if you try to touch it, I'll make your brains fly about! There!--you may go and tell him what you've done, by bringing a blackguard like that to walk up and down the court. You think yourself safe enough, master; but I'll have a turn out of you yet, some of these days. I've a great mind to have it now, whatever may come of it, so you had better be off as fast as possible."

The pedlar thought so too, and moved towards the door; but when he had reached it, and got the handle of the lock in his hand, he turned round, saying--

"You're a fool, and have lost a good hundred pound. As to the fellow walking before the window, I never saw him in my life, and he may be the constable, or the muffin-man, for aught I know; so you have spoiled your own market, and are a fool for your pains."

The man sprang at him like a tiger; but Joshua snatched up a heavy chair, and threw it against his shins with such force as to send him hopping about the room in agony, during which time the pedlar escaped into the outer shop, and thence into the street, without waiting to take leave of Mr. Mingy Bowes.

No attempt was made to pursue him, though the ruffian in the long loose coat continued to swear most vehemently, and rub his shins to allay the pain he still suffered. The dealer in marine stores, at the same time, carefully locked the door of the back room in which they were, and then opened the iron door of a tall cupboard, which seemed destined as a place of security for the most valuable articles he possessed. On the various shelves, indeed, which were all of the same metal as the door, appeared a number of rare and curious articles, which no one would have expected to find in a little shop in the back street of a country town. He paused not, however, to contemplate his treasures; but with a rapid and quiet motion, though with strength greater than he seemed to possess, laid hold of the middle shelf and pulled hard. The whole of the iron lining of the cupboard with the contents instantly moved forward, apparently rolling upon castors, till the back was what builders would call flush with the wall. A very slight effort then turned the whole of this moveable case round upon a pivot in the right hand corner, leaving not only the aperture which it had previously filled exposed to the eye, but a considerable depth beyond, apparently a passage to some other part of the building.

"There, get in, Sam," said Mr. Mingy Bowes. "Hide away for a minute or two, and I'll see what that fellow Jones is about out there."

His companion did not seem at all surprised at anything that he saw or heard, but hobbled into the vacant space in the wall, as if he were as fond of a burrow as a rabbit. Mr. Bowes rolled back the iron cupboard into its proper place and shut the door upon it; and, the room having resumed its ordinary appearance, he issued forth through the shop into the street, and speedily found his way to the back lane, which the constable was still perambulating.

"Good morning, Mr. Jones," he said, with a look of haste and eagerness; "have you seen a stout man in a brown coat with grey stockings and gaiters just pass by?"

"No," answered the constable; "no man has come this way."

"You had better look after him if he does," said Mingy Bowes, "for he came offering me things to sell which I didn't choose to buy. I'm sure he's stolen them, and I thought you might be watching for him."

"Oh, no," answered the constable; "I'm looking for young Wilson, who lives up there in number four. He came home drunk last night, and thrashed his wife till she was nearly dead. She was taken to the hospital this morning, and as the surgeon says she's in great danger, the magistrates will have him up. He's keeping out of the way, however; but he'll be starved home soon, for he hasn't a penny in his pocket, and nobody will trust him, I'm sure."

Mingy Bowes laughed, and the constable laughed; for there are some people to whom sorrows which would make most men melancholy, and crimes which ought to make all men melancholy, are very good jokes.

Mr. Bowes was well satisfied too with the information, although upon other points he was a little inclined to be sulky. Hurrying home again, he soon set free his concealed companion, who had by this time recovered from the blow upon his shins, and who now walked quietly--I might say absently--to the fire, and took his old seat again; but Mr. Bowes was not well pleased with him, and proceeded to read him a lecture.

"I wonder how you can be such a fool, Sam," he said. "Jones has nothing to do with the cove who was here just now. He's looking for young Wilson; and just because you thought it was a trap, you must go and throw the pocket-book into the fire, when you might have got a hundred pound for it. Now you've done for yourself. The gentleman will put the beaks upon you, and they'll soon nab you, you may depend upon it."

"He daren't," said the other, with a twist of his mouth; "and you're a fool, Mingy, for talking about what you don't understand."

"Not so great a fool as you," answered Mingy Bowes, boldly; "for what was the use of burning the book? That was no good at all: whatever you intend to do, you might as well have kept it."

"There you're out," said the other: "'twas the very best thing I could do with it. You're not up to snuff yet, Master Mingy, I can tell you. I didn't read what was in the book for nothing; and I've got this young fellow, whoever he is, in a vice that'll squeeze him pretty hard, as you'll see before long. I could hang him to-morrow if I liked--though that, indeed, would be no great good to me or anybody else; but I'll sweat him, notwithstanding."

"I don't understand," said Mingy Bowes. "If you could hang him, he could hang you, I fancy; and that wouldn't suit you, Master Sam--at least, I should think not."

"No, certainly," replied the other man; "but I'll let you know all how it is, Master Bowes, for you must give me some help;" and he proceeded to explain to the receiver of stolen goods that he had found in the pocket-book that paper which had been given by Mr. Hayley to his son, just on the eve of Henry's flight from England, and which has already been laid before the reader.

It is true, the man knew nothing of the story, or, if he ever had heard anything of it, had forgotten it altogether; but the paper itself showed that a forgery had been committed, and that the document had been given to exculpate, in case of need, one who had voluntarily borne the imputation of the crime to save a parent. The names were there before him, and consequently, so far as the past was concerned, he had full information. Then as to the present, and the means of connecting the history of Henry Hayley with the personage who had been robbed on the preceding night, there were several papers, comprising letters addressed to Colonel Middleton at a hotel in London, and some memoranda of things to be done, which, without any great stretch of imagination, might be discovered to apply to the other paper referring to the forgery.

As I may have to notice the contents of that pocket-book hereafter, I will not pause longer upon them now, but merely say that the explanation of his worthy friend was quite satisfactory to Mr. Mingy Bowes; and that he applied himself, with due zeal and diligence, to concoct with Mr. Samuel a plan for their future proceedings, in the execution of which he flattered himself he might obtain even more than he should have gained by his commission, had the hundred pounds offered by the pedlar been accepted without hesitation.

There, then, for the present we will leave them, perfectly satisfied as they were that they had got a firm hold upon a victim who would not be able to escape from their clutches till they had drained him as dry as hay.

CHAPTER XXI

Henry Hayley did not forget his promise, and by eleven o'clock was sitting by the side of Mr. Winkworth, who had on that day, for the first time, come to breakfast in the sitting-room of the hotel which had been appropriated to Charles Marston and himself.

Charles was seated at a table at some distance, writing a letter, and the old gentleman was reposing upon a sofa after the fatigue of the meal. He was somewhat paler and not quite so yellow as when Henry had last seen him; but certainly his whimsicality and petulance did not seem to have at all diminished during the illness and suffering he had lately undergone. He was very glad to see his young acquaintance, however; shook him warmly by the hand, and seemed more gay and lively than he had been during the morning.

"Well, colonel," he said, "I wanted very much to see you--to ask you a question. You are a military man, have been in service some years--seven, I think you told me once--and have doubtless been in a good number of engagements. Now, tell me--were you ever wounded?"

Henry pointed to a scar on his cheek, replying--"Only once, my dear sir, and that very slightly."

"Now, see what a whimsical jade Fortune is!" exclaimed Mr. Winkworth. "You go about the world for seven years, seeking wounds and bruises. It is your trade, your profession, the object of your life, to get shot, or slashed, or poked with a pike, and you receive nothing but a scratch on the face; while I, whose business it is to avoid such things--who hate war and bloodshed, and strife in all shapes, and have an especial objection to being wounded at all-- cannot travel for a year, to see sights, in the most pacific guise and manner, without getting twice shot and once nearly killed."

"These things, certainly, are very unaccountable," said Henry Hayley. "I have known two men, one of whom never went into battle without getting wounded, while the other appeared to bear a charm which seemed to turn steel and lead aside; and yet he perhaps exposed himself more than the other."

"But it is not only between two men that the whimsical harridan plays her tricks," said Mr. Winkworth: "it is even between two shoulders. I am sure I do not know what my unfortunate left shoulder has done to offend her, or why the right one has not quite as good a title to be wounded as the other; but certain it is, the same poor suffering fellow comes in for every bad thing that is going, while the other lolls comfortably at his ease, and never even sends round to ask after his brother's health."

"I trust, however, from what I see," replied Henry, "that neither has suffered very much this time, my good sir, and that you will soon be better."

"I don't know--I don't know," replied Mr. Winkworth: "if the doctors will let me alone, and that boy does not tease me to death, I dare say I shall do very well; but there's a great chance of one or the other killing me--if I am fool enough to let them."

Charles looked up from his writing, hearing this attack upon himself, saying--

"Heaven knows, my dear Winkworth, I have not been teasing you, except to get you to do what the surgeon bids you."

"Well, is not that enough?" exclaimed Mr. Winkworth with a smile. "Why should you tease me to do what I know to be wrong--to follow the directions of a man in whom I have no confidence, or to bathe my shoulder, morning, noon, and night, with a lotion that only does it harm, while plain milk-and-water is making it quite well? No, no--thank heaven, I am not old enough, or fool enough, or young enough, or mad enough, to put any confidence in doctors, who go groping in the dark, and kill a great many more than they cure. Besides, you have been teasing me about a great number of other things. Did you not tell me just now that your father was in the 'Gazette?' That was enough to tease any friend of yours; and then, to see you take it so quietly and jauntily, as if it were a matter of no moment at all, is enough to drive one mad. I'm sure your good uncle, Mr. Scriven, does not look upon it so lightly."

"Certainly not," answered Charles Marston; "but then, in the first place, the mind of my good uncle is of a very different complexion from mine; and, in the next place, he does not know a great many things which I do, and which greatly tend to alleviate the matter. At all events, one thing is a great comfort. Come what will, my father never can be in want; for the generous settlement he made upon me long ago guards him now against that; and I have other things to tell him, which I trust will wipe away all memory of the disappointment and sorrow which this event must have caused him."

"Ho, ho!--secrets!" exclaimed Mr. Winkworth, while Henry Hayley looked at his friend with a kind but very meaning smile: "if the secrets be worth knowing, I will find them out. I have all the curiosity of an old bachelor or an old maid, I can tell you, and I will answer for it, Master Charles, I shall be in possession of the whole intelligence before your letter reaches Calcutta."

"That is very likely, my dear sir," answered Charles; "for, in the first place, the secret will soon be very well known, and I promise you shall be one of the first to hear it; and, in the next place, there is little chance of my letter going to Calcutta at all, for Mr. Scriven tells me my father is on his way to England. I wonder I have not heard myself."

"Then, where do you intend to send your letter?" asked Henry Hayley, in some surprise. "If your father is on his way, it will most likely miss him."

"I shall send it to his agents at Liverpool," answered Charles. "He may get it or not before he reaches London; but when I can testify my gratitude for all his kindness, and my affection for all his worth, and perhaps soothe his grief and relieve his anxiety, I will not delay an hour--though you know, Middleton, I hate writing letters."

"I know all about it," said Mr. Winkworth, starting as if from a deep reverie. "I have fathomed your secret; I have made it all out. Hazel eyes, an oval face, a straight little nose, lips running over with fun and impertinence. I've made it out--I've made it out, Master Charles!"

"A lady, sir," said a waiter, entering, and addressing Mr. Winkworth, "wishes to know if she can see you--her card, air: she's waiting in the carriage below."

"A lady!" exclaimed Mr. Winkworth, taking the card. "Good heaven! have they found me out already? What terrible women these Europeans are! They cannot let an old bachelor live in peace amongst them for three days without attacking the citadel of his heart with all the forms of war. Lady Anne Mellent!--Present my most humble and respectful compliments to her ladyship, and say that I am forbidden by the laws and ordinances of Hippocrates to descend to the door of her vehicle; but that, if she will do me the honour of walking up, I shall be delighted to see her."

That waiter always made a point of staring very much at Mr. Winkworth, and of thinking him the most extraordinary man in the world. However, he retreated speedily, and in a moment or two after returned, announcing Lady Anne.

She entered with a gay and laughing look, her colour a little heightened, and a bonnet which became her exceedingly; so that, certainly, if she had any designs upon the old gentleman's heart, her forces were well prepared for action.

Mr. Winkworth, however, though occasionally a little bitter and sarcastic upon the fair sex, was the pink of politeness and old-fashioned courtesy in his demeanour towards them; and, rising from the sofa, he met Lady Anne near the door, and taking her hand gallantly, pressed his lips upon the tips of her fingers, saying--

"This is, indeed, a great and unexpected favour, my dear Lady Anne; and I am quite as grateful for it, allow me to assure you, as if I had been impudent enough to ask it, and you had been cruel enough to hesitate for a month."

"An excellent beginning, Mr. Winkworth," said Lady Anne, "for I am going at once to put your gratitude to the test. You will think me somewhat exacting, but still I will prove your sincerity. I am going to have a party to spend a week down at a place of mine in the north. Some very pleasant people are to be there, I can assure you: one Colonel Middleton," and she turned a laughing look towards Henry; then added, nodding her head to Charles, "one Mr. Marston; besides an exceedingly pretty girl called Maria Monkton, and the dearest and best of old ladies in the world, Lady Fleetwood, who would fain remain behind in London, having an infinity of things to do, but whom I am determined to have down with me, just to keep her out of harm's way. Now, Mr. Winkworth, you must be one of the party; and I promise you I will flirt all day with you, except when I am coquetting a little with Colonel Middleton or Charles Marston."

"Humph!" said Mr. Winkworth. "I suppose that with ladies' speeches, as with their letters, the pith lies in the postscript," and he turned a keen look from her face to that of Charles.

"Their speeches and their letters both deserve an answer, at all events," replied Lady Anne; "and I think you very rude, Mr. Winkworth, for making a saucy speech about ladies' postscripts, instead of catching at my invitation with due reverence and delight."

"I will atone, I will atone," said the old gentleman, "not only by accepting immediately, but by speaking nothing but soft and complimentary speeches all the time I am your guest. But you must give me a few days to recover, my dear young lady, for you see here I am, forbidden to set a foot out of doors for the next three days."

"Oh, yes," answered Lady Anne. "Charles Marston knows all the arrangements, and will bring you down at the proper time and season."

"Like a tame bear in a travelling-cage," said Mr. Winkworth. "However, dear Lady Anne, as I said before, I'll do my best to stand upon my hind legs, and behave civilly to all men."

"You won't be half so delightful at any time as when you growl," answered Lady Anne, laughing. "But come, Colonel Middleton; I intend to take you away with me."

Charles looked up with a feeling of mortification which he could not altogether banish from his face, and Lady Anne saw it, half-amused, half-vexed. Odd as she was, and accustomed to indulge every fancy without restraint, she nevertheless understood sufficiently well the nature and feelings of love to know that she was putting Charles Marston to a sore trial, and to be sorry for it. However, she might still have persevered, for many motives induced her to do so, had not Mr. Winkworth suddenly turned an inquiring and almost sarcastic look to Charles's face, which Lady Anne chose to interpret, "Is this the way she treats you?"

That look decided Lady Anne at once. She could bear to tease Charles Marston a little; she could bear even to put his confidence in her affection and constancy to a very painful ordeal; but she could not bear the thought of making Charles seem contemptible in the eyes of any one, even for his complaisance to her. As soon, then, as she had drawn on her glove, she went up to the table where Charles was sitting, and laid her hand with the most undisguised affection on his shoulder.

"Can you come with us, Charles?" she said, slightly bending her head, and looking down into his face, with infinite grace both in the attitude of her figure and the expression of her countenance; "or must you stay and finish this long letter? To whom is it? It is too long to be to a man, and I don't allow you to write to any other woman, without first obtaining my consent."

"It is to my father, dear Lady Anne," answered Charles Marston; "but it can be finished any time before six o'clock this evening."

"Well, then, come with me," she replied; "but remember I don't permit you to call me Lady Anne. You may make it Anne if you like, or Anne Mellent, or Anne anything you please; but drop the 'ladyship,' or you shall be 'Charles Marston, Esquire,' with me for the future."

Charles started up to get his hat, which, polished by the care of his servant till it shone like a mirror, lay with his gloves and stick on a small table behind him; and Lady Anne, turning again to Mr. Winkworth, observed--

"You think me very odd, I am sure, Mr. Winkworth; but it all proceeds from nature, habit, and calculation; and you'll find me ten times odder than you now think, when you've known me a little longer."

"I do think you very odd," said Mr. Winkworth with a gay look, "but very charming."

"There!--that's the first of the civil speeches," said Lady Anne; "that'll do for to-day, Mr. Winkworth--no more of them!"

"Yes, one more," rejoined the old gentleman--"one more. You two young men, go away and leave this gay lady with me. I am going to make her a declaration, so stay at the top of the stairs for fear she should faint."

With a smile Charles Marston and Henry Hayley did as they were bid, while Lady Anne advanced towards Mr. Winkworth, saying--

"What can you want with me, you very funny old man?"

The answer they did not hear; but when, in about two minutes, Lady Anne rejoined them at the top of the stairs, her eyes were full of tears, and her cheeks bore traces of the same dew of the heart. Her manner, however, was too gay and sparkling for those tears to be tears of grief; and when Charles asked her what had happened to move her so much, she answered playfully--

"There, Charles!--not a word! He's an excellent old man that; and he loves you, and will do for you more than you know. But now let us on our way. I am first going to my own house for a little, and then to dear aunt Fleetwood's, so you shall go with me to both places."

CHAPTER XXII

Leaving the lady and the two gentlemen to follow whatever path the gay and somewhat capricious elf who ruled the whims of Lady Anne Mellent chose to dictate, we will, with the reader's good leave, stay a little with Mr. Winkworth, to whom we have not been altogether as civil as we might have been. We have left him alone, weary and wounded, with very little to do, though a good deal to think about.

Now, to say truth, the fact of having a good deal to think about is not in general a source of consolation to a sick or wounded man, unless it be of so important and pressing a nature as to postpone corporeal suffering or mental occupation. A general somewhat smartly wounded may go through a battle, hardly discovering the injury he has received; for the immense interests that press upon the mind withdraw all attention from the body's pain; but were he to be carried to the rear, to know nothing of what was going on, to receive no momentary excitement, to have no engrossing object pressed upon his attention every instant, the very pangs which would have been unfelt, in the fiery interests of an all-important fight, would now in idleness weigh down the very spirit which in activity would have subdued them.

Were you ever wounded, reader? I mean something, of course, more serious than the cut of the schoolboy knife, or any of the little ordinary accidents of civilian life. If you have, you will know that, though sometimes for a minute or two you are hardly aware that you are injured, yet gradually very unpleasant sensations succeed to the first numbing effects of the wound: a burning heat, a swollen and tingling stiffness of all the neighbouring parts, come on--a sort of horny sensation, as if the whole flesh around were changed into an exceedingly sensitive but cartilaginous substance. Gradually the inflammation affects the constitution, the whole frame sympathises with the wounded part, the stomach turns sick and weary, the head aches, the limbs are full of lassitude. At the same time the spirit sinks terribly, at least in ordinary cases; amusements, occupations which we were once fond of, afford us relaxation no longer; and that terrible symptom which doctors call precordial anxiety deprives us of rest and tranquillity.

The latter miseries Mr. Winkworth had been spared, though he felt all the first five or six in the catalogue. His constitution so far sympathised with the local action that he occasionally felt sick, had a distaste to all sorts of food, and held tea, of which he was usually very fond, in utter abhorrence. His spirits did not flag, however, for they were of a very active and untiring nature. They had borne him through a good many sorrows, which he had felt very keenly, but which he had never suffered to cast him down. Thus, with a book which he changed as often as he found it tiresome, and with a pen and ink which he employed not unfrequently, and with thoughts which he occupied on subjects totally different from his own situation, he had contrived to wear away the time between sleep and sleep, without much weariness.

When he was now once more left alone, after Lady Anne and her two companions had departed, Mr. Winkworth sat for a few moments on the sofa, and then rising, his left arm supported by a sling, to relieve the wounded shoulder of the weight, walked several times up and down the room.

"She is a very charming girl indeed," he said, or rather murmured, for the words can hardly be said to have been spoken; "and he is a very lucky lad. She will not be unhappy either, for I do not know a better or a kinder disposition than his. With abundant wealth, good health, and good tempers, there is every earthly prospect of happiness. God will, of course, temper it, as he mercifully tempers all lots, lest man should become self-confident. It is needful, that alloy of grief and disappointment--as needful as the baser metal mingled with the gold, lest it should be too soft and wear away too rapidly. It is needful; for, if we found perfect happiness here, how terrible would be the summons to leave it all for the untried hereafter! Yet this business of the bankruptcy seems to have shaken him a good deal--not for himself, that is evident; for as to his own fate he is full of high hopes. I must try to cheer him on that score.--Well? well?"

He turned sharply round, for at that moment the door opened behind him, and the voice of the waiter said--

"There is a lad, sir, below, who says you told him to come here, and that you intend to make a servant of him. I should have sent him away, but he has got a paper with your name, which he says you wrote."

"Send him up," said Mr. Winkworth, and then added, speaking to himself, "The young man has been somewhat tardy. I must lecture him; for diligence and attention I will have, and if he begins thus, how will he go on?"

A moment after, Jim Brown was ushered into the room, with a tolerable-sized bundle under his arm, wrapped up in a piece of an old cashmere shawl. Some country boys, finding themselves for the first time in the highly-decorated sitting-room of a London hotel, would have gazed round at the various objects it contained, with bumpkin amazement, and in the present instance it might have been very excusable to do so; for, besides the ordinary ornaments of the room, there were enormous numbers of different articles, all strange to the boy's eyes, and of the most miscellaneous character that it is possible to conceive. Charles Marston had more than half filled it with things of bronze, marble, alabaster, painted canvass, and carved oak, from France, Italy, and Greece, together with Greek and Albanian dresses, Syrian carpets, turbans, caps, sabres, yataghans, and other things, which would extend the catalogue down to the bottom of the page; and Mr. Winkworth himself, though he had travelled with but little baggage, and had not opened a tenth part of the cases which were awaiting his arrival, had contrived to get out a number of hookahs and long pipes, with not a few strange-looking commodities from India, Burmah, and Ceylon.

Jim Brown, however, did nothing of the kind. That he was a rude, uncultivated country boy I do not mean to deny; but he possessed that peculiar characteristic which I look upon as one of the most valuable qualities, when guided by good judgment, with which any human being can be gifted--a quality which, in dealing with the world at large, sooner or later overbears all the impediments which lie in the way of success--the prejudices, the inattention, the indifference, the very reason, in many instances, of our fellow-men; and which, in its action upon ourselves, is no less triumphant, overbearing the most intrusive of all our weaknesses--the thought of self. The quality he possessed was earnestness--earnestness of purpose, earnestness of thought, earnestness of feeling. If it could not be called the great principle of his nature, it was at all events the great quality of his character, and it subdued all things within him to itself.

He looked not round the room for one moment; his eyes instantly fixed upon Mr. Winkworth, and he advanced straight towards him, his mind bent upon one subject too resolutely to stray to any other.

The old gentleman's brow was rather cloudy when he entered, and, as we have seen, he meditated a reproof; but he was a good deal of a physiognomist; and as he marked the expression of the boy's countenance, he said to himself--

"He is about to assign a reason, or make an apology, or show a motive for his delay. Let us hear what he has to say for himself;" and he remained silent.

"Sir, I intended to have been here before now," said the boy, when he had come within two or three feet of the sofa. He did not know that, according to rule, he should have staid a good deal nearer the door. "I was afraid you would be angry; but then I thought, when you heard why I staid, you would forgive me. You see, sir, when they took away poor Bessy, they took all the things of hers they could find, and some of mine too. I thought they had taken all; but when I came to put the place in order, that I might come away here, I found a whole heap more of her things, and a good many papers of hers, hid away under the bed. I took them away to our parson's, to ask him to keep them for her; but he was out, and not likely to come back, so I had my eight miles' walk for nothing. The coach passed a little earlier than usual, and so I missed it that day, and the next day Joshua Brown advised me to bring on the things to you and give them into your care, and also to ask at all the posting-houses which he and I passed, where the gentleman had taken poor Bessy, that when I came I might know and be able to tell you where she is, for you and the other gentleman seemed to think a good deal about her. This kept me so long, but I hope you will forgive me."

"Well, well--reasons sufficient," replied Mr. Winkworth. "I like punctuality, my good lad, but I'm not altogether a hard taskmaster. And so you have brought the poor woman's things here--have you? Are they in that bundle?"

"Yes, sir," replied the boy, laying the things down upon the table; "and I've got a little gold box in my pocket, too, belonging to her, with what Joshua Brown says are diamonds on the top."

"Let me see--let me see!" said Mr. Winkworth; and the lad immediately produced from his pocket the vinaigrette which he had previously shown to the pedlar, and placed it in Mr. Winkworth's hands.

All fashions have their day, and pass away, sometimes giving place to things better than themselves, sometimes to worse. Even the workmanship in hard metal is subjected to the capricious rule, and the fashion of gold and silver seldom lasts above two or three years. It is very probable, however, that some of my readers may have seen snuffboxes, lockets, and cases for miniatures--ay, or even vinaigrettes--which displayed, on one side or the other, a tablet of bright blue enamel, on which appeared a cipher formed of diamonds. The top of the box now produced was thus ornamented; and Mr. Winkworth, examining it closely, said--

"Very fine stones, indeed! 'M. M.'--what can that mean? Charles assured me that her name was Hayley."

"So it is, sir," replied Jim; "for the gentleman who took her away called her Miss Hayley."

"'M. M.!' I don't understand it," said Mr. Winkworth. "Now, then; let us look at these in the bundle."

And he untied the corners, when a mass of very miscellaneous articles displayed itself, amongst which there appeared none that could be of any great value, except one or two packets of written papers, rolled up in small bundles and tied with dirty pieces of ribbon. One seemed to consist of letters which had been transmitted by the post, for on the outer cover there was an address, with the official stamp. The others seemed to consist of manuscripts, without any direction or indication of the contents upon the outside, but were written very closely, in a good, clear, masculine hand.

Mr. Winkworth paused and gazed at the papers for a moment or two, as if in doubt and hesitation. Then, turning to the boy, he asked--

"Can you tell me what these packets contain, Jim Brown?"

"No, sir," answered the boy: "I did not open them, for I thought I had no business."

"Right," said Mr. Winkworth; "right. Now, Jim, I should like very much to open them, from various motives, some of which you can conceive, and some of which you cannot. I should like to see this poor thing's history, which is, most probably, herein written. I should like to know what brought her to madness, destitution, and solitary wandering. Moreover, there is a chance that, by something contained in these papers, we might learn how her condition could be ameliorated, and who are the relations and friends who might have a right to take care of her in her present condition and provide for her future comfort. That chance would afford a good excuse to many men for examining these documents. But a man of honour and honesty, Jim, will be always very scrupulous in satisfying himself that there is something more than an excuse--nay, a full justification--for doing that which under ordinary circumstances would be dishonourable. Now, the man or woman, Jim, who would look into the private papers of another person, without full and convincing proof that to do so is absolutely necessary for the benefit of that person, is dishonest--is a rogue, Jim--is one unworthy of trust or confidence. I have no such proof; and therefore I will not examine these papers until I have, or until I am by some means authorized to do so. Ring the bell, boy--there it hangs, by the side of the fireplace."

Jim in vain looked for a bell, for he had never before seen a bell-rope in his life; and he took Mr. Winkworth's words literally, supposing that he should find a bell hanging by the fireplace--probably something like a church bell, for that was the instrument of sound with which he was best acquainted.

"I don't see a bell, sir," he said.

"Pshaw!" cried Mr. Winkworth, laughing: "pull the rope that's hanging there. I forgot that you had not been long caught."

The bell was soon rung, and a sheet of large cartridge-paper procured, in which the old gentleman made the boy fold up carefully the various documents he had brought, as the wound in his shoulder prevented him from doing so himself. This packing up was very neatly accomplished by Jim; but when it came to the sealing, notwithstanding all the good instructions of Mr. Winkworth, who stood by with a seal ready to press upon the wax, the poor boy made a sad mess of it, and burned his fingers awfully.

"Never mind, Jim; never mind," said Mr. Winkworth. "In my young days, when people were in the habit of walking the bounds of the parish, the officers used to whip one of the boys of the charity-school at every point which might become doubtful, in order that the tail might help the head to recollect. Now, your fingers will put you in mind of this sealing in case of need. However, there are two or three other things to be thought of. Have you found out where they have taken her to?"

"Yes, sir," answered the boy. "The last driver I talked to told me that the gentleman had ordered him to go to a house with barred-up windows.--Stay! I wrote down the name of the place on a bit of paper."

Mr. Winkworth eagerly examined the address the boy produced.

"Brooke Green," he said; "Brooke Green. That's not far. I've a great mind to go there at once. Hang the doctors! who cares what they say? I'll go. Ring the bell, Jim."

The bell was rung once more, and the waiter ordered to have a pair of post-horses put immediately to Mr. Charles Marston's carriage; for Mr. Winkworth did not stand upon any great ceremony with his young friend.

"Now take this boy down and give him something to eat," continued Mr. Winkworth.

"Yes, sir," said the waiter.

"You're a respectable man, I think?" said the old gentleman.

"Yes, sir," said the waiter.

"With a wife and children?" asked Mr. Winkworth.

"Yes, sir," said the waiter.

"Then take care of that boy while I stay here, and see if you cannot get him immediately, from some ready-made shop, a tidy suit of clothes, and have him prepared to go out with me in an hour."

"Yes, sir," said the waiter.

"You may go as far as fifty rupees," said Mr. Winkworth.

"Yes, sir," still said the waiter--though, heaven knows, he knew no more what a rupee is than Adam knew what a wife was before he fell asleep in the garden of Eden.

Mr. Winkworth was by temperament, and still more by habit, somewhat impatient; and on this occasion he certainly did not let the hour pass before he rang the bell, and asked if the horses and the boy were ready. If the truth must be told, he was apprehensive lest Charles Marston should come in and attempt to dissuade him from going out at all. Now, there was nothing on earth Mr. Winkworth so much disliked as being dissuaded; for he always took his own way, and a very odd way it generally was, so that he looked upon any attempt to dissuade him as trouble to both parties without benefit to either. However, it turned out that the horses were ready, but the boy was not; and he had to wait another quarter of an hour before Jim returned with the porter, whom the waiter had sent to guide him. The moment he arrived, Mr. Winkworth put him in the dickey of the vehicle, told the postboy where to drive, and got into the inside himself. Just as he was whirling round the corner of Albermarle Street into Piccadilly, who should he see walking soberly along, with Colonel Middleton, but his young friend Charles Marston!--and, with a laugh at the consternation which he saw in Charles's countenance, he shook his finger at him and rattled on.

Brooke Green was speedily reached, and at the door of the house, which had one of those portentous names usually given to lunatic asylums, the carriage drew up. Here, however, some difficulties presented themselves; for, although Mr. Winkworth and the boy were at once shown into the master's parlour, that personage demurred to letting them see Miss Hayley, though he did not venture to deny that she was in the house.

Though a very odd man, Mr. Winkworth, in matters of business, was a very sensible man; and though, as I have shown, an impatient man, yet in difficult circumstances, strange to say, he never lost his temper.

"Well, sir," he said, "I will ask you one question: by what authority do you detain the lady here?"

"By sufficient authority for my justification, sir," replied the master.

"It must be sufficient for my satisfaction before I go hence," replied Mr. Winkworth; "for I warn you I am a person never turned from my object. My belief is, that you have no lawful authority whatever; and, if you persist in your present course, I must take very unpleasant means to ascertain whether you have or have not."

"What means may those be?" asked the man, drily.

"The sending for a constable," answered Mr. Winkworth, "and giving you in charge for assault and false imprisonment."

"You will think twice before you do that, I fancy."

"No, I shall not," answered Mr. Winkworth: "I never think twice of anything. But you may save me some trouble, and yourself some annoyance, by answering a few very simple questions, which I have every right to demand."

"Well, I have no objection to answer any reasonable question," said the master, who did not like the notion of being given in charge, though he had affected to treat it lightly.

"First, then," said Mr. Winkworth, "has the lady been seen by any physician?"

"Not yet," replied the master of the house, "but one will visit her in an hour or two."

"Then by whose authority do you detain her in the mean while?" demanded the old gentleman.

After an instant's hesitation, the reply was--

"By that of Mr. Scriven, a connection of the lady."

A grim smile came upon Mr. Winkworth's yellow face.

"I am quite as near a connection of the lady as Mr. Scriven, sir," he replied, "and I now demand to see her, without further delay. If you accede, I shall take no further steps of any kind till she has been visited by the medical man of whom you speak, and until he has given a certificate as to her state. If you refuse, I must take those measures at which I hinted."

"Oh, very well," replied the master, who had by this time made up his mind: "if you promise me that, I will certainly admit you."

Mr. Winkworth, who right well understood the whole process which had been going on in the man's mind, merely nodded his head with a dry smile; and saying to the boy, "Come along, Jim," he followed the master into the interior of the building. It was not a very large establishment, nor had it many patients in it; but the whole bore more or less an aspect of neatness and cleanliness, although the part which they first passed through was very much superior in furniture and decoration to that at which they afterwards arrived. It was in the poorer part of the house, where patients paying very small sums were confined, that they found poor Miss Hayley.

She had a room to herself; but the master, while unlocking the door, thought fit to explain that they had not yet had time to put her in a ward.

Mr. Winkworth entered the room first; and the poor woman, who was seated near the window, turned a timid glance upon him, but immediately withdrew her eyes, not appearing to recognise him. The old gentleman, however, advanced kindly to her, saying--

"Don't you remember me? Here is your young friend Jim, come to see you."

Miss Hayley suddenly turned round at the name, and the moment she beheld the boy, started up, ran towards him, and cast her arms round his neck. The large tears fell from her eyes, too, and they seemed to relieve her brain; for the wild, scared look with which she had at first regarded Mr. Winkworth passed away.

"Oh, Jim!" she said, "I thought they would never let me see you again! But come here, my dear--come here; I want to speak with you;" and drawing the boy into the farther corner of the room, she whispered to him eagerly for several minutes.

"He has got them all," said the boy, at length, pointing to Mr. Winkworth: "he has sealed up the papers without reading them."

"What would you wish done with them?" asked Mr. Winkworth: "anything you direct I will see performed."

Poor Miss Hayley, however, made no reply, giving him a doubtful glance, and again whispering eagerly to the boy.

"Shall I tell him so?" asked Jim, after having listened attentively for a minute or two.

"If you can trust him," replied Miss Hayley, gazing at Mr. Winkworth with her large black eyes; "but not here--not here. Quite quietly, where nobody can hear, and see that there's nobody listening at the door; for he's a very cunning man, that Mr. Scriven, and a hard, cruel man, too."

"You see, sir, she's quite mad," said the master of the house, addressing Mr. Winkworth in a low tone. "You can have no doubt of that, I suppose."

"I have no doubt that her reason is impaired," replied the old gentleman; "but, at the same time, my good sir, I have many doubts as to whether her state of mind justifies or requires her detention in a place of this kind, and I am quite sure that it affords no excuse for excluding her friends from seeing her."

"That must be according to the doctor's orders," replied the other. "I have no wish to prevent people from seeing her--only Mr. Scriven thought it might irritate her."

"Pooh! pooh!" answered Mr. Winkworth, "Mr. Scriven should know better; and, besides, he has no authority here. He is no relation, no connection, and has been anything but a friend to her and hers. That she shall be well treated and comfortably lodged, I and other friends of her family will insist upon; and I authorise you to let her have more fitting accommodation than this room, making myself responsible for any reasonable expense that such an alteration may entail. I do not wish to interfere beyond a certain limit; and as long as I find that her friends are freely admitted to her, and that she is well and kindly treated, I shall be satisfied; but if any severe restrictions are attempted, I shall immediately apply for a commission to inquire into her state."

"I have not the honour even of knowing your name," rejoined the master of the house, "and of course must be responsible to those who placed the lady here."

"If you will come down-stairs, and furnish me with pen, ink, and paper," replied Mr. Winkworth, "you shall have my address, and the directions I have to give in writing, so that there can be no mistake, and that you may be ensured against loss."

This proposal was very satisfactory to the master of the house; and the boy Jim, being left with poor Miss Hayley at Mr. Winkworth's request, the other two went down-stairs, and were absent for a little more than a quarter of an hour. When they returned, it was somewhat difficult to induce the poor old lady to part with the boy. She held his hand in hers, and asked him to stay with her, so piteously that Mr. Winkworth's kind heart was grieved to take him away. He promised to send her some books, and she petitioned earnestly for paper, and for drawing and writing materials. The master of the house, too, promised to let her play for an hour every day upon the organ, adding--

"You used to be very fond of music when you were here before."

"What! then this is the house in which she was confined at first?" said Mr. Winkworth.

"To be sure, sir," answered the man. "She got out in the most cunning way possible, and she will need a deal of watching, I can tell you, to prevent her doing so again. Come, ma'am--you must let the boy go;" and, drawing Jim away from her, he saw him and Mr. Winkworth out of the room, and then locked the door.

"Come into the carriage with me, my lad," said the old gentleman, as the boy was going to take his seat behind; and during the whole way back to his hotel, Mr. Winkworth continued in very earnest conversation with his young companion, which left him grave and thoughtful for the rest of the day.

CHAPTER XXIII

Henry Hayley sat beside Maria Monkton, alone. Lady Anne Mellent and Charles Marston had left them together, as soon as they found that Lady Fleetwood was out: their own hearts told them how pleasant are the few uninterrupted moments of happy communion which love can snatch from the giddy and importunate world. Charles Marston had promised to return for Henry in an hour; and the young soldier was eager to take advantage of precious opportunity, to say a part, at least, of all that remained to be said between him and her he loved. Maria, however, was sad, or at least very grave. The agitation of being thus left alone with him, perhaps, might have some share in that seriousness, for woman's love only grows bold by degrees. Perhaps the uncertainty of his fate and future prospects might have some share; for how full of emotions is the anxiety with which we watch the current of events affecting a beloved object--events over which we have no control or power--especially when from ignorance or inexperience we cannot calculate the amount of dangers that menace and difficulties that beset!

However, Maria was very grave, as I have said, and Henry, remarking it, hastened to make an effort to remove what he imagined might be the cause of the sadness he beheld.

"How I have longed for this moment, dear Maria!" he said; "and yet, now it is come, I fear it will last so short a time that I shall not have space to say all I have to say. Indeed, dear girl, it becomes more and more necessary, every moment, that we should have some means of communicating with each other unrestrained by the presence of others. How may this be, Maria? for I foresee that from time to time it may be absolutely needful for me to have at least a few minutes to explain to you things that may appear strange in my conduct--to show you that there is no cause for fear, even when things seem going wrong--to communicate to you, in short, the hopes and expectations that are in my own bosom, whenever they assume a tangible form."

"You must tell me the fears, and the dangers too, Henry," said Maria. "You cannot tell what I suffered during the whole of dinner-time, while such sharp questions and answers were passing between you and my uncle.

His suspicions are evidently aroused. As to how I can see you, except at such moments as these, I do not know what to reply. If it be needful, indeed, I can drive down into the country for a day, at any time, and see you there; but, as we are all going soon to Lady Anne Mellent's, it seems, there will be plenty of opportunity."

There was a slight peculiarity in her way of pronouncing Lady Anne Mellent's name, an emphatic dwelling upon the words, which did not escape Henry's ear; and he gazed at Maria for a moment, with a look almost as grave as her own; then, laying his hand lightly upon hers, he said--

"Do you not think Lady Anne's manner strange towards me, Maria? Do you not think mine strange towards her?"

The colour came warmly into Maria's cheek.

"No, Henry," she said, after a moment's pause. "I might think both strange, were any other person concerned than dear Anne Mellent--but I know her so well! I know that she is so good, so kind, so true, so sincere, and yet, in habit of thought and general course of action, so unlike other people, that what would be strange with others is not strange with her; and I feel sure, Henry, that there is some strong and good motive both with you and her for all you do."

Still Henry gazed at her gravely and thoughtfully.

"There is something more, Maria," he said. "Stay, dear girl--let me place the case before you as strongly as it can be placed, to show you that I see the most unfavourable light in which it can be viewed. I return to you after many years of sad and painful exile, with a reputation tarnished and doubtful-- with a story vouched for by my own word alone. You receive me as if not a day had passed--as if not a breath had sullied my name. You believe my exculpation; you listen to my love; you give me confidence, comfort, hope; and yet, while telling you that I love you--you alone--you, with my whole heart and soul--I am more frequently with another, passing long hours with her, conferring, consulting with her, although she is one whom, good, kind, and amiable as she is, I profess to regard in a very different manner--less warm, less tender than that in which I regard yourself. Acknowledge that it has struck you as very strange, Maria; that it has pained you; that it has almost made you doubt me."

"No, no, indeed, Henry," she said: "it has not done so. You could have no motive, no object in deceiving me, even if I could believe you capable of doing so."

Henry smiled faintly.

"I might tell you," he said, "that there are many causes for such conduct; that Lady Anne, from her father's old intimacy with mine, possesses information most valuable to me, upon the only points where difficulties stand in my way or dangers menace me; that I have always the opportunity of seeing her alone, of consulting with her, and making arrangements to secure the future. All this is true; and I might add that, though you may think this close communication dangerous with one young, gay, beautiful as she is, yet there is no risk for a heart given entirely to you, which has never loved another, and never will. But I will put it upon a totally different ground. I will only say, trust me, dear Maria; fully--entirely--as you did when there was every cause to doubt and suspect me. Believe that I am incapable of any baseness, especially to one whose generous kindness and undoubting confidence have been the brightest reward of that rectitude of which I am conscious, and the sweetest compensation for all that I have suffered and deserved. Trust me, and do not doubt me; and in a very few days all shall be explained."

"Indeed, Henry, I have never doubted you," replied Maria, earnestly: "never, upon my word. I have been a little anxious, a little sad, and my feelings have been so mixed that they would be difficult to explain. The evident suspicions of my uncle alarm me: my aunt Fleetwood, too, recognises you, I am sure. You can easily imagine that, not fully knowing what is taking place, what means you have of proving your innocence, what your intentions are, what your course is to be, I have felt agitated, frightened; and besides----"

She paused, and did not conclude the sentence.

"There is something more," said Henry. "Say, what besides, Maria?"

Maria laughed, but not gaily, and shook the bright curls back from her face, with some degree of agitation. "I was going to say," she replied, "that besides all this, the way you replied several times to my uncle last night troubled and alarmed me a good deal. There was a mocking sort of sarcasm, which I thought likely to irritate him rather than otherwise--to provoke him to pursue his inquiries farther. It was unlike yourself, too, Henry. You were always frank, earnest, calm. Even in your very gaiety there was a clear, open candour, peculiar to yourself. Last night there might be playfulness, yet there was a degree of sneering superciliousness, too--a touch of scorn for the opinion of others--a little like Lady Anne's own manner to those whom she despises, which struck me very much. I love Henry Hayley's natural manner better."

Henry laughed gaily, and pressed his lips upon her hand. "It shall all come back again, dearest Maria," he replied, "in a very, very short time; but in the mean while you must not let that manner pain you any more, even though you should see it carried still farther. You have said you do not know what my intentions are, what my course is to be. Now, dearest Maria, listen; and do not be angry with me, even if you think my course is a rash and imprudent one. My intentions are very strange. Whenever I meet your uncle, I propose to treat him exactly as I did last night--to irritate him, if you will--to goad him on, in short, upon the course in which his suspicions would lead him--to drive him to take the initiative in proving who I am, and to throw no obstacles in his way, except such as may stimulate him to proceed the more fiercely. In this course I even intend to make you art and part, with a sort of bold and almost impudent recklessness, which, believe me, I should never dream of were the circumstances different. I know not whether Maria will forgive me, nor how she may herself be disposed to act; but wherever I meet her, especially where Mr. Scriven is present, my feelings towards her will appear undisguised: I will seek her as an object of deep and ardent attachment; and though, of course, my conduct shall be regulated by the ordinary proprieties of life, so as not to pain her feelings by calling the gaze of the multitude upon us, yet no one shall see me near her and doubt that she is dearer to me than any other being upon earth. How will Maria act with so strange a man?"

Maria smiled gladly; for, though there was much that she did not comprehend, many motives that she did not see, objects that were hidden, yet through the mist there gleamed things pleasant to her eyes--hopes, assurances, affections, that seemed bright and happy. He could not so act, he could not so speak, without deep love, without strong expectation.

"She will act as you would wish her, Henry," she replied. "A promise once given is with me binding for ever, nor will I shrink from avowing it--no, nor attempt to conceal it. But I will not endeavour, Henry, either to say or to determine how I will act. I will let my conduct towards you take its natural course. The feelings in my heart, the confidence, the trust, will ensure that it shall be such as will not be disagreeable to you; and I am sure that whatever you think it right to do will be so guided as not to render it painful to me."

"Except in regard to your uncle, dear Maria," he replied. "Perhaps in his case it may be so, but it will spare much hereafter; and of this be assured, that no consideration whatever would induce me to blazon forth my attachment in the eyes of the world, did I not feel fully assured that when all is made clear, and every cloud blown away, I shall stand forth not unworthy of the affection of such a heart as yours--not unqualified, even in point of wealth and the world's esteem, to seek your hand."

"As to wealth," said Maria, smiling, "that need be no consideration, Henry. I have enough, and more than enough, for both; and I suppose, of course, that when you resume your real name and station, you will resign the fortune which you hold as Frank Middleton."

"I do not know," answered Henry. "That fortune was not obtained by any deceit. He who left it to me knew right well that I was not Frank Middleton, and I can prove that such was the case. However, that will be a matter for after consideration; though, were I to do as you say, Mr. Scriven would undoubtedly exclaim loudly against your marrying a beggar, though he might not be able to prove that you were marrying a felon. But what say you, Maria?" he continued gaily. "Might we not pursue another course? Might you not give this dear little hand to Colonel Middleton, great-nephew of a grandee of Spain? Might you not go with him to that bright, sunshiny land, and spend the rest of life amidst groves of oranges and myrtles, by the side of clear streams, with the cork-tree spreading out its broad, rugged branches overhead, and the wild blue mountains falling into every fanciful form against the distant sky? There, amidst the marble palaces of races long passed away, with minaret, and dome, and fretted arch, and fountains sparkling, in the sun, the breeze loaded with fragrance, and the night sky gemmed with lustrous stars, life might fly away like a summer dream, and all the dark realities in the fate of Henry Hayley be forgotten."

"You are mocking me even now, Henry," said Maria, shaking her head. "Do not put such a question to me again, unless you put it seriously; and if ever you should do so, I will take two minutes to consider, and then give you an answer. But, hark! there is my aunt Fleetwood: I know her servant's knock."

"Well, then, remember, dear Maria," said Henry, "that to her as well as to others I may behave strangely. Nor be you surprised at anything you may see, nor think that I am changed except in mere appearances. All will be fully explained in time, and in the mean while, dear Maria, trust me."

"I will, I will!" answered Maria with a smile, and almost at the same moment Lady Fleetwood entered the room. She seemed somewhat disconcerted at finding Colonel Middleton there, and she would fain have been a little cool and distant in her manner; but it was a very difficult thing for her kind-hearted ladyship to feel or appear cold to anybody. In the case of Henry, it would have been less easy than in any other; for, in spite of all she could do, there was a natural warming of the heart towards him whom she had loved and caressed as a boy, which she could not overcome. His manner, too, was very engaging; and he spoke to her so like an old friend, with so much of the easy confidence of long-tried affection, that she could not either persuade herself he was other than Henry Hayley, or make herself angry lest his evident love for Maria should spoil her favourite scheme of uniting her niece and nephew.

To do Henry merely justice, he did not in the least attempt to conceal from Lady Fleetwood his affection for Maria; but on the contrary, to use the ordinary term, made love to her more openly and desperately when her aunt alone was present to watch them than he would have done in the presence of any other human being.

Poor Lady Fleetwood witnessed it all with sad dismay. She had fortified herself strongly in her little plan for Charles and Maria; and the great indifference which her niece had shown for all other men, the rejection of two or three very eligible proposals, and the light and laughing way in which she usually treated the subject of marriage, when her aunt, in simplicity of heart, forced it upon her, had all tended to strengthen her belief in the security of her position. Now, however, she saw so terrible an attack made upon it, that she began to entertain the notion that she could not maintain it; and Maria, although she was not one to flirt even with a lover, suffered, every now and then, a word, a look, a smile to escape her, which made poor Lady Fleetwood tremble for the fate of all her little arrangements.

Shortly after her return some visiters came in, and they were succeeded by others; but still Colonel Middleton did not give up his post, and remained there, with his manner a little subdued towards Maria, indeed, but still without any attempt to disguise his attentions.

If there was any change in Maria's manner towards him, it became rather warmer than colder in the presence of her visiters. She did not attempt to conceal her preference, and poor Lady Fleetwood was more uneasy than ever. When she found, moreover, that Henry was to be one of the guests at Lady Anne Mellent's, she was actually roused to an attempt to carry the war into the enemy's territory, though, poor thing, heaven knows she was anything but fitted for an enterprising general.

"Oh! then you are going down to Lady Anne's, Colonel Middleton?" she said, with a meaning smile. "You seem very intimate there. Have you been long acquainted with her?"

"I saw Lady Anne at a ball in Rome, more than a year ago," replied Henry; "and she is, as you remark, exceedingly kind to me--of which her invitation on this occasion is a proof; for, as soon as she had secured you and Miss Monkton, Lady Fleetwood, she sent to tell me so, and to invite me, knowing how delighted I should be to meet you there, and how desolate London would seem to me during the absence of yourself and your fair niece."

The slightest possible smile curled his handsome lip as he spoke, and Maria could not refrain from looking a little amused, also. Lady Fleetwood felt that she had better let him alone; and in a few minutes after, to her great relief, Charles Marston was announced.

He had not entered the room, however, when a fluttering apprehension, seized upon Lady Fleetwood, lest her nephew should perceive that he had a rival in the young officer, and some quarrel should be the result. She therefore determined, with her usual kindness, to try and explain to Charles that Colonel Middleton was only there accidentally, and soften matters as much as possible. But Charles was in the most provoking humour in the world, and seemed resolved to demolish all his aunt's hopes and expectations completely.

"Oh, my dear aunt," he said, nearly aloud, "I left him here an hour ago, or more, promising to call for him again."

Lady Fleetwood looked aghast, and murmured--

"On purpose?"

"Oh, dear, yes!" answered Charles, laughing. "Listen, and I'll tell you a secret in your ear, dear lady," he continued in a whisper: "see if I am not the kindest and most considerate man in the world. I found that you were out, and that Maria was here alone, so I went away, and left Middleton with her, thinking they might have something to say to each other. So now that's a hint for you, dearest aunt; and I'm quite sure that a kind, good-natured creature like yourself will take every little quiet opportunity of letting them have a few minutes' conversation alone from time to time."

Poor Lady Fleetwood was struck dumb, and sinking down into a seat, she began to play with the stopper of a large scent-bottle which stood upon the table.

In the mean while, Maria and Henry were conversing with some people at the other end of the room; and Charles and his friend soon after took their departure, while poor Lady Fleetwood said to herself--

"Well, I suppose there is no use in trying to mend the matter now; but I must certainly talk to my brother about it, and hear what he thinks. I never could have believed that Maria would throw herself away upon a man whom she has only known a few days--and half a Spaniard, too!"

CHAPTER XXIV

When I was a boy at school, I used, like other boys, to employ very unprofitably some of my leisure hours in keeping silk-worms. In a neighbouring garden there was a large mulberry-tree, and for a certain sum--I forget what--I, as well as other boys, was permitted to go in and gather as many leaves as I thought necessary as food for the emblem of the English literary man: I mean the silk-worm who spins golden threads for the benefit of others, and whose tomb is valued after he himself is gone. But it is not with the silk-worm I have to do now. The leaves which I gathered as a boy are my illustration. I remember very well that I used to place them one upon the other in a pile, and try to gather them as nearly of the same size and shape as I could; but, do what I would, I never was able to find two that were exactly alike. A point would stick out here, and a point would stick out there. Some would be a little longer, some would be a little shorter; and I used to marvel, even in those young days, that in such a simple thing as a leaf there should be such infinite variety.

I have marvelled more at human nature since, in which, with all the training and forcing and moulding of society, with similar education, similar laws--I might almost say similar accidents--we never find two characters exactly alike, any more than two leaves perfectly the same on a tree.

Were this a contemplative age, I would venture to meditate upon the subject much farther, for it is a fine one and a strange one. But this is not a contemplative age. It is an age of action, wherein no thought that does not apply to the mere business of the day is worth a farthing. I do not mean to abuse it. It is quite as good as any other age that ever was, or perhaps ever will be; but still this is its character. It has lost something, if it has gained something. Let those strike the balance who keep such accounts accurately. I am of the age, so I must onward; and I only put down these meditations because there are some men of a contemplative turn, such as I once was myself; and because even men of the most earnest activity have their contemplative moments, when that which is suggestive interests more than that which is objective.

It is difficult to find words to express the infinite; and, although it may seem a pleonasmatic expression, I must say that all the varieties of human character have infinite varieties within themselves. However, the easily impressible character--that which suffers opinions, feelings, thoughts, purposes, actions, to be continually altered by the changing circumstances around--the chameleon character, if I may so call it--is perhaps the most dangerous to itself, and to those it affects, of any that I know. It goes beyond the chameleon, indeed. The reptile only reflects the colours of objects near, retaining its own form and nature. The impressible character, on the contrary, is changed in every line, as well as in every hue, by that with which it comes in contact. Certain attributes it certainly does retain. The substance is the same, but the colour and the form are always varying. In the substance lie the permanence and the identity: all else is moulded and painted by circumstance.

Now, substantially there never was a kinder or a better heart in the world than that of Lady Fleetwood. She was ever anxious for the happiness of those around her. She was too anxious, in fact; for, never thinking they could secure it for themselves, she was always seeking to do it for them--in her own way. In this, too, she differed from many other persons, that the foundation of her ill-directed activity was not exactly vanity. It was not so much that she thought she knew better than they did what would contribute to their happiness, as that she was always making mistakes as to what their real wishes were. As soon as she was thoroughly convinced and completely comprehended--which seldom happened--what her friends truly desired, no one would labour more zealously to accomplish it than she would; but always in a wrong direction, be it remarked. Thus it was nearly as dangerous to let her know one's wishes as to conceal them.

This may seem a somewhat singular character; but yet, I believe few who have lived long have not met with some specimens, modified by circumstances, probably; and indeed there is a spice of this same disposition in more people than we know; there may be in ourselves. If you wish to prove the fact, give a commission to a friend, he would do anything to serve you, but he never executes the commission as he received it.

When Henry Hayley left her drawing-room with Charles Marston, Lady Fleetwood, who had fully made up her mind that her niece Maria ought to marry her nephew Charles, and that she would have married him, too, if he had asked her--which, by-the-bye, wasn't the case--was very much disappointed to see a towering impediment rising up in the way of such a consummation; and she resolutely and at once determined to go that very day and consult with her brother, Mr. Scriven, in the desperate hope of still bringing it about.

She remained firm in her purpose till the visitors who were in the room took their leave also; but then, *unfortunately*, a conversation took place between her and Maria, which changed all her views and purposes.

Take note, reader, that each word is considered--even that word "unfortunately."

When the visitors were gone, Lady Fleetwood thought she might as well say something to Maria about Colonel Middleton. She thought she should, at least, learn what her views and intentions were, and very likely her own advice and remonstrances might still affect Maria's decision. Heaven help the poor lady! she was but little aware that Maria's stronger mind and more energetic character had guided her like a child for many years, without ever seeming to do so, indeed, but gently, gaily, laughingly.

She had some little difficulty in beginning, for there was a sort of vague consciousness of weakness about her, which occasionally made her timid in her activity. However, she at length said--

"I did not expect to find Colonel Middleton here this morning, my love."

Maria, who knew every turn of her aunt's mind as well as that of her own sandal, saw what was coming; and a slight glow spread over her face, deepening the colour of her cheek and tinging her fair brow and temples.

"Why not, my dear aunt?" she asked, knowing that it would never do to show any timidity.

"Why, if he was here for an hour before I came in, his visit must have been an early one," replied Lady Fleetwood.

Maria mused for a single moment, but then determined upon her course at once.

"He wished to see me, my dear aunt," she said; "and therefore he came at a time when he thought I should be at home."

Lady Fleetwood began to perceive that the matter was rather hopeless; and shaking her head, with a deep sigh she replied--

"I am sorry to hear it, my love. I had hoped----"

There she stopped, and looked so disconsolate that Maria in her own kind and gentle manner crossed the room, sat down beside her, and laid her hand kindly upon her aunt's.

"You had hoped what, my dear aunt?" she said; and then added, with a gay smile, "that I should marry Charles?"

"Why, I certainly did hope it, Maria," answered her aunt; "and I know that your uncle wished it also."

"Your wishes, my dear aunt, would always have much weight with me," replied Maria; "but I am afraid my uncle's, upon such a subject as this especially, would have none. As to Charles and myself, however, though I am very sorry that any wish of yours should be disappointed, you will, I am sure, admit that I never gave you any reason to believe that such a thing as a marriage between him and me could take place: indeed, quite the contrary. Charles and I are utterly unsuited to each other, though I have a great regard for him, and he the same for me. But, even were such not the case, my dear aunt, certainly no marriage can or ought to take place where neither party is willing; and Charles, depend upon it, would be quite as unwilling to marry me as I should be to marry him."

"But that is no reason, my dear, why you should marry this Colonel Middleton, whom you have only known for a few days," said Lady Fleetwood, almost sharply.

"Certainly not," answered Maria, her colour a little heightened; "nor did I say that I am going to do so. But yet I may see a great number of good reasons for doing so, and no reason against it, in any impracticable scheme which friends, however kind, may have thought fit to frame for me and Charles. But tell me, my dear aunt, what objections have you to urge against Colonel Middleton?"

"Why, that you have known him so short a time," replied Lady Fleetwood, causing a faint smile to flutter about Maria's pretty lips; "and then he is half a foreigner. You can know nothing of his character, his disposition, his fortune, his station--nor, indeed of anything about him."

Maria leaned her head thoughtfully on her hand, and mused for a minute or two, without reply.

Lady Fleetwood thought she had made great progress, that her niece's resolution was shaken, and that by a word or two more she might triumph.

"Indeed, Maria," she said, "you must think better of this matter, and not give this young man such encouragement. I will do everything I can to dissuade you, and I must get your uncle to help me. I have no doubt the man is some foreign adventurer, who thinks to raise himself from adversity by marrying an English heiress."

"Fie, fie, my dear aunt!" cried Maria, almost indignantly: "this is unlike yourself. Is it generous, is it kind, is it even just, to speak thus of a man of whose character and situation you know nothing? But now, my dear aunt, I will tell you, I know everything about him--his family, his fortune, his character, his station. He is no needy adventurer, but a distinguished officer, with ample fortune and a high reputation. The Conde de Fraga told me so last night; and if he has met with adversities in life, and sorrows bitter and undeserved, it shall be my task, and a sweet one, to console him and make him forget them."

Lady Fleetwood was aghast at the result of her own efforts, for she had never seen Maria so much moved before; and she felt, also, that there was some truth in the reproachful words of her niece.

"Well, my dear Maria," she said, in a timid tone, "I did not know that you had so completely made up your mind, or I should not have said what I did. As to Colonel Middleton's character, of course, as you say, I can know nothing. I only spoke from what your uncle said, for he seemed to think very ill of him."

"I thought so," replied Maria. "I was quite sure, my dear aunt, that it is not in your nature to injure or traduce any one even by a word. My uncle is harsh and prejudiced; but surely you will not listen to unfounded suspicions, the justice of which he cannot bring forward a proof to support."

"I know very well your uncle does dislike him very much from his likeness to poor Henry Hayley," said Lady Fleetwood.

"For that very reason I should love him," replied Maria, warmly. "And now, my dear aunt," she said, taking Lady Fleetwood's hand affectionately, "do not pain and grieve your Maria by throwing any needless and useless obstacles and objections in my way. Be assured that I know well what I am doing, and shall be perfectly prepared to justify it. But, even were such not the case--were Colonel Middleton poor, as you have supposed--you would not, I am sure, provided he can prove himself, as he assuredly can, an honourable and upright man--endeavour to thwart the affection of two people who love each other deeply and devotedly. That such is the case on my part you may be perfectly sure; for no consideration would ever make me give my hand to a man who did not possess my whole heart. You yourself, my dear aunt, have shown that you can feel the deepest and most enduring affection; and you ought to know how painful it is to hear objections, suspicions, and prejudices urged against a man whom one loves."

The tears came into Lady Fleetwood's eyes.

"I do indeed, my dear Maria," she said; "and now that I know you do love him, far be it from me to do anything to mar your happiness. Far, far from it! I will do everything I can on earth to facilitate your views. But still it is very strange that you should become attached to him so soon and so strongly. Why, I have seen many a man paying devoted attention to you for months, without being able to obtain anything but the coldest possible return, and in the end a decided rejection."

"No man had any right to make me reject him," replied Maria; "for I have always taken care, my dear aunt, to give no encouragement to such proposals, and have done my best to avoid them; for you may well believe that nothing could be more painful to me than to inflict pain upon another."

"But still it is very strange that you should become attached to Colonel Middleton so soon," answered Lady Fleetwood, returning pertinaciously to her point.

Maria smiled.

"There is a secret, my dear aunt," she said, "which I must not tell you or any one yet; but you shall be one of the very first to know it, and when you do, it will explain all that now seems strange."

Lady Fleetwood meditated, saying--

"A secret! Well, my dear, I don't wish to pry into any secrets; but be sure that I will do whatever I can to help you;" and warming in her new zeal as she went on, she said, "Whenever Colonel Middleton comes again, I shall go out of the room, just to leave you alone with him, for you may have things to say to each other."

"No, no, my dear aunt; pray do not do that!" exclaimed Maria: "only let matters follow their course quietly and easily. Take no notice of the feelings between Colonel Middleton and myself; and I promise you that, if I have anything to say to him, or he to me, which requires to be said in private, I shall very quietly take him into another room; for I am not in the least ashamed of my choice or afraid of avowing it."

Notwithstanding this admonition, excellent Lady Fleetwood was determined to be of service to Maria and her lover. Now that she was fully convinced of which way her niece's happiness really lay, she was all eagerness to promote her views. There was a necessity for activity in some direction upon her; and, had she but possessed the rare quality of discretion, she might indeed have helped the lovers very much; but unfortunately the worthy lady's first consideration was how she might be active immediately, without waiting for opportunity, which is always very indiscreet. No way presented itself to her imagination for some moments; and while Maria retired to her room to dress for going out, and moreover to recover from a greater degree of agitation than she had suffered to appear, Lady Fleetwood went on considering what could best be done to remove all difficulties from her niece's way. As mischief would have it, the only thing she could think of was to go and persuade Mr. Scriven that it would be the best possible thing, after all, for Maria to marry Colonel Middleton. She felt not the slightest doubt in the world that she should be quite successful; for, although she had enjoyed plenty of opportunities of judging of her brother, she was not yet convinced of the indisputable fact, that Mr. Scriven could never be persuaded. Whether it was that his brains were harder than other men's, or that he never formed a wrong opinion in his life, or that there is a peculiar organ of persuadability which he did not possess, certain it is that he was never known to yield one step when once he had taken up his ground.

However, as I have said, Lady Fleetwood felt perfectly confident of success. She was convinced herself, and she thought the same arguments which had produced that effect on her must be convincing with others. She did not remember, indeed, that she was not unlikely to forget one-half of them. Nevertheless she thought, "I will not say a word about it to Maria. It will be a pleasant surprise to her to find that her uncle offers no opposition. I will just wait till she has gone out, and then drive to the city at once."

CHAPTER XXV

At the door of a hotel in St. James's Street, towards that hour of the day at which waiters, butlers, and valets, have the least to do, stood a group consisting of several of those respectable personages, with their hands behind their backs, enjoying the air of the fine spring day, and making impertinent comments upon everybody who passed. Amongst the rest was a tall, thin man, of middle age, who had originally possessed very dark hair as well as a dark complexion, but whose hair and whiskers were now thickly mottled with grey. His face was good and intelligent, his eyes were black and sparkling, his features aquiline and high. Though he was an Italian, his face had not at all the Italian cast; and, well-dressed and gentlemanly in appearance, he looked more like an old French nobleman, who had escaped the first Revolution, than the foreign servant of an English gentleman, which was in reality his condition. He and one or two more were standing on the top step of the flight which descended from the door of the hotel to the street, when a small, sleek, oily-looking man, dressed as a respectable tradesman, approached and spoke to one of the younger waiters, who, upon the lowest step, was making signs to a chambermaid in the area.

"I don't know, I am sure: there's his gentleman," said the waiter. "Mr. Carlini, this person is asking for your master. Is he at home?"

"No," replied the other, with a very slight foreign accent; "he has gone out."

"Can you tell me where he is to be found, sir?" asked the tradesman in a deferential tone; "I want to speak with him on important business."

"He has gone to Lady Fleetwood's, in ---- Square," said the Italian; "but if your business is not very important indeed, he will not thank you for going there after him;" and he turned round to carry on his conversation with the others near.

"Why, the colonel is always going to Lady Fleetwood's, Mr. Carlini," said the head waiter, with a jocular air. "I should not wonder if you found a mistress there some day. I recollect her a very handsome woman, in Sir John's time. What do you think of it? Is it likely to be?"

"Perhaps so: I know nothing about it," replied Carlini, "for I never inquire into my master's affairs."

"Oh! it's all settled, I can tell you," said a pert puppy, who formed the third at the top of the steps. "I heard my master talking about it with young Count Fraga this very morning, and it's to be very soon, too."

The gentleman who had been speaking to the waiter below heard all this conversation, and then turned away. It might seem a matter of little importance to a man of his apparent pursuits in life, who married another in the higher ranks of society; but yet he seemed very well satisfied with what he had heard; and he chuckled a little as he walked up St. James's Street, crossed over to the corner of Abermarle Street, and then took his way towards Berkeley Square.

"It only wants working well," he murmured to himself; "it only wants working well, and we may make a pretty penny of it. I mustn't trust it to that thick-headed fool, Sam, though. He'd make a mess of it. Going to be married in two days! Well, that's extraordinary. I dare say the old lady wouldn't like to be disappointed, and would pay a handsome sum down to save her lover from being scragged. But I mustn't let Sam have anything to do with it, he's so rude and unpolishable. There he stands: I must have a chat with him before the matter goes farther."

And walking on, he found a tall, stout man, who has been already described as holding negotiations with Joshua Brown, the pedlar, of rather a fierce and intemperate character. He was not badly dressed upon the present occasion, having clearly put on his Sunday's best for his trip to London; but, nevertheless, he could not by any means get rid of a certain blackguard air, any more than the ominous black eye, which shed a halo of many colours around it on the cheek and temple. As soon as he saw his friend and fellow-labourer, Mr. Mingy Bowes, he advanced towards him with a quick step, asking eagerly for intelligence, in language which, perhaps, would not be altogether comprehensible to most of my readers.

"Mum!" said Mingy Bowes, holding up his finger, and looking along the pavement under the walls of Lansdowne House, where a policeman was seen sauntering slowly and *nonchalantly* along, his eyes turned towards the wall, as if his sole business in life was to count bricks set in mortar. "Come along, Sam; let us go and have a whet at the 'Pig and Whistle.' The cove's out, but I've got hold of something that, if tidily worked, may fill both our breeches pockets."

"I'll have mine filled first," said the man he called Sam; "for it's my job anyhow, Mingy, though I don't mind your having a cut out of the whiddy."

"To be sure, to be sure," answered Mingy Bowes; "that's all fair. I don't want more than a quarter; and I'll manage it so, if you'll let me, that I'll answer for it my quarter shall be more than ever I took in three months out of the shop--the bank into the bargain."

His companion merely gave a grunt, for the policeman was by this time near; and they walked on together, across various streets and through various alleys which led into Oxford Street.

It is curious and sad that in some of the most fashionable parts of the town of London, within a stone's throw of the mansions of the opulent and great, are, or at least were some twenty years ago, an immense mass of the lowest and most squalid houses in the metropolis. Close by Grosvenor and Manchester Squares, and lying between them and Bond Street, are a number of places in which it was dangerous, as the writer once found to his cost, for a respectably-dressed person to set his foot. There, congregated tier above tier, in small, dark, unwholesome rooms, are whole classes of people, in comparison with whom the denizens of Saint Giles's may be looked upon as aristocracy. If you walk along one of these courts or alleys, the first things you remark, on the right hand and the left, are the two confederates in demoralization and degradation, the pawnbroker's and the gin-shop, both tolerated and encouraged by the British government on account of those iniquitous and burdensome taxes grouped under the name of excise--taxes which, whatever they may do for the revenue, tend more to hamper industry, to debase the people, to make rogues of honest men, to prevent the employment of the poor, to give monopoly to the rich, to obstruct salutary laws, and to disgrace the legislature, than any imposts that ever were invented by the great British demon, Taxation.

The fact is, ministers dare not deal with the gin-shop nuisance as they would with any other nuisance, for fear of diminishing the revenue; and when they come before parliament and boast of an increased revenue from the excise--which they call the barometer of commercial prosperity--they boast, in fact, of how much they have been able to wring from the vices, the follies, or the hard labours of the industrious classes. They say neither more nor less than this: there must have been more demand for labour, because the labouring classes have been able to drink more gin, to smoke more tobacco, and to swill more beer.

This is a very irrelevant tirade, but it would be written.

Beyond the pawnbroker's and the gin-shop, you enter into the heart of the den; probably meeting, at the first two or three steps, some half-clad women, with foul matted hair, strange-shaped caps which were once white, and yellowish handkerchiefs loosely spread over the otherwise uncovered bosom. Perhaps there is a short pipe in the mouth; but there is gin in every hue of the face, and the eyes are bleared and inflamed with habitual intoxication.

There may be a miserable baby in the arms, or on the back, the naked feet and legs appearing from beneath the rags that cover it--sallow, sickly, sharp-faced, keen-eyed--the nursling of misery, despair, and vice--the destined victim of every evil passion and every degrading crime. Above, below, around, from every window in cellar, in attic, in the middle floors, come forth the varied murmurs, in different tongues and tones: the slang and cant of English rogues and vagabonds; the brogue of Ireland, or the old Irish language itself; the shouts of wrath or merriment; the groans of anguish; the cries of pain or sorrow; the gay laugh; the dull buzz of tongues consulting over deeds of evil, telling tales of despair and woe, or asking counsel how to avoid starvation.

As you go on, innumerable are the different forms you meet, in every shape of degradation: the fierce bludgeoned bully, the dexterous pickpocket, the wretched woman who acts as their decoy, the boys and girls serving an apprenticeship to vice, the hoary prompters of all evil, who, in the shape of receivers, profit by the crimes of the younger and more active.

Look at that girl there in the tattered chintz gown. She can scarcely be sixteen; and yet, see how she reels from side to side in beastly intoxication! And then that elderly man in the shabby brown coat, with the venerable white hair, who goes walking along by the side of the gutter, and every now and then stops and gazes in, as if he saw something exceedingly curious there. He is a respectable-looking man, with a gentlemanly air and carriage. A thief, and a man suspected of murder, are just passing him; but he is quite safe: they know he has nothing to lose, and his emaciated body would not fetch two pounds at the anatomist's.

What is it has brought him to this state? Look in his face; see the dull, meaningless eye, the nose and lips bloated with habitual sottish tippling. That man can boast that he never was drunk in his life, but for more than forty years he has never been quite sober. Hark to the screams coming forth from that house where one-half of the windowpanes at least are covered up with paper. They are produced by a drunken scoundrel beating his unhappy wife. She was once an honest, cheerful, happy country girl, and now--I must not stay to tell the various stages of degradation she has gone through, till she is here, the wife of a drunken savage, in one of the lowest and vilest dens of London. Hark how the poor thing screams under the ruffian's blow, while one of his brutal companions sits hard by and witnesses it, laughing! Three days hence, by one too-fatally-directed blow, that man will murder the wretched woman in the presence of her two children, and then will go to end his own days on a scaffold, leaving those wretched infants to follow the same course in after years.

I must not pause upon these things more. It was through such scenes as I have described that Mingy Bowes and his companion took their way, without the slightest fear or trepidation, for it would seem that they both knew the haunt right well. They went up a very narrow sort of court out of Oxford Road, and then turned into a broader and more reputable-looking street, though heaven knows it was bad enough. About half-way down was an open door, over which were written some letters required by the excise, and by the side of which, on a board about two feet square, appeared a curious painting.

On a background, intended to represent sky and cloud, though in reality it looked more like a torn blue coat with a white shirt peeping through the rents, appeared a tolerably well painted sow, standing on her hind legs, with a flageolet in her mouth, whence this pleasant resort of rogues and vagabonds took its name of the "Pig and Whistle." Mingy and his friend went in, pushed the first swing-door open, then passed a second, for there was no impediment in the way, at least for the moment, though there were bolts and bars in plenty about, which might possibly be used at times to shut out suspicious characters. The sense of words, of course, differs in different places, and perhaps by the term "suspicious characters" two very different classes of persons would be meant by the police and by the landlord of the "Pig and Whistle." The latter, at all events, did not seem to consider Mr. Mingy Bowes and his friend Sam as within the category; for he made them a very reverent bow as they entered that apartment which bore an ironical inscription, designating it as "the Commercial Room." With Sam he seemed quite familiar, and to Mingy Bowes was highly deferential, for gentlemen of Mingy's calling are very important personages in the great community of thieves and scoundrels. As soon as he had brought the liquor which his two guests demanded, the landlord, well skilled in the usages of his own peculiar world, retired from the room, which for the time had no other tenants than those just arrived.

"And so the cove was out, Mingy," said Sam, who had by this time recovered in some degree from his first disappointment; "but what's this you've found out that you think you may work well?"

Mingy took a sip of his brandy-and-water, looked into his glass, and seemed to consider, like one of Homer's heroes, before he began to tell his story. When it began, however, it was not a very long one.

"Why, as far as I can make out, Sam," he replied, at length, "the young man is a-going to be married to a rich lady, a good deal older than hisself."

"D--n him! what's that to me?" asked the ruffian.

"A great deal," answered Mingy Bowes; "for I think it was ten to one your scheme broke down with the young man, while I am quite sure we can make it answer with the old woman."

"Broke down! How the devil should it break down?" asked Sam, with great indignation. "Why, I had nothing to do but to tell him that I'd blow him altogether if he didn't give three or four hundred down."

"But he might think you couldn't, Sam," said Mingy Bowes, in a sly tone. "You may say you would soon have shown him that you could, and that you'd tell him his own real name, and all that you made out from the pocket-book. But then, you see, Sam, it's very much more than probable that the fellow who came after the book has told him by this time that you put it in the fire. Then the young man will lay his calculation this way:--'As this cove has burned the book, he can't prove anything but by his own word. Now, he can't come forward to swear, even if his swearing would be of any good; for if he swears at all, he must swear that he knocked me down and took my pocket-book, and then what's his oath worth? If I give him a penny, he will be sure to come bothering me for more.' That's what he will say, Sam, and devilish right, too." 4 "Not quite so right after all," answered the man; "for if I can't prove nothing myself, I can put those upon the scent as will. He wouldn't like that, Mingy, and I shall just tell him so. If there's anybody can prove that he's the same man who ten years ago was called Henry Hayley, they can hang him--that's all; for the paper that showed who did forge the gentleman's name was burned in that book. Now, take my word for it, Mingy, he won't let it come to that for the sake of a cool hundred or two."

"Do you recollect whose name it was that was forged?" asked Mingy Bowes, fixing his shrewd eyes upon the big man's face.

"To be sure I do," answered the other: "it was Scriven and Co.; and hang me, if the young fellow makes any mouths at it, I'll find out where Scriven and Co. put up, and tell them all about it."

"For heaven's sake, don't do that!" cried Mingy Bowes, with a look of consternation. "It was bad enough burning the pocket-book; but if once you tell, you've given the whip out of your own hands altogether, my man. Let me try it with the old lady first. I think we might manage to get a thousand pound out of her to save her young man, if we can but get her to believe that we can grab him when we like. If you like to leave her to me, Sam, I'll take you a bet I'll screw something out of her."

The ruffian seemed a good deal impressed by the cogency of Mr. Bowes's arguments, especially in regard to the impropriety of suffering his valuable secret to slip from him in any fit of rage.

"No, no; it won't do," he said, "I can see that clear enough, to go and tell Scriven and Co. till I've tried everything else; and as to the old lady, Mingy, I don't care if you try her, but I'll try the young man too; and I say, Mingy--remember, fair play's a jewel, and it's understood I am to have three-quarters of whatever we get, and you one quarter; so no kicking, Master Mingy."

"Honour--honour!" said Mingy, laying his hand upon his heart; "but now let's have something to eat after this brandy-and-water. I dare say the landlord has got some cold roast pork. He generally has."

His pleasant anticipations were fulfilled. The landlord had cold roast pork, and it was speedily placed upon the table before him and his companion, together with a fresh supply of brandy-and-water. Mingy calculated upon discussing all points which wanted further elucidation, over cold pork and mustard; but here he was disappointed, for hardly had each helped himself abundantly when the room was flooded by a stream of the usual guests, who seemed just returned from some successful enterprise, so that any further private conversation was at an end. All sorts of things were called for by the new-comers. Mingy and San were saluted by several, who had some slight acquaintance with them. Beer, gin, brandy, flowed abundantly. Some stood, some sat; all talked together. There was a great deal of swearing, a great deal of laughter, a great deal of abuse. One-half of them seemed to be quarrelling with the other half, though in reality they were only what is called chaffing; but from one especial corner of the room a continual strain of angry words was heard to rise, which went on, with greater and greater vehemence, till at last a blow was struck and returned. Two or three who were near rushed forward, perhaps to see what was going on, perhaps to keep the peace; but somehow the pugnacious spirit seemed to spread. Fists seemed to be flying about very thick; and in the midst of the uproar and confusion, the cause of which nobody appeared clearly to understand, the two men with whom the riot had originated came struggling forward out of their corner, driving back the crowd, knocking over the tables and benches, smashing the glasses, and squeezing flat the pewter ware.

Mingy Bowes did not like the scene at all, although he was often compelled to witness such; for, besides being small and fragile, he was a very peaceable person, and thought force of cunning much superior to force of arm. Besides, he calculated upon having his character compromised, and he soon saw that such was very likely to be the case.

His more pugnacious companion, Sam, who never could resist a row when it was either within sight or hearing, had just started up and rushed into the midst of the affray, exclaiming, "I'll soon settle that," when Mingy Bowes, having raised his eyes to the window, in the vain hope of finding some means of exit, perceived two or three ominous-looking heads gazing in, and at the same time heard the sound of a rattle. He would have given worlds to reach the door, but that was impossible, for the combatants were exactly in the way; and in a minute after his worst anticipations were realised; for, just as the landlord was attempting to restore peace, an overwhelming force of police poured in, and the whole body of vagabonds there assembled, inclusive of Sam and his friend, were marched off to the station-house.

CHAPTER XXVI

There was a fatality about Lady Fleetwood's views and wishes. We see the same often; and foolish people imagine that there is something in the character of the individual which so assuredly makes the schemes of certain persons fail of effect. It is all a mistake. No man has a mind sufficiently capacious. No man has power sufficiently extensive, let his wit, wisdom, judgment, command, be as elevated and as infinite as they may, to grasp and rule the circumstances which surround even the smallest of his plans, the most insignificant of his actions, and say, "This shall succeed." He cannot say with certainty, "I will walk out of that open door."

He may design according to the probabilities which are apparent to him; he may exercise a keen judgment; he may bring long experience to bear upon the subject; he may calculate by all that the keenest and the justest observation has taught him, and he may combine by the powers of a well-regulated and long-exercised reason: but when he has done this, he has done all. The rest belongs to fate--which, in other words, is the will of God. The man who has well and thoughtfully watched the progress of events must know that there is not a straw so small that it may not throw down a giant in his course; and if Napoleon Bonaparte, the pampered child of undeserved success, did really say--which I do not believe--"I propose, and I dispose too," he had used to very little purpose the experience of a life.

Still, it must be admitted that Lady Fleetwood's plans were not always the best calculated: she took too much for granted; she had an enormous number of very frail ladders, with which she proposed to scale the high walls that opposed her, and which always broke down at the very first step she set upon them. In the present instance, however, she was disappointed, not at all by her own fault. She set out to see Mr. Scriven at an hour when, perhaps, during the last six or seven-and-twenty years, he would not have been found absent from his counting-house on any three lawful days. Nevertheless, Mr. Scriven was not there when she arrived in the city. The head clerk knew not where he had gone, nor when he would return, so there was no sending for him, no waiting for him; and all that Lady Fleetwood could do was to leave word that she very much wished to see him, if he could call upon her during the following morning. The head clerk promised to give him the message faithfully, and Lady Fleetwood went out. The next moment, however, she returned again, to say that she should be glad if he could call about eleven; then she returned again to add, that she would thank him to send for her down into the library; and a third time she returned to beg that he would not say to any one she had called to ask for him.

The head clerk knew Lady Fleetwood well, and very readily promised to deliver all her messages; but they did not get very accurately to Mr. Scriven's ears, notwithstanding; and on the following day the excellent lady, having got her niece Maria to go out earlier than usual, and given her servants due directions, sat in the library ready to receive her brother--in vain.

Eleven, a quarter past eleven, went by; and Lady Fleetwood, who was as impatient as a girl of eighteen, tripped lightly up to her own room, proposing to go out and call upon her brother, as he had not attended to her summons. The distance was not great; she knew the exact way he would come; she should either meet him as he came or catch him before he went into the city.

Poor Lady Fleetwood! she was rarely if ever destined to do what she intended to do. The servant opened the door for his mistress to pass out, with his hat and long cane, as was customary in those days, ready to follow. But, lo and behold! upon the step of the door, with hand ready stretched out to seize the knocker, appeared a little, neatly-dressed man, with a shrewd, intelligent countenance. Lady Fleetwood set him down at once for some tradesman, or some tradesman's shopman; and being, as I have shown, very careful and economical, she paused to make inquiries, saying--

"What do you want, my good man?"

"I wanted to speak a few words with Lady Fleetwood," said Mingy Bowes; for he it was, delivered from incarceration.

"My name is Lady Fleetwood," replied the lady, while Mingy took off his hat very reverently; "but you see I am going out just now, and therefore----"

"Ma'am, it's a matter of great importance," said the man, interrupting her: "it would be much better for you to hear what I've got to say at once."

"Well, what is it?" asked the old lady, somewhat impatiently.

"I can't tell you here, ma'am," replied the other. "You'd not like it if I did. If I could say a word to you alone, it would be much better."

"This is very strange," said Lady Fleetwood, beginning to feel some degree of alarm, though curiosity predominated, most decidedly. She looked over the person of Mr. Mingy Bowes with an inquiring glance, but there was nothing very formidable in the little man's appearance. When dressed in his best, as on the present occasion, he was decidedly dapper. Now, nothing that is at all dapper can ever be awful; and therefore, having considered him well for a minute, Lady Fleetwood repeated.

"It is very strange. However, come in here with me. John, stand you near the door, and if my brother comes, show him up-stairs; but don't you go away from the door yourself, for--for I do not know what this person wants."

Thus saying, she walked into the dining-room, and Mr. Mingy Bowes followed, with perfectly well-bred composure.

He shut the door carefully behind him, while Lady Fleetwood seated herself in an armchair; and pointing to another, on the opposite side of the room, in order to keep the table between her and her visiter, begged him to be seated. The worthy gentleman accordingly sat down, brought the inside of his hat over his knees, and bending forward, so as to get his head as far across the table as possible, he said, in a low voice--

"I think, my lady, you're acquainted with a Colonel Middleton: aren't you, my lady?"

"Yes, sir," said Lady Fleetwood, with a look of surprise; "I've the pleasure of knowing him very well."

"I think, my lady," rejoined Mr. Bowes, putting on a cunning and amiable look, "there's like to be a nearer connection--isn't there, my lady?"

Lady Fleetwood's face flushed with surprise and dismay, to find the secret of Maria's engagement to Colonel Middleton already known to such a person as the man before her.

"Good gracious!" she exclaimed, "who told you that? Did Colonel Middleton himself?"

"Oh, dear, no, my lady," replied Mingy Bowes. "I never saw Colonel Middleton in all my life, that I know of."

"Then, in the name of heaven, what do you want?" demanded Lady Fleetwood.

"Why, just a little bit of business, ma'am," answered the dealer in marine stores; "but before I go on, I should like very much to hear whether what I have been told by those who ought to know, about there being such a connection on the carpet, as I may say, is true or not."

Thus pressed, Lady Fleetwood replied, after a good deal of hesitation--

"Why, I believe it is," to which assertion she added a strongly confirmatory nod of the head.

"Very well, my lady," continued Mr. Bowes, as soon as he was satisfied on this point; "then the thing comes to this: you see, that gentleman--that Colonel Middleton--he's quite a gentleman, I believe, and I don't mean to say anything against it; but there's a bit of a secret about him, and that, a secret which might put him in very great danger if it were to be known to every one. Ay, that it might," he continued, seeing the consternation on Lady Fleetwood's face growing deeper and deeper every moment: "why, it might cost him his life, ma'am, and no mistake."

"Really, this is very terrible!" exclaimed the poor old lady, not knowing what to say or what to do.

"Why, it is, indeed," replied Mingy Bowes; "but I dare say it can be managed very easily for a small sum."

"I really do not understand what you mean, sir," said the worthy lady, her thoughts getting more and more into confusion every moment.

"Why, now, I'll explain it all to you in a minute," replied Mr. Bowes, in a tone of kind familiarity. "You see, the case is this, ma'am: this gentleman--this Colonel Middleton--happened by chance the other night to lose his pocket-book. How he lost it is neither here nor there; but a friend of mine, a very respectable young man, found it, and looking in to see whose it could be, he found a whole heap of letters, and papers, and things, which showed him the whole story about this Colonel Middleton, and how, though he's a very nice young man, and all that, his life's in danger in this here country, on account of something that happened ten years ago."

Lady Fleetwood sat confounded, for her mind and her imagination had made great progress during the man's statement. Like a finely-balanced magnetic needle, which has been slightly deranged by some accident, her judgment had wavered about a good deal, but it pointed right at last. First, she came to the conclusion, from the man's speech, that Colonel Middleton was not what he appeared to be, and then that he was certainly Henry Hayley. How to act, what to say, however, she did not know, and all she could utter was--

"Well?--well?"

"Well, as you say, ma'am," rejoined Mr. Mingy Bowes, "the matter, no doubt, will be easily settled; for my friend, who found the book, is quite inclined to be reasonable. He's quite a shy, timid young man, and he asked me to arrange the matter for him. 'You know, Bowes,' he said to me, 'when one has got hold of such a secret as this, it is all fair that he should make something out of it; but I don't want to behave at all unhandsome, so I wish you would go and see what can be done, and I'll content myself with a trifle, Bowes,' he said."

"Is your name Bowes?" asked Lady Fleetwood, who, as I have before remarked, had a terrible habit of darting off at a tangent.

"Yes, ma'am," replied her visiter; "my name is Bowes--Mingy Bowes, at your service."

"It's a very good name," said Lady Fleetwood; "there was a Mr. Bowes I used to know very well, who lived down near Durham. I wonder if you are any relations."

"No, ma'am; none at all," answered Mingy Bowes; "I never had no relations at all."

"Oh, dear, yes; you must have had some relations at some time;" and Lady Fleetwood set hard to work to prove to Mr. Bowes, that at some time or another he must have had some relations, if nothing better than a father and mother--a fact which he did not attempt to controvert, but returned at once, like a man of business, to the more immediate subject of discourse.

Lady Fleetwood's little excursion, however, had done her good. It had suffered her mind to repose and compose itself; and if she made any mistakes now, it was not because she was agitated and confused.

"Well, you see, my lady," continued Mingy Bowes, "I said to the gentleman who found the book, 'Why don't you go yourself?' 'No, no,' says he; 'you go: I only want what's fair, and I'll leave you to judge of that;' so then I said to him, 'What would you think of a thousand pounds?' So then he answered, 'Well, that will do, though it ought to be fifteen hundred.'"

This was coming to the point, Mr. Bowes imagined, and doubted not that Lady Fleetwood would take the matter up at once, as he intended it. He was a little surprised and disappointed, however, when, after he had made a dead stop, and waited for a moment or two, the excellent lady coolly demanded--

"And pray what have I to do with all this? What made you come to me about it?"

Mr. Mingy Bowes, however, was rarely puzzled for an answer; sometimes plunging into the rigmarole, sometimes taking refuge in the most laconic brevity.

"Why, you see, ma'am, we talked that over too," he said. "My friend wished me to go to the colonel at once about it; but I said, 'No, that won't be delicate--if there's any friend we could get to break the matter to him.' 'Well, then,' says he, 'go to Lady Fleetwood--she's the person. You may give her my solemn word of honour, that if I have the thousand pounds I'll not say a single word to nobody; and it's very likely,' says he, 'that she'll never say a word to him about it, but give the money herself, as she's going to marry him.'"

"What! I?" exclaimed Lady Fleetwood, almost with a shriek; "did he mean I was going to marry Colonel Middleton?"

"Yes, my lady," replied Mr. Mingy Bowes, almost as much astonished as she was: "why, you told me so, almost this minute, yourself."

"You impudent person!" exclaimed Lady Fleetwood, angrily. "I should as soon think of marrying you as Colonel Middleton. I am quite old enough to be his mother."

"But what you said about the connection," said Mingy Bowes, with a good deal of perturbation, seeing that he had made one mistake, at least, and not knowing how far it had gone.

"Oh! now I see," exclaimed Lady Fleetwood. "My good friend, you and I have been playing at cross purposes all this time. I have no personal interest in Colonel Middleton whatsoever, though I am told he is going to be married to a relation of mine."

"Then, hang me if I've not wasted my time!" said Mingy Bowes, starting up from the table. But just at that moment a bright thought--one of her own peculiar bright thoughts--came across Lady Fleetwood's mind. "I must not let this man go away altogether disappointed," she said, "for fear he should go and make terrible mischief. I see the whole business as clear as possible now. This Colonel Middleton is poor Henry Hayley, and Maria knows it. That is the secret she would not tell me; and she knows, or thinks, that he can prove himself innocent of the forgery in a few days. Now, if I let this man go away dissatisfied, he may very likely spoil all their plans. I know nothing about it: how should I know? And if Maria had thought fit to tell me all, I might have known how to act; for I'm sure no one was ever more thoroughly convinced that poor Henry Hayley, however much appearances might be against him, never did think of forging my brother's name, than I have always been. As to giving the man a thousand pounds, that is out of the question, for I haven't got it to give; and if Henry is innocent, as I am sure he is, there can be no need of it; but yet, if I send him away disappointed and angry, he may make a fuss, which is always exceedingly unpleasant."

She puzzled herself sorely as to what was best to be done under these perplexing circumstances; but at length a notable scheme presented itself to her mind, for the purpose of gaining time, and suffering the plans of Maria and Henry Hayley to develop themselves undisturbed.

"Early, the day after to-morrow," she thought, "we set out with Lady Anne for the North; and if I tell this man to come here at noon on that day, we shall be gone, Colonel Middleton and all. In the mean time I can consult about it, and, should there be any necessity, leave a note or a message, to give explanations and to make arrangements. The man must see that I cannot decide upon anything at once."

Although thought is very rapid, and though this and a great deal more passed through the mind of Lady Fleetwood in a very few moments, yet the pause was sufficiently long to attract the attention of Mingy Bowes, and make him linger still, in the hope of bringing his negotiation to some more satisfactory conclusion. Although he was terribly tempted to say something more, yet like a wise man he refrained, from a sort of intuitive perception that the weakness of the other party might do something for him which his own strength could not accomplish. He did not walk to the door, however, as his first sudden start up from the table had seemed to promise; and at length he was rewarded by hearing Lady Fleetwood's voice once again.

"I can have very little to do with this business," she said; "but, at the same time, as the gentleman is a very intimate friend, and is likely to be a connection of some members of my family, I have no objection whatever to talk to him upon the subject, and see what he thinks fit to do."

Mingy Bowes was very well disposed to listen to this offer, as, to say truth, he had only come there for the purpose of opening a negotiation, to be carried to greater advantages at a future period. A little bluster, however, he thought, might be as well; and he replied, gruffly--

"Well, ma'am, I hope you'll make haste about it then for we haven't much time to spare, and my friend must do one thing or the other. So, if the gentleman says yes, well; and if he says no, well. We can but go and tell Messrs. Scriven and Co. the whole story after all."

"Dear me!" exclaimed Lady Fleetwood, "you seem to know all the people about here quite well. Mr. Scriven is my brother. However, I shan't be able to see and consult anybody till the day after to-morrow. So, if you like to come here at twelve on that day, you shall have an answer, yes or no."

"That's a long while, ma'am," said Mingy, with a good deal of affected sullenness. "I should think, for that matter, a lady like you might give such a trifle herself, without waiting to consult at all."

"You're very much mistaken, sir," answered Lady Fleetwood, sharply. "In the first place, I am not called upon to give anything, as the gentleman is no connection of mine whatever; in the next place, I do not know whether it would be right to give anything at all; and, in the third, I should not know how much to give. But at all events you have my answer, and can come at twelve o'clock the day after to-morrow, or not, just as you think fit."

"Oh, I'll come," said Mingy Bowes; "but you'd better tell the gentleman, my lady, that if he does not come down handsome, he's done to a dead certainty."

"I don't understand what you mean, sir," said Lady Fleetwood; "but, at all events, I cannot talk any more upon the subject, and therefore shall beg to wish you good morning. Thus saying, she rang the bell sharply, and made a ceremonious curtsey to Mr. Mingy Bowes, saying aloud to the servant who appeared--

"Show that person out, and if he comes at twelve the day after to-morrow, let me see him."

CHAPTER XXVII

"There's a person below inquiring for your excellency," said Colonel Middleton's foreign servant, entering the sitting-room where his master sat writing a note.

"Who is he, Carlini?" asked the young officer, looking up; "is it the same man who was here before?"

"No, sir," replied the servant. "This is a taller, stouter man, dressed somewhat like the other. He says you know him, and that his name is Joshua Brown."

"Oh, show him up--show him up," said Colonel Middleton; "I will see him by all means."

The servant retired, and in a moment or two returned with our good friend the pedlar. But Joshua Brown's face, upon the present occasion, bore an expression which, in the course of their short acquaintance, Colonel Middleton had never seen it assume. It was a sort of hesitating, undecided expression, very different from the frank and easy, though unpresuming, manner which he generally displayed in addressing persons whom he looked upon as his superiors.

Henry remarked it; but at the same time he treated the man exactly as he would otherwise have done, saying--

"Sit down, Brown: I am very glad to see you. Have you brought me any information?"

"A little, sir," replied the pedlar; "but I am sorry to say it is not all good. About the pocket-book----"

"Oh, never mind the pocket-book for the present," said Colonel Middleton; "that is of very little consequence, compared with the certificate."

"I am glad to hear you say so, sir," answered the pedlar: "I hope you may think so still, when I've told you all. As to the certificate, there it is. I thought I should know my way back. I don't forget very easily; and I walked yesterday, straight as a line, to the place where I thought it was to be found. The old clerk's dead, and a dapper young fellow in his place, who found it out in a minute. You owe me half-a-crown, sir, for that."

"A great deal more," said Colonel Middleton, his eyes fixed thoughtfully upon the paper. "St. Mary's, Westfield," he continued, reading aloud: "how far is that from town?"

"About sixteen miles, sir," replied the man. "Is that the gentleman's name you expected to find?"

"Exactly," replied Henry, placing the paper in his writing-desk: "it only confirms what I knew before."

"Humph!" said the pedlar, in a very peculiar tone; but he added something more, and Henry, looking up, said--

"Now for the pocket-book, my good friend."

"Why, I suppose you guess, sir, by this time, that I have not got it," replied the pedlar; "and I am sorry to say we shall never get it now."

"Indeed!" exclaimed Colonel Middleton, in a tone of surprise and disappointment. "How has that happened? Have they destroyed it?"

"They have, sir," said Joshua Brown, "and that in my presence, too;" and he looked in the face of Colonel Middleton with a keen and inquisitive expression, as if seeking to form a judgment, from what he there beheld, regarding some doubtful questions in his own mind.

"That is unpleasant," said Colonel Middleton, in a grave but ordinary, matter-of-fact tone, as if he had lost in the pocket-book the value of a thousand pounds or more.

Now, let the reader remark and remember, that a man's face and manners bear a very different expression when he has lost something very valuable, which he regrets much and would give a great deal to recover, and when something has occurred which generates apprehension. The passions are different, and so are their effects. In one instance they have reference to the past, and in the other reference to the future; and nothing can be more different than the looks of regret and fear.

Now, all that Colonel Middleton felt or seemed to feel was regret.

"Well, tell me how it all happened," he said. "Curious, that they should burn it in your presence, when they had the certainty of getting a considerable sum of money for it."

Joshua Brown set to work to convince him that nothing in the world could be more natural; but he did not altogether succeed.

"I am afraid," said Colonel Middleton, "that these good gentry must have discovered that there was something very important to me in that pocket-book; but why they should burn it I cannot conceive."

It was curious to remark the changes of expression which came over the plain and almost harsh features of the pedlar, during his conversation with Colonel Middleton; and certainly, if the face is in any degree the index of the mind, he underwent more changes of emotion that day than were at all customary with him. A look almost of anxiety now came into his face as he answered--

"I am afraid, sir, that they had found out how important the pocket-book was to you, and had arranged all their plans to make what they call a good job out of it. Nevertheless, I don't think that they were quite clear as to all the little particulars, so that, perhaps, they can't do as much mischief as they would."

Colonel Middleton paused in thought for a moment, and then said, with a grave look--

"As far as I can remember, the contents of that book were quite sufficient to afford them the means of discovering the whole particulars of a transaction long past, which I do not wish to revive. But what could make them destroy the pocket-book I cannot conceive; for the contents must have induced them to believe that its preservation would be much more profitable to them than its destruction."

"I'm afraid, sir," replied the pedlar, frankly, "that I did not altogether manage the matter for you well. You see, sir, I was ignorant of the circumstances. You had told me how much you would give, and I did not like to offer more, especially when the rascal who had got the book tried to exact more by threats."

"By threats, did he?" said Colonel Middleton. "How much did you offer, my good friend?"

"I offered a hundred pounds, sir, as you said; and, to make them think that I had no interest in the matter, I pretended to require something for myself out of the money. There was my mistake, I think."

"Oh, no," replied Henry, with a degree of indifference which surprised the pedlar very much; "I think you did quite right. I would not have given more than a hundred pounds. That was quite enough."

"Then the blackguard must have been making a great mistake," said Joshua Brown, with a relieved look; "for he seemed quite sure that you would give a great deal more, and said there was that in the pocket-book which might hang you or save you."

"And you half believed him, my good friend," replied the young officer, looking at him with a smile, while the colour mounted up in the pedlar's brown cheek. "But if you had considered one moment, Brown, you would have seen that, had that book contained, as the ruffian said, the means of hanging me, he would never have thought of destroying documents that gave him such a power over me. No: to be plain with you, the book did contain full and satisfactory proofs of my innocence of an act once imputed to me. By destroying them the villain did me a great disservice; but, thank God, they are not the only proofs, and those that still exist I trust will be sufficient."

"Well, sir," said Brown, "I am sorry I attended to the man at all; and, if I had but thought a bit, as you say, I must have seen that his conduct and his words were not consistent. However, what made him burn the pocket-book was the sight of a constable walking up and down before the house. The two scoundrels chose to think that I had brought him there, and that as soon as I had got the book I should give them into custody; so away it went into the fire in a minute, and I could not get it out, for they were two to one; and though Master Mingy Bowes is a little one, his comrade is worth two of me at any time."

"So, one is a little man?" said Colonel Middleton, thoughtfully. "Try and describe him to me. Yet, stay a minute," and ringing the bell, he ordered the waiter to send his servant. As soon as Carlini had entered the room, Colonel Middleton said, "Now go on, Mr. Brown. I merely wished my servant to hear your description of this good gentleman. You mark it, Carlini, and let me know whether it seems to be the same person who was here this morning."

The pedlar, who, as I have before shown, was a very minute and accurate observer, proceeded to give a full and particular account of the personal appearance of Mr. Mingy Bowes, while the Italian stood by and listened, bending his head gravely and approvingly, from time to time, as the other proceeded. When at length Joshua Brown paused, Carlini turned to his master, saying--

"The same, sir, exactly;" and then at a sign retired.

"Now then, Brown, who is this person?" demanded Colonel Middleton; "for it seems he is not the person who actually had the pocket-book."

"No, sir; he's the 'fence,'" replied the pedlar; "that's to say, the receiver; and it was at his house I saw the other man, whose name I do not know, any more than that it is Sam."

"Well, this man called here to-day," said Colonel Middleton; "and I suppose the object now is to extort money from me by threats."

"Don't you doubt it, sir," said Joshua Brown. "That's a game which is always playing in London; and those horse-leeches, as soon as once they are fixed, never let go till they have drained every drop of blood out of a man's body. There are many thousands of them in this city who live by nothing else. Many a man they break down in health, as well as in fortune and happiness, and many another they drive to commit suicide."

"Weak and pitiful must their victims be," said Colonel Middleton, somewhat contemptuously; "for none but a mere slave to fear would yield to threats which, he must know, would necessarily go on increasing in virulence."

"I'm not quite sure of that, sir," replied the pedlar. "All men have their weaknesses, and I believe all men have their timid side. It is a part of the trade of such fellows as these to find out where a man is likely to be afraid, and hunt him down upon that. I have known many a very brave man who would have fought anybody or anything, but who could not face an accusation."

Colonel Middleton meditated for a moment or two, and then replied--

"These scoundrels will find themselves very much mistaken, if they fancy that such fears will influence me."

"I think they will, sir," replied the pedlar; "but I would advise you to be careful what you do with them, for I think a cunninger thief was never known than that same Mingy Bowes; and if he cannot manage one way, depend upon it he'll try another."

"Without success," answered Henry. "But now, my good friend, as to you I am considerably indebted for many services, I would fain settle that account before we part, that you may not think me ungrateful."

"Oh, sir, I have no claim to make," replied the pedlar: "I am very glad to have served you, and the loss of time has not been much. I should like, however, to know how this other business goes on, and I should not be sorry to see Master Mingy Bowes myself, and talk to him a bit upon what he's about; for I might give you some sort of hint that would be serviceable."

Henry Hayley seemed to think for a moment over the proposal before he answered; but at length he replied--

"Well, be that as you like. It can do no harm, and might perchance do some good. I suppose that, beyond all doubt, one or both of the two villains will be here ere long again, and if you were to remain at the hotel, and meet them unexpectedly when they come, they might feel not very pleasantly surprised. My servant shall take care of you, if you like to stay. As for myself, I shall away at once to St. Mary's, Westfield."

The pedlar smiled.

"I will tell you what, sir," he said: "you may want me in that business too, before long; and so, when I go away from here, I shall tell your servant where I am to be found when needed."

"I do not think you can be of any more service to me there than you have been already," replied Henry; "but, nevertheless, I shall be very glad of your address."

"We shall see, sir; we shall see," said the pedlar. "Don't think me impertinent; but I know something of almost everything under the sun, and more of this matter than a great many."

"Indeed!" said Henry; "pray tell me how that may be."

"No, no, sir," answered the pedlar; "not just yet. I'll only ask one favour of you, which is, that you will always let me know where you are to be found for the next six weeks, and I'll do the same by you."

Henry laughed, saying--

"Well, my good friend, I will agree to the compact, though it is somewhat unequal.--Carlini," he continued, speaking to his servant, who entered with a note, "take care of this good gentleman, who has been of great service to me lately; and if that person returns who was inquiring: for me this morning, let Mr. Brown deal with him, as he knows something of him."

"Yes, your excellency," replied the valet; "but Lady Anne's servant is waiting for an answer."

Henry unfolded the letter and read.

"I will go directly," he replied. "Send a chaise after me, Carlini, to Lady Anne's. I shall not be home to dinner--most likely not till eight, but certainly by that time. In the mean time, take care of Mr. Brown."

Thus saying, he retired for a moment into his bed-room, returned with his hat and some papers in his hand, and set out at once, leaving his servant and the pedlar together.

CHAPTER XXVIII

Perhaps no two animals upon the face of the earth have fewer points of attraction for each other, in all ordinary circumstances, than a plain English peasant and an Italian valet. When Joshua Brown and Carlo Carlini were left together in the sitting-room of the master of the latter, there was but one single link of sympathy between them, and that a very remote and indirect one. Every Italian, I believe--not from nature, perhaps, but from the circumstances and accidents of his country--has more or less of the pedlar in him. He is always dealing with some kind of wares, religious, political, moral, philosophical, even if they be not commercial in the ordinary sense-- wherein he is very sharp, too. He is always exalting these wares with praise, and magnifying his own information and capabilities; and he is, nine times out often, trying to make you believe that pinchbeck is gold, and that an Italian is an old Roman.

I speak generally, without meaning to say for one moment that there are not many exceptions; but still, between such a man as Joshua Brown and such another as Carlo Carlini, there seemed to be but one tie, namely, the pedlarism which I have mentioned. There were, however, in reality, other and better ties, which they found out after a time; and, strange to say, the most powerful of these was honesty of purpose.

"Will you come down with me, sir, and take a glass of wine?" said Carlo Carlini to the pedlar, well knowing what his master's injunction to take care of his guest implied; "or perhaps you have not dined, sir, and would like something more solid."

There was a certain dignity and grace about the man, nothing abated by his foreign accent and look, which had a good deal of effect upon the pedlar, whose general notions of valets and valetry were not very sublime.

"Really," thought Joshua Brown, "this is quite a grand sort of a man. One would take him for a prince in disguise, if one didn't know better. He seems no way proud, however, but just like his master."

Here his contemplations came to an end, and he replied with a low bow--

"Thank you, sir; I have not dined. As to wine, it's very little of it I get, for there's less of it in our country than in yours, I take it, and not very good either."

"There is plenty of very good wine in England," said Carlini, shaking his head solemnly backwards and forwards; "only very dear, Mr. Brown. But my master, who is a rich man and a liberal one, does not grudge me my glass of wine, knowing that I have been accustomed to it all my life as well as himself; for we both come from countries where there is nothing else but wine to be drunk except water."

"Is not your master an Englishman, then?" asked Mr. Brown.

"No; a Spaniard, to be sure," replied Carlini with a start: "what made you think he was an Englishman?"

"Why, his language, his name, his manner, his look," said Joshua Brown, "all made me feel sure he was an Englishman."

"Oh, as to his language," said Carlini, "he speaks Italian, Spanish, and French, just as well as he does English; and then as to his name, that's his father's name, and he was an Englishman. His manners and appearance may be English, too; but, nevertheless, he has lived with Spaniards all his life, having been brought up as the nephew and heir of Don Balthazar de Xamorça. But come--let us go down, Mr. Brown. You shall have some dinner, and then we will have a quiet glass of wine together, as you call it in England."

Joshua Brown followed his new friend down to a small room on the sunk story, meditating very profoundly as he went. There was something that puzzled him greatly. He could not make the two broken ends of Colonel Middleton's story fit at all, and at last he convinced himself that the servant must have made a mistake. "He cannot have been long in Colonel Middleton's service," he thought; "I will find out how long he has been with him."

In pursuance of this resolution, Mr. Joshua Brown, after having comforted the inner man with some very soft and savoury viands, and as soon as a glass of not bad wine was placed in his hand, looked across to Signor Carlini with a very shrewd expression of countenance, winking his eye over the rich juice of the grape, and saying--

"A very good master, yours, Mr. Carlini, I should think. One does not meet with such every day."

"No, that one doesn't," answered Carlini, heartily. "No one has an easier or a better place than I have."

"I suppose you've had it a long time," said the pedlar, in an inquiring tone.

"About five years," replied Carlini, "but I knew him three or four years before that. Ah, Mr. Brown! one sees strange changes in this world. When first I saw my present master, he brought into my counting-house a draft for twenty thousand dollars, and I paid it as if it had been no sum at all. The next time I saw him, I was a waiter at an inn; and when he paid the bill he gave me a dollar for myself, without knowing me again."

"That is a strange history, indeed," said the pedlar. "How came you to have such a fall, sir?"

"Oh! revolution, revolution!" replied Carlini; "revolution, by which poor men think to better their condition, but which always ends in making them the first sufferers. It was the revolution in the New World that ruined me; but as it only brought me down to the same rank from which I rose, and indeed not quite to that, I have no cause to grumble. Mine's a very strange history altogether."

"It must be so, indeed," answered Joshua Brown: "I should like of all things to hear it. I always like to hear people's histories, Mr. Carlini--not for curiosity's sake only, but because there is always something in them to show us how good God is to all his creatures, and to make us contented with our own lot; and also to hear a real history from a man's own mouth is to me like seeing a picture, especially if there are many ups and downs in it to represent the mountains and the valleys."

"Well," said Carlini, "take another glass of wine, and I'll tell you something of it, for it is worth listening to."

"And so is your master's, too, I should think," rejoined Mr. Brown, whose curiosity was directed more towards the history of Colonel Middleton himself than that of his servant.

"Not half so much as mine," answered Carlini; "for his has been all prosperity from beginning to end, and mine has been continually changing, as you will see."

CARLINI'S STORY

>

"The first thing that I remember was running about in the streets of Naples, a ragged boy, without shoes, stockings, jacket, or hat. I suppose I had a father and mother, if I did but know who they were; but of that they took very good care I should never be informed, and, to tell the truth, I have no great curiosity on the subject. My name was universally admitted by all my companions to be Carlo, which in your language means Charles; and when I was about eight years old, a much bigger Carlo than myself having joined the band of little vagabonds to which I had been attached from infancy, I acquired the name of Carlini, which in your language means Little Charles. Till I was nine years old, where I slept, how I was clothed, and what I fed upon, were three miracles, not at all less curious than the liquefying of the blood of St. Januarius; but at nine years old my first change of fortune took place. The two Carlos in the same troop could not agree. Carloni thrashed Carlini, and Carlini immediately deserted. I remember very well, the second day after I had quitted my band, standing, with a faint heart and a feeling of exceeding solitude, before the shop of a barber, who, I found afterwards, had just lost his apprentice by fever. My back was turned to the shop, for I little thought that any good would come out of it for me, when I suddenly found something touch me, and turning round I saw a basin stretched out through one of the small open panes, while the voice of the barber exclaimed, 'Here, boy, run and fill that with fresh water at the fountain.' I need not say how gladly I ran, and filling the basin I brought it back; but, to make sure of some reward, I did not give it in at the window again, but carried it in at once by the door. There I found a stout, tall man, just shaved, to whom the barber with great respect handed the basin of water, into which his face and eyes were immediately plunged. Seeing the barber very zealous to show every attention in putting his customer's dress to rights, I thought I could not do better than ape his civility, by going down upon my knees and brushing the dust off the stranger's shoes with the ragged sleeve of my shirt, which certainly was not much more dirty when I had done than when I began. However, my attention pleased the stranger, and he gave me a piece of copper of the value of a penny. It was the first money I recollect ever having had in my life, and I fancied it would have bought half of Naples. The same barber's shop became a sort of treasury to me. For two months I continued to plant myself before the window, either lying on the stones in the sun and pitching little bits of bones to and fro, or standing and watching to see if I could be of service. The shaver was a kind old man enough, and did not forget me. From time to time he would throw any little job in my way, such as holding a gentleman's horse, brushing his shoes, or carrying a message; and when there was nothing of this kind to be done and I looked very hungry, he would give me two or three handfuls of *pasta*, or a lump of bread. He found me active, diligent, and faithful; and, contriving to live, principally upon his charity, and to save all the little sums which I got, I was at length enabled to purchase some articles of decent dress, and appear at my old post with a much more respectable exterior. The old man was delighted, not only with the change in my appearance, but with the self-command which had furnished me with the means; and, taking me into his shop, he asked me a great number of questions about myself, preparatory, as it turned out, to engaging me in his service. He could not have found one whose mind was more open to instruction than mine. It was like a bag, ready to be filled, for there was actually nothing in it. I could neither read, write, nor calculate. I knew no tongue but the jargon of the *lazzaroni*; and I didn't even know my own name--which was, perhaps, no great evil after all. Well, at the end of three days from that time I was fully installed as barber's boy. I learnt to shave, to dress hair, to sharpen razors, to make perfumes and cosmetics, to bleed, and on an occasion to draw a tooth. All this my master taught me gratis, he having my services at the same rate. Nevertheless, he fed me, and though neither very delicately nor very abundantly, the food was so superior to any I had ever had before, that in despite of a lean nature I grew fat. The little gratuities I received from time to time furnished the small stock of clothes I wanted, and enabled me to get some instruction in matters which did not come within the sphere of my worthy master. I taught myself to read; I learned to write; I acquired a competent knowledge of arithmetic. I picked up a little French amongst the people at the port; for a Frenchman thinks that every one is bound to speak his language, and that he is bound to speak none but his own. I learned a great deal of Spanish, without any difficulty at all; and at the end of five or six years I flattered myself that I was a very accomplished barber. My old master was now beginning to be stricken in years, and much less active than he had been; so that at length we divided the work between us, he remaining at home, to shave and dress those who came to the shop, and I going out to the more courtly customers, who required attendance at their own houses. The business still remained very good; and I cannot help flattering myself that I had some share in keeping it up and increasing it. My old master seemed so far sensible that this was the case as spontaneously to offer me one-fourth of the receipts, for which I was most grateful, although I had three-fourths of the labour. I had a sincere affection for the old man, for he was the only father I had ever known; but he was not destined to remain long with me. I was not nineteen when the old man died. His relations claimed his shop and his implements, even to an old, worn-out shaving-brush, which would have rubbed the skin off a rhinoceros; but the business remained with me. I took the shop next door, stocked it, and beautified it, with the money I had saved, and was shaving, powdering, and pomatuming from morning till night. Most unluckily, a Spanish grandee, who passed a winter in Naples, placed his head and chin under the immediate superintendence of Carlo Carlini. I was soon taken into great favour; and, as this nobleman was about to return to his own country in the spring, he exerted all his eloquence to persuade me that my talents were quite thrown away in the city of Naples.

Madrid, he said--Madrid was the only fitting theatre for the display of my genius. It was the Elysium of barbers, where I was certain to find myself completely happy.

"He offered even to take me in his own suite, defraying all my expenses by the way; and he promised that I should shave every friend he had in the world, and powder and perfume all his mistresses, who were many. In an evil hour I yielded. Off we set for Madrid, and very well did my Spanish patron keep his word till we reached that city. I fared sumptuously along the road; and, the system of favouritism being universal in Spain, I was considered his highness's favourite, and treated accordingly; but, unfortunately, after our arrival in Madrid, wars and rumours of wars broke out very soon, and the duke was prevented from carrying out his views in my favour by the strong hand of death, which seized him just as I had established myself in the Spanish capital, and was obtaining a little of the promised custom. My days of prosperity were now at an end. My little capital gradually diminished; my patients did not increase; my stock of smart clothing wore out, and six pairs of while silk stockings--absolute necessaries to a Spanish barber--were reduced to three. As the very utmost neatness and cleanliness are required in that country, you may easily suppose that my silk stockings made frequent visits to the wash-tub; and my *lavandera*, who was the most punctual of women, had the strictest injunctions to return that indispensable part of my apparel at a certain hour on the day after she had received them. She was, be it remarked, a very pretty woman, and had captivated the heart of one of the royal guard, whom I not unfrequently saw at her house, and found him an exceedingly amiable, good-humoured young man. One morning, as my good fortune would have it, my silk stockings did not return. The preceding day had been rainy; and, although it does not often rain in Madrid, yet when it does there is plenty of mud in the streets. A prince and a duke were waiting to be shaved; and after waiting in a state of acute anguish for half-an-hour, I was obliged to sally forth in my dirty stockings. I lost two of my best customers; but fortune and misfortune are always intimately mingled in the affairs of this life. What I thought my ruin was the dawn of my most prosperous day. I rushed down to the *lavandera*. I scolded like a madman about my silk stockings. I demanded that she should instantly produce them. She could not do so, and I accused her of having pawned them. Thereupon she burst into tears, and acknowledged that she had lent them to Manuel G----y, the royal guard, who was to appear that day on duty at the queen's dinner. A mysterious hint had been given him, by an old lady of the court, to dress himself as handsomely as possible, intimating that his future success in life might depend very much upon his personal appearance. As soon as I learned that they had been lent to G----y, for whom

I had a real regard, my wrath evaporated. 'Let him keep them as long as he likes,' I said, 'and tell him, when my silk stockings have made his fortune, I hope he will make mine; but in the mean time, my good girl, though I have only two pairs left, you must contrive that I have a clean pair each day.' The girl afterwards assured me that she had given him my message, and that G----y said he would not forget me. But what was my surprise, not a week after, to hear that he had received a lieutenant's commission in his corps!--and then, with the most marvellous rapidity, came the intelligence of his being a captain, colonel, general, a grandee of Spain, a prince, a prime minister. During all this time I heard nothing of him, and I concluded----"[1]

"Here is that person again, sir, inquiring for the colonel," said the inferior waiter, whose peculiar task it was to attend upon the 'gentlemen's gentlemen.'

"Send him in; send him in," said Carlini, stopping in his story. "You, Mr. Brown, have to deal with him, you know."

The moment after, the door was again opened, and Mr. Mingy Bowes entered, his face suddenly assuming a look of extreme surprise on perceiving the person of the pedlar before him.

CHAPTER XXIX

It was a fine summer afternoon, when a carriage-and-four--a thing by no means uncommon in those days, though as rare as a bustard at present--dashed into the small town of Belford, at that sort of pace which shows well-paid postboys, if not well-fed horses. I find, by a statistical account of that part of Europe which lies between the Aln and the Tweed, and which in former days was frequently subjected to inundation from the great northern reservoir of mosstroopers, that, under the beneficial influence of a more civilized state of society, the small town of Belford had increased and prospered, till, on the day of which I am writing, it was computed to contain no less than one hundred and seventy-three-houses, and nine hundred and forty-seven inhabitants. The greater proportion of the inhabitants possessed no stockings, and very few shoes. I say the greater proportion; for it had been an immemorial privilege of that portion of the citizens of Belford which had not yet attained the age of fourteen, to wear upon their legs and feet the covering with which nature had provided them, and none else. Some of the higher classes, with that neglect of their rights which they often show, had suffered the privilege above mentioned to fall into desuetude. The children of the clergyman always, and of the Presbyterian minister sometimes, wore shoes and stockings. So also did those of the doctor, the lawyer, the two principal shopkeepers, and the landlord of the inn; but all, or very nearly all, the rest adhered to their right, with strong determination; and after the carriage ran a multitude of boys and girls, whose feet had never been tightened and spoiled by compression in cotton or leather. It was not, indeed, that the climate of Belford was particularly like that of Eden, which dispensed, as we all know, with the necessity of any great superfluity of garments. On the contrary, the north wind visited it fresh from home; so much so as to have generated a despair of cultivation, which after efforts have proved to be very unreasonable. Andrew Fairservice's crop of early nettles gave, in those days, a very fair specimen of the sort of horticulture practised at Belford; and, not very many years before the period of my tale, an old woman used to walk through the town with a basket on her arm, crying, at different seasons of the year, the following rare and in many instances unknown fruits, the names of which, be it remarked, I give in her own peculiar dialect, though I cannot convey to the reader any idea of the tone, something between a song and a squeal, in which she offered her produce to the public. "Hips, haws, slees, and bummle-berriers; cherries, ripe grosiers, nipes (turnips) sweet as honey!" were the sounds she uttered, and in them consisted very nearly the whole catalogue of fruit brought to market at Belford.

Notwithstanding all this, the town contained a very good and respectable inn, where at one time were no fewer than sixteen pair of post-horses, as at that period it was generally made the first stage northward from Alnwick--rather a long one, it is true, being charged fifteen miles, but many persons preferred it to Charlton.

Bells must certainly have acted a very important part in the history of former times, as they rival the most distinguished personages and the most splendid objects in the traditionary veneration of innkeepers; and neither harts nor hinds, black bulls nor red lions, dolphins nor fountains, bushes nor cocks, great generals nor gold and silver crosses, can boast a greater number of votaries--nay, not even the crown, the sun, or the moon. The image of a large bell, then, painted in blue, and lipped and rimmed with gold, served as a sign to the principal inn at Belford; and underneath its auspicious bulk drew up the carriage on the day I have mentioned.

"Horses on, sir?" asked the ostler, running out, and addressing one of the smart-looking, six-feet-and-a-half-high footmen at the back of the carriage.

The man made no reply; and mine host of the "Bell," seeing his ostler repulsed, advanced to the door of the vehicle (while the two servants got slowly down), and demanded, in a most deferential tone, if he should put on four more quadrupeds to hurry on the handsome post-chariot towards the north. He looked in, too, with some degree of curiosity; but, whatever he expected to see, nothing was perceived within--excepting always a lady's-maid--but a very pretty-looking girl, apparently twenty or one-and-twenty years of age, with a gay, bright, sparkling countenance, and a crimson velvet four-cornered Polish cap, bound with rich sable fur and ornamented with a tassel.

"No, I thank you," said the lady; "be so good as to open the door. I shall stay here to-night. Let me see what rooms you have got. Where's your wife?--I suppose you have got a wife."

The innkeeper informed her that her supposition was correct, and shouted very loudly for Mrs. Gunnel, while the carriage door was opened, and the servants assisted their mistress to alight.

"Had not I better go and see the rooms, my lady?" said the maid, more for the purpose of announcing her mistress's rank to the numerous bystanders than with the hope of saving trouble, for she well knew the lady would see the rooms herself; and with all reverence Mrs. Gunnel led the way for the unexpected guest, up the stairs, through the corridors, and into the different rooms, while Mr. Gunnel followed, descanting upon the excellence of the beds and the comfortableness of the accommodation.

"This room for myself, that little one for my maid, the large one beyond for a lady who will be here in an hour or two, and all the rest of the house for my servants," said the young lady, in a very princessly way. "Oh! this is the sitting room, I suppose," she continued, entering an adjoining chamber, and sitting down in a great armchair, covered with white dimity. "I wish it had not been so long, and a little broader, Mr. Gunnel," she continued, eyeing the host from head to foot.

Mr. Gunnel certainly did think her the oddest lady he had ever seen; but it is wonderful what an impression oddity, joined with wealth and station, makes upon the great mass of human beings. As I have said elsewhere, strength of character is the most commanding of all things; and it is probably the latent conviction, that a man must have strength of character to be odd, which renders oddity so impressive.

"Very sorry, my lady," replied Mr. Gunnel, with the most profound respect, "but it is the only one we have got, except a very little one at the end of the passage and the commercial room down-stairs."

"It will do, it will do, Mr. Gunnel," said his pretty guest, playing with a gold pencil-case, which she had got chained round her wrist.

"Now tell me something about yourself. How old are you, Mr. Gunnel?"

"Lord, my lady!" exclaimed the landlady, "if Gunnel tells you that, he will tell you more than ever he would tell me in his life."

"Well, I don't want to embarrass him," answered the young lady, with a smile, "but I'll put another question, which shall do as well. How long have you been in this house, Mr. Gunnel?"

"Oh, as to that, my lady," replied the landlord, "I have kept the 'Bell' three-and-twenty years, come next twelfth of October; but times are sadly altered since I first set up."

"Oh, yes," replied the young lady; "they are always altering. But now, Mr. Gunnel, have fresh horses put to my carriage, to take me first to Detchton-Grieve, and then to Belford Castle--to wait and bring me back. Have dinner ready for me and the lady, who will be here in an hour or two, at half-past seven; and in the mean time collect whatever you have got in the shape of upholsterers and cabinet-makers, and let them know that I shall have some orders to give them to-night."

"Bless my heart!" said the landlord, "if I don't think it is Lady Anne Mellent! We shall be so happy to see somebody at the old place again. Why, my lady, it is just ten years and three or four months since your ladyship's grandfather died, and not a soul has lived in the castle since but old Mrs. Grimes and her two daughters."

"I know that, Mr. Gunnel," said Lady Anne, rather gravely; "but I doubt not that you will soon see it inhabited again, during a part of every year. Now order the horses, and have the things ready, as I have directed. My servants will put the place in order here while I am away."

In about ten minutes Lady Anne was once more in her carriage, now disencumbered of its packages, and, with one man-servant behind, was rolling away towards the place which she had mentioned, called Detchton-Grieve. At the distance of about three miles from Belford the carriage left the high-road, and turned into a narrow country lane, about half-a-mile up which appeared a pair of iron gates. Passing through these, Lady Anne saw before her a very broad, smooth, hard road, well kept, but displaying no trace of cart or carriage wheels. This road descended a gentle slope of park meadow, and then plunged in between two dark masses of old gigantic trees, through which it continued its course for nearly half-a-mile. When it issued forth again, another wide open space of hill turf was spread out to the eye, dotted here and there with clumps of large trees; and at a little distance in advance rose a mansion, by no means equal in appearance to that which the extent and beauty of the park would have led one to expect. It was a brick-built house of ancient date, very irregular in its form, with gables here and gables there, and large stacks of chimneys placed in the most extraordinary positions. The windows were small, but innumerable; and at one side of the house rose a tall, square brick tower, very much like the tower of an old Kentish church, in great part covered with ivy.

Up to the front of this building dashed the carriage at a great rate, in the midst of a scene so still and solitary, that, but for the house, one might have fancied the place a desert. The sound of a great deep-toned bell soon brought to the door an old-fashioned man-servant, with a powdered head, silk stockings, and lace garters round his knees; and in answer to Lady Anne's question, if Mr. Hargrave was at home, he replied in the affirmative. The young lady then alighted, and followed the man through a stone hall, past some ten or twelve doors, to a small one, which gave her admission into a little study half filled with books and old pieces of armour--the servant merely saying, as he threw open the door, "A lady wishes to speak with you, sir."

The personage to whom this was addressed deserves some description, for I do not think there is one of the genus left. He was, at the time of which I speak, of the age of sixty-eight or sixty-nine, so that his youthful memories must have referred to a period considerably anterior to the close of the last century. Whether it was a clinging to these youthful memories or a peculiar taste of his own which guided the old gentleman in his choice of dress, I do not well know, but certainly it was very different from anything that Lady Anne was accustomed to see. His coat, besides its unusual cut, was distinguished by the material, which was of uncut velvet, and by the colour, which was of a yellowish green. His hair was powdered, and drawn back into a large mass behind, which was bound round and round with a black ribbon. Two large, well-powdered curls appeared above the ears, but the forehead was left completely bare. His waistcoat was of white satin, richly embroidered; and his knee-breeches as well as his stockings were of black silk, while in the shoes and at the knees were richly-cut gold buckles. In short, he looked like a man who had been laid up in a bandbox for fifty years, and taken out as he had been put in, ready dressed for a ceremony.

No glance of recognition beamed in Mr. Hargrave's eyes as they lighted on Lady Anne, and he scanned her curiously through the spectacles with which his face was usually adorned. As the reader knows, his visiter was no great respecter of ceremonies, ever acting or speaking upon the first impulse, and taking it for granted that whatever she said or did was sure to please, partly from a conviction of her own sincerity of purpose, and partly from having always found that her oddities were very successful with the general world, and more especially with elderly gentlemen. Lady Anne, therefore, took a quiet and somewhat long survey of the person before her, till he, not very well satisfied with the scrutiny, demanded, in a gay and lively tone, a touch of the paternal mingling with a sort of light *badinage*, which was the mode in his early years--

"Well, little girl, what do you want with me? Here is your humble servant, at your disposal in every respect but love or matrimony."

Lady Anne understood him in a moment, and seating herself in the armchair opposite, she replied--

"Were it a case of either love or matrimony, I probably should not seek you, Mr. Hargrave; but the case is quite the reverse. I have come to see you upon business of some importance. You do not know me, but I know you;

and what I desire you to do is to get into the carriage with me, and take a drive of twelve or thirteen miles: nay, more--you must do it, whether you like it or not."

The old gentleman looked at her with an expression of amusement, and then said--

"Do you know I have not dined?"

"Nor I," answered Lady Anne; "though I wonder at you, for the men who wore velvet coats always dined at three or four o'clock; but you know, my good friend, that ladies always have their own way, and so I intend you to dine with me to-day. Wherever I am, I always arrange everything for everybody, according to my own plan; and though people are frightened at the beginning, they are always very well pleased in the end, I assure you. So now tell your servant to bring you your roquelaure and your hat--is it round or cocked?"

"Do you know, you are very saucy," said Mr. Hargrave, in reply. "Where do you intend to take me? What do you intend to do with me?"

"I shall tell you nothing about it," replied Lady Anne: "I intend it to be a clear case of abduction, in order that an action may lie, and be decided upon the merits. I will say and do nothing which can raise the slightest technical quibble, but direct you immediately to get your hat and cloak, and if you do not make haste I shall give you sufficient cause to swear that you go in personal fear."

"That will depend upon the nature of the vehicle," rejoined Mr. Hargrave, who seemed perfectly to enter into her humour. "Is it an open carriage or a shut? Is it a dog-cart, a gig, a phaeton, a landau, a coach, or a post-chaise?"

"Neither the one nor the other," replied Lady Anne: "it is my own travelling carriage; and you shall be at full liberty to drop into the corner and fall sound asleep, or to talk to me the whole way, as your courtesy may decide."

"But how far? how far?" exclaimed the other; "that at least you can tell me."

"Why, as far as Milford Castle," answered Lady Anne with a gay and good-humoured smile; "but we shall be back in plenty of time for dinner, so you shall not lose the meal which no Englishman can go without."

"Milford Castle!" exclaimed the old gentleman. "What! Lady Anne! Come and give me a kiss."

"No--you must come for it," replied Lady Anne. "Five years ago I would have given you one, but you did not come to London to seek it, and now you must take it if you want it."

The old gentleman rose from his seat, and with a light and elastic step crossed over and kissed her cheek. "My dear child," he said, "I am really glad to see you. I was a friend of your father and your grandfather, and a sort of connecting, harmonising link between them, being some fifteen years younger than the one and some eighteen years older than the other. I was the mediator when they quarrelled, which, I am sorry to say, was not unfrequently; and although I am, and always have been, a man of the old, while your father was a man of the new world, I believe he had as much confidence in me as in any man, and a great regard for me likewise. He wanted me to be one of your guardians; but inveterate habit, my dear child, ties me to this seclusion; and I knew I must either neglect duties which it would be criminal to neglect, or break through rules which at my age it would be no longer graceful to abandon. The spirit and essence of Englishism, if I may so call it--that which marks our distinctive character, that which renders all we do so progressive, and at the same time so permanent--is the system, or principle, or habit--call it what you will--of small communities acting together, in some things separate from, in some things dependent upon, the great mass of the nation. Our municipal institutions are but better organised types of that which exists even in country districts, where, round a few men of property and intelligence, whose duty it is to maintain order and peace, and as far as in them lies to spread happiness and prosperity around them, are collected a multitude of persons of various grades of wealth and intellect, who have a right to look to those above them for advice, assistance, protection, and support. Now, no man, placed by God's will in the position of a country gentleman, has any title to abstract himself from the mass amidst which God's will has planted him, and whom his influence, his custom, his example, his advice, may benefit. I felt that I ought not to undertake the discharge of any duties incompatible with those which heaven had assigned me, and therefore I declined to be one of your guardians, although I must ever retain a sincere affection for all your family."

"I am sure you do, Mr. Hargrave," replied Lady Anne; "and therefore, in my impudent way, I came boldly to see you. I think you were quite right not to undertake the guardianship of a giddy girl, when you had duties so much more important to perform; and I only wish all our country gentlemen entertained such views of their duties. However, I must now seriously ask you to drive over with me to Milford Castle, as I have something to do there which may require the presence of a magistrate."

"I am ready this moment," said Mr. Hargrave, ringing the bell.

"Well, then, countermand your dinner," said Lady Anne, "for I am determined that you shall dine with me."

"I have not dined out of my own house for six or seven years," replied the old gentleman, "and it will be a long way back at night from Milford."

"Oh! that is not where you are going to dine at all," answered his fair visiter. "I have taken the whole inn at Belford; and, although an inn dinner may not afford many attractions, yet, let me tell you, my own cook will be down in an hour, and depend upon it he will not be content to see chickens roasted to a rag, and raw beefsteaks set before his mistress, even in Northumberland. To-morrow I shall take up my head-quarters at Milford. Upholsterers, carpenters, cabinet-makers, will be as busy as ants till three or four o'clock, and about five I expect a great number of people down, who will make the old place cheerful again, after the long reign of solitude and dulness. I will therefore take no denial, for I have a great deal to talk to you about, before these people come down; and I have nobody with me now but my good old governess, whose presence will be no impediment."

Mr. Hargrave's hat and cloak were then brought, and after having, much to the astonishment of the servants, announced that he should not be home to dinner, he followed Lady Anne to her carriage, and set out for Milford Castle.

As they drove along, the worthy old man was somewhat anxious to ascertain what Lady Anne could want with a magistrate at Milford; but his fair companion seemed to be in one of her wayward moods, and would give him no information whatsoever. The moment that he found she was reluctant, with the true courtesy of the old school he changed the conversation; and, notwithstanding a great degree of oddity, and very peculiar views on many points, proved anything but an unpleasant companion. He spoke of the county in which he lived, the changes which had taken place in it during his own lifetime, the progress which it was making, and the improvements which still might be made.

Lady Anne was a good deal surprised at the liberality and extent of view which he displayed, in conjunction with his partial adherence to old habits, even in insignificant things; but Mr. Hargrave was a man of a singular mind--one of the few who judged of all things solely upon their merits. He did not think that anything was worthy of being retained because it was old, or adopted because it was new; and he accidentally explained to his fair companion his views of all those alterations which people in general are too apt to look upon as progress, when very often the direct reverse is the case.

"That which *is*, my dear lady," he said, "has always one great, direct advantage over that which *may be*--certainty. Long experience of anything existing has shown mankind all its benefits and all its evils; but, besides this, there is an indirect advantage in retaining that which is--namely, that it has adjusted itself to the things by which it is surrounded; and there is a direct disadvantage in change--namely, that one can never calculate what derangements of all relations may take place from any alteration of even one small part in the complicated machine of any state or society. Nevertheless, I hold that when it has been shown that many things have altered, with or against our will, general alterations must take place to readjust the relations which have been changed; and also that when, in favour of any change that is proposed, there can be shown a reasonable probability of advantages sufficient to counterbalance the inherent evils of change, we are fully justified in taking the forward step, and may hope to reap benefit by it. If we change for the mere sake of change, we are Frenchmen. If we remain stationary from mere attachment to old customs, we are Chinese. I think the English nation is better than either--neither like youth, greedy of novelty, nor like age, tenacious of prejudices; but like maturity, guided by reason, either in tranquillity or action."

The saucy girl beside him laughed.

"I have no doubt it's all very true," she said; "but I am not a politician, and really do not much care, my dear sir, whether we stand still, go forward, or go backward. It will make no more difference to me than whether you wear a velvet coat or a cloth one."

Mr. Hargrave now laughed in turn, and looking down at his sleeve, he said--

"This is velvet, is it? Well, my dear, I did not know it. I have remarked, indeed, occasionally, that my dress is somewhat different from that of other people, and now I will tell you how it has happened. A great number of years ago--some fifty, I dare say--I was just as full of fancies and vanities as you or any other young person of the present time, and perhaps was a little bit of a beau, and might affect some singularity of apparel. I can talk of the matter very coolly now, for age has extinguished passions, and softened even bitter memories. I met with a very painful disappointment. A young lady to whom I was sincerely attached, and who, I believe, was sincerely attached to me, died in a moment, on the very morning appointed for our marriage. I bore the bereavement, I am sorry to say, neither as a Christian nor as a philosopher; and I soon found that, if I went on mingling with the world, as the idle and light portion of society is generally called, I should lose what little senses I still possessed. I determined to make a great struggle, and a great struggle it was. I applied myself to the most important subjects I could find out or devise. I studied divinity, I visited the poor, I visited hospitals, I visited prisons. For ten years I would never suffer my mind to rest, even for one moment, upon what I considered a trifle; and my directions about my clothes, whenever I wanted anything new, were to make them exactly like those which I was wearing. At the end of these ten years, when my object was gained and my mind had somewhat recovered its tone, I did perceive that my dress was somewhat old-fashioned; but I thought it was not worth while to change, and I have never given any fresh directions since. Thus, at any time during the last fifty years, you would have seen me in a coat of exactly the same cut, of the same colour, and of the same texture. Four times in the year it comes in regularly, is placed upon the clotheshorse in my room, and I put it on, often without knowing that it is new, unless it pinches me under the arms. I certainly shall not change it now, because nobody would know me if I did; for one's face forms so small a part of one's personal appearance, that old Hargrave's coat and waistcoat are much more easily recognised, I fancy, than old Hargrave's eyes and nose would be."

"You're a dear old man," said Lady Anne; "and I love you, velvet coat and all."

"I am glad to hear it," replied Mr. Hargrave, "for I have loved all your family, my dear, very truly."

In such sort of conversation passed the time, till at length a pair of great gates appeared, and the carriage rolled through into the park.

"This is Milford Castle, my dear," said Mr. Hargrave, "and I wish you joy on your first visit to the home of your ancestors. I am afraid, however, you will find some marks of neglect, at all events on the outside of the house; for a master's eye is like sunshine, and his absence like storm. The one produces all that is bright and beautiful, the other is sure to leave some traces of devastation."

"It is very bare," said Lady Anne, looking out of the windows of the carriage; "and how stunted all the trees look, leaning to one side as if they had a great inclination to lay themselves down and die!"

"The prevailing wind," said Mr. Hargrave, "which morally and physically bends all things to its influence, has beaten upon them for so many years that they may well have yielded to it; but you will find the scenery improve as we go on. We are merely at the outskirts of the park. Do you not see that deep wood filling up the hollow? That is the first grove; this is merely a sort of wild chase we are passing through."

Rolling on, the scenery did, as he said, improve greatly, and from time to time Lady Anne Mellent caught a distant glimpse of an old grey mansion, seen and lost alternately, as the carriage mounted or descended the manifold slopes of the park. At the end of a quarter of an hour, a thick, wild wood cut-off the view of all other objects; and in a minute or two more the two postboys put their horses into a quick canter, up a steep rise, and Lady Anne suddenly found herself at the gates of her father's house. It may well be supposed that she gazed at it with interest, and the aspect pleased her well; for it was a large, stately, dignified-looking mansion, with manifold doors and windows, and a broad terrace before it. But on looking into the park she was somewhat mortified to see that several hundred acres of ground around the house had been lightly enclosed; and, though various herds of deer could be perceived in the distance, nothing but sheep, rather too numerous for the pasture allotted to them, appeared in the foreground.

The servant rang the bell sharply, and having opened the carriage door by Lady Anne's directions, aided his mistress to descend. She was very grave; and indeed it is hardly possible to look up at an old building, especially when it has been the habitation of our own immediate ancestors, without feeling impressed with a chilling sense of the vanity of human hopes, desires, and efforts. An old mansion is a sort of cemetery of dead aspirations, every stone a memento of joys and wishes passed away.

Of course, nobody answered the bell; but a shepherd lad was seen running towards the back of the house, and Lady Anne forbade the footman to ring again. After a minute or two of expectation, a large-made, bustling woman opened the great doors, with a face glowing like the rising sun, and hands which she continued to wipe in her apron, evidently in a very pulpy and washerwoman-like state. She looked at the handsome carriage, the arms it bore, the livery of the servant, and concluded she had the heiress before her; but still, not to seem too ready, she demanded--

"What's your will, sir? What do you wish, ma'am."

"I wish to go over the house, my good lady," replied Lady Anne. "I suppose you are Mrs. Grimes. I am Lady Anne Mellent, your mistress."

"Dear me, my lady! I wish you had let me know you were coming," said the good woman. "Why, there's nothing in order for your ladyship, and we have nobody to help to put things right. Lord, sir! I didn't know you," she continued, turning to Lady Anne's companion: "you are Mr. Hargrave, I believe."

"I wonder you did not know me," replied the old gentleman drily, looking down at the sleeve of his velvet coat: "I am always ticketed; but do not keep Lady Anne standing here."

"Do not make yourself uneasy, Mrs. Grimes," said Lady Anne. "I have not come to stay to-day; but I shall walk over the whole house to judge what is necessary to be done. Be so good as to show me the way. Come after me, Matthews."

Mrs. Grimes was evidently taken very much by surprise, and by no means prepared to receive the lady of the house; for, to say the truth, she had converted the servants' hall into a wash-house, and was actually engaged in washing and ironing for her own and the steward's family.

While her two nieces and two country girls, in consequence of the first hint of the shepherd lad, were busily engaged in effacing as far as possible the traces of their occupation, Mrs. Grimes led the young lady into the large, old-fashioned hall, on the left of the entrance, and made great ado to open the windows. The assistance of the man-servant, however, rendered the process shorter than she desired; and Lady Anne stood in the midst, gazing round at the old pictures upon the walls, the stately black oak chairs, and the enormous mantel-piece, with its Cupids, and columns, and baskets of fruit, all carved in white marble.

"Where does that door lead to?" demanded Lady Anne.

"To the great drawing-room, my lady," replied Mrs. Grimes, with a low curtsey; "and beyond that is the little drawing-room, and then the great dining-room. On the other side of the entrance hall are the library, and the breakfast-room, and the little library."

"There is a small dressing-room," said Lady Anne Mellent, "adjoining the bed-room in which my father slept when he was here. Do you know which that is?"

"Oh, yes, my lady," replied Mrs. Grimes: "it's the dressing-room that has what we call the sealed cabinet in it; for there is a great piece of parchment nailed across the doors, with seals over the nails."

"Exactly," said Lady Anne. "Take my servant with you, open the windows of that room, and then come back to show me the way."

As soon as the woman and the footman had retired, Lady Anne took a letter from her pocket, and placed it in Mr. Hargrave's hand, saying very gravely--

"You have wondered, I dare say, my dear sir, why I brought you hither. Read that letter, which my poor father left to be given to me after his death. You will therein see that it may be needful that I should have some one with me to witness the fact of my opening this cabinet, and to certify what are the contents that I find in it. I could apply to no one so well as to a magistrate, an old friend of my father's and my grandfather's, and one universally respected."

Mr. Hargrave took the letter, which had evidently been written some years, and looked at the back, which bore the following words: "To be delivered to my daughter, Lady Anne Mellent, when she attains the age of twenty, or previous to her marriage, if she should marry before attaining that age. It is my wish that she should read it when alone."

The old gentleman then opened it, and read it near the window, pausing every now and then to consider the contents; and while he was doing so Mrs. Grimes re-entered the room, saying, "The windows are open, my lady."

"Well, wait without for a minute or two," said Lady Anne, and then turned her eyes again to the face of Mr. Hargrave, who continued to read. When he had done he folded up the letter again, and returned it, saying--

"Part of the facts mentioned in that letter, my dear, I suspected long ago, from various circumstances which came to my knowledge; but as I suppose there is no chance of your title being disputed, I think your precaution in bringing an old gentleman with you was unnecessary."

"I wished to take every reasonable precaution," replied his fair companion with a smile; "and as, to tell you the truth, my dear sir, another person may be very much affected by my acts, I thought it but right to be sure of what I was doing."

"Oh, ho!" said Mr. Hargrave, laughing; "then I am afraid I have no chance for this fair hand."

"You are too late in the field," answered Lady Anne, gaily; "but come--let us to the cabinet."

"Stay--I must have pen and ink first," said Mr. Hargrave; but pen and ink were not very easily procured at Milford Castle, for Mrs. Grimes was not of an epistolary turn, and her accounts were kept upon a slate. One of her nieces, however, supplied the deficiency; and ascending the long, broad oaken staircase, Lady Anne and Mr. Hargrave followed the housekeeper to a small dressing-room adjoining the principal bed-rooms.

I would not be the man over whose heart a feeling of sad and solemn interest does not steal when for the first time he enters a chamber once tenanted by a friend departed; ay, though long years may have passed since the remembered form darkened the sunshine on the floor. With him, if there be such a man, affections must be written in water, or the heart be unsusceptible of love. Such was not the case with Lady Anne Mellent, nor with her old companion; and they both paused in the midst of the room, and thought for a time of those whom they could never see more.

The old man's tears were dried up, but he saw a drop gathering in Lady Anne's eyes, and laying his hand tenderly upon hers he said, "Come, my dear," and led her towards the large old ebony cabinet which stood between the windows.

Across the two folding-doors, just above the lock, was a broad strip of parchment, sealed on either side with the arms of the Earls of Milford: and upon the parchment was written, "To be opened only by my daughter.-- Milford;" for the late earl, though he died at Harley Lodge, had felt, when last he visited Milford, that the sand in the hour-glass was for him waning fast.

Lady Anne approached the cabinet, and with her own hand removed the parchment. She then with a small key, which had remained, ever since her father's death, attached to her watch-chain, opened the doors, while Mr. Hargrave beckoned up Mrs. Grimes and the footman, saying--

"Come a little nearer, and bear witness that I place my name upon every paper found in this cabinet."

Only one packet, however, was found therein. Most of the drawers were totally empty; but at length, in a small drawer fitted up with ink-glasses and pen-cases, a bundle of four or five papers was found, which Sir. Hargrave untied, and without looking at the contents of any, placed his signature upon each document, certifying that it had been found by Lady Anne Mellent in his presence, in a certain cabinet referred to in a letter from Frederick Earl of Milford, in her possession, and that the cabinet had not been previously opened since it had been sealed by the late earl.

This being completed, Lady Anne begged her old companion to keep possession of the papers, at least till they arrived at the inn; and then once more closing the cabinet, she left the room.

Her spirits seemed to rise, now that the task was over, and she went on gaily and lightly from chamber to chamber, causing all the windows to be thrown wide open, commenting upon everything she saw, and asking a multitude of questions, to all of which Mrs. Grimes had not very satisfactory answers ready.

When she had gone over the whole house, somewhat to the amusement and somewhat to the fatigue of good Mr. Hargrave, she sat herself down in one of the great, richly-gilt armchairs, which stood in the principal drawing-room, and exclaimed laughingly--

"Now, like Alexander Selkirk, 'I am monarch of all I survey;' but like him, too, my dear sir, I lack subjects sadly. Send some one for the steward, Mrs. Grimes; and, to guard against all the many contingencies, some of which are always happening in the country, if the steward should not be at home, let his son come up; if he has no son, or his son be out, let his wife come; if no wife or son be found, let a daughter, a nephew, a niece, an uncle, a cousin, or some relation of some kind; and especially let each, all, or every of them come directly, for I have an infinity of orders to give; the spirit of hurry is upon me; and, let the whole inhabitants of the manor and all their horses work as hard as they will, they will have great difficulty in doing what I intend to have done, within the time I shall allow. Now, my dear Mrs. Grimes, don't stand and stare, but send for the steward, as I tell you. You, Matthews, go and see what is wanting, as far as you can judge, in the butler's, cook's, and housekeeper's departments. I know there is plenty of wine in the cellar, and I can see from the window that there is mutton at the door."

These last words were addressed to Mr. Hargrave with a slightly sarcastic smile; and she then added, laughing--

"I intend to sleep here to-morrow night with all my household."

Mr. Hargrave shook his head, saying--

"I scarcely think you will find that possible, considering that not a single bed in the whole house has been slept in for many years."

"Do you pretend to believe, sir," asked Lady Anne, gravely, "that anything is impossible when a lady wills it? Let me tell you, it shall be done. I will make the gamekeepers into house-maids, the shepherds into scullions, the steward into an upholsterer, and the labourers of the land into kitchen-maids, laundry-maids, dairy-maids, and housekeepers. Do you suppose that I, who never was contradicted in my life, will be so on my first visit to my own castle? But, to tell you the truth, my dear Mr. Hargrave, I trust more to a whole regiment of servants of mine, who are coming down from London, and to two tumbrels of London ammunition, than to all the auxiliaries of Northumberland."

Thus she gaily went on till the steward appeared in haste, with that half-dogged, half-plausible look which a man puts on when he is suddenly brought into the presence of authority, which may demand an account not very easy to be rendered.

He bowed low to Lady Anne, and even lower to Mr. Hargrave; but Lady Anne attacked him at once about the sheep.

"Whose sheep are those, Mr. Blunt?" she demanded, "and how came they to be where they are?"

"Why, you see, my lady," said the steward, evading the real point of her question, "the rest of the park is reserved for the deer, and I thought your ladyship would not like it to be meddled with."

But Lady Anne was not to be put off; and she demanded,

"But how come they to be in the park at all, Mr. Blunt? I thought the whole of the park was reserved for deer."

"Why, so it used to be, my lady," answered the steward; "but you see, my lady, I just thought it would be clean waste of good feed not to have a few sheep in."

"And how long has this been carried on?" demanded Lady Anne.

"Why, I can't just say, my lady," replied the steward, "not having the books handy."

"And to whom do they belong?" demanded Lady Anne.

"Why, for that matter, they may be your ladyship's, if you like," said the steward; "they are not that dear, of the money."

Lady Anne burst into a violent fit of laughter at the man's pertinacious evasions--so gay, so light-hearted, so good-humoured, that, joined with the shrewd glance of her eye, it quite upset good Mr. Hargrave's gravity, and utterly confounded the steward, who clearly perceived, with no very pleasant feeling, that she saw through him to the very backbone.

Waving her hand to stop any further explanations, she said--

"Very well, Mr. Blunt; very well. I have not the least doubt that they are very excellent sheep, and that you have very excellent reasons for everything; but I think they are out of place in my park, and therefore, I must beg that you will have every one of them removed before noon to-morrow; the whole of the fences which you have planted taken away, and every vestige removed which your woolly tenants may have left behind. The ground must also be rolled with a large roller. I should desire also to have the carriage-drive, from the side both of Belford and Wooler, rolled likewise, the branches which overhang the road trimmed away to the full height of the top of a carriage, and some gravel put down in those deep ruts at the bottom of the valleys, between this and the great gates. Moreover, you will be so good as to send up all the poultry, eggs, and butter which are available, and direct the gamekeepers to bring up all the trout they can catch. They must also shoot a buck, and see for a leveret or two. Of course the poultry-yard is well stocked, as the farm makes such a large item in the accounts. All that I have mentioned must be done before to-morrow night, as I am about to take up my residence here to-morrow, and expect friends during that evening or the morning after, who will stay with me for some days. The park paling on each side of the gate, too, must be mended, and a new lock put upon the gates themselves."

"Heaven preserve us, my lady!" exclaimed Mr. Blunt; "it will be quite impossible to get all this done before to-morrow night."

"I am very sorry to hear it," replied Lady Anne, "for it must be done, and somebody must be found to do it. So, if you cannot accomplish it, I must----"

"Oh, I didn't say I couldn't accomplish it, my lady; only it'll be desperate hard work, and there is hardly time."

"I am very sorry to hear that too," replied Lady Anne, "for there will be at least forty other things for you to do in the course of the morning, and they must all be done too. You will have the goodness to collect all the workpeople in my employment here at the castle, by one o'clock. I have a note of how many they consist of; and, moreover, I should like to have all the active men in the neighbourhood, of whatever professions they may be, here at the castle to help the others. That is all for the present. I will give further directions to-morrow. Stay, Mr. Blunt: you have, of course, guinea-fowls at the farm, and young ducks?"

But no guinea-fowls had Mr. Blunt; and young ducks, according to his account, were never to be had in that part of Northumberland before St. Somebody's fair, the name of which he mentioned, but I forget.

Lady Anne shook her head.

"Guinea-fowls must be found," she said, "and you must make some young ducks, if you haven't got them. Plovers' eggs, of course--you have plenty of plovers' eggs."

Mr. Blunt looked aghast, but he did not like absolutely to deny the fact, and therefore replied--

"They have some over at Wooler, my lady, but they don't come down here."

"Then send over to Wooler for all they have got," said Lady Anne; and with these orders she dismissed him.

"Now, Mrs. Grimes," she said, turning to that good lady, who had been standing by in a state of great consternation, "you will have the goodness to leave all the windows open till sunset, to spread out all the beds upon the floors of the rooms, to brush the dust off all these hangings, chairs, and pictures; to have all that green removed from the steps, to make the cobwebs disappear in different directions, to have large fires lighted in every bed-room and in the principal sitting-rooms, and to let me see the house in complete order when I arrive to-morrow. Now, Mr. Hargrave," she continued, "I have tired out your patience; let us drive back to Belford; and you, Matthews, stay here, and see that all is done as I have directed. You know what I want."

"Yes, my lady," replied the man; and hurrying forward he opened the door of the carriage.

As soon as she and her old companion were seated, Lady Anne leaned back on the cushions and laughed.

"I have given them enough to do, I think," she said; "am not I an excellent housekeeper and woman of business, Mr. Hargrave? I was only afraid of making some mistake, and asking for some bird or beast in June that does not come to England till November."

"I am afraid," said Mr. Hargrave, "that they will never be able to fulfil all your orders in the time; but to give them was a very fair punishment for the neglect--perhaps I might use a stronger word--which they have shown."

"It is the only punishment I shall ever inflict," replied Lady Anne; "for, as you say, if masters and mistresses choose to neglect their own affairs, how can they expect that others will take care of them? But now listen, for I have got a long story to tell you, which, with all the questions you intend to ask, and all the answers I intend to give, will just occupy one hour and a half, and by that time we shall be at Belford."

CHAPTER XXX

In the mean time----

It is curious to begin a new chapter with such words as, "In the mean time." But yet, dear reader, they are the most comprehensive, and nearly the most important, in any language. They comprise the present infinity, all except one small point, and even that they affect in all its consequences. The man who is an actor in the great world's drama performs his solitary deed; but all the results of that deed are modified by what is doing *in the mean time*. The man who is a recorder of other men's actions chronicles what is done by one or another; but still, to judge, even in the least, of the essence and the bearings and the consequences of the deeds recorded, we must ask, what was doing *in the mean time?* A stone rolled out of its place, a casual and thoughtless jest, the sport of a child, a grain of sand wafted by the wind, *in the mean time*, may overset all that we are labouring to perform, frustrate our best devised schemes, render fruitless our most skilfully performed actions.

Do you doubt it, reader? Listen, then. I will take one of the assertions I have made, and work it out. There was a rich merchant who had an only daughter. He laboured for twenty years to make her a great heiress. His hopes and his happiness were all built upon her. His efforts were all for her, nor were they unwisely directed. He cultivated her mind. He improved her understanding. He enlarged her heart. He looked round for some one who was to make the happiness of her who was his happiness. He was difficult in his choice, careful in his examination, scrupulous in his judgment. With rare good fortune, he found what he sought--a man, noble but not proud, good but not rigid, gentle but not weak: one, moreover, who sought her for herself, not for her wealth; and, to crown all, one whom she could love. The merchant was very happy. No difficulties arose. The marriage-day was appointed; the settlements were drawn up, and he and the bridegroom went to read them over together. They were all that either desired, and the father shook hands with his future son-in-law, expressing his perfect satisfaction. *In the mean time*, at the very moment when their hands were clasped in each other, a little boy of eight years old, an orphan nephew of the merchant, lighted a piece of paper at the fire in the drawing-room. The paper burnt his fingers, and he let it fall. It dropped upon his clothes; they caught fire, and he screamed. His cries brought his fair cousin rushing from the adjoining room. She caught him in her arms, endeavouring to stifle the flame; her own apparel took fire; and before night the merchant was childless. Let no man ever calculate upon success, for he never can tell what is doing *in the mean time.*

In the mean time, while Lady Anne Mellent was acting as we have seen in the most remote part of Northumberland, two series of operations were going forward in London, with which it is necessary the reader should be acquainted; but, like the long-eared animal between the two bundles of hay, I am sorely puzzled which to go on with first. We left Lady Fleetwood just ready to go out, after having dismissed Mr. Mingy Bowes. We left Mr. Mingy Bowes just entering the room where Carlo Carlini and the pedlar sat, with a look of surprise upon his countenance.

Which would the reader like to go on with? Let us toss up. If the luck should be against the reader's inclination, he has nothing to do but invert the order of this and the following chapter. Now, then--heads or tails? Lady Fleetwood wins the day!

After Mingy Bowes had taken his departure, the excellent lady sat for a moment or two to recover breath and composure; for both were in a somewhat exhausted state, at the end of her conversation with the respectable person who had just left her. She then rose, rang the bell, and walked out, taking her way direct towards the house of Mr. Scriven. As she went, indeed, she became a good deal agitated. She had previously made up her mind to act most diplomatically with her brother, had arranged all her plans, was fully convinced that she comprehended every particular of Maria's situation, and saw through all her secrets; but her conversation with Mr. Mingy Bowes had shaken and confused all her thoughts, views, and purposes, so that she could lay her hand upon nothing; and when she did find the skein of thought, it was so tangled and twisted that she could not unravel it for the life of her.

In these circumstances it would have been only wise to have gone back quietly to her own house, and left matters exactly as they were, without meddling with them at all: but, as I have shown, the demon of activity was upon her, and spurred her on to help her friends and relations, against their will. So, forward she was carried upon her way, by the power of the locomotive within, till she reached Mr. Scriven's door, and John rapped loud and strong. Then, indeed, she would have given her ears to have got away, or to have found that her brother was out.

No such good fortune awaited her. The door was opened almost immediately; Mr. Scriven was at home, and she was shown up to his drawing-room. He had got three printed papers before him, the London "Gazette," the "Shipping List," and another, I don't know what, besides a little scrap of white paper, not bigger than my hand--for Mr. Scriven was very careful of his paper--on which he was jotting down various cabalistic signs and a number of figures, which nobody in Europe could have made anything of but himself. The result did not seem satisfactory to him, however, for his face was certainly gloomy; and, pointing with the butt-end of his pencil to a chair, he uttered the laconic and incomplete sentence, "In a minute," and then went on with his calculations again.

Lady Fleetwood sat down; and perhaps no worse mode of torture could have been devised by Mr. Scriven than that of making her wait in silence; for she did not employ the interval calmly and orderly, in thinking what she had best do, but suffered *pros* and *cons*, and the recollections of everything that had taken place between Maria and herself, and Mr. Bowes and herself, and all the deductions she had formerly drawn, and all the doubts which had since sprung up, and a great many other considerations besides, to settle down upon her like a swarm of bees, and sting her till she was half mad with the irritation.

Her mind was in a very swollen and inflamed state when Mr. Scriven stopped, folded up the paper, and put it in his waistcoat pocket, drew in the nose of his pencil, like the head of a tortoise into its shell, and then, looking straight at Lady Fleetwood, said--

"Well, Margaret, what do you want? I could not come at eleven, for, as you see, I had something else to do; but I suppose your business is important, or you would not hunt me down here."

His uncivil speech gave Lady Fleetwood an opportunity of escape, if she had had wit enough to avail herself of it: and indeed she did make an effort, though it was not a very successful one.

"Oh, I don't want to disturb you at all," she said; "I did not know you were particularly engaged."

Had she stopped there, it would have been all very well; for her brother, in his dry, unpleasant way, was just about to say that he *was* particularly engaged, and the matter might have dropped. But Lady Fleetwood was a terrible person for standing upon the defensive. She did not at all like the very insinuation of trifling; and she added, unluckily--

"Of course, what I wanted to say was important, or I should not have asked you to come, and should not have come here."

"Well, what is it?" asked Mr. Scriven. "I suppose you have got into some important scrape, and want me to get you out of it."

"Not at all," answered Lady Fleetwood, with an indignant air: "I wished merely to speak with you, not about myself, but about Maria and Colonel Middleton."

"Oh!" said Mr. Scriven, not well pleased at the collocation of his niece's name with that of an object of antipathy; "pray, what has Maria to do with Colonel Middleton, or Colonel Middleton with Maria?"

Now, his bitter, sneering way at times roused even Lady Fleetwood into something like resistance. But, unfortunately, Mr. Scriven knew that such was the case, and knew that in her fits of indignation his sister would tell him all he wanted to hear, more plainly, straightforwardly, and concisely, than she would under any other circumstances--that she was thrown off her guard, in short. He therefore occasionally irritated her upon calculation, for Mr. Scriven was a great calculator. In the present instance, the way in which he put the question, more than the question itself, induced her to reply--

"Now, my dear brother, if you're inclined to hear patiently and act reasonably, I will go on; for I came here with the purpose of persuading you not to struggle against what you cannot resist, but to let Maria seek her own happiness in her own----"

"Now, my dear sister," answered Mr. Scriven, in a somewhat mocking tone, "I am inclined to hear patiently if the story is told briefly, and to act reasonably however it is told; for I think you ought to know that I always act upon reason, and that reason is my sole guide. Thank God, I have neither imagination, nor caprice, nor fine feelings, nor delicate sentiments, nor any of the trash with which your very tender and extremely sensitive people befool themselves. Reason is the only guide I ever applied to, and I don't think she is likely to leave me now. As to letting Maria seek her own happiness in her own way, I have no means of preventing her. If she is going to make a fool of herself, I shall tell her so; and having told her once, I have done my duty, and there the matter ends. She is of age. She can do what she pleases; and I have only to do the best that I can to prevent anything she does from affecting her more injuriously than it otherwise might. Now, then, our ground is clear; what's the matter?"

Lady Fleetwood hesitated, but it was too late to retreat.

"Why," she said--and be it remarked, that whenever woman makes use of the little word "why," as an expletive, she knows she is coming on difficult ground--"Why, I cannot help seeing--that is to say, fancying--that is to say, believing--that Maria has a partiality for Colonel Middleton," said Lady Fleetwood; and during her stammering enunciation of this proposition Mr. Scriven sat provokingly silent and quiet. He did not help her even by a look.

"What makes you think so?" he inquired laconically.

"Oh, many things," answered his sister, taking courage a little.

"Many things!" rejoined Mr. Scriven, "that is the refuge of the destitute. Let me hear one or two of these things."

"Why, you know, my dear brother, one judges from what one sees," said Lady Fleetwood; "women's eyes are sharp in such matters."

Mr. Scriven was well-nigh tempted to condemn women's eyes in the vernacular; but he never swore, or used imprecations of any kind; and therefore he asked, simply--

"But what have the sharp eyes seen?"

"I have seen them talking together, you know, and all that," answered his sister.

"So have I," answered the merchant; "and I have seen her and half-a-dozen young men talking, and all that."

"Well, but then her looks and her manner," said Lady Fleetwood, driven to the wall; "and, besides, I have had some conversation with her upon the subject."

"And she told you that she intended to marry him?" demanded Mr. Scriven; "is not that the plain truth?"

"No, she did not in so many words say that," was the reply; "but she did not deny it, certainly."

Mr. Scriven got up and walked across the room three or four times--not fast, be it remarked--not with the slightest agitation of word, look, or manner; but calmly, considerately, as if he were thinking of the Royal Exchange. He asked himself if that was all his sister had come to tell him--if it was likely she should come upon such an errand. But he knew her well, and was not unaware of her peculiar talent for increasing difficulties by trying to smooth them away. He saw it was likely in her, though unlikely in any one else.

"Well, I suppose, before she does such a thing," he replied at length, "we shall hear something more of this Colonel Middleton. He is wonderfully like Henry Hayley; but the evidence of everything but one's own senses is the other way."

"And if he were Henry Hayley, my dear brother," said Lady Fleetwood, wonderfully revived and encouraged by the progress which from his calm tone she had made. "I am quite sure you would not be disposed to persecute the young man. I, for one, feel quite sure he did not commit the forgery. If it was any one, it was his father, for Henry could have no need for such a sum of money, and we all know poor Mr. Hayley had, for you told me yourself that he was given to gambling."

A new light broke upon Mr. Scriven. His sister did know more than she had said. There was a secret trembling on her lips; he saw that, or at least imagined it; and he knew that to frighten her would drive it back again at once. His course was determined in a moment.

"Very true," he said, thoughtfully; "that never struck me before. Hayley was capable of anything--he was a notorious gambler. What you say is very likely, Margaret; and if that be the case, far from persecuting the young gentleman, I would--but no matter for that--persecuting is quite out of the question. The matter has been over so many years, you know, that it may almost be said to be forgotten. However, that has nothing to do with the business; for, as I said just now, though very like poor Henry Hayley, it is evident that Colonel Middleton cannot be the same person: all the proofs are against it, and you and I must have committed a blunder in thinking so even for a moment."

"I don't know that," said Lady Fleetwood, with a very sagacious air: "I have still my doubts, brother."

"Pooh! pooh!" cried Mr. Scriven. "I made inquiries of the young count and countess. It cannot be: you are quite mistaken, depend upon it."

"Do not be too sure," replied his sister. "Something very strange happened to me this very day; and I cannot help thinking that some bad people have got hold of the secret, and intend to extract money from the poor young man. Now, I know that, if you did discover it, you would never make use of it for any bad purpose;" and she looked up in her brother's face with the most appealing look in the world.

"Most assuredly I would not," replied Mr. Scriven, solemnly; and he meant it too, for to have hanged Henry Hayley he would have looked upon as a highly meritorious act. "But what is this that has happened to you, Margaret? I am afraid you are making one of your mistakes."

The words, "one of your mistakes," were very galling: and Lady Fleetwood hastened to prove that she was making no mistake at all, by telling her brother all that had taken place between her and Mr. Mingy Bowes.

Mr. Scriven listened with profound attention; but his mind was carrying on two processes at once. He was weighing every syllable his sister uttered, to judge whether her tale could leave any doubt whatever of the identity of Colonel Middleton with Henry Hayley; and he was arranging and preparing his own plan of action, to be ready to reply accordingly when she had done. Long before her story was concluded, Mr. Scriven had made up his mind. Not a doubt remained. Henry Hayley was alive, in England, within his grasp; and that grasp was a fell one, which did not easily let go. But although he had now extracted all he wanted from Lady Fleetwood, yet he had a strong conviction that she was even more likely to spoil his schemes than those of any other person, if he allowed her to get the least glimpse of his game, and therefore he replied--

"Indeed, Margaret, this seems something like the truth: and now we must think what can best be done, under such dangerous and difficult circumstances. I would not, if I were you, say a word to the poor young man of what I had discovered. It would only alarm him to no purpose. Nor, indeed, would I have any more dealings with that rascal who called. Ladies are not fit to meet such men, and indeed it is dangerous----"

"Oh, I told him to come at twelve the day after to-morrow, on purpose," replied Lady Fleetwood, "because then I and Maria will both be gone into the north, to this party of Lady Anne's; so he will find no one but old Mrs. Hickson and the maids. As to telling Colonel Middleton, I shall not have any opportunity for three or four days. He is going down too; but you see it would not, of course, be proper for Maria and him to travel together, so we shall first meet at Milford Castle."

"Very improper, indeed," said Mr. Scriven, musing. "Pray, Margaret, where is this man to be found who called upon you this morning?"

"Dear me! how should I know?" replied Lady Fleetwood: "of course I did not ask him."

"I do not see the *of course*," said her dry brother, "and indeed it would have been much better to ask him; for, you see, it is in some degree endangering your young friend. However, I will be at your house when the man comes the day after to-morrow, will see him and settle all with him, so as to ensure that nothing goes amiss."

Now, Lady Fleetwood knew her brother to be very clever at settling all matters of business; but in this case Mr. Mingy Bowes had specifically demanded the sum of one thousand pounds; and it was not within possibility for any one who knew Mr. Scriven well to believe that he would pay a thousand pounds on any account, if he could help it. She therefore said, in a somewhat timid tone--

"But the money, my dear brother--what is to be done about the money which these men demand? I do not see how it can be got, without telling Colonel Middleton what they say."

"Leave it all to me," said Mr. Scriven, somewhat impatiently. "Do not say a word to Colonel Middleton, for it would only fill him, and Maria too, with anxiety; and it is very likely, after all, that no money will be needed. The very act of attempting to extort money by threats of accusation is punishable by transportation; and the good gentlemen will not like the prospect of that, when it is clearly stated to them. Leave it to me, Margaret, I say; and now I must go to the city."

Lady Fleetwood, in accordance with this last hint, left him, and bent her steps back towards her own house. At first she walked joyously and well satisfied, as if she had performed a great feat; but gradually, as a doubt stole in as to whether her brother was the best person to whom she could have revealed secrets affecting Henry Hayley, her self-satisfaction began to sink considerably, and she asked herself, what use might Mr. Scriven make of the information if he chose?

It is one of the unpleasant consequences of such a character as Mr. Scriven's, that even those who, from the ties of blood or old intimacy, feel that sort of negative regard which springs less from esteem and affection than from mere habit, always rely on them imperfectly. The indiscreet, in their paroxysms of loquacity, may give them their secrets; the timid, in order to disarm their opposition or win their assistance, may furnish them with dangerous information; but both, as soon as it is done, doubt the prudence of the act, and wait in trembling uncertainty for the result.

It occurs also, nine times out of ten, with persons of the disposition and character of Lady Fleetwood, that they are discreet at the wrong moment; the angel visits of discretion come at times when they are unserviceable; and so poor Lady Fleetwood found it. She had told her brother what she had better have left untold; but after having done so, she did not dare inform more trustworthy people of the fact, lest she should draw down blame upon her own indiscretion; and she resolved to let things take their course, especially as Maria and Colonel Middleton would both be at a distance from London, so that some time must pass before they heard indirectly of what she had thought fit to do. Indeed, she rather hurried all the preparations for their departure from London, for fear anything should force an explanation before they went; and very glad she was when she and her niece, safely packed up in the carriage, had passed the first turnpike on the great north road.

CHAPTER XXXI

It one could really be a spectator, a mere spectator, of what is passing in the world around us, without taking part in the events, or sharing in the passions and the actual performance on the stage; if we could sit ourselves down, as it were, in a private box of the world's great theatre, and quietly look on at the piece which is playing, no more moved than is absolutely implied by sympathy with our fellow-creatures, what a curious, what an amusing, what an interesting spectacle would life present! But we never, in this fashion, see the whole of the play. Sooner or later we jump up on the stage and take a part in the acting, and are inclined, all throughout, to do so, like a child or a savage, or Don Quixote at the puppet-show.

From time to time, indeed, we do see a detached scene or two as spectators, and then most exceedingly entertaining it is. Such was the case with Carlo Carlini, as he sat reclining with dignified ease in an old-fashioned leathern chair, with a long, comfortable, sloping back, looking alternately at the two faces of Joshua Brown, the pedlar, and Mr. Mingy Bowes, when they met, so unexpectedly to the latter. Carlini, as the reader is aware, was totally unacquainted with the peculiar circumstances in which the two now encountered each other; and therefore the expression of their countenances had all the advantage of mystery. Joshua Brown sat gazing upon the new-comer with a look of old Roman sternness, which was not lost upon Mr. Bowes. The expression of the latter was full of surprise, joined with a considerable portion of apprehension; for his first idea was that the pedlar was there for the purpose of handing him over to a police-officer and bearing testimony against him. Now, knowing himself assailable upon many points, Mr. Bowes was by no means fond of police-offices the investigations at which are sometimes carried a good deal farther than is either agreeable or convenient to persons of his profession. The first effect, therefore, of the apparition of the pedlar was surprise; the second was fear; but surprise was of course over in an instant, being the most evanescent of all things; and fear was soon banished likewise by reliance on his own skill, and on the arms which he believed were in his hands.

"Good evening, Mr. Bowes," said the pedlar, who was the first to speak; "I did not expect to meet you here to-day, when I came in just now. Don't you think it may be a little dangerous both for you and for your friend Sam to show yourselves in London, so soon after what took place down near Frimley?"

"I don't know why it should," said Mingy Bowes, with the most innocent air in the world: "I have only come to speak to the colonel upon the little business you know of."

"What colonel?" demanded Joshua Brown, speaking civilly, and motioning Mr. Bowes to a seat; for it was his object to make the "fence," as he was called, say all he had to say, and lay open his game as far as his discretion would permit him.

They were both men of the world, however; and Master Mingy, having had a great deal of very delicate work to do in his lifetime, was not a little cautious. He thought, indeed, that there could be no great harm in answering the question as nakedly as it was put; and he consequently replied--

"Why, Colonel Middleton, to be sure."

"Oh, Colonel Middleton!" said the pedlar; "I suppose I have no business to ask what you want with Colonel Middleton."

"I should think not," said Mingy Bowes.

"Well, at all events, Colonel Middleton is out," said Carlini: "he won't be home from the country till it is late, and as soon as he does come home he's going out again."

"Ha!" said Mr. Bowes, who was fast getting over his apprehensions: "nevertheless, I must have a word or two with him, sir, and that as soon as possible."

"You'll find that difficult," replied Carlini, "unless you tell me what your business is; for he will not see any one whom he does not know, without inquiring what he wants."

"Then he may find he's got into the wrong box," said the "fence," in rather a menacing tone.

"'Box?'" said Carlini; "what does he mean by 'box?'"

"He means what he does not understand himself," said the pedlar, leaning his two hands upon the table, and slowly and deliberately rising from his seat, as if he were somewhat stiff and weary. He then took a step or two towards the door, with a heavy, unconcerned air.

Mr. Mingy Bowes did not at first remark the proceeding; but, as Joshua Brown got between him and the way out, he felt a little nervous, which nervousness was greatly increased when he saw the pedlar put his hand upon the key in the lock.

"What are you going to do?" he exclaimed, starting up; "I don't choose to be locked in."

"Sit down, Mr. Bowes," said Joshua Brown, in a tone very quiet, but very stern; and at the same moment he turned the key in the lock, drew it out, and put it in his pocket. He then walked back to his seat, in the same sort of stiff, heavy manner.

There was something very impressive in that sort of semi-limp; and Mr. Bowes sat himself down again, and began playing with the buttons at the knees of his drab breeches, apparently to pass the time while waiting for an explanation.

Before he gave one, however, Joshua Brown poured himself out half-a-glass of wine, and took a sip or two, without the least hurry in the world; but at length he said--

"Now, Mingy Bowes, I dare say you want to hear why I have locked the door. It's only because I've got a word or two to say to you, which might, perhaps, make you bolt before you had heard the whole, and that would not suit me. You're a dealer in marine stores, I take it?"

"Well, I know that," said Mingy Bowes; "all the world knows that."

"Good!" said Joshua Brown; "and you keep a thieves' bank, and receive stolen goods, and run a little tobacco, and come and go between gentlemen 'on the lay' and those who take the goods up to London. There--don't interrupt me, for all the world knows that, too. Many a gold thimble, and many a silver one too, you've helped off the shelf in your day: that I know as well as you, and can prove it too when I like. But there's one thing I desire very much to hear--that's to say, what is just now behind that long iron door in your back parlour?"

This was thrown out at random, simply to create apprehension; for Joshua Brown had not the slightest idea that within that cupboard was to be found anything but stolen goods. It had even more effect than he expected, for Mr. Bowes turned as white as a sheet, thinking, not unnaturally, that some of the most treasured secrets of his dwelling had been by some strange chance discovered. Still, however, caution was uppermost, and he sat as mute as a fish.

"However, that's not the question now," said Joshua Brown; "what I want to ask is, what are you up to just now, Mr. Bowes?"

"I don't see what that is to you," said the worthy whom he addressed. "I mind my business, you mind yours."

This was the sort of timid boldness of a cat in a corner, but Joshua Brown was not all moved thereby.

"It's a great deal to me," he answered; "for the case is this, Mr. Bowes: I and another gentleman, a friend of mine, were robbed the other night, in the lane just beyond Knight's-hill. Some of the goods you got and sent up to London; some you didn't get." (Mr. Bowes gave a start, for this was touching the reputation of subordinates.) "Now, I and the other gentleman are in the same basket; and I'm resolved that I'll either have the information I want or the goods back again--all of them--or that you and Sam and the other three shall go across the water to Botany, even if nothing worse comes of it."

Mr. Mingy Bowes paused and considered for a single instant, and he determined that, in the first instance at least, he would try the dogged vein; for, to know nothing of anybody or anything is very often a rogue's first resource.

"I don't know anything about what you mean by 'Sam and the other three,'" he replied: "you must be joking, I think; and as to myself, I should like to hear what you intend to do; for you can't hurt me, I take it."

"That's easily told," answered Joshua Brown, coolly. "I intend, if you do not tell me what you're up to, to call for an officer, give you in charge, and tell the police that, if they choose to send down a gentleman in plain clothes to your place, and put out the gentleman you've left there, they'll soon get plenty of evidence of your trade, and catch the whole gang of you. I dare say a sergeant of the force can carry on your business for a week or a fortnight quite as well as you can."

This was certainly a very frightful announcement to Mr. Mingy Bowes. It was a stratagem he had never dreamed of, and his heart sank a good deal; but yet, for two or three minutes, he could not tell how to enter into the sort of compromise which seemed to be offered to him, without acknowledging the justice of the charges against him. An excuse for yielding without confessing seemed wanting, but at length he found one, though it was rather lame.

"It would be the ruin of me," he said, "to be kept out of my business for a month in that way. Come, speak out; what is it you want me to tell you?"

"I want to know," replied the pedlar, "what you are up to, coming hanging about this hotel. You know quite well, Mr. Bowes, I saw Sam burn a pocket-book belonging to a friend of mine. At the same time he told me what sort of a story he thought he had got hold of in that pocket-book; and, though he was wrong altogether, and only making a fool of himself, I want to know what 'lay' you and he are upon now."

Mingy considered for a minute or two. A lie first came up to his lips, of course; but then he recollected that all parties concerned were likely very soon to hear everything which had passed between him and Lady Fleetwood. It is true, he never liked dealing with any but principals; but that was a small matter compared with a compromise in the circumstances of grave difficulty which surrounded him; and he therefore replied--

"Well, I don't mind telling you all that, if you promise upon your life and soul not to stop my going back to my own business."

It was now the pedlar's turn to consider; for, to tell the truth, there was a certain feeling of false honour about him which made him shrink from the idea of being an informer; but yet he did not like to give out of his own hands the power of restraining Mr. Mingy Bowes's actions in the case with which he was then dealing.

"Why, the case is this," said the pedlar: "you see, Mr. Bowes, whenever I promise anything, I always do it, come what will; and now you are asking me for a great thing in return for a small thing. I look upon it that I have got you by the neck, Mr. Bowes, as I may say; for I can swear that I saw, at your house, one of the men who robbed me and t'other gentleman, with part of the stolen property in his possession; and that you, knowing it to be stolen, helped him to drive a bargain about restoring it. Now, you want me to acquit you of all this, for nothing but telling me something which I shall know before to-morrow's over. That's too much."

It certainly was an awkward way of putting the question, and Mingy Bowes did not at all like the look of things. He had recourse to silence, as the best resource; and after waiting a minute or two, the pedlar proceeded thus:--

"I am inclined to be liberal, Mr. Bowes, and don't wish to be hard upon any man; so, if you'll make a fair offer, I'll promise upon my word of honour not to hurt you."

"The job is," said Mingy, with a sudden burst of frankness, under the influence of fear, "that I can do anything you like myself, but I cannot answer for that man Sam. He's a wild, headstrong devil, worse than a pig, for he'll neither be led nor driven, nor pulled back by the leg."

"So I should judge," said Joshua Brown, "and one can't expect any man to do more than he can do. Therefore, if you'll promise to tell us all you know, and to work with us afterwards in any way I tell you--this gentleman here's a witness--I'll let you off altogether, and not mix you up in the matter at all."

It was a hard pill to swallow; for, although Mr. Mingy did not possess much even of that honour which is said to exist amongst thieves, yet he had to remember that his reputation as a trustworthy receiver of stolen goods was at stake. Considering, however, that promises are but air, and that while that made by the pedlar, in presence of a witness, would at any time give him a fair opportunity of turning king's evidence, a thousand means of evading his own engagements might present themselves, he took the pledge offered to him, and informed Joshua Brown of all the plans and purposes of himself and his excellent confederate, and all that they knew, or thought they knew, of Colonel Middleton.

While this detail took place, Carlini sat by and listened; but at the latter part of the statement he laughed aloud.

"Why, what a set of fools you must be!" he said: "my master's a Spaniard by birth, and has lived almost all his life in Spain. He was in Mexico at the time you talk of. That I can prove; and the whole story you have got up could be blown to pieces by gentlemen now in England."

The pedlar bit a piece of hard skin off his thumb, which in his case was tantamount to an expression of doubt; but he said nothing, for he was very well satisfied that Mr. Mingy Bowes should be led to disbelieve the truth of the story he had heard.

"Are you serious?" said the marine store dealer, addressing Carlini.

"Quite," said the Italian, with a scornful look: "your friend has made some blunder, Mr. Bowes. His excellency, my master, has got cousins in London who have known him from his birth; and, do what you will, you cannot make him out anything but what he is. So, as this blackguard is going himself, you say, to Lady Fleetwood, the day after to-morrow, you can let him go. He'll only get himself into a scrape, and nobody else."

"Well, I've only told you what he told me," said Mingy Bowes; "but I don't think he told me the whole, and I did not see the inside of the book that he burned."

"Stop a bit," said Joshua Brown: "at what hour did you say he was to be there?"

"At twelve o'clock," answered the marine store dealer.

"I was to go with him to introduce him; but I thought I would just come here and see the colonel myself, to have a little deal with him if possible in the first place."

"It is well you did not see him," replied Carlini; "for, depend upon it, he would have thrown you out of the window. He's not a man to be frightened, I can tell you."

"I should think not," said Joshua Brown, with a laugh; "but now, Mr. Bowes, as all things are clear, and as we understand each other, I have nothing more to say, only that you must not go out of town till I tell you; and you must come and see me to-morrow morning at ten o'clock."

Mingy Bowes promised.

"I am very punctual," said the pedlar, with a meaning look; "and, as I shall certainly want to speak with you, if you don't come I must look for you, and get people to help me."

Mingy understood him completely, repeated his promise, with a full determination of keeping it for fear of worse consequences, and received the pedlar's address--No. 43, Compton Street, Seven Dials.

"Now, mind," said the pedlar, as the worthy "fence" took up his hat to depart, "you're not to say a word to Sam of anything that has happened till I see you to-morrow. Perhaps I may then allow you to tell him what a fool he is making of himself; perhaps I may let him go on and trap himself."

Mingy Bowes was all obedience; for the confident tone of the Italian servant had greatly shaken his reliance on his friend Sam's conclusions, and his own somewhat perilous position had rendered him wonderfully ductile. A good deal chapfallen, he took a very polite leave of his two companions, and left them alone to discuss the scene which had just passed. The first observation came from the lips of Signor Carlo Carlini, who exclaimed, in an indignant tone--

"What a set of blackguards you have in this country of England! My countrymen are bad enough, and so are the Spaniards; but it seems to me brave and honourable to attack a carriage, perhaps escorted by a dozen or two of dragoons, when compared with this attempt to rob a man of his money by accusing him of a crime. A bandit is a gentleman to such a fellow as that."

"There are a great number of such, I am afraid," replied the pedlar. "These things are happening every day in London; and I have known two or three cases in which a gentleman in the same situation as yourself has made a great deal of money, and set up a hotel, upon the strength of some letters which he had found belonging to his master. You cannot form a notion of all that is going on every day in this great city; but wherever you get a great number of men together, you are sure to gather a great quantity of rascality. But, as to this business, we must talk to the colonel, and see what he thinks it better for us to do. So, with your leave, I will stop till he comes back, and should like in the mean time to hear the rest of the story you were telling me."

"With all my heart," replied Carlini. "Let me see where I was. Oh--I remember I was just telling you how G----, the life-guardsman, rose to be a prince and a grandee of Spain."

CARLINI'S STORY, CONTINUED

"Spain is a very curious country, sir--a very curious country indeed. Things happen there every day that could happen in no other spot of the globe. It is like one of those things which I think you call magic lanterns, where the scenes are always shifting, and nothing on earth remains steady for an hour. You may see a little ragged boy running in the street, and not long after he'll be walking about the court; a great man in velvet and lace, without anybody but himself knowing how it happened. There are only four things necessary to it--impudence, cleverness, youth, and good luck. Well, as I was saying, G----, the life-guardsman, in a very few months rose from nothing at all to be a prince and a minister. The old nobility grumbled and growled, and all the new people tried to stop his progress, till they found it was useless; but in the end the old and the new, both together, bowed down and licked his feet. All this time, as I have said, I heard nothing of him; and I thought he had quite forgotten me, and was just as selfish and cold-hearted as such sort of people generally are. But I made a mistake, sir, and think it but right to do justice to a man against whom everybody cries out. One day, as I was walking along the street in which his palace was situated--for he lived in a palace by this time--I saw a fine horse standing before the little door (there was a great door, where the carriages went in), and three or four servants, all magnificently dressed, by the side of it. Just as I was going to pass, who should come out but the prince himself, in a general's uniform, all gold, and feathers, and jingling spurs! I drew back, with my brass basin under my arm, to let him go by, thinking he would take no notice of me. His eye fell upon me, however; and he knew me directly and stopped. 'Ah, Carlini!' he said, 'is that you? Why, you have never been to see me. I haven't forgotten you, and if I can do anything to serve you, I will. Come to me here to-morrow at ten o'clock;' and then he told the servants to let me be admitted. There are some people who, as the French say, suffer fortune to knock at their door and do not open, but I am not one of that kind; and putting on the best clothes I had, I left my brass basin and my razors behind me, and went away the next morning to see the prince. I suppose there were at least twenty people in his ante-room, waiting to see him, and amongst them a great number of noblemen and high officers; but I went through them all, after a page, and was shown straight in. I could hear some of them say to their neighbours, 'Why, that's Carlini, the barber! We shall not see the prince for an hour, if he's only just going to be shaved;' but I laughed in my sleeve and went on. I found the great man stretched at his ease, in a dressing-gown of gold brocade, and I stood near the door, bowing down to the ground; but he said, 'Come near, Carlini--come near and sit down;' and he began to talk to me just as familiarly as ever. He even spoke about the silk stockings, and said, 'Ay, those silk stockings made my fortune, and I won't be ungrateful to them or you.' He then went on to speak of a great number of other things, and joked and laughed with me till I believe the people in the ante-room thought I was telling him all the scandal of the court, as barbers often will do; but at last he began to be more serious, and questioned me about what knowledge I possessed. He had not much himself, so that I don't wonder he was surprised to find that I could read and write, speak several languages, and keep accounts as well as any *contador*. At length he dismissed me, saying, 'I won't forget you, Carlini--I won't forget you; and if ever you think have done so, come back at this hour, and they will let you in.' But I had no occasion; for three days had scarcely passed when he sent for me, and told me that the king had graciously permitted him to name the viceroy of the Indies, and that he had appointed a certain nobleman (whose chin, I was very glad to find, had never come under my razor), upon the condition that he gave him the nomination of his *intendente*--that is to say, a sort of steward. 'Now, Carlini,' he said, 'if this suits you, you shall have the place;' and he told me how much it was worth--besides pickings. 'You had better take it,' he said, 'if you don't mind going to Lima; for it is the best thing I can offer you, and heaven knows how long I may be here to offer you anything. Fortune is fickle, and as she raised me up, so she may cast me down; but if you take this, you at all events open for yourself a new path in life, which may perhaps lead to greatness and wealth.'

"I was very much inclined to cast myself at his feet and give him honours more than his due; but you need not ask me whether I accepted the proposal, which placed me in a position that I had never even dreamed of obtaining. I was introduced to the newly-created viceroy, gave him apparently the fullest satisfaction, and set out with him tor Lima, applying myself heartily to learn, before I reached the shores of the New World, the business which I was likely to be called upon to transact. By close attention I made such great progress, that my new patron, although at first somewhat cold towards me, who had been forced into his service, became attached to me, and relied upon me entirely. During two years I transacted the whole business of his household, amassed great wealth, and as the business of my actual office was as small as the emoluments were great, I had plenty of time both to push my fortune and to enjoy my leisure. The *intendente* of the viceroy was a very great man. His favour and his influence were sought for by all classes of people. A great portion of the wealth of the province passed through his hands; and, enlarging my views with my opportunities, I established a bank in Lima, rendered a large house in Mexico a mere branch of my establishment, and, passing from the one city to the other whenever the business of my *intendencia* permitted, became one of the greatest dealers in the precious metals to be found in all the colonies. But I had fallen upon those changeful times which left none of the world's goods firm and stable. Revolutionary ideas began to get abroad; and, with a miscalculation very common in those who have been born and acted under one period while passing to another, I thought the things which I had been accustomed to retained sufficient vitality to last, even though the germs of a new order of events were destroying their roots and pushing through the ground. At all events, gratitude towards the viceroy, who had been most kind and generous towards me, would have induced me to pursue the same course which I did follow, even if I had known that circumstances were against him. His friends would have been my friends; his supporters, those to whom I granted support. I was in the world of wealth; the power of wealth was greater than the power of authority; and as, by his generous carelessness, the wealth was at my command while the authority was at his, I might be said to be more powerful in the Indies than himself. I call heaven to witness that I did not use this great power amiss. Undoubtedly, I supported the existing state of things. By it I had risen; on it my fortunes were founded; and no one had a right to attribute to me as a crime gratitude to those who had befriended me, and the support of institutions under which I lived and prospered. But then came the revolution: the colonies took advantage of the weakness of the mother country--a weakness which their establishment had first caused, and which their support had nurtured. They cast off the yoke; they forgot all former benefits; I became loaded with odium; my bank was pillaged; my property was sequestrated; my house was sacked; and I was cast into one of the dungeons of the old inquisition, where I remained for nine months, in a state of horrible neglect and privation, which it is impossible to describe. My food was scanty, the attendance I received grudging and unwilling. I had no bed, no accommodation of any kind. The mud, in some parts of the horrible cell to which I was consigned, was several inches deep, and the straw upon which I slept was at the bottom soaked in water. I went into that dreary abode a healthy and powerful man, in the early prime of life; I came out a skeleton, hardly able to drag my feeble limbs along. By this time some degree of order was restored, and a show of law was established. It was necessary to try me, as I had been so long confined; and idle charges were fabricated to justify my long detention and the pillage of my property.

Not even the skill and the malice of those who seek to justify wrong could devise an accusation that was tenable. My accounts were all in order; and, although no person had a right to investigate them but the viceroy, whom they had expelled, they could not even found a charge upon them. As a base excuse, however, for refusing to do me justice, they declared that I had systematically denied all assistance to the leaders of the revolution, in my capacity as a banker; and, after having been one of the most wealthy men of the land, I was cast upon the world utterly penniless. There are some men, however, who act by divine laws and not by human ones. I am afraid that they are to be found only in the lower portion of the middle class. There are none more cruelly tyrannical than the people; none more selfishly careless than the upper class. The latter are the best masters, because in their carelessness they are generous while they have the means. The former are the worst, because their minds have never been expanded by prosperity, and because their passions are capricious in proportion to their numbers. But in the middle class you find the men who have lived by right and equity, and are sensible of the benefits of right and equity: nay, more--who will follow them sometimes even when they don't see good consequences to themselves. I wandered through Lima, without a friend as I thought, and certainly without a penny; but passing by the door of a goldsmith, to whom I had once lent money, he called me in and made his house my home. He and I consulted with regard to my affairs. Most of those to whom I had lent large sums had fled; others had joined the revolutionary party and were beyond my reach; but there were a few who owed me trifling debts, of thirty or forty crowns, which I had no power of reclaiming, for all my papers were in the hands of the state; but nine out of ten of those who could do so paid me, and I gained sufficient money to come to Europe and to subsist for a few months. It was necessary that I should adopt some new trade. I landed in France, went to Paris, offered myself as a servant, and became courier to an English gentleman. I travelled with him for two years, made myself thoroughly acquainted with his language, of which I had learned a good deal before in Naples, and at last lost him, for he was drowned on a party of pleasure, passing from St. Malo to Jersey. I then became courier to a German count, but I only remained in his service for three months; and at the end of that time, after gambling unsuccessfully, he left me to provide for myself. I now found that I was better fitted for a barber than for a courier, and was thinking of resuming my old profession, when the place of waiter at an inn was offered to me at Bordeaux. There I happened to meet with my present master. He did not recollect me in the least, but he was kind and courteous to everybody; and, as the landlord endeavoured to cheat him enormously, one day, in a fit of spleen or indignation, call it what you will, I warned him of the fact, and was dismissed for my pains by the good master of the house. Some days after, I met his excellency in the streets. He remembered me as the waiter, though not as the banker, asked my circumstances, and on my telling him the whole story of my dismissal, engaged me as his servant. With him I have remained ever since; and, as I told you before, a better master does not live. I have been with him in a good number of different countries; and I know quite well that if I act faithfully to him I shall always find him act generously towards me. I am too old to push my fortunes as I did when I was young; and circumstanced as I am, I find--although in life I have very often seen the contrary--that for me, at least, according to your English maxim, honesty is the best policy."

"I have always found it so," replied the pedlar; "but yet one sees people get on wonderfully by the other course. Now, this very man who was here just now is as great a rogue as any in the world, and yet he has risen from a shoeblack, and made a good deal of money, I am told, by pure lying and rascality. I wonder if that story he told about his visits to Lady What-d'ye-call-her is true or false."

"Lady Fleetwood, do you mean?" said Carlini. "Oh, we can easily find that out. I know two of her servants very well--her own footman and the housekeeper. The footman can tell whether this Mr. Bowes has been there, and very likely a good deal more; for I have remarked, Mr. Brown, that the servants of all nations, in whatever else they may differ, are alike in listening at doors. Let us walk down to the old lady's house. We can be back before his excellency returns, I dare say."

The pedlar thought the proposal a very good one, and they accordingly set out. Whatever was the fruit of their expedition--of which more hereafter--they received confirmation strong of the truth of Carlini's judgment as to the eavesdropping propensities of English as well as other servants.

CHAPTER XXXII

"I really must and will remonstrate, my dear Winkworth," said Charles Marston, entering the room where his old yellow-faced friend was sitting. "How you can risk your health and your life by neglecting the express directions of a surgeon you have called in to attend you, I cannot conceive, unless you wish to make people believe you are quite mad, or meditating suicide."

"We are all mad, Charles," said Mr. Winkworth, "every one after his own fashion; and every man, judging his neighbour by his own madness, thinks him insane on account of the very actions which most show his sanity. You are by nature, habit, and education, utterly idle. Idleness is your madness; and you would not put yourself the least out of your way to perform the most important business in the world. Therefore it is you think me mad for neglecting advice in which I have no confidence, in order to transact business which I thought important. Business, business took me out, I tell you. Look there;" and he pointed to an ocean of old papers by which he was surrounded; "and if I choose to kill myself, Charles Marston, what is that to you? I am not your son, nor your ward, nor your wife; and no man, let me tell you, has a right to meddle with another man's actions, unless he is affected by them."

"But I am affected by this," replied his young companion. "You have promised to take a journey with me into the country; and if you lay yourself up on a sick bed, you will not only defraud me of your society, but you will prevent me from going too, for I must stop to nurse you."

"Pooh! pooh!" cried the old man: "I can nurse myself; I have nursed many other people, too, long before you were born; and I think I can do so still in my own case. But I tell you I don't intend to be ill. And now, what are you going to do? for, as soon as I get through these papers, which will take me about half-an-hour more, I may want to talk to you."

"I shall wait here, then," replied Charles; "for my uncle Scriven sent to say he would call about this time."

"I won't see him!" exclaimed Mr. Winkworth, impetuously. "Have him taken into another room. I won't see him: at all events, not yet. It would do me more harm than all the journeys in the world."

"Ho, ho!" cried Charles, laughing; "so then you have come to the conclusion that my opinion of my worthy uncle is not quite so wrong as you at first thought it?"

"I never thought it wrong," said Mr. Winkworth, who was in one of his polemical humours. "I had no business to think about it, because I had no data; and all I concluded was that it was either a great pity a nephew should think so of his uncle, or a great pity that an uncle should give a nephew reasonable cause so to think. Now I have data;" and he laid his hand upon some of the papers before him. "These documents belong to that poor thing we met upon the common, Miss Hayley. How she has saved them, how she has preserved them, in all she has gone through, I don't know; but it now seems to me very clear why your uncle wants to keep her in a madhouse."

"Indeed!" exclaimed Charles Marston, a frown coming upon his brow and a flush into his cheek. "Pray let me hear, my dear sir; for although I do not doubt that Mr. Scriven is a very honourable man, as the world goes, yet I know he always has his motives. Be good enough to tell me what they are in this instance."

"No, I won't," answered Mr. Winkworth, abruptly; "at least, not at present, Charlie. You shall hear more by-and-by; but before I speak upon any subject, I like to know it thoroughly myself; and before I act in any matter, I like to consider how I had best act."

"But where is Miss Hayley? How did you find out?" exclaimed Charles Marston.

"She is in a madhouse at Brooke Green," replied Mr. Winkworth; "and I found out by the boy Jim, who tracked her with the instinct of true affection. Now, that is all that you need know for the present."

Charles thought for a moment, and then said, in a mild tone--

"I wish, Winkworth, you would tell me more; for your words lead me to believe, in some degree, that the honour of one member of my family, at least, is somewhat affected by this business. Yet I cannot insist, as I am debarred from acting as I should like to act in behalf of this poor thing."

"Why debarred?" said Mr. Winkworth.

"By my father's unfortunate situation," replied Charles. "I look upon it as my duty, my dear sir, to make over the income of my poor mother's whole property, which my father assigned to me, to him for his life. I have thus nothing on earth to bestow upon poor Miss Hayley. Otherwise I had proposed, out of old affection for her and hers, to settle upon her what would make her independent."

Mr. Winkworth got up and walked once or twice across the room; then, turning sharply round, he said--

"You shall do it, my dear Charles. Do you know I intend to leave you all I possess? There--no words about it. I told Lady Anne so, a little while ago; and now tell me what your father allowed you. Not a word about any other subject."

Charles paused for a moment, as if overpowered by his emotions; but Mr. Winkworth waved his hand impatiently, and he replied--

"Nearly two thousand a-year, my dear sir: the whole interest, in fact, of my mother's fortune."

"Then I will allow you the same," said Mr. Winkworth. "I adopt you as a son. You won't be the worse for two fathers, especially when one is away; and I am a nabob, you know, who could eat gold if I liked, were it not that the food is indigestible; and, to tell the truth, I've been so long accustomed to feed upon rice, and to wear one coat the whole year, that I fear anything like dainty diet and rich apparel would be the death of me. Hark! there is somebody coming to the door--that's your uncle, I'll warrant. Take him quickly through the room to that one beyond: don't introduce him, and let me finish what I am about."

The last words were spoken just as Mr. Scriven was entering the room; and as he was by no means deaf, he must have heard them. He gazed coldly upon Mr. Winkworth, however, as he advanced towards his nephew; but the old gentleman merely raised his head for an instant, made a slight bow, and resumed the reading of the papers before him, while Charles led his uncle into a small room beyond.

As may be supposed from all that had lately passed between uncle and nephew, Charles did not feel very cordial towards Mr. Scriven; but that gentleman cared very little about it. He did not trouble himself about affections. They were not in his way of business.

"Well, Charles," he said, "a lawyer has been to me to inquire into the particulars of the property settled upon you. I hope you are not going to borrow money."

"Not a penny," replied Charles Marston, drily.

"Then what is this lawyer's object?" asked Mr. Scriven. "Was he sent by you? If so, why?"

"He was sent by me," replied Charles, "and for this reason: my father, on my coming of age, having plenty of money himself, settled upon me the income of my mother's property, to which he was entitled during his life.

Now he has not plenty of money, and I am going to give him back what he gave to me. It must be done legally, and therefore I have employed a lawyer. You, as the trustee, have the papers, and he must see them."

"Very good," said Mr. Scriven; "and pray how do you intend to live yourself?"

"By my wits," answered Charles, "as many other people do, I believe."

"Oh, plenty, plenty!" said Mr. Scriven. "Pray, have you seen your friend Colonel Middleton lately?"

"Yes; I walked with him for an hour this morning," answered Charles, his colour a good deal heightened at the insinuation which lay couched in his uncle's abrupt question.

"Then he has not gone down to Frimley again, to look for Miss Hayley?" said Mr. Scriven, with a meaning smile.

Charles paused, a good deal struck. This was a new link in the chain of evidence proving that Henry Hayley and Frank Middleton were one; but he feared the use his uncle might make of the fact, if he could once establish it, and replied--

"You still suspect him of being Henry Hayley, I see; but I fancy you would have great difficulty in proving it."

"I have no interest in proving it," replied Mr. Scriven, in an indifferent tone; "it would not benefit me. However, as you have now explained what this lawyer wants, he shall have copies of the deeds. Of course, you have a right to do what you like with your own; but, if you will follow my advice, you will take care what you are about; for if your father's creditors get hold of the capital, it will benefit neither him nor you."

"I will take care," replied Charles.

And merely saying "Good-bye," Mr. Scriven walked away, passing Mr. Winkworth without taking any notice.

When Charles Marston rejoined his old friend in the other room, which he did not do till he had stood and pondered for several minutes, Mr. Winkworth looked up suddenly, and addressed himself at once to the very point which had been the subject of his young companion's meditations.

"Can you tell me anything, Charles," he said, "of a young man whom I find frequently mentioned in these papers--a nephew of Miss Hayley's, named Henry?"

"I can tell you much, my dear sir," replied Charles; "and, strange to say, I was thinking of him at that very moment, from some words that my uncle let fall. Henry Hayley was the son of my uncle's partner, and an old schoolfellow of mine. He was accused, when he was little more than sixteen----"

"I know all that; I know all that," said Mr. Winkworth, hastily: "it is all written down here, and I remember seeing something of the story in the newspapers. He fled to the Continent from the pursuit of justice; but what became of him then?"

"It was said he died," replied Charles Marston; "and the officer who was sent in pursuit of him declared that he had seen his dead body at Ancona. My uncle, however, contends that he is still alive; and certainly the likeness between him and our friend Colonel Middleton is very extraordinary."

Mr. Winkworth mused for a minute or two, turned over the papers before him, and examined some passages carefully.

"From what I know of Middleton," he said at length, "your uncle's suspicions must be wrong. Henry Hayley would have sought for the aunt who seems to have loved him so well."

"Middleton went down to Frimley a few nights ago," replied Charles. "I had told my good aunt Fleetwood of our meeting with Miss Hayley on the common, and I doubt not that she mentioned the fact in his presence."

Mr. Winkworth mused again, but he was uncommonly taciturn upon the subject.

"I must speak to Middleton about all this," he said. "There is some mystery here, which should be solved. I wish, Charles, you would send your fellow to see if he can find Middleton and bring him hither."

Charles immediately acceded; but the servant returned with an intimation that Colonel Middleton had gone into Hertfordshire.

"I left the message, however, sir," he said; "and the waiter assured me it should be delivered as soon as the gentleman came back."

Some hours passed in the usual occupations of the day. Mr. Winkworth sat and read, wrote, and thought, while Charles Marston went in and out upon various matters of business, dined with his aunt Fleetwood and Maria, and returned somewhat late to the hotel.

To his surprise, Charles found Mr. Winkworth still up; and, as he was going to commence a serious remonstrance, the old gentleman lifted up his finger with a smile, saying--

"Middleton has been here, and the surgeon; so say not a word, or I disinherit you--cut you off with a shilling. Listen, therefore, to my new resolution. Lady Anne Mellent sets out to-morrow morning."

"I know she does," replied Charles.

"Your aunt and cousin go at six on the following day," continued Mr. Winkworth; "but they are young people, especially Lady Fleetwood--I never saw any one so young in my life. You, I, and Middleton, are old, and cannot bear travelling; therefore we will all take our departure about five to-morrow evening. Not a word! It is all settled--Middleton and I arranged it all, and the surgeon said it was a capital plan; for, as I told him I must and would go, either that night or the following day, having made up my mind to be at Belford on Thursday next, he declared it would be better for me to travel slowly than quickly, and to begin in the cool of evening. In short, he perfectly approved, declared I was going on quite well, and left me with an impression which I never entertained before--that he is an honest man and a clever doctor."

Charles saw that it would be vain to oppose, and contented himself with asking--

"But what did Middleton say of himself? Could you make anything of his history?"

"My dear Charles, he is an enigma," replied Mr. Winkworth; "and, as I am the least of an [OE]dipus of any man that ever lived, I very soon gave him up. One thing, however, is clear: he is a gentleman in every respect, and a very distinguished one. He is, moreover, as rich as Cr[oe]sus, a Jew, or a nabob. I told him plainly the doubts, or rather suspicions, which have been entertained; and he merely laughed at them, seeming to be highly amused at your uncle's conduct at Lady Fleetwood's house, which by his account must have been exceedingly strange."

"Very strange indeed, and by no means agreeable," replied Charles; "but did Middleton tell you nothing at all about himself?"

The old gentleman laughed.

"Oh, yes," he said: "he told me many things; but the most important he would not tell, and so the rest was of little use. Now, Charles, I shall go to bed; for you know it is quite needful for a feeble old man like me, with a bad habit of getting wounded in the shoulder, to take care of himself."

"Which of course you never do," replied his young companion, smiling. "I shall not meet you at breakfast, however, sir, for I go early to Lady Anne's to see her off."

"Good, very good!" said Mr. Winkworth, and walked away into his bed-room, while Charles remained for a moment or two, with that strong inclination to think which often comes upon a man about midnight. He soon found, however, that thinking was a most fruitless occupation, and he too retired to rest.

CHAPTER XXXIII

It is a most unfortunate and ever-to-be-lamented thing that the fairies have quitted England. How it happened I do not know, nor is the period of their departure exactly ascertained; but I cannot help thinking that it was about the time of the Great Rebellion, when the whole people of the country were so busy about other things that they had hardly time to eat their breakfasts, and none to knock holes in the bottoms of their egg-shells, so that the fairies had a fleet of little ships ready prepared for them to cross the Channel when they thought fit. Nor is it at all wonderful that they should choose that time for going, with the Fairy of Order at their head; for every one knows that the good little people are strongly averse to anarchy and confusion, and dissension of every kind; so that, when Oberon and Titania quarrel, I have it upon good authority, the whole of the royal train, except Puck, who stands by and laughs, hide themselves away under harebells and columbines, and only peep out with one eye to see when the storm has blown over.

However, certain it is that they are all gone--left our shores, I fear, for ever. Nothing can be done by magic now. The milk remains unchurned; and no more is seen before the fire,

> Stretched at his length, the lubbard fiend.

All the business of the world goes on at a jog-trot, and that trot is very often a slow one.

So Lady Anne Mellent found it at Milford, for the people were not at all accustomed to work fast or obey promptly; and they did not believe the stories told by the servant whom she had left behind, in regard to her impatience of disobedience and delay. Early in the morning, a whole host of servants, headed by the butler and housekeeper, arrived at Milford Castle; but when Lady Anne herself appeared, with good Mrs. Brice, her former governess, she found everything in the most woeful state of confusion. There was no end of embarrassments. Almost all the servants were congregated in the great hall, waiting for her coming, and all were full of complaints of Mrs. Grimes and the steward.

"I never saw such neglect in my life, my lady," said the tall, stately housekeeper, dressed in a quaker-coloured silk, shot with amethyst and green. "This good woman, this Mrs. Grimes, tells me that she used almost all the coals in the house last night and this morning, and that there are heaven knows how many miles to send for more."

"There is not a bit of charcoal in the house, my lady," said the cook, advancing in his white nightcap and apron; "and Mrs. Barker here says it is my fault for not bringing it in the fourgon: now, I could not lumber the fourgon all the way from London with charcoal."

"Where are the toilet-covers for my lady's room, Mrs. Barker?" said Lady Anne's maid, addressing the housekeeper in a loud tone, aside.

"I declare," said one of the footmen, in an audible tone, just behind the butler's back, "I don't think that either oil or candles were remembered."

"Nor blacking," said another.

"Nor soap," said a very broad housemaid.

"The meat is all fresh-killed," grumbled the cook.

"And the poultry has been sent in with all the feathers on," added the kitchen-maid, with a sort of hysterical scream at the thought of the eternity of plucking before her and the scullion.

Lady Anne burst into a fit of laughter, which no sense of dignity could restrain. It was evident that there were no fairies there to favour her; though, heaven knows, if there had been one in the island, he or she would have been there with counsel to support the gay-hearted, good-humoured lady of the castle.

Seeing that her merriment was becoming infectious, Lady Anne made a great effort to suppress it, and was turning away towards the drawing-room, telling the housekeeper to follow her, when a girl ran in exclaiming, apparently in reference to something which had passed just before the lady's arrival--

"Butter! they say there's not a pound of butter within twenty miles!"

It was too much for human endurance; and, making the best of her way into the drawing-room, Lady Anne sat down and wiped the merry tears from her eyes, while the housekeeper stood before her, looking exceedingly rueful.

"Let me have my writing-desk," said the young lady, at length. "Now, Mrs. Barker," she said, "have the goodness to let me know everything that is wanting in your department and the cook's."

"Oh, my lady, I can't manage the cook," exclaimed the housekeeper, in a tone of spiteful dignity; "he has been raging like a wild beast all the morning. I am sure I was very glad when your ladyship came, for I thought he would have eaten some of us up."

"Cooked you, I suppose you mean," replied her lady: "I will very soon manage him, if you cannot. Go and make me out a list then of what you want yourself, and remember that it be complete. Send the butler here."

The butler, when he entered, received nearly the same orders; and then the cook, being introduced, made his complaint in formal terms in regard to the state of everything in the house. The very pots, pans, and kettles, were not according to his mind. The meat was all new-killed; no fish had yet appeared; butter was not to be had; eggs were scanty; and the vegetables which the garden produced had been out of season in London for a full month.

Lady Anne listened to him with the utmost patience; but when he had done, she said in a grave tone--

"Monsieur Hacker, I wonder to hear you speak in this way. I had always thought that a man of your great skill could, out of an ox's head or foot, produce at least three courses. It is in emergencies such as the present that the genius of a great man appears. Go, sir, and out of such materials as you have show me what your art can do. I shall dine at eight. But in the mean time, as there will be servants going both to Bedford and Wooler, you can make out a list of all that is absolutely necessary, and send it to both places. Gradually we shall get what is required from London; but at present remember, I expect to see a triumph of art."

"My lady, you shall not be disappointed," said the cook, laying his hand upon his heart: "it is only that Mrs. Barker enrages me with her *inepties.*"

"Very well," replied Lady Anne; "see that she does not enrage you any more, lest your lady's service should suffer."

The man retired; and with a gay glance to poor Mrs. Brice, who had been confounded at the symptoms of rebellion she had witnessed, Lady Anne gave way to another burst of merriment, which she had repressed in the man's presence, in order to treat him with that dignified consideration which is especially required by men-cooks, the vainest of all creatures upon earth, not even excepting dancing-masters, romance-writers, and poets.

Some degree of order in the proceedings of the household was soon re-established. The lists were made out--very formidable, it must be confessed, in length and details; and a copy of each was sent off to Wooler and Belford. Some fine trout were brought in, in the course of the morning, and also a salmon. It was found just possible, when people set about it willingly, to obtain butter and coals within a less distance than twenty miles; and although, from, time to time, during the rest of the day, a fresh want was discovered, and a little noise was made about it, like an occasional roar of thunder after a storm has passed by, all went on very tolerably considering, till at length, about five o'clock, a cart was seen wending towards the house, the driver of which bore a note to Lady Anne.

"My Dear Child" (it ran)--"I saw very clearly yesterday that you know not Northumberland, that you forgot Milford has not been regularly inhabited for more than ten years, and that 'tis in somewhat of a remote district. I have, therefore, sent you over some of the produce of my farms to supply deficiencies for to-day; and to-morrow I shall come and dine with you, and inquire what can be done to render you service, by your faithful servant and admirer,

"Charles Hargrave."

Columbus, when he first discovered the shores of a new continent, hardly felt as much satisfaction as Mons. Hacker when he saw the contents of that cart--the well-fed, well-fattened, well-kept mutton--the fine river and sea fish--the white poultry, the fat pigeons, the ducklings, the guinea-fowls, the eggs, the butter, the green goose, the fine vegetables, the hot-house fruit. Everything was there that could be thought of; and he went from one article to another, murmuring, "*Cotelettes à-la-braise--en compottes--matelottes--rôtis aux cressons à-la-Celestine. Mon Dieu!* if we had truffles, it would be complete!"

And the heart of the cook rejoiced with a pure and high devotion for the honour of his art and of his mistress; for he knew that on that day Lady Fleetwood and Maria Monkton were expected to dine at Milford; and for the latter lady he entertained that reverent affection which all really chivalrous cooks feel towards beauty. His last and severest trial was to discover that nothing but brown bread was to be procured in the neighbourhood, for which there was no remedy; but, nevertheless, that was not his fault; and when, about half-past seven o'clock, the rush of wheels was heard, and Maria's carriage drove up to the gates, he felt a proud satisfaction at the odours which were rising up around him, as an incense which had not risen from the altars of Milford for many a long year.

The dinner was laid in the great dining-hall, for Lady Anne had determined to make the first impression of her ancestral castle as imposing as possible upon her young friend.

The reader may ask, Why? and may say, Was it like her--so gay, so joyous, so thoughtless, so careless of show, ceremony, or parade? Nevertheless it was so. She had laid it all out. She had even condescended to a little trickery. Although, at that season of the year, there was light enough remaining in the sky, at a quarter past eight, when they began their dinner, to proceed with the first course at least with no aid but from the beams of heaven, yet she had ordered two windows at the side to be shut up, leaving unclosed only the large oriel window at the end, filled with deep-coloured stained glass. Over the table, which looked almost like a speck in the centre of the great hall, hung an old-fashioned but richly-ornamented silver chandelier, with eight branches lighted; but yet the beams only illumined the table; and a sort of uncertain twilight pervaded the remoter parts of the hall, except where a sideboard loaded with ancient plate appeared, lighted by several old candlesticks. Lady Anne had so contrived it that, in coming from the great drawing-room to the hall, the little party passed through several other rooms but faintly lighted; and in so doing, Lady Anne managed that Maria should occupy the middle place, between her and Lady Fleetwood. As they entered the hall, too, she looked up in her young friend's face, while her eyes ran over the fine old chamber--which, with its lights in the centre, its mysterious gloom at the end, the richly-covered table and sideboard, the number of servants in their handsome liveries, the large antique chandelier of silver and its silver chain, the tall stained glass oriel at the end, and the evening light faintly streaming through, only just sufficiently to throw long lines of yellow, purple, blue, and even red, upon the floor and ceiling, and those three graceful women entering arm-in-arm--looked more like some painter's dream of the ancient time than anything that is seen in our own stiff and tinselled days.

"What a beautiful hall!" exclaimed Lady Fleetwood, looking round. "Isn't it cold?"

And at the same moment her foot passed from the rim of marble which ran round the whole chamber, and took the first step on the ocean of Turkey carpet with which seven-eighths of the floor was covered.

"I think not," answered Lady Anne: "at all events, I shall try, dear Lady Fleetwood, to keep it warm and gay while I am here. Isn't it a fine hall, Maria?"

"It is indeed," replied Maria: "the span of the vault is so great, it makes me feel as if I were in Westminster Hall."

"Oh, no, no!" cried Lady Anne--"not amongst lawyers in black gowns. But come, Maria: you take that end of the table, and be mistress of the house. I will act master for the present; and Lady Fleetwood shall be our guest. Do you know, dear lady," she continued, seating herself, "I intend to be very gay while you are all here, and to have a grand ball, and a number of dinner-parties, and that we shall amuse ourselves all the morning, and sing and dance and flirt all the night, and have all the great people of the county who will come. Won't that be very delightful, Maria?"

"Very splendid indeed," said Maria, with a smile.

"Like the splendour of a sky-rocket when it bursts," said Lady Anne, quite gravely. "But why did you call it splendid, Maria? Why did you not say, pleasant--charming--delightful?"

"Because I am sure I should like Milford quite as well without any such gaieties," replied Maria Monkton. "You know I am not particularly fond of large parties, Anne; and, although one must mingle with them, and some of them are pleasant enough, yet I hardly think they deserve the epithet of charming or delightful."

"Cynic!" said Lady Anne Mellent, and proceeded to eat her dinner, with a somewhat pouting air, as if she were hardly well pleased. She was soon as gay again as ever; and when they returned to the drawing-room she opened the window, and gazed out with Maria upon the starry sky, which looked almost misty with its innumerable lights, and upon the wide-spread park with its undulating slopes, and the tall dark masses of the trees cutting black upon the luminous heaven.

They had been silent for some time, while Lady Fleetwood sat at the other end of the room, netting one of the innumerable purses which had afforded her a grand source of occupation through life.

But suddenly Lady Anne's lips moved; and she said aloud, as her eyes remained fixed upon one spot of the sky, thronged with stars--

"Oh, ye bright and glorious wanderers of the night! had you voices, as men dreamed in days of old, to tell the fate of those born under your influence, how gladly would I ask the destiny of those who here stand and gaze upon you! Say, Arcturus!--wilt thou take me in thy car, and let me see the storms and tempests that wait my onward course and that of the dear girl beside me? Or thou, planet of love and hope, just climbing the hill of heaven!--wilt thou tell me whether the seeds which have been sown in our hearts under thine influence will bud and blossom into the flowers we dream of? Shall we go on hand in hand together, even unto the end, as hitherto we have lived, in deep affection? Shall the ties which bind us in nearer kindred unite our hearts still more closely? or, shall the love that knows no sharer wean us of our youthful tenderness towards each other? I ask not to hear what will be the frowns or smiles of Fortune--whether the dull earth's wealth will be augmented or diminished--whether we shall meet reverse, accident, or care--ay, or even poverty or early death. I only ask, shall we love and be beloved? for surely that is to know enough of fate;" and turning away towards Maria, she leaned her brow upon her fair friend's shoulder.

For a moment or two Maria was silent; and then she said, in a low tone--

"If the stars could have answered you, would you have asked them, Anne?"

"Yes, yes," eagerly replied Lady Anne. "Would not you, Maria?"

"I think so," answered Maria; "yet sometimes, perhaps, it were better not to know our fate."

"Oh, no, no!" exclaimed Lady Anne; "doubt is always horrible."

"Yes; but there may be trust without knowledge, faith without comprehension," replied her fair friend. "I have both, although the future is very dark and impenetrable to me just now."

"Oh, it shall be bright!" cried Lady Anne. "Mine shall be the voice of those brilliant stars, which, rolling millions of miles above all earthly things, may well see, stretched out beneath their eyes of living light, the past, the present, and the future of each existing thing. Oh, yes; it shall be bright, Maria! For you the future hours are weaving a many-blossomed wreath. First is the early bud of love, now full-blossomed to a rose; and then the clustering lily-of-the-vale, to speak domestic happiness and peace; the passionate violet, hiding its intense blue eyes in the shade, and spreading rapture's perfume round; and the proud imperial lily, portrait of high station and the world's esteem: the pansy, too, imaging the sunshine of the breast, and pure, enduring faith; and the linked hyacinth with its many buds. All, all are there, sweet sister, for you and him you love: and the wandering seasons, as they pass along, shall not unfold a flower or ripen a fruit that shall not fall into your hand----"

"If your wishes can command fate," said Maria, "it is the voice of hope and not of the stars you speak, dear Anne."

"Nay, nay--I am a prophetess just now," replied Lady Anne. "Beware how you doubt Cassandra, lest she predict woes as well as blessings. I see a little cloud coming, and the stars tell me it is very near. It sweeps over the face of the moon; but the moon scatters it, and the blue sky drinks it up."

"Dear me! is the moon risen?" exclaimed Lady Fleetwood from the other side of the room; and Lady Anne's fanciful visions were gone in a moment.

"Oh, dear!" she said to Maria, with a low voice and a sigh, "I forgot we were in this world, but always something brings us back to it. No, she is not risen yet, dear Lady Fleetwood."

"I thought you said you saw her," said Lady Fleetwood.

"I was only romancing," replied Lady Anne: "this is an age when our young women dream dreams, but now I'll talk sober sense. You know, Lady Fleetwood, that I am going to have three gentlemen to stay with me to-morrow; and you must act quite the lady of the house, for decorum's sake--be a very discreet chaperon, and not take the slightest notice if I choose to flirt most desperately with Mr. Winkworth or any one else. I'll do the same, and not take any notice when you flirt with any one--or Maria either."

"I am sure, dear Lady Anne, Maria never flirts," said Lady Fleetwood, in the most matter-of-fact way in the world.

"Bless her heart! then she shall do it for once, just to keep me in countenance," exclaimed Lady Anne; "but remember you are to be chaperon, Lady Fleetwood, and to look as demure as possible."

"But where is Mrs. Brice?" said Lady Fleetwood: "I haven't seen her since we came."

"Oh, dear me! I forgot Mrs. Brice," said Lady Anne. "Well, she will do quite as well for a chaperon, and so you shall have leave to flirt too; but the truth is, she's so tired with her journey, and so frightened with the desolation we found reigning in these halls, that she said she would not come down to-night, and dined in her own room. To-morrow she will be as brisk as ever, I dare say, and that will just do; for I expect Mr. Hargrave, whom I am in love with, and intend to marry, to dine with us also."

"Mr. Hargrave!" "Intend to marry!" exclaimed Lady Fleetwood and Maria, both together.

"Certainly," said Lady Anne: "he is the dearest, cleverest, most beautiful old man in the world, in a velvet coat, embroidered waistcoat, and black velvet breeches; just like a fine piece of Dresden china well preserved. He is, moreover, the soul of honour and the spirit of good judgment. If I had the most difficult and delicate thing in the world to do, I would entrust it to Mr. Hargrave."

"I have seen him," said Lady Fleetwood; "I remember him quite well in poor Sir John's lifetime, but Sir John did not like him."

"My dear father did," replied Lady Anne, "and consulted him on all his affairs; so you see I could not do better than marry him, for I am sure I want some one to manage me. Don't I, dear lady?"

Maria smiled; but Lady Fleetwood expressed a general opinion that all young women ought to marry, especially if they had lost their parents; and after some more conversation of the same rambling kind, they separated and betook themselves to their beds.

CHAPTER XXXIV

About a quarter of an hour before the time appointed, Mr. Scriven entered the door of his sister's house in ---- Square. The door was opened by a maid-servant, for Lady Fleetwood always took her own man with her: one of Maria's had also gone with the carriage, and the rest were at Bolton Park. Mr. Scriven was generally as taciturn and dry towards servants as towards associates; but on this occasion, as he was going a little out of his usual track, he thought fit to say--

"I know your mistress is absent; but she desired me to speak with a man who is coming to see her this morning at twelve."

"Yes, sir--I know," replied the maid, with a curtsey; "her ladyship told me before she went away."

"More fool she," thought Mr. Scriven, as the maid opened the door of the dining-room and showed him in; but he judged that a rejoinder was requisite, and therefore he said--

"When the man comes, you will be so good as not to say that your lady is out, but merely ask him to walk straight in here. Are the drawing-room window-shutters open?"

"No, sir; we don't open them when my lady is out of town," said the maid, dropping another curtsey; "but I'll go and do it directly."

"Do so," replied Mr. Scriven. "Have you got the key of the library?"

"No, sir," said the girl, looking towards a door which led into a small apartment behind the dining-room: "perhaps it's open, though my lady generally locks it when she goes away;" and she went forward and tried the door, but it was locked.

"Go and open the shutters," said Mr. Scriven; and sitting down, he looked attentively at his boot, which was exceedingly well polished.

Just as twelve o'clock struck--it might be a minute or two before--two men entered the square, and approached direct towards the house. They did not ring, however, for some minutes; but one of them looked up and passed it. They then paused, and seemed to consult for a minute or two; gazed round the square; looked one way and then another; waited a minute, till two men who were carrying along a large looking-glass, like a dead man on a stretcher, had got to some distance; and then, turning back, they knocked and rang at the street door.

In answer to their inquiry for Lady Fleetwood, the maid said--

"Pray walk in. Her ladyship expected you, I think."

"Yes, yes," replied the taller man, who looked upon this announcement of the lady's punctuality to her appointment as a very favourable indication. "Yes, yes, she expects us;" and he strode into the hall, followed by Mr. Mingy Bowes.

The maid shut the door, and then led the way to the dining-room; but much was the surprise, and not a little the consternation, of the two worthy personages, when, instead of a respectable old lady with a very delicate complexion and a fine lace cap, they saw the tall, thin, gentlemanly person of Mr. Scriven standing exactly before them, and looking straight in their faces. They both paused for an instant, as if not well knowing whether to turn tail and run away or not; but Mr. Scriven decided the matter by saying--

"Come in, gentlemen. Lady Fleetwood was obliged to go out of town, and she therefore begged me to confer with you upon the business which one of you mentioned to her a day or two ago. I am a relation, as much interested in the matter as herself, and perhaps more. Pray be seated."

The maid shut the door, and the two men sat down, Mingy Bowes on the very edge of his chair, his body inclined forward at an angle of forty-five, his hands upon his knees; and his huge companion, Sam, casting himself at once into a seat, throwing his long arm over the back of his chair, and gazing upwards round the cornice, as if he were a plasterer or an architect. Both kept silence.

"Well, gentlemen," said Mr. Scriven, who had also seated himself, "will you be good enough to explain your business?"

"Why, as to that," said Sam, in his usual rude and abrupt manner, "I thought you knew d--d well what my business is. Didn't you tell the old girl, Mingy?"

"Yes, I told her exactly what you said," replied Mingy Bowes.

"Well, didn't she tell you?" asked Sam, addressing Mr. Scriven.

"She gave some explanations," replied that gentleman; "but you know ladies' heads are not very clear, and therefore I would rather hear the whole particulars from yourself. She said you had got a pocket-book, which contained papers affecting the honour, and perhaps the life, of a gentleman who may probably be closely connected with my family."

"Ay, that's it," cried Sam; "and I told him to tell her that if she liked to come down handsome I'd say nothing about it; but if she didn't, I'd go and blow the whole to Scriven and Co. Those are the people whose names were forged."

"Indeed!" said Mr. Scriven, in his usual calm and deliberate tone: "well, the matter is worthy of some consideration."

"Devilish little time will I give for consideration," replied the brute. "I'll have the money down this very day, and a promise of it before I go, or else I'll be off to Scriven and Co. at once."

"Well, well," answered Mr. Scriven, "don't be impatient. I have no doubt we shall come to terms of some sort before we part. As a man of business, however, I must know what you can prove and what you cannot, before I agree to anything."

"There, you fool!" whispered Mingy Bowes, in a low tone; "I told you what you would do when you threw the pocket-book into the fire."

"You're the fool," answered Sam, fiercely; "and a d--d fool too!" And then, turning to Mr. Scriven, he added, "What you say is all fair--two sides to every bargain. So I'll tell you what I can prove, and then you can let me prove it or not. I can prove that a man going about here, calling himself Colonel Middleton, is the very same man who ten years ago went by the name of Henry Hayley, and that he was then accused of committing a forgery upon Scriven and Co. Now, I said the papers in the book would either hang or save him; for in it was jotted down his own account of the whole matter, showing that this Colonel Middleton is just the same man; and that, if he had not run away as he did, he would have been tried for the forgery, and been hanged for it too, perhaps, had it not been for another paper that was in the book."

"Pray, what was that?" asked Mr. Scriven.

"Why, a paper in a different hand," replied the man, "written by the young man's father, who calls himself Stephen Hayley, I think, and says that he himself committed the forgery, and got the young man to take the bill to the bankers' to be changed, without his knowing that it was forged. It's a long story; but then he goes on to say that he persuaded the young man to run away and take the blame, to save his father's life; and that he gives him that paper to show his innocence, in case he's caught."

Mr. Scriven mused for a moment or two with a frowning brow. For once in his life, the first impression was a right one; and had he acted upon it, he would have done justly and wisely.

There was so much probability in the story that he felt a difficulty in disbelieving it, though he might wish to do so, and a repugnance to pursuing plans incompatible with that belief; but, as he paused and thought, selfishness mastered conscience; the wishes grew more strong, and overpowered belief.

"That paper must be a fabrication," he said, aloud; and then, addressing the man more directly, he added, "Have you got it? Let me see it. I will return it to you again, upon my honour."

"Why, no--I haven't got it," replied Sam. "I burned it: I threw it, and the pocket-book too, into the fire, because I thought the d--d fellow they sent wanted to nab me."

"Then, how do you dare to come here," asked Mr. Scriven, "when you've nothing to show as proof of your story?"

"Come, come--none of that," exclaimed the man, looking at him fiercely. "I've got enough to show that this Henry Hayley and Colonel Middleton are the same man. I didn't burn them in the pocket-book. I was resolved to keep some hold on him; so I took them out first, while Mingy was gone into the shop for the man he sent. So, if, without any more palaver, you don't strike a bargain, and tell me what you or he will give, I shall be off to Scriven and Co. directly, and let them know all about it. He may then prove his innocence or let it alone; but he'll find that a devilish difficult matter, now the other paper's burned to a cinder in Mingy's grate."

"Can you show me those papers you have got?" said Mr. Scriven, in a much more placable tone.

"Here they are," replied the man, taking a little roll from his pocket; "but, unless I get a thousand pounds for them, I won't show them to any one till I show them to Scriven and Co."

"Well, then, show them to me," replied the gentleman. "My name is Scriven, and I am the person whose name was forged."

The fellow gazed in his face with a look of horror and consternation, and demanded, with a terrible imprecation--

"Then are you Scriven and Co.?"

"I am the head of that house," replied Mr. Scriven, "and the 'Co.' has long ceased to exist."

"Well, then, you have done me in a d--d unhandsome manner," said the man, "and I should like to twist your neck about for your pains."

"I have done no such thing," answered Mr. Scriven. "I told you that I am Lady Fleetwood's relation, which is true, and that I am here to act for her, which is true also. Moreover, if you will listen to me for a moment, you will see that, although you will not get a thousand pounds from me upon any pretence whatever, you may make a reasonable profit by this business notwithstanding. First, understand that I do not care one pin whether this Henry Hayley, alias Middleton, be hanged or not, except merely for the sake of justice. He showed himself exceedingly ungrateful to me, and forged my name for a large sum; for that paper, pretending to be his father's confession, is all a fabrication--but I did not lose anything. It was the bankers who lost, and they offered a reward of two hundred pounds for his apprehension, which offer is still in force. I offered the same sum; perhaps it was foolish to do so, for in truth I had nothing to do with it, but still I will not go back from my word; and if you will follow out exactly what I tell you, I may add a hundred pounds more, in order to open my niece's eyes, and save her from the snare that this man has laid for her. That will make five hundred pounds, which is all you will get. Will you do it or not?"

"What do you say, Mingy?" said the one scoundrel, turning to the other.

"Here, Sam--let me talk with you a bit," said Mingy Bowes, walking towards the window. The other followed him, and for nearly ten minutes they conferred together, very eagerly and in a low tone, while Mr. Scriven coolly took some tablets from his pockets, and amused himself with making notes and adding up sums. At length they returned again to the table, and Sam began to speak; but Mr. Scriven waved his hand for silence, and went on with his calculations, saying--

"Five and two are seven, and nine are sixteen, and six are twenty-two, and seven are twenty-nine. Nine, and carry two.--Now, what is it?"

"Why, you see, sir," said Sam, in a very deferential tone, greatly impressed with the merchant's coolness, "I'm afraid I can't."

"Why not?" demanded Mr. Scriven.

"Because, sir, I suppose you'd want me to give evidence," said Sam, "and that might be rather ticklish for me. I don't want to put my own neck into a noose, nor to take a swim in a ship at the expense of government."

Mr. Scriven thought for a moment or two.

"I understand you," he said at last. "In fact, you knocked the young man down and took the pocket-book and other things from him. He mentioned the fact. Did he see you?"

"No, that he didn't," replied Sam, promptly; "and he can't prove that I had any other things but the book."

"Then it seems to me the matter's very easy," said Mr. Scriven. "Let us be frank with each other, my good friend. The case stands thus:--You got the pocket-book, and he can prove it; so you won't help yourself a bit by holding back that fact, for the officers are after you by this time, depend upon it. Now, by coming forward and first proving a crime against him, you help yourself very much; for if he's convicted of felony first, he can't give evidence against you, and he would have to prove that he was robbed of the pocket-book before he could punish you for taking it."

"The only thing to do is, to get up a good story as to how you came to have the book," said Mingy Bowes. "Can't you say you found it upon the common that same night?"

"I dare say you've put away all the other things by this time," said Mr. Scriven.

"Ay, they are safe enough," answered Sam.

"Well, then, your having nothing else but the pocket-book, which would be valueless to any who did not examine the papers, will corroborate your story," observed Mr. Scriven; "for people may naturally conclude that those who took the things threw away the pocket-book on the common when they found there was no money in it."

Sam looked at Mingy Bowes, and Mingy nodded his head approvingly, saying--

"That'll do, I think, Sam."

"The only way of saving yourself and getting the money," said Mr. Scriven, "is to go at the thing boldly. The very fact of your making the charge will be a presumption in your favour. People will all say, of course, that you would not have ventured to do so if you had taken the thing unlawfully, and I will do what I can to help you, you may depend upon it; but remember, you must act according to my directions, and I will answer for it that no harm shall happen to you."

"Hang it, sir!" said the man, "one so often hears it said, 'No harm shall happen to you,' and then a great deal does, that I am half afraid."

"What else have you to propose?" asked Mr. Scriven, in his driest tone. "If you reject good counsel, you must have some scheme or plan already formed. I know not what it is, but think it somewhat more than dangerous, whatever it may be; for I can see no way of extricating yourself but that which has been named."

"Lord bless you! I've no scheme, sir," said the man, who, to say the truth, was a good deal bewildered by the new point of view in which the question had been placed before him. "What do you say, Mingy?"

Mingy Bowes shook his head doubtfully, without venturing a reply; and Mr. Scriven, seeing clearly that the unexpected discovery of his name, together with the disclosure of all their secrets, had, as it were, left the men no choice but to follow his plan or to fly, thought he might as well throw in the last inducement--as he would have done, in selling one or two thousand bales of goods, by giving a bale or two over and above the bargain.

"You will remember, sir," he said, addressing Mingy, "that in advising your friend, I myself have no choice in this matter. If he enables me to break off the match between this man and my niece by coming frankly forward, it will, of course, be a duty and a pleasure for me to help him to the utmost of my ability; but if, on the contrary, he holds back, I must take part with Colonel Middleton, and must do what I can to prove my niece's husband worthy of her affection."

"That's to say, you'd hang me if you could," replied Sam.

"Undoubtedly," answered Mr. Scriven, in his usual dry manner.

"Well, that's hard," said the man; "but you seem to have got me in a cleft stick, and so I suppose I must do what you please."

"Ay, that's right," replied Mr. Scriven. "I tell you conscientiously, and upon my honour, that I think it the only way to save yourself; and then you get five hundred pounds into the bargain, you know."

"I'll do it, or I'll be hanged!" said the man, warming enthusiastically at the thought of the money. "They can but give me what they call a life-interest in the colony, and I don't much care for that. Come, it's a bargain. I'll help you to fix the young man so that the beaks can't have the least doubt in the world that he is the chap; and whenever he's fixed, I'm to have the five hundred."

"There's the offer of a reward by Messrs. Stolterforth and Co. the bankers who cashed the bill," said Mr. Scriven; "so you see that it will be necessary to do what we propose, as soon as possible. Now let me see the papers, because there can be no use in concealing them."

"There they are," replied Sam. "Look you here. He has been careful enough; but he says in this one, which looks like a sort of day-book, that he determined at a certain time to go back to England, under the *assumed* name of Colonel Middleton."

Mr. Scriven looked over the papers carefully, and as great an expression of satisfaction appeared upon his countenance as he ever suffered to take possession of his usually inanimate features.

"That's all right," he said, turning one down: "now, if there's nothing to upset the scheme, you'll get your five hundred pounds to a certainty; and though that is not a thousand, it is better than nothing."

"A devil of a deal," said the man, delighted with the notion of the money; "but you haven't looked at the one next to it. It's got something in it too. That is something. But I think now, Mingy, as this is settled, we had better pack up our tools and be off."

"No, no, stay," said the other; "there are two or three things more to be settled. You must come to me at six o'clock this evening, when we can finally arrange all our plans; and, if you take my advice, you will not go to any coffee-shop, nor to any of your usual haunts; for depend upon it this Colonel Middleton, as he is called, has set many a trap for you."

"I don't think he dare," said the man, "being quite sure I know such a deal about him."

"Oh, he'll try to have the first word as well as you," replied Mr. Scriven; "but we must prevent him. He is gone down to Northumberland for a day or two, perhaps to keep out of the way rather than anything else; and the best plan for us to follow will be to go after him at once, pounce upon him in the country, give him in charge, and if possible get the country magistrates, who know nothing about him, to commit him. You come to me at six, as I have said, and in the mean time I will go away to the police-office, and get the notes of the former proceedings. Now, good-bye for the present; but do not think that you can bolt and leave me in the lurch, by going away out of town or out of England; for I shall have one or two sharp hands looking after you, and depend upon it, wherever you went they would find you out."

"Oh, I shan't bolt," replied Sam. "You have got me under the pitchfork, and must do what you like. I'll be at your house by six, if you tell me where it is."

"Willingly," answered Mr. Scriven, writing the name of the street and the number of the house down in pencil. "You'll find me there at six o'clock precisely; but remember, I'm very punctual, and I do not wait for any one."

"I'll be there to the minute," answered the man, "for I've nothing else to do; but I suppose I come upon honour, and that nobody will try to stop me from coming away again."

"Neither by any fault nor any indiscretion of mine," answered Mr. Scriven; "but you must take care in the mean time for fear they should shut you up. If you and I can set off to Northumberland at once, while the iron is hot, you will be out of the way yourself, and we shall take this lad quite unprepared, and have him before a justice ere he knows what he's doing. It must depend upon circumstances, however--I mean, from what I see in the city. If all's right, and if I can go away, we will set out this very night or to-morrow morning."

"That's all right, sir; that's all right," said Sam. "I'll be there to the minute; and now I suppose we had better go away, for I see you've got your hat in your hand, and I suppose your time's short."

"Very, considering all I have to do," replied Mr. Scriven; "and as I know this matter is important, the sooner it is got through the better."

"Certainly, sir, certainly," answered Sam; "you shan't wait for me. So, good morning to you."

Mr. Scriven did not half like to let him go, but there was no help for it. He had once thought of giving him in charge to a constable; but that, he saw, might spoil all his plans, and he abandoned the idea directly. There were no securities to be taken of such a man except his fears or his interests; and both of these, Mr. Scriven imagined, he had to a certain degree enlisted on his side. Nevertheless, when he saw him depart, he felt a good many unpleasant doubts as to whether he should ever see his face again, unless at the bar of some police-court.

CHAPTER XXXV

There was a morning of longings at Milford Castle: something--somebody--was evidently expected. It began at the breakfast-table. Lady Anne was down first, but Maria had been up earliest; and when she at length entered the cheerful little room, she found her fair hostess gazing thoughtfully out of the window. A heavy dew had fallen during the night, and it was lying filmy and bright upon the lawns and slopes of the park, like the misty radiance with which fancy invests the unseen things of life. Was it at that dewy silvering Lady Anne was gazing so intently? or at that deep shadowy wood, the tops of whose ancient trees were just seen above the rise, the road dipping down into them as if to take a bath in their cool verdure? It was the road towards Belford, and her eyes were anxiously turned in that direction--perhaps her thoughts also.

Maria went up to her and kissed her; and then, twining their arms together, they both stood at the window, and both thought for nearly five minutes without speaking a word.

At length Lady Anne said--

"It will be a hot day," and then she laughed at herself for talking so wide of her thoughts; and gazing into Maria's lovely eyes with a faint smile, she added, "Henry cannot be here till the day is at the hottest."

Maria smiled in return, but it was a faint, fluttering smile, in which fear and hope were blended; for she was very, very anxious about him she loved. His confident and hopeful manner had not communicated courage to her woman's heart, and many an uneasy and apprehensive hour had she passed when thinking of the difficulties of his situation. Oh! how we love that which excites our anxiety! How the chasing hopes and fears, the cares, the watchfulness, bind the object of them to our heart!--and all these, during the last few days of her short existence, had Maria felt intensely for Henry Hayley. Whenever he was absent from her for any time, she was full of apprehensions for him: she expected to hear that he had been arrested, that the struggle which she dreaded had commenced, that the game of life or death was staked; and though she might preserve the external appearance of calmness, yet was the poor girl sadly moved within.

Maria would not reply to her friend's words, for she feared her own self-possession; but nevertheless she was apparently calmer during that morning than Lady Anne herself. Her manner was composed; she spoke, she answered quietly; and it was only by an anxious look or a slight start, when she thought she heard the sound of carriage wheels, that she betrayed how much she felt at heart.

Lady Anne, on the contrary, though her usual April mood was still present, was assuredly more inclined to be on the showery side of the sweet month than on the sunshiny. Sometimes she would talk wildly and laugh gaily; but at others she would sink into profound fits of thought, gaze forth into the vacant air, and answer questions quite astray.

Even Lady Fleetwood seemed in a degree to feel the irritating effects of expectation. Once, in the middle of breakfast, without a word having been uttered regarding travels or travellers, she suddenly lifted her head and said, "I wonder at what hour they will arrive;" and some time afterwards, when walking for a moment on the terrace with Maria, she observed, in the same abrupt manner, "They will have a fine day for their arrival, at all events."

As the day wore on, and the hour at which they might be expected passed, Maria grew more thoughtful, more anxious, more grave; and Lady Anne, after watching her friend's face for a moment, said, "Come, Maria; this will not do. Let us go and amuse ourselves in some way. We will walk down to the steward's, see the hens and chickens, talk about lambs, and be quite pastoral. Nay, we shall not be absent when they arrive; for I will set a boy upon the tower to watch the road, and whenever he sees a carriage coming he shall run up my grandfather's old flag. The top of the tower can be seen from the steward's house, they tell me; and as it is only half-a-mile, and the carriage can be seen two miles off, we shall get back in time."

Maria made no objection. They went down to the steward's house; and they did talk about chickens and lambs, and were quite pastoral. But time wore on. No flag was displayed, and they returned to the house somewhat sadly. They found Lady Fleetwood seated in the drawing-room, working at the purse--her Penelope's web: but the old lady's face was very grave, too; and, to tell the truth, her imagination had gone careering in the same direction as Maria's. When she looked up, then, and saw all the anxiety that was written in her niece's fair face, the milk of human kindness in her bosom overflowed, and she must needs comfort her.

"My dear Maria," she said, "do not make yourself so uneasy. I know what you are thinking about and what you fear; but there is really no cause for alarm. My brothers conduct towards Colonel Middleton was very strange that day at dinner--I suppose, because he thought we had shown a want of confidence in him; but I saw him just before we left town, and he was quite kind about the whole business, assuring me he would do the best he could for our friend, even if it should turn out that he is the person whom we all suspect he is, for I told him all I knew, and all I fancied."

"Good heaven!" exclaimed Lady Anne.

"To him? To my uncle?" demanded Maria, with a look of consternation, clasping her hands together. "To him did you tell all?--the very last man to whom a word should have been spoken till all was settled!"

"Well, my dear child," said Lady Fleetwood, very much distressed, "I did it, I am sure, with the best intentions."

"Oh, your best intentions--your best intentions, my dear aunt!" exclaimed Maria, judging her uncle's character better than her aunt, and seeing with anguish all the fatal consequences which might ensue. But, almost as she spoke, the roll of carriage wheels was heard, and then some vehicle or vehicles dashed up to the doors.

It could not be resisted, under the circumstances in which they were: all proprieties and decorums were forgotten, and the three ladies, by one impulse, ran to the windows. There were two travelling carriages on the terrace, and the first person who sprang out was Henry Hayley.

Maria had resisted strongly. Expectation, anxiety, even the terror of her aunt's communication, had not drawn a tear from her; but when she saw him whom she loved and feared for, there before her safe and well, the bright drops rose up in her eyes.

Was it wonderful that she should feel so? Perhaps not: and yet the most wonderful things that I know of in the world are the emotions of the human heart--surpassingly mysterious. We are habituated to them; we feel or we mark them in others every day, and our wonder ceases; but who can account for them?--whence do they arise?--in what deep well of the soul have they their source? Take any emotion you will and drive it home--you will be puzzled to trace it to the end. We say, it is natural for man to have a fondness for this, a repugnance to that; but in so saying we assume the whole groundwork--we assert, but do not explain. Why did Maria so feel for the man before her? Why had she feared for him as she was incapable of fearing for herself? Why would she at that moment have willingly sacrificed her life for him? Why was the sense of rejoicing so overpowering, when the immediate anxiety for him was at an end? How had he contrived, in so short a space, to change the whole current of her feelings--to concentrate, as it were, every thought and affection, which had previously ranged wide and far, diffused over all things that surrounded her, upon himself alone--to transmute his interests into her interests, and to bind their future fates together by a strong and indissoluble tie, inseparable for ever?

So it was, however; and at that moment, as Maria stood at the window and saw him spring from the carriage, she felt that it was so, more than she had ever felt before. In a few moments the whole party were assembled in the drawing-room; but these few moments had been enough to calm the minds of those who had been waiting, to that point, at least, where joy is unmingled with agitation. Lady Fleetwood was delighted to see everybody, but especially Colonel Middleton, to whom she was now profuse in kindness and attention, in order to make up for the little *faux pas* which her niece's words showed her she had committed. She was the best-hearted, kindest woman in the world; but she did not see, or she would not see, that Colonel Middleton's whole thoughts were upon Maria, and that the first five minutes were in some sort Maria's due. Lady Fleetwood talked to him; she inquired after his journey, as if he had been a sick man or lame; she assured him more than once how glad she was to see him in Northumberland, as if she had utterly despaired of seeing him there at all; and she effectually contrived to prevent him, for a full quarter of an hour after his arrival, from doing more than merely shaking hands with her he loved.

Poor Maria bore it with the fortitude of a martyr; and even Lady Anne did not venture to interfere, lest by coming to her rescue she should only make matters worse. She was like the man who saw his companion carried away by a tiger, and did not dare to fire lest he should kill his friend instead of the brute.

Mr. Winkworth still had his sleeve cut open and his arm in a sling; but he looked exceedingly brisk and gay, and, with his mixture of odd eccentricity and old-fashioned courtesy, paid his compliments to Lady Anne, congratulated her upon having so fine a park, in which, to use his own expression, her deer, her horse, and her wits might range about at liberty; and then, turning to Mrs. Brice, who was by this time in the room, left his fair hostess to converse with Charles uninterrupted.

At length, however, compassion moved him; and in order to draw the fire from Colonel Middleton, he advanced, and began chatting to Lady Fleetwood in a gay and easy strain.

"I feel what it is to be old, my dear madam," he said: "here you have not spoken two words to me, while this gay young gentleman monopolises you entirely. Now, that is not right. I claim my share, and here I come to take possession of it;" and he seated himself beside her on the sofa.

Henry instantly turned to Maria; and how they managed it I do not know, but in the space of less than a minute they were standing talking to each other at one of the windows. It was a difficult man[oe]uvre to effect, in the presence of such an active adversary as Lady Fleetwood; but it was accomplished, nevertheless, with such skill and precaution that dear Lady Fleetwood did not remark what they were doing, nor make any attack upon either flank as they retreated. Had she seen them, there were a thousand chances to one that she would have done so. She would have asked Colonel Middleton some question, or called Maria to talk with Mr. Winkworth, or, worse than all, would have whispered to her niece to explain to her niece's lover that what she had said to Mr. Scriven was said entirely with the best intentions.

Five or six pleasant minutes did Henry and Maria pass in low, earnest conversation; but at length the latter said aloud--

"Oh, yes--I dare say we can; we have only been a very little way." And then, turning towards the spot where Lady Anne stood, she said, "Colonel Middleton is proposing a walk in the park, if you are not tired, Anne."

"Not at all," replied Lady Anne; "let us all go and take a ramble. It is nearly as new to me as to any of you, for I have not been here before since I was three years old; and, to say truth, I don't remember much about it. Come--bonnets and shawls, and let us go. Gentlemen, the butler will show you the apartments prepared for you, which I trust will be found tolerably comfortable, although, when I arrived here myself, I felt almost in despair lest that epithet should never be applicable to the house again. Of one thing, however, I can assure you, namely--there are no rats, for they were starved out two years ago, and emigrated to some other country."

Thus saying, she tripped away. Maria followed. Lady Fleetwood, too, declaring that a walk would be very delightful, went to get ready.

"Do you come, Mr. Winkworth?" asked Colonel Middleton, in a somewhat anxious tone.

Mr. Winkworth looked at him ruefully.

"I had not meditated such a feat," he said; "but I'm of a self-sacrificing disposition, and the most gallant man in nature, as you all know. Therefore, as our excellent friend Lady Fleetwood is going, and as without me there would be but two gentlemen to three ladies, I must ensure that one is not without an attendant. Pray, Charles, can you tell me whether Fox, who wrote the 'Martyrology,' was not a Northumberland man? I think, at all events, I should be added to his book as a sort of supplementary martyr. But here is the butler to show us our rooms, and I will hasten to get ready."

The chamber to which Colonel Middleton was shown was a large, old-fashioned room, hung with tapestry, through which protruded several gilt iron brackets, supporting old family pictures. Some were very good, and some in an inferior style of art, though probably the best which could be found at the period when each picture was painted. There were two Vandykes, and the rest were by Kneller, Lely, and their disciples; but they all had an interest for Colonel Middleton, who went round from the one to the other, stopping a moment or two before each, and gazing on the mute and motionless countenances. To me, and I believe to many other men, there is a strange fascination about old family portraits. I could gaze upon the effigies of the dead for many an hour, striving to read in the lines and features the life, the fate, the character of the being there represented. Such seemed to be the feelings of the young officer as he walked round. He commented, however, in his thoughts, upon the countenances before him.

"They have been a handsome race," he said to himself, "with a strong family likeness in all the men--all more or less like Lady Anne, too; here in one feature, there in another, and then again in the expression. This one in the formal dress of the last century is perhaps less like than any, and yet he must have been nearer in relationship than the rest. He looks stern and harsh, a man of a strong will and fiery temper."

As he thus thought, his eye rested upon a little gilt scroll at the bottom of the frame; and he there saw written--

William Earl of Milford, born 1754, died 18--

It was the year during which he himself had come down to Milford Castle in search of the son of that very man. The inscription awakened another train of thought; and seating himself in a chair, he leaned his head upon his hand and gave way to meditation.

He was roused the moment after by some of Lady Anne's servants bringing up his luggage, and raising his head he asked--

"Pray, has my servant arrived? He was to come down by the mail."

"No, sir," replied the man; "he has not come yet. Shall I put these in the dressing-room?"

"If you please," said Colonel Middleton. "Where is the dressing-room?"

"It is here, sir," said the servant, turning up a corner of the tapestry, and opening a small door, which displayed a little room into which the sun was streaming warm and bright.

It is strange what trains of thought very insignificant circumstances will produce. The sight of that small but cheerful chamber, compared with the large and gloomy one in which he stood, struck the young officer much; and he said to himself--

"Thus it is often with human fate. The narrow and confined sphere of humble life is often gay and happy, while the wider and loftier one of wealth and station is cold, gloomy, and cheerless." The next moment he heard the voice of Charles Marston calling him; and, going down-stairs, they set out upon their walk.

Mr. Winkworth managed admirably. One would almost have supposed him a daughter-marrying dowager, so admirably did he keep Lady Fleetwood in play, while the younger party roamed on before. He walked slowly, too, which is a great faculty in such circumstances; and as Lady Fleetwood herself was not generally disposed to walk fast, it suited her very well.

"Colonel Middleton is an old friend of yours, I find, Mr. Winkworth," said Lady Fleetwood as they went on. "Have you known him many years?"

"Not many, according to the almanac, my dear madam," replied the old gentleman, "but a great many according to the computation of the mind. I look upon it, my dear Lady Fleetwood," he continued, in a moralising tone, "that thoughts, words, and actions are the real measures of time; and that the sun's rising or setting, the mere whirling round of the great peg-top on which we creep about, has nothing in the world to do with it. According, therefore, to my way of computing, I have known Colonel Middleton a great many years, and ten times as long as I have known some men with whom I was hand-in-glove before he was born. You understand me?"

She did not in the least; but she replied, "Oh, yes: you mean that you have known him many years, but that you have lost sight of him."

"Not so," replied Mr. Winkworth. "It is not many months since I first made his acquaintance; but I have seen a good deal of him in that time, have heard much of him from friends of longer standing; and a more honourable, high-spirited, gentlemanly man does not exist."

"Oh, dear! I am glad to hear you say so."

"Why so?" demanded Mr. Winkworth: "did you doubt it?"

"Oh, no; not in the least," replied Lady Fleetwood: "I never did, I can assure you, not even when----"

For once in her life, Lady Fleetwood checked herself in full career. She was on the highway to tell Mr. Winkworth everything she knew of Henry Hayley's history; and all the present, as well as all the past, was about to be detailed for the benefit of his companion, when she recollected herself and held her tongue, though the bridle was hardly strong enough to keep in that very hard-mouthed horse.

Mr. Winkworth did not seem to have much curiosity, for he instantly changed the subject, saying--

"What a beautiful park this is! One does not expect to find such a spot in so remote a part of the country. Lady Anne's fortune must be very large."

"Oh, dear, yes!" replied Lady Fleetwood. "Her mother had nearly eight thousand a-year of her own, and Lord Milford had a very large property. His father was a strange, recluse sort of man--spent very little himself, and allowed his son a small income for a young nobleman. Until he married a rich banker's daughter, I believe he had not more than fifteen or sixteen hundred a-year allowed him; and he was rather extravagant, too, in his habits, so that he was a good deal in debt. At one time, people thought the old earl would have left everything he could away from him; for he was a sad tyrant, and quarrelled with his son very often; but then the young lord pleased him by his marriage, and everything went well after that. They say the old man saved at least three-quarters of his income every year, living down here amongst these hills the whole year long, like an old rook in the top of an elm-tree. He died of some disease of the heart, it is said."

"I should think so," replied Mr. Winkworth, drily; "but it does not seem, to have been hereditary, or at all events it became extinct in that branch."

The excellent lady would, in all probability, have contrived to be puzzled with this reply, had not a little man[oe]uvre of the advance-guard attracted her attention and interested her feelings.

Hitherto, Maria and Lady Anne had been walking on arm in arm, with Colonel Middleton by the side of the former and Charles Marston by the side of the latter, when suddenly, to Lady Fleetwood's infinite surprise, Lady Anne disengaged herself from her fair friend, went round, and took Colonel Middleton's arm. Then, pointing with her parasol to the right, she walked away with him, leaving Charles Marston sauntering on by Maria's side.

"Dear me!" said Lady Fleetwood; "Lady Anne is really very strange. Let us go on and overtake them. I am afraid Maria will feel hurt."

"Hurt!--why?" asked Mr. Winkworth, quietly, and Lady Fleetwood, feeling the difficulty of explanation, did as all weak and many cunning people do--insinuated what she did not choose to say, by replying with a meaning look--

"Oh, there may be reasons, Mr. Winkworth."

At the same time she walked on at a pace which was very quick for her, but which failed to overtake Charles and Maria, who, talking together earnestly, and apparently very confidentially, took their way in a direction quite opposite to that which had been followed by their fair hostess and Colonel Middleton.

Upon observing these indications, Lady Fleetwood paused and hesitated. A new solution of many difficulties presented itself to hope and imagination.

"What if Charles and Maria were to marry after all?" she thought. "It might not be quite fair, indeed, to Colonel Middleton; but still, here he had voluntarily gone away with another lady, almost as if to avoid Maria and her cousin;" and the worthy aunt gradually slackened her pace, saying--

"Well, it does not much matter."

Oh, Lady Fleetwood! Lady Fleetwood! Had you but been contented in everything to take all matters as easily as you did in this instance, how much better it would have been for you and all your friends and relations!

Soon after, the excellent lady and her companion reached the top of a small hill, perhaps a barrow, from the summit of which a great part of the park was visible, and there she saw Lady Anne and Colonel Middleton walking slowly along towards the deep pines through which the private road to Milford Castle from Belford passed in its way up to the house.

Suddenly, just emerging from the trees upon the road, appeared two men, who, as soon as they perceived Lady Anne and her companion, quitted the road, as if to meet the two others; and, if such was their intention, they succeeded; for the lady of Milford and her guests went straight forward towards them, and one of the strangers advanced, pulling off his hat with a low bow. A moment or two after, the young lady left her companion with the two men, and walked leisurely away towards the house.

Lady Fleetwood was puzzled. She could not make out what it all meant, and she expressed her surprise to Mr. Winkworth, saying--

"I wonder what's the matter. Had we not better go and see?"

"I think not, my dear lady," replied Mr. Winkworth: "there can be nothing of any importance the matter, or Lady Anne would not leave the party so quietly. Besides, if I am not very much mistaken, one of those men is Colonel Middleton's valet. The figure is just of his height and appearance."

As the next best step, Lady Fleetwood judged it would be better to return to the house immediately, thinking that there at least she should get information, but she was disappointed; for, though she sought Lady Anne as soon as she reached Milford Castle, the young lady had betaken herself to her own room, and the elder did not venture to intrude upon her privacy.

CHAPTER XXXVI

The dressing-bell rang in Milford Castle; but before its iron tongue had told the guests to make ready for the great business-meal of the day, all of them had sought their chambers, and Lady Anne Mellent was nearly dressed. Five minutes after, she sent her maid to knock at Colonel Middleton's door and tell him that she was going down, and would be glad to speak with him in the drawing-room as soon as he was ready. The maid thought it rather strange, although she was well accustomed to her mistress's various oddities; for, though she knew Lady Anne to be very eccentric, yet she had never before suspected her of coquetting with any one. With abigail penetration she had discovered, by some means or another, that Charles Marston was a favoured suitor; and now to be sent to tell a young, handsome, distinguished-looking man to make haste in dressing, for the purpose of having a *tête-à-tête* with her mistress before any one else was down, shocked her ideas of propriety very much. Pounds per annum and perquisites, however, are better than all the proprieties in the world, and accordingly she did as she was bid. But few minutes elapsed before Colonel Middleton was in the drawing-room. The maid's ear was certainly too near the keyhole within five minutes after; but she could hear nothing except the indistinct buzz of a low but eager conversation. She then tried what one sense could do to make up for the defect of another, and applied her eye to the aperture which had refused intelligence to her ear. She had the whole farther end of the room before her; but, to her surprise, there she saw Colonel Middleton standing with his back against one of the window-frames, and Lady Anne near him, leaning upon a large carved and gilt chair, while good Mrs. Brice sat writing a note at a table much more in advance.

A moment after a carriage drove up, and the maid ran away, just catching a sight of the velvet coat of Mr. Hargrave as he entered the door.

With stately step the old gentleman followed the servant, who admitted him to the drawing-room, and was met joyously by Lady Anne, who said--

"I am glad you have come, and have come soon."

"Did you suppose I would break my written word, fair châtelaine?" asked the old gentleman, in a somewhat reproachful tone. "Have I been true to a velvet coat and a queue for so many years, to have my faith doubted now-a-days?"

"No, no," said Lady Anne; "but I wish particularly to introduce you to this gentleman, Colonel Middleton, who, though magnanimously prepared to fight his own battles against a very formidable enemy, has listened to my persuasions, and is going to take you into his councils and solicit your advice and assistance. There--go with him, Henry, into the library; tell him the whole story, and the intelligence you have received to-day of the machinations against you."

While she was speaking, Mr. Hargrave from time to time looked with a somewhat inquiring glance from her face to that of Henry Hayley, and then a faint smile came upon his fine though faded features.

"No, no!" cried Lady Anne, laughing, as she remarked it; "you are quite mistaken. He is not the man, and a great deal handsomer. But you will hear all about it in a minute, for the whole must come out now, and you will know the why and the wherefore."

"Come with us," said Henry, addressing her: "we shall need you in our council indeed."

"Well, then, dear Mrs. Brice," said the beautiful girl, "if Lady Fleetwood and the rest come down, say that I will be back in a few minutes."

Lady Fleetwood did come down, and then the other members of the party, one after another, and to each Mrs. Brice delivered Lady Anne's message.

"I wonder where Colonel Middleton is," said Lady Fleetwood, at length, after Mr. Winkworth, who was the last, had been down five minutes.

"He is with Lady Anne in the library," said Mrs. Brice, simply; and Lady Fleetwood's fair and delicate complexion showed a blush as deep as if she had been a young girl just caught in attempting to elope.

Maria remarked her aunt's colour, and she coloured a little too, from sympathy more than anything else; for she felt certain that all her young friend's thoughts and feelings were high, and pure, and noble; but yet she did not wish that Lady Anne would make other people think she was coquetting with Colonel Middleton.

Charles Marston walked towards the window, and tumbled over a footstool; and even Mr. Winkworth seemed a little discomposed.

A few minutes after, the butler threw open the doors, and without looking round, pronounced in pompous tones--"Dinner is on the table, my lady;" but the next moment he perceived that Lady Anne was not in the room, and stood confounded.

"You had better knock at the library door and tell Lady Anne," said Mrs. Brice, in her usual quiet tones.

"Knock at the door!" thought Lady Fleetwood: "well, this is very strange!"

Still they were kept waiting for some minutes; and then--to the infinite relief of some of the party, it must be confessed--the doors on the other side were thrown open, and Lady Anne appeared, leaning on Mr. Hargrave's arm and followed by Colonel Middleton.

"I am afraid you have thought me lost," she said; "but I and my two counsellors here have been considering weighty matters for the good of the nation. Mr. Hargrave, allow me to present you to Lady Fleetwood, who says she had the pleasure of knowing you in years long past. Not a word to her till you are in the dining-room, for the dinner is getting cold. This is my dear friend, Miss Monkton, of whom we were talking two nights ago. Mr. Winkworth--Mr. Hargrave. Charles Marston, let me introduce you to Mr. Hargrave, my future husband."

"A promise before witnesses!" said Mr. Hargrave, with a smile; "but now, my dear lady, let me lead you to the dining-room, for I do not intend to give you up to any one."

The procession was soon formed, and the party sat down to dinner. Lady Anne was peculiarly gay and lively; but every now and then a shade of grave thought came upon her for an instant, which she cast off again as soon, her high spirits seeming to bound up more lightly than ever from the momentary depression. She had contrived to place Colonel Middleton next to Maria, and, if the extraordinary truth must be told, to get Charles Marston next to herself. Once or twice, too, when the conversation at the table was general and Mr. Hargrave was engaged with some one else, she exchanged a few words with Charles Marston in a low tone.

Thus, shortly after the fish and soup had been removed, she said--

"What made you look so gloomy when I came in before dinner? Traitor and rebel! your faith has been wavering."

"Because you are a little tyrant," replied Charles, in the same tone, for his heart now beat freely again; "and you sport with the pain of your subjects."

"They inflict the pain upon themselves," said Lady Anne; and the next moment, there being an interval of silence, she turned to speak with Mr. Hargrave.

Some time afterwards, she took another opportunity to say, "I think, Charles, you will stand by a friend in time of need."

"What do you mean?" he asked, for she spoke very gravely.

"I cannot explain," she said; "but you may be tried within four-and-twenty hours."

"Oh, I understand," replied Charles, and his eye glanced towards Colonel Middleton. "Do not fear; I will stand by him to the last, if I can be of any assistance."

They were again interrupted, and the dinner passed over without anything worth chronicling, till the ladies rose to retire from table. Lady Anne paused for a moment before going out, saying to Mr. Hargrave, "Do not forget the two notes, my dear friend."

"They are gone already," answered Mr. Hargrave: "as I came out I gave them to your butler, bidding him send them by one of my postilions."

When the ladies were gone, Mr. Hargrave naturally resumed the seat which he had occupied at the end of Lady Anne's table, and Mr. Winkworth drew his chair near him.

"Charles Hargrave," he said, laying his hand upon that of the old gentleman, "you have forgotten me."

Mr. Hargrave turned, and looked at him steadfastly. "I have indeed," he said, "though I thought I forgot nothing, and have sometimes lamented, my dear sir, that my memory was too tenacious, especially of affections."

"Yet we were once very intimate," said Mr. Winkworth, "though you are well-nigh twenty years my senior--older in years, I mean, though perhaps younger in body; but it is not wonderful, for I have withered away during nearly thirty years in India, so that, when I take up a little miniature portrait that was painted about the time I knew you, and then look in the glass, I do not know which it would be better to do, to laugh or to cry."

"It is very strange," said Mr. Hargrave. "Will you not recal the circumstances to my mind by some fact? Your voice, I will own, sounds familiar to my ears; but----"

"It is of no consequence just now," replied Mr. Winkworth: "by-and-by, when we can have a little chat alone together, I will bring it all up before you in a minute, like the landscape on the rising of the sun. Suffice it for the present that you are sitting beside an old friend."

Still Mr. Hargrave seemed puzzled, and returned to the subject more than once; but the other only laughed, and in a very few minutes they rose to rejoin the ladies. Then, while Colonel Middleton and Charles Marston walked away to the drawing-room, Mr. Hargrave took the other old gentleman by the arm, saying--

"Now you must give me satisfaction. You have attacked the honour of my memory, and I must have an explanation, lest I should think my faculties are failing."

"Well, let us sit down, then," said Mr. Winkworth; and seating themselves at the table, they remained there for a full hour. When they rejoined the party in the drawing-room, the two old men seemed as gay as any of them; and with music, and a game of chess between Mr. Winkworth and Lady Fleetwood, the evening passed lightly to its close. Half-past eleven o'clock came, without Mr. Hargrave's carriage being announced; but three notes were brought to him by the butler, who informed him at the same time that his servant had returned from Detchton-Grieve.

Mr. Hargrave only said, "Very well;" but Lady Fleetwood thought fit to tease herself about the old gentleman's going home so late. In truth, she looked upon the remote part of the country in which she was as little better than a barbarous land, and the journey back to Detchton-Grieve in as formidable a light as a retreat through a pass in presence of an enemy. Nor could she help expressing her sense of Mr. Hargrave's courage in undertaking such a perilous enterprise; but the old gentleman replied—

"I must decline the glory, my dear lady. I am going to sleep here to-night, and perhaps may spend to-morrow here likewise. This is the first time, dear Lady Anne," he continued, turning to his fair hostess, "that I have slept out of my own house for five-and-twenty years; but what would I not do," he continued, gallantly kissing her hand, "for an approving look from those bright eyes?"

"When we are married, you know, you shall always stay at home," said Lady Anne; "and now I have taken care that everything should be made as comfortable for you as possible. I wish I could have got a drawing of your room at Detchton; then you should have found all things precisely in the same state."

"When Cicero wrote his essay upon the 'Consolations of Old Age,'" said Mr. Hargrave, smiling, "he did not, so far as I remember, include that of being made love to by all the beautiful girls in the neighbourhood. But I am afraid he thought that there might be some portion of bitter under the sweet, and that they only ventured to do so from a knowledge that we are very harmless animals, and may be petted without peril. But now, sweet lady, I will seek my room; for, though I flatter myself I am very hale and healthy under seventy winters, yet I must not forget the good old maxim, that 'early to bed and early to rise' is the way to obtain many desirable things."

This was the signal for the general dispersion of the party; but Henry Hayley contrived to obtain an opportunity of saying in a whisper to Maria—

"Come down early to-morrow, dear Maria. I must speak with you for a few moments as soon as possible. Events are thickening around us, and you may be frightened at some things that are likely to happen, unless I have an opportunity of preparing you for them."

The colour mounted a little into Maria's cheek, but she answered frankly--

"I will come. Where shall I find you?"

"In the library," replied her lover, and they parted for the night; but Maria certainly did not take the best means to ensure early rising, for she lay awake for more than an hour, in anxious and painful thought.

CHAPTER XXXVII

The clock had not struck eight when Maria entered the library at Milford. The servants had just quitted the room: and through the open windows came the perfumed breath of summer, bearing from wild banks, no one knew where, the odours of the honeysuckle and the eglantine. The soft, early beams of unconfirmed day stole in, and streaked the floor with long rays of light; and a merry bird was singing without, in harmony with the fragrance and the sunshine. Joyful to the light heart, soothing to the memories of sorrow, the sweet, calm things of nature are painful to anxiety and dread. They raise not, they speak not of hope. The song of the bird, the odour of the flower, the gleam of the sunshine, are then like the farewell, the parting kiss, the last long look.

Maria felt sadly depressed as she entered the room. At first she did not see her lover, for he was standing in one of the deep windows; but the opening door and her light step instantly called him forth to meet her.

"Thanks, dear one and kind one!" he said, drawing her towards him and kissing her; "you are earlier than I expected, my Maria, but not earlier than I hoped. You are pale, my love: have you rested well?"

Maria shook her head with a sigh.

"How could I rest well with such apprehensions, Henry?" she asked. "I watched with thought till nearly two, and thought again awoke me. But tell me now, Henry, what danger menaces? Your words last night alarmed me sadly."

"No danger, I trust, dear Maria," he answered; "and I did not mean to express any apprehension or to excite any in you; but I thought it best to let you know that the hour of struggle is approaching, in order that you might be prepared for it. Indeed, dearest Maria, it is for your agitation that I fear and feel, more than for any peril to myself, of which I believe here is little or none; but I cannot help being grieved that your love for me should bring even one cloud over the sunshine of a life that I would fain render all bright. I saw how you were agitated when I arrived yesterday; I saw that you had been anxious and apprehensive regarding me; and I asked myself what right I had to make you, whose fate has been shaped in the fairest mould of fortune, take part in the darker lot of one who has been too often the sport of adversity."

"Every right--every right, Henry," she answered warmly; "or at least the best right--the right of affection. But let me share all your thoughts. Do you know, in spite of all you have said, I am half jealous of Anne Mellent. Not that I dream you love her; for I have trust and confidence enough to know that you would never tell me you love me were such the case--and, indeed, what motive could you have? Nor is it that I fancy she loves you; for I have known her from infancy, and never saw the least cloud dim her pure, high heart; but, Henry, it seems as if you had more confidence in her than in me."

He had listened with a smile till she uttered the last words, but then he eagerly replied--

"No! oh, no, dear Maria! do not fancy that for one moment. But perhaps I have been wrong. I should have told you before that she knows more than you do, from other sources. Her father was intimate with one now no more, of whom I will utter no reproachful word, although, to save and screen him, the bright early part of youth has been sacrificed by me. In a word, Maria, she possesses a power over my fate which no other human being has; and frankly and generously she is disposed to use it for my best happiness; making no condition, but only asking as a favour that I will let her unravel the web in her own way. Can I-- could I--refuse her, dear Maria? But yet it is needful that we should often consult together; for, though she suggests most of the steps to be taken, and has bound me by a promise to be silent to every one as to the motives on which she acts, it is very necessary that I should point out to her, from time to time, consequences which, in her somewhat wild and fanciful moods, she does not see."

"Well," replied Maria, with a faint smile, "I suppose an explanation must soon come, and I do believe she loves me as a sister."

"She does indeed," replied Henry; "and this very day all will be explained, I doubt not. But now, dear girl, let me tell you that which is likely immediately to occur. By some means, your uncle, Mr. Scriven, has become fully convinced of my identity with the poor lad whom he pursued so eagerly ten years ago. I know not well how he was first put upon the track, but I imagine by some imprudence----"

"Oh, my aunt Fleetwood! my aunt Fleetwood!" said Maria, with a sigh. "She, I know, told him--with the best intentions--all that she suspects herself; but still she has nothing but suspicion, nor can he have more."

"Yes, indeed," replied Henry; "he has conviction and proof--whether legal or not I do not know; but at all events such is the case, and of course my conduct must soon be determined. Indeed, Mr. Scriven himself is resolved to bring matters to an issue; and from the information I received yesterday in the park, he will probably be here this very day, to point me out as Henry Hayley and charge me openly with a felony."

"And what do you intend to do?" demanded Maria, with an expression full of terror. "Oh, Henry! would it not be better to go away?"

"No, dear girl--no!" he answered; "that cannot be. I will never fly again: indeed, I have now no object. I will meet him face to face, hear all he has to say, let him make his charge, and cast it back upon his own head."

Maria gazed at him in some surprise, for he spoke very sternly; and she asked, in a low and anxious tone--

"But how will you meet the charge, Henry? Will you defy him to prove your identity? or will you acknowledge your own name, and disprove the charge of forgery by the papers of which you told me?"

"Alas, dear Maria! those papers are destroyed," said Henry; and in a few words he told her the fate that had befallen his pocket-book. "Most unfortunately," he added, "I took it with me that very night I was attacked. It was the first time I had carried it for some years; but I was anxious to trace out my mother's family, and in that pocket-book I had put down all the information I had ever gleaned upon the subject."

"But this is ruin, Henry; oh, this is ruin!" exclaimed Maria, in an agony of alarm. "Indeed, indeed, it will be better to fly! Oh, do, Henry--do! I--I will go with you if you wish. He will never, surely, persecute his niece's husband."

"As bitterly as a stranger," answered her lover, gravely; "but no, Maria--dear, generous girl!--no! I will not take advantage even of that kind, noble offer. Nor do I think----"

"But how can you prove your innocence without those papers?" she asked, interrupting him, "especially that declaration of your father?"

"I think I can," he answered; "nay, I am sure I can--thanks to dear Lady Anne. How I shall act must be regulated by circumstances. We have determined to let him evolve his own plans step by step. Excellent Mr. Hargrave is fully in our confidence; and by his advice I will in some degree be guided. What I wished to say now, however, more particularly, is this, dearest girl--I think it would be better for you not to be present at the scene which must ensue upon your uncle's arrival."

"No, Henry--no!" she said; "do not ask that of me. I have promised to be yours--I am yours; and in weal or woe I will stand by your side."

"But it is not alone on account of anything that may happen to me that I make the request," answered Henry, "but because, dearest girl, there may be words spoken, regarding your uncle's conduct towards me and mine, which it may be painful for you to hear. He forces me to meet him as an enemy. If he shows forbearance, so will I; but if he does not--if his hatred and his vindictiveness push him to the last extreme--the accumulated wrongs of many years will find a voice, and a more powerful one, perhaps, than he imagines."

"Stay--let me think a moment," she replied; and then added, after a very short pause, "No, Henry--I thank you much; but I will adhere to my first purpose--I will be present at the whole. It may be painful--nay, it must be so in every way; but still I say, I will stand by your side in all, and will not be scared away by any fears of pain to myself."

"May you have your reward, dear, noble girl!" replied Henry; "and if a life devoted to you can prove my gratitude, that evidence shall not be wanting. My only anxiety is to spare you pain, my Maria; for I tell you, for myself I have no fears. I am sure--I am confident--that my character and my conduct will come out of the trial pure and unstained; and, were it not for the agitation that must befal you in such a scene, I should wish you to hear every word that may be spoken both against me and for me. But I will not try to shake your purpose. It is noble, and high, and like yourself; and I am sure that a compensation will follow for the painful emotions you must undergo, by joyful and well-satisfied feelings hereafter. And now, dear Maria, come out for a while to walk on this sunshiny terrace. We need now have no concealment from any one, for the time is very near when all must be explained."

"Your words comfort me, Henry," replied Maria, "and yet I cannot help feeling alarm; but I will try not to think of what is coming, and enjoy our short hour of happiness without the alloy of painful anticipations."

For twenty minutes they walked backwards and forwards upon the terrace in the bright sunshine. The morning was cool, for the sun had not yet heated the sky; the air was fresh and clear, for the ground was high. The clouds, as they floated along, mingling with the sunshine, produced gleams of purple and gold upon the slopes of the park and the brown mountain tops rising beyond; and Maria, now less anxious, felt that there is a voice speaking of hopes and consolations within the blessed and beautiful bosom of Mature, such as no mortal tongue can afford. Their conversation, too, was very sweet; for both strove to banish, even from memory, that there were dangers in the future, and to fill the present with happy dreams; while still through all came the mellowing shade of past emotions, gently and lightly touching the heart, and making the thrill of strong affection all the more exquisite. At the end of that time Lady Anne joined them, without bonnet or shawl, as gay as ever, as bright, as joyous.

"Is not this delightful, Maria?" she said, as she felt the morning air fanning her cheek, "Who would lag in cities, with their dull clouds and close atmosphere, when there are such scenes and such air as this? When I have lived in London for a fortnight, I wonder at myself. I feel as if I were a stuffed chameleon in a glass case, and have a great inclination to tell my maid to take me out and dust me."

While she was thus speaking, she turned her eyes once to Henry's countenance, and then added abruptly--

"You've been telling her. I see it in both your faces. Whenever Maria's eyebrow goes up in that way, I am sure there is something very busy in her mind. You have been telling her."

"Not more than you permitted," replied Henry. "I have only been preparing her for what must come."

"Foolish man!" cried Lady Anne; "do you not know that you should never prepare a woman's mind for anything? Pain and fear are not like butter or gold, that you can spread out to an infinite thinness. You only augment them by stretching them out through time, without diminishing their weight one grain. Let everything take a woman by surprise; then she will bear up much better under it, for it is once for all."

"But often," replied Henry, "the surprise greatly increases the pain; and I did think that it was absolutely necessary, not only to tell her what was coming, but to assure her that, whatever appearance things might put on, there was little real danger."

"If you were driving a pair of fresh young horses in a curricle, would you say to her, 'The brutes have run away, but do not fear; I will get you safely round that corner, which looks as if it would dash our brains out?' But never mind. I tell you, dear Maria, that there is not the least danger." Such was Lady Anne's reply.

"And now," she added, "let us go and take a walk farther in the park."

"Will you not put something on?" asked Maria. "You will catch cold."

"Not I," answered Lady Anne: "I am so full of warm, high spirits, that nothing, cold can get in. I feel like a general, who is sure of winning, just preparing for a battle. So let us go."

They walked for nearly an hour, and as they were returning they saw a gentleman's carriage standing before the door of the house.

"That's either Sir Harry Henderson or Colonel Mandrake," said Lady Anne. "I hope Mr. Hargrave is down, for I never saw them or heard of them before, yet I have invited them both to breakfast; but still we must get home and be civil. I did not know it was near nine o'clock."

The carriage moved round towards the stables; and as they entered the door of the house, Lady Anne asked a servant who was standing there if Mr. Gunnel had arrived.

"Yes, my lady," replied the man; "he is waiting in the housekeeper's room."

"You go and talk to him, Henry," said Lady Anne; "Maria, come with me, and help me to entertain these county magistrates."

Lady Anne, however, did not find the persons she expected in the drawing-room. Lady Fleetwood was there, and Mr. Winkworth, but neither Mr. Hargrave nor the two gentlemen just arrived. It would seem as if excellent Lady Fleetwood had a sort of presentiment of a coming bustle, for all her good intentions and her little anxieties were in a flutter. She declared that she had been very anxious about Maria, when she heard she had gone out so early, and begged her to recollect that Northumberland was very different from the neighbourhood of London, and that colds were easily caught, but not easily got rid of; adding a number of sage observations of the same kind, much to the amusement of Lady Anne. Then turning upon her fair hostess, she informed her, "that one of the servants had been seeking her, as two gentlemen had just arrived to breakfast," adding, "that they seemed friends of Mr. Hargrave's, who had gone away with them to the library."

"Well," answered Lady Anne, "I dare say he'll soon bring them out again, and so I shall wait here till he does." Nor was she disappointed in her expectation; for in about five minutes Mr. Hargrave returned, with one tall and one short elderly gentleman, who were introduced to Lady Anne in turn, and then to her various guests. Colonel Middleton entered as the ceremony was going on, and to him especially Mr. Hargrave presented the two magistrates, whose demeanour somewhat surprised Maria; for, while tall Colonel Mandrake addressed her lover with a sort of dignified deference, fat little Sir Harry Henderson was all bows and scrapes. Henry received them frankly, but calmly; and a moment or two after, Lady Anne led the way to the breakfast-room. There the meal passed pleasantly enough, no one seeming anxious but Maria; no one showing herself fidgetty but Lady Fleetwood. That dear lady, indeed, did her best to create several little disorders; but, even with the best intentions, she was unsuccessful. A treat, however, was in store for her; for breakfast was just over, and the party had hardly sauntered into the drawing-room, when a post-chaise-and-four rushed up to the doors, and in a minute after the butler appeared, announcing Mr. Scriven.

CHAPTER XXXVIII

Maria turned very pale on hearing her uncle's name, and her eyes unconsciously glanced towards her aunt. But poor Lady Fleetwood had turned paler still; for she seemed to divine in an instant all the consequences which acting unadvised in the affairs of others, with nothing but the best intentions to support her, had produced; and when she saw that Mr. Scriven, on entering the room, was followed by Mr. Stolterforth, the banker, her heart sank farther still.

The movements of all parties in the room were characteristic. Mr. Hargrave sat calmly for a minute on his chair, scanning Mr. Scriven with a curious and inquiring eye.

Henry stood firm and erect, with no other appearance of that emotion which the struggle about to commence must necessarily have produced than a slight contraction of the brow and the least possible curl of the lip.

Charles Marston, who was talking with Lady Anne, murmured in a low tone, as soon as he saw the banker following the merchant, "Scriven and Co. once more!" and took a step forward to Henry Hayley's side.

Mr. Winkworth broke off a conversation with Mrs. Brice, put on a large pair of spectacles, and stared full at Mr. Scriven, with a keen, searching look.

The two county magistrates conferred together in a low tone, glancing from time to time at the entering party; and Lady Anne, with graceful ease, but with a colour somewhat heightened, advanced a little before the rest to receive her not unexpected visiter.

Mr. Scriven himself could not be said to be graceful, but he was perfectly unembarrassed. He was pursuing his system, following his game, acting in the same character which he had sustained through life. He had nothing, he thought, to be ashamed of or afraid of--nothing to agitate him but eagerness; and although, it must be confessed, he was more eager in this instance than on ordinary occasions, yet his eagerness was much less intense than that of most men, when seeking even less important objects.

"Good morning, Mr. Scriven," said Lady Anne, in a calm tone. "Good morning, Mr. Stolterforth" (he was her banker). "To what may I owe the pleasure of seeing you? I fear funds must have fallen terribly, or else risen so high that you cannot invest for me, Mr. Stolterforth."

"I am sorry to say that our business at your ladyship's house is of a much more painful nature," replied Mr. Scriven; "but it is not with you."

"Whatever happens in my house must be business of mine," answered Lady Anne, "and therefore I must beg to know it."

Mr. Stolterforth, who had an infinite reverence for Lady Anne's hundreds of thousands--even more, indeed, than for her beauty, though he admired both--remarked a certain twinkle of the eye, which was not satisfactory to him; but Mr. Scriven pushed his point coolly, and, advancing towards Henry Hayley, he said--

"My business is with this person. Sir, I am now in a position to charge you directly with being here under an assumed name and character. Your real name is Henry Hayley. Is it so, or is it not?"

Greatly to the surprise of Maria, and to the utter astonishment of Lady Fleetwood, Colonel Middleton answered, in a cool, determined tone--

"It is not."

"Well then, sir," replied Mr. Scriven, "I am in a condition to prove the fact; and, moreover, that in the month of August, 18--, the same Henry Hayley was charged upon oath with forgery, and a warrant obtained for his apprehension."

"You will prove, sir, what you are able to prove," replied Colonel Middleton, with the same degree of coolness, for everything like agitation had vanished from the moment the struggle began. "However, as you are making a serious charge, you had better, in the first place, consider it well, and the grounds upon which it is founded; and, secondly, you had better make it in a more proper place than the drawing-room of Lady Anne Mellent."

"What! and give you an opportunity of running away again?" replied Mr. Scriven. "There, my good sir, you are mistaken; for I do not intend to lose sight of you till I lodge you in jail."

Hitherto poor Lady Fleetwood had been totally overcome, but she now rose from her chair trembling, and exclaimed--

"Oh, my dear brother! for heaven's sake, don't! You promised me, you know, that you would----"

"Hush!" exclaimed Mr. Scriven. "Margaret, you're a fool. You had better leave the room. No, stay--your evidence may be wanted; I was told at the house of a gentleman named Hargrave, a magistrate for this county, that I should find him here. If he be present, I must beg his assistance in this case."

"My name, sir, is Hargrave," replied that gentleman, rising; "and I am, as you say, a magistrate, and the chairman of the magistrates of this district. I am quite ready to afford any assistance in my power, in a legal manner. Here are also two of my brother justices present--Sir Harry Henderson and Colonel Mandrake--whose opinion will be valuable. May I ask what charge you have to make against this gentleman, Colonel Middleton?"

"I charge him, sir, with forgery," replied Mr. Scriven, "committed rather more than ten years ago, by putting my acceptance to a bill, with intent to defraud Messrs. Stolterforth and Co.; one of the partners of which house is now here with me."

"Where was the forgery committed?" demanded Mr. Hargrave.

"In London, sir," replied Mr. Scriven.

"Then, I am afraid we cannot entertain that charge," said Mr. Hargrave. "Informations should have been sworn, sir, in the county where the act was committed; but I am very willing to give any help in my power. Have you a copy of the depositions, or a warrant against this gentleman, or a copy of the informations--in fact, anything for us to go upon?"

"I have not," answered Mr. Scriven. "I was not aware of such technical niceties, and set out at once, with my friend Mr. Stolterforth, as soon as I had procured evidence sufficient to justify his apprehension; and I do think that, by a fair construction of the law, you yourself can grant a warrant, rather than suffer a person who has already escaped the hands of justice to abscond again."

"It may be so," replied Mr. Hargrave; and then, after speaking a few words to his brother magistrates, he added, "It is my opinion, Mr. Scriven, and that of the other two justices here present, that you should so frame your charge as to bring it more immediately within our cognizance. You state that Colonel Middleton is here under an assumed name; and, if you suspect that name is assumed for any illegal purpose, an information upon oath to that effect will quite alter the case, and enable us more satisfactorily to deal with the charge. Are you prepared to make one?"

"I am," answered Mr. Scriven. "I charge him with being here under an assumed name, upon fraudulent purposes towards my niece, and also with the view of avoiding apprehension upon a more serious accusation."

"That will do," answered Mr. Hargrave; "but we must conduct matters a little more formally."

"One word, if you please, my dear sir," said Henry, advancing a little. "For my own part, I have not the slightest objection to your dealing with the whole case, although several persons whom I might wish to call upon as evidence are now in London; and as this is merely, I take it, a preliminary examination, I promise you, if you like to go into the whole case, I will myself take no steps whatsoever hereafter, in consequence of a want of jurisdiction."

"We shall see as we proceed," replied Mr. Hargrave. "Mr. Scriven's information must be reduced to proper form; but it very luckily happens that our clerk has come over this morning on some business; and with Lady Anne's permission we shall convert her library into a justice-room, and deal with the case at once."

"I trust it is to be an open court," said Lady Anne; "for where so serious a charge is made against one of my guests, I feel, of course, personally interested."

"Oh, undoubtedly it is an open court," replied Mr. Hargrave; "for I could not suffer an investigation of so serious a nature to be carried on in secret, even if the accused were my most intimate friend. We will adjourn then to the library, if you please, which will be more convenient, and I will send for the magistrates' clerk. You shall sit upon the bench, fair lady, although I almost think the interest of the matter may be too much for you."

"Oh, dear, no!" replied Lady Anne: "I can bear up against harder things than this. Come, Maria;" and she linked her arm in that of her friend.

The emotions of Maria Monkton during the whole of this scene would be difficult to describe minutely. Much pain, much agitation, she certainly had suffered, and the colour had risen warmly in her cheek when her uncle had coupled her name with Colonel Middleton; but, upon the whole, her courage had rather risen than fallen, and her composure had in a great degree returned. Henry's perfect coolness, and the gentlemanly dignity with which he treated her uncle's charge, had not been without their effect upon her; and she had remarked with surprise, but with satisfaction also, that the accusation had not called forth an expression of wonder from the magistrates before whom it was made: in short, that they all seemed in some measure prepared for it.

The party then proceeded to the library, Lady Fleetwood, as they went, endeavouring to communicate something to Mr. Scriven in a low tone, and that worthy gentleman turning rudely away from her. The magistrates took their seats on one side of the large, old-fashioned library table. The clerk was sent for, and almost immediately appeared; and after a good deal of trouble he contrived to reduce the somewhat loosely-worded charge of Mr. Scriven to a technical form. When this was done, the accuser was sworn to his information; and Mr. Hargrave then, turning towards him, said--

"Now, Mr. Scriven, will you have the goodness to bring forward your proofs?"

"In the first place," said Mr. Scriven, "the likeness is so exceedingly strong that there can hardly be a doubt. From the likeness alone I am ready to swear that I believe the person calling himself Colonel Middleton to be no other than Henry Hayley."

"We have so many cases of mistaken identity," said Mr. Hargrave, "that it will require very strong evidence to establish the fact by mere resemblance. Pray, how long ago is it since you saw this Henry Hayley?"

"Somewhat more than ten years," answered Mr. Scriven.

"Humph!" said Mr. Hargrave: "what age was he then?"

"I believe, between sixteen and seventeen," answered the merchant.

"Are they of the same height?" inquired the magistrate.

"Oh, dear, no," was the reply: "Henry Hayley was decidedly shorter; but, if you recollect his age, that is easily accounted for."

"Humph!" said Mr. Hargrave again. "Have you any other persons ready to swear to the identity?"

"Yes," was the reply. "Mr. Stolterforth here must remember him very well."

"We are ready to take his deposition," said Mr. Hargrave; and Mr. Stolterforth, coming forward with some hesitation, deposed to the best of his knowledge and belief that the person before him was the same Henry Hayley who had absconded ten years before.

Mr. Scriven then called upon Charles Marston, who came forward without hesitation, and was asked as to the resemblance.

"They are very like, certainly," he said with a smile; "but still, either my sight is not as good as my uncle's, or else my spectacles do not magnify as much as his; for I must confess that, though I was at school with Henry Hayley, and have been long acquainted with Colonel Middleton, I did not perceive the likeness till Mr. Scriven pointed it out. I always thought him like somebody I had known, but could not tell whom."

"Have you any question to ask the witness, colonel?" said Sir Harry Henderson, turning to the accused.

"Merely this," replied Henry: "you have said that you have known me long, Marston. Have you frequently seen me in society?"

"Oh, dear, yes," replied Charles: "in the society of Englishmen, Spaniards, and Italians."

"Then by what name did I usually go, and how was I recognised and received?" was the next question.

"By the name of Colonel Middleton," replied Charles Marston; "and under that name you were always recognised and received as a very distinguished officer in the Spanish service, and the nephew of Don Balthazar de Xamorça, a grandee of Spain, by the marriage of his niece with an English gentleman. I have conversed with several noble Spaniards, who claim close kindred with you by the mother's side; and----"

"This is all hearsay," said Mr. Scriven, "and I object----"

"Hold your tongue, sir!" said Colonel Mandrake, sharply. "The magistrates will object when they think the evidence inadmissible. Go on, if you please, Mr. Marston."

"I was only going to say," continued Charles, "that I can take upon myself to swear that Colonel Middleton succeeded to a considerable portion of the property of Don Balthazar, on account of his relationship, for I heard it from persons who shared with him."

"Humph!" said Mr. Hargrave again. "I think, as far as we have gone yet, Mr. Scriven, you have made out a case of strong resemblance, but nothing more."

"I will do more presently," replied Mr. Scriven, drily; "but I will first call my sister, Lady Fleetwood."

In a state of bewilderment and agitation perfectly indescribable, Lady Fleetwood advanced to the table, in that exact frame of mind from which a skilful advocate can extract anything upon earth. She would have sworn, under a little management, that the sun was black and the moon blue; and, to say the truth, if Mr. Scriven had been wise, he would have let her alone, for at that moment she was a sort of revolving gun, and there was no knowing in which direction she would fire. As to keeping her to the point, that was quite out of the question. She said she thought it was exceedingly cruel and unpardonable of her brother to bring forward that charge, when he had formally promised her not to do so, and that she never would have told him a word about Colonel Middleton being Henry Hayley, if he had not given his word that he would do everything he could to help him.

"Then you know him to be Henry Hayley?" said Mr. Scriven, fixing his cold eyes upon her.

"I know you would do anything to prevent his marrying Maria," said Lady Fleetwood, now really angry. "You would swear away his life, though I am quite sure he never committed the forgery at all, and I believe you're sure of it too."

"But you are sure he is Henry Hayley?" reiterated Mr. Scriven: "remember you are on your oath, Margaret."

"I believe you must answer the question, Lady Fleetwood," said Mr. Hargrave.

"Well, I do believe he is," said Lady Fleetwood; "but I am sure I never would have told my brother about the man coming to my house, and threatening to inform against the poor young gentleman, if he had not promised to help him."

"That will do," said Mr. Scriven, coolly; and one of the magistrates inquired whether the accused had any questions to put to the witness.

Henry, however, declined; and as Lady Fleetwood was retiring, he took her hand, saying in a kindly tone--

"Do not agitate yourself, my dear lady. You have not done me the slightest harm."

"I am very glad of it," replied Lady Fleetwood, warmly; "for I am sure I did it all with the best intentions."

"I suppose you have other evidence to produce, Mr. Scriven?" said Mr. Hargrave.

Mr. Scriven hesitated. He felt he was coming upon the most dangerous part of his case; for, though he had been bold in anticipation, he was less so in act.

Mr. Hargrave, however, continued:--

"I must look upon the testimony of Mr. Marston, that Colonel Middleton has long gone under the name he now bears, and is believed to be entitled to it by persons who have not only known him from youth, but have had the best means of and strongest motives for ascertaining who he is, and for resisting his pretensions if they were false, as something very positive; against which we have a mere expression of belief on the other side. We must have something more, sir, to satisfy us."

"Besides, I want to hear something about this man who used threats," said Colonel Mandrake.

"I am coming to that this moment," said Mr. Scriven, seeing that he must necessarily proceed if he was determined to succeed, and remembering that his companion, Mr. Stolterforth, was well aware that he had what appeared strong corroborative evidence against the man whom he accused. "I think I have proved sufficiently that the likeness is so strong as to justify reasonable suspicion; and I must observe that you have not heard one witness yet who, having known the defendant more than ten years under the name of Middleton, can establish that he is not the same man as Henry Hayley. I therefore think you would be justified in granting a warrant against him; but I will produce further evidence if it be needful."

Here the clerk whispered a word or two to Mr. Hargrave, who inquired, apparently in consequence--

"Pray, Mr. Scriven, under what circumstances was the warrant against this said Henry Hayley quashed or dropped?"

The merchant hesitated for a moment, as if not very sure whether it would be better to enter into the details or not; and his first reply was vague and unsatisfactory.

But Mr. Hargrave pressed him home.

"The clerk informs me," he said, "that he remembers the case quite well; and that the warrant was dropped because the officer entrusted with the execution of it, after having pursued the fugitive into Italy, found him there in a dying state, and subsequently saw his dead body and witnessed his funeral. Do you admit these facts or do you not, sir?"

"I admit that the officer saw a dead body, which he was told was that of Henry Hayley," Mr. Scriven replied; "and he might witness the funeral for aught I know; but I maintain that there was a juggle in all this."

"Well, sir," answered Mr. Hargrave, "this is, at all events, strong presumptive evidence that Colonel Middleton cannot be Henry Hayley."

"Of course," said Colonel Mandrake; "for if Henry Hayley died in Italy, Henry Hayley cannot be living here. We have not yet come to the resurrection of the just, Mr. Scriven."

"We may have come to the resurrection of the unjust, however," replied Mr. Scriven, uttering a joke, for the first time in his life; "and that, I think, I can prove, notwithstanding all opposition."

"We must certainly have more evidence, or dismiss the charge," said Mr. Hargrave: "there is nothing before us which we can either deal with ourselves or send to another court. I say this much, although Colonel Middleton has not yet commenced his defence."

"Well, then, more evidence you shall have," answered Mr. Scriven. "I will beg you to send for the man whom we brought hither from London in our chaise."

This request was immediately complied with; and in a minute or two the worthy gentleman who has been named Sam was brought into the room, with Mr. Scriven's servant, who had received especial directions not to lose sight of him, following close upon his heels.

This worthy personage, being brought to the table and sworn, declared that his name was Samuel Nugent, and that he was by trade a general dealer. He said, also, that on a certain night which he named he was crossing over Frimley Common, when he accidentally kicked something with his foot, which on examination he discovered to be a pocket-book; that in it he found a number of papers, which he proceeded to describe, and all of which, as he stated, tended to show that Henry Hayley and Colonel Middleton were the same person.

"The book itself," said the man, "and a good many of the things in it, I threw away; but I kept these, because I thought they were curious, and then a friend of mine told me I might turn a penny by them."

"We usually say, turn an honest penny," said Mr. Hargrave, gravely. "The word *honest* you have judiciously left out. Show me the papers."

The papers were accordingly handed up to him, and he and his brother magistrates examined them carefully.

"Here is, I find, a memorandum-book, in which there are some entries which may very well bear the construction attempted to be put upon them. I find the remarkable words, 'The assumed name of Colonel Middleton;' and here are two letters addressed to Henry Hayley, at Eton, and several other things referring to Colonel Middleton and to Henry Hayley, which, taken with other circumstances and the striking resemblance, throw considerable suspicion on the case. I am afraid, Colonel Middleton, I must call upon you for some clear and explicit explanation. What is your defence?"

"Remember, sir," said Sir Harry Henderson, "that you are not obliged to make any statement, and that whatever you say will be taken down, and may be used against you at an after period."

"I have no objection to such being the case," replied Henry, calmly, while Maria, terribly agitated at the serious turn which affairs seemed to be taking, closed her eyes and bent down her head upon her hands. "I will simply ask a few questions, and bring forward a few facts to show the character of the man who stands before you, and the nature of the transaction in which he and Mr. Scriven have been engaged. I do not know," he continued, fixing his eyes sternly on the merchant, "sufficient of the law of England to be sure that it will justify me in requiring that gentleman to be held to bail upon a charge of subornation of perjury; and the witness before you to be committed for perjury; but I think I will show you very soon that there is ground for such a charge against each."

Mr. Scriven turned very white, but whether it was from fear or anger it might be difficult to say. He certainly affected the appearance of the latter passion, and was beginning to exclaim furiously against the insolent daring of the accuser, when Henry exclaimed--

"Cease, cease, sir! You have been like the rattlesnake, and have given warning of your design before you sprang at me. I have not forgotten the night at Lady Fleetwood's. However, now I will proceed to make good what I say. Joshua Brown, come forward!" and as he spoke, the pedlar advanced to the table. "Do you know the last witness?" continued Henry.

"Yes, sir," replied the man.

"Well, then, explain to the magistrates who and what he is," was the rejoinder.

"Why, gentlemen, he's a well-known thief," said the pedlar. "He and three others attacked myself and this gentleman, Colonel Middleton, near a place called Knight's-hill, on the night of Friday, the 3rd; knocked us down, pillaged us of almost everything we had, and were only prevented from murdering us, I believe, by some other people coming up. Amongst other things, they took the colonel's pocket-book, and he employed me to get it for him. So, on inquiring at the house of Mr. Alston, a silversmith and jeweller, in the town of ----, I found that the most likely place to hear of it was at the shop of a receiver of stolen goods, named Mingy Bowes."

He then went on to describe all that had occurred on that occasion, and ended with the fact of the pocket-book having been thrown into the fire and consumed.

Mr. Scriven was somewhat alarmed; but he was too shrewd and clear-sighted to suffer any advantage to escape.

"Your worships will remark," he said, "that it is here admitted that my witness had in his possession a pocket-book actually belonging to the person calling himself Colonel Middleton; and that there were papers in that pocket-book of such consequence as to induce him to offer a hundred pounds to regain it. You will also remark that I know nothing of the witness except what he himself has told me. I cannot know how he became possessed of the pocket-book or of these papers; and as he has stated that he threw the book away, but retained these, without stating whether it was into the fire he threw it or not, it seems to me that the truth of his statement and the genuineness of these papers are rather confirmed than otherwise by the evidence just given."

"Oh, you can tell very well how he became possessed of the papers," replied the pedlar, looking him full in the face, "because, you know, you told him what he was to say here. Why, didn't you, in Lady Fleetwood's dining-room, the other morning, put him up to saying that he found the pocket-book as he was crossing the common?"

This was said in the most simple and natural manner in the world, but its effect upon Mr. Scriven was very terrible. His lips turned livid, and for a moment he remained speechless and motionless, holding the edge of the table as if for support.

"What is that? what is that?" exclaimed Colonel Mandrake. "He told him what he was to say here, did he?"

"Yes, your worship," replied Joshua Brown. "He told him in Lady Fleetwood's dining-room, on Wednesday morning last. They can't deny it, either of them."

Mr. Scriven was utterly confounded, and for the moment had not a word to reply; but Sam Nugent, who was as bold in lying as in other things, answered at once, with an oath--

"I do deny it. It's false!"

"How came you to know, or rather how can you know, what took place in Lady Fleetwood's dining-room?" demanded Mr. Scriven, taking courage from the man's bold tone.

"Because I was in the next room, sir, and heard every word of it," answered the pedlar, with the utmost composure.

"Pray, how happened you to be there, my good sir?" demanded Mr. Hargrave.

"I went on purpose, sir, with another witness," replied Joshua Brown, deliberately. "The way was this:--The man Mingy Bowes--that is, the 'fence,' as they would call him, or receiver of stolen goods--called twice upon the colonel there, to try and frighten him out of some money. He did not see him either time; but the last time he saw me, and a very unpleasant sight it was for him. I was sitting with the colonel's servant when he was shown in; and having got my hand upon his neck about the robbery, I soon brought him to reason, and made him tell me all about their plans. I found that he and this young gentleman were to go to Lady Fleetwood's on Wednesday morning last, and that they hoped to get a thousand pounds out of her on account of the papers they pretended to have. So I made my arrangements accordingly, knowing that my lady was to be out of town, and that they were to see Mr. Scriven, which I learned by accident; and so I told Mr. Carlini, the colonel's servant, not to say a word to his master, for fear he should not like it, but just to ask leave to stay one day behind him in London. It was granted readily enough; and as Mr. Carlini knew her ladyship's housekeeper and one of the other servants, we got admission----"

"And you went to listen to what I said, you scoundrels!" exclaimed Mr. Scriven.

"No, sir, begging your pardon," replied the pedlar, quite civilly: "I did not go to learn what you said, for I had no thought you would say anything like what you did say. I went to hear what this man said to you, that I might detect his trick and punish him as he deserved. However, I heard enough to surprise me very much; for I never fancied a gentleman would condescend to trade with a thief, and promise him five hundred pounds if he would swear away another man's life."

There was a dead silence in the room for a minute after these strong words, and then Mr. Hargrave looked round to the other magistrates, saying--

"This is becoming very serious, gentlemen."

"Very serious indeed," said Colonel Mandrake, slowly; and Sir Harry Henderson echoed his words, adding--

"Is the person who was with you on this occasion in the room?"

"No, sir," replied Joshua Brown; "but he is in the house, and can be called in a minute."

"Let us hear you out first," said Mr. Hargrave. "Be so good as to relate the whole conversation you overheard."

The pedlar did so, with wonderful accuracy; and Carlini, having been called in, gave exactly the same account.

At first Mr. Scriven was silent, confused, and overpowered; but he soon recovered himself. He was not a man either to believe or to admit that he had done a wrong thing, and by the time the tale was told he was prepared to face it.

"Well, gentlemen," he said, addressing the magistrates, "I do not well see what this has to do with the case. If I did suggest to the man a way of accounting for having the pocket-book in his possession, it does not at all prove that these papers are not genuine."

"It is proved, sir, that you suggested to him to take a false oath," replied Mr. Hargrave, very sternly; "it is proved that he did take a false oath; and the credibility both of the man's evidence and your own is very seriously affected by his character, his conduct, and your dealings with him. Call in a constable there! I shall give him into custody, and send him to London upon the charge of the robbery, if not of the perjury. With you, sir, I really do not know how to deal;" and he leaned his head upon his hand and thought gravely.

"It is not ten minutes ago, sir," said Mr. Scriven, sharply, "that you refused to entertain a charge against this person calling himself Colonel Middleton, because the act with which he was charged had been committed in another county."

"I did not refuse to entertain the charge," replied Mr. Hargrave: "I informed you of what was the usual course, and I believe the strictly legal one. Magistrates, however, must sometimes overstep mere technical difficulties; and in the case of this man, Samuel Nugent, I have no doubt at all, but will send him to London in custody, upon my own responsibility. In the same way, also, I have now determined to enter fully into your charge of forgery against Colonel Middleton, if the prosecutor and he are both desirous of our doing so; otherwise, I certainly shall take no steps whatever."

"I suppose, sir, I am the prosecutor in this case, technically speaking," said Mr. Stolterforth, stepping forward; "and as such, I shall be perfectly satisfied with your decision upon the whole case, whatever that decision may be. I was very unwilling, I must say, to open the matter again at all, and would have let it rest had not Mr. Scriven pressed me earnestly to proceed. It is so long ago that it might very well be dropped; and, moreover, I always entertained some doubts as to whether the party charged was the one really criminal. The evidence certainly was strong; but I had known the boy long, and it was hardly possible to believe him guilty. In regard to the question of identity, I certainly thought the proofs brought forward by Mr. Scriven very convincing; but my view has been altered since I came here, and now I entertain many doubts. Under these circumstances, I am the more anxious that the whole matter should be investigated at once, and I pledge myself to abide by the decision of the magistrates present."

"And whatever their decision may be," said Henry, "I shall be satisfied with it."

There was a momentary pause, as if no one knew well how to commence the somewhat irregular proceeding agreed upon; but at length Henry took another step forward to the table, and taking Mr. Stolterforth's hand, he said--

"My dear sir, you have done me justice, and from my heart I thank you for your good opinion. To simplify all your proceedings, however, I will at once admit that I am Henry Hayley."

"I beg your pardon, my dear sir," said Mr. Hargrave, laughing; "but you are under a mistake. You are not Henry Hayley. My brother magistrates and myself have just this moment agreed that you are not, and I can take upon myself to affirm, of my own positive knowledge, that we are right."

"Then why admit it?" asked Mr. Scriven, harshly, while Mr. Stolterforth and most of the party present looked perfectly bewildered.

"Nay, let me make the admission, my dear sir," said Henry, addressing Mr. Hargrave. "This painful scene has already continued too long, and I have only suffered it to do so in order to show the vehement animosity excited against me. I will, therefore, in order to curtail every unnecessary detail, admit, moreover, that I was charged with forgery upon a due and formal information upon oath, that a warrant was granted against me, and that I fled the country----"

"That is enough, I think!" exclaimed Mr. Scriven: "the matter ought now to be sent to a competent court."

"Stop, sir!" said Henry, sternly, "and be so good as to hear me out. I admit, I say, that I fled the country, but not to escape the arm of the law, for I had with me full proof of my innocence; and, as you have heard from the witness Joshua Brown, the man who burned the pocket-book, of which he had robbed me, acknowledged that there was in it a document purporting to have been written by the late Mr. Hayley, which clearly stated that the forgery was his, that I knew nothing of it, and that I had consented to abandon my country, and rest under the imputation of crime, in order to save a father from death."

"All very pretty," said Mr. Scriven; "but we have not the paper to examine. We cannot ascertain whether it was genuine. I myself believe it to have been a fabrication, and the evidence was overpowering against you. You fled at once to Northumberland, thence went to Wales, thence to London, thence to the Continent, changing everywhere the notes in which the forged bill had been paid."

"I wish, sir, you would not interrupt me," said Henry; "you have surely had sufficient license of the tongue to-day. Allow me, at least, to make my own statement connectedly. Mr. Hayley one day gave me a draft upon your house, of which he had been very lately a partner, apparently accepted by yourself, to discount at Messrs. Stolterforth's bank. At the same time he entered into an explanation of some of his affairs, which I already knew to be seriously deranged, telling me that he must absolutely have two thousand pounds more within a week, and that as soon as I had got the draft discounted I must go down with all speed to this very house, and borrow that sum for him of his friend Lord Mellent, then in attendance on his father at this house. Mr. Stolterforth kindly discounted the bill at once. I now believe the money to be obtained from Lord Mellent was destined by Mr. Hayley to take up the bill before the forgery was discovered; but I knew nothing of that, and set out that night for Belford. When I arrived here, I found that the Earl of Milford was dead, and that his son had set out to convey the body to the family vault near Caermarthen. As I had been told that the necessity of Mr. Hayley's case was urgent, I followed, changing, as Mr. Scriven says, several of the notes which Mr. Hayley had given me, at different places, to pay my expenses. I missed Lord Milford at Caermarthen, but passed him, while in the mail on my road to London, as he was being carried into an inn with concussion of the brain, his carriage having been overturned and nearly dashed to pieces. It is false, however, that I changed any notes whatsoever after I went to the Continent; for Mr. Hayley had himself provided for me foreign gold, so that I had no notes whatever to change."

"I recollect, I recollect," said Mr. Stolterforth; "I have a memorandum of it here. Several notes were traced to a money-changer, who said he had received them for napoleons from an elderly man, of whom he could give no particular description, and could not identify him."

"I went to London in the most open manner," continued Henry, "in the public mail-coach, with my name at large on my portmanteau, and proceeded from the post-office at once to Mr. Hayley's house. There I found him up and waiting for me, and for the first time learned the crime he had committed. Everything was already prepared for my instant departure; and he besought me, in an agony of distress and agitation, to save him from disgrace and death. Could a son refuse a father under such circumstances? I could not, and I fled."

"The statement seems exceedingly likely," said Mr. Stolterforth, "The only improbable part of the whole is, that Mr. Hayley should send his son, a boy of sixteen or seventeen, to borrow a sum of two thousand pounds from Lord Mellent, when it would have been much more natural and proper for him to go himself."

Lady Anne Mellent smiled, and Henry replied--

"There was a cause; but, even without any peculiar motive being assigned, the fact did not strike me at the time as the least extraordinary, for I had been all my life a peculiar favourite with Lord Mellent. He had been uniformly kind and generous towards me, and had more than once told me, if ever I should want advice or assistance of any kind, to apply to him without scruple. Mr. Hayley told me to make it my own request to the young lord, and I was prepared to do so, without much doubt of the result."

"I think the whole story most improbable, from the beginning to the end," said Mr. Scriven; "and I must say it should be thoroughly sifted in a court of justice, before we admit the truth of a tale, every word of which is wanting in confirmation."

"Confirmation it shall have to the fullest extent," said Lady Anne Mellent, coming forward to the table with a packet of papers in her hand. "Happily for myself and others, I can give that which you so bitterly demand, sir."

She was a good deal agitated, but it was evident that anger had some share in her emotion; for as she spoke, she fixed her bright, beautiful eyes steadily upon Mr. Scriven; her nostril expanded, and her lip quivered.

"In the first place," she continued, "it shall be confirmed that this gentleman came down here to seek Lord Mellent. Stand forth, Mr. Gunnel, and tell these gentlemen who you are, and what you know of this transaction."

"The good, stout person of Mr. Gunnel now made its way forward to Lady Anne's side; and he said--

"My name is Gunnel, and I am the landlord of the Bell Inn at Belford. I remember quite well a young gentleman of sixteen or seventeen, though he was very tall and manly for his age, coming down to my house by the mail, in the month of August, about ten years ago. That gentleman is very like him. I should say, certainly, 'tis the same man grown older. When he got out he asked how far it was to Milford Castle, and said he must go on directly, for he had to see Lord Mellent upon business. I told him it was sixteen miles, and that he couldn't go on that night, for that all our horses were out. He took dinner, and asked very often if the horses had come in. He seemed very anxious to see Lord Mellent; but, as it was a stiff journey and there had been a run upon the road, I did not like the horses to go before they had had a night's rest. He did not change any notes at my house, but paid me in gold; and I never heard any inquiries made about it till Lady Anne asked me the other night if I recollected the facts. When he went from my house he came straight over here in a chaise of mine; but I heard from the postboy afterwards, that finding the old lord was dead, and the young lord gone with the body into Wales, the gentleman had gone on in the chaise to Wooler, seeming very anxious to catch his lordship as soon as possible. That's all I know upon the subject."

"And quite enough, too, Mr. Gunnel," said Mr. Hargrave, with an approving nod of the head.

"I am quite satisfied," said Mr. Stolterforth.

But Lady Anne exclaimed--

"No, not yet. There shall not be a shade of suspicion left upon his name. May I ask you, Colonel Mandrake, to read that paper aloud? You were acquainted with my dear father, and must know his handwriting at the bottom. The other signature I can prove, for the witness is now in the house, and shall describe what he saw and heard."

"I will read the paper at once, my lady," replied Colonel Mandrake. "I see your father's handwriting, and would swear to it anywhere from the peculiar turn of the *d*.

"'The confession of Stephen Hayley, made in the presence of Charles Earl of Milford, on the 11th day of October, 18--, at Harley Lodge, in the county of Hertford. I, Stephen Hayley, upon the solemn promise of the Earl of Milford never to divulge what I am now about to write, until after my death, except in case a young gentleman, known by the name of Henry Hayley, now supposed to be dead, should again reappear in this country, do hereby acknowledge and confess that I did forge the name of Mr. Henry Scriven, with the word "Accepted" on a bill of exchange, which, was discounted for me by the said young gentleman at the house of Messrs. Stolterforth and Co. bankers; and that he, the said Henry Hayley, was totally and entirely ignorant that the bill was forged, when he so discounted it; and that he never either knew, or, to the best of my belief, suspected, that the said bill was forged, till the very morning on which he departed for the Continent. Moreover, I acknowledge and confess that he left England at my earnest entreaty, and solely with the view of saving my life, I having previously furnished him with a paper to the same effect as this present, in order to ensure him from danger if he should be apprehended and brought back. I solemnly declare every word herein above written to be true; and I authorise the Earl of Milford to produce this paper in case the said Henry Hayley should not be dead, and should ever return to England, and to make whatever use of it he may think fit after my death.

"'Signed, Stephen Hayley.

"'Witnesses, { Milford.
Thomas Alsager.'"

"My father's signature can be proved by Alsager," said Lady Anne. "Let Thomas Alsager be called. Mr. Hargrave, will you put what questions to him you think necessary?"

When the name of Thomas Alsager had been pronounced, a stout, portly man, Lady Anne's butler, advanced to the table, bowing to the magistrates.

"Thomas Alsager," said Mr. Hargrave, "did you ever witness, in the presence of your late master, the signature of a gentleman named Hayley?"

"Yes, your worship," replied the man; "I did."

"Is that your handwriting?" demanded Mr. Hargrave.

"It is," answered the butler.

"Describe what occurred on that occasion," said Mr. Hargrave.

"Why, your worship," replied the man, "my lord had been very ill, from an accident by which he had nearly been killed; but he had been recovering rapidly, and had walked out once or twice in the park, when one morning at breakfast he had taken up a newspaper, just as I was putting some things on the table; and all in a minute he started up, as if he had seen something frightful, threw the paper down under his feet and trampled upon it. I never saw him in such a way before; and he cried out, 'Send a man on horseback immediately for that villain Hayley! Tell him to come down to me directly; and say, if he does not come, I will come and fetch him.' My lady was in the room, and she tried to quiet him. He did get a little more composed, and he wrote a note, and sent the carriage instead of a man on horseback. Mr. Hayley came back in the carriage, and when he got out I saw he was pale and trembling. I showed him into my lord's little room, and there he remained for about an hour; and as I passed and repassed I could hear my lord's voice very high at times, till at last he rang the bell as if he would have shaken it down. I ran in as fast as possible, and I found Mr. Hayley on his knees before him, crying, 'I will indeed--I will do it this minute.'

"Then my lord answered, 'Very well, sir; if you have told the truth, you can have no objection to write it. You may go away, Alsager.' In about half-an-hour after, he rang again, but much more quietly; and when I went in I found Mr. Hayley sitting with that paper before him, not spread out, but doubled down, so that I could only see the last words; and my lord said, 'I wish you to witness this person's signature, Alsager. Now, Mr. Hayley.' Then Mr. Hayley put his hand upon the paper, and said, 'All I have written in this paper is true, so help me God;' and then he wrote his name. My lord wrote his, and I wrote mine and went away. In a few minutes after, Mr. Hayley went too; but my lord would never see him afterwards, though he called once or twice."

No further questions were asked of the butler; but Sir Harry Henderson remarked--

"Here is your name upon the back of the paper, Hargrave, I see."

"That was merely for verification," said Mr. Hargrave, "in order to be able to prove how, when, and where this and other papers were found."

"Rather singular, indeed," said Mr. Scriven, whose bitter spirit was not yet fully worked out, "that the earl should leave such a paper about, when his old schoolfellow's life depended upon it." "He did not leave it about, sir," answered Lady Anne. "He placed it in a cabinet here at Milford, a short time before his death, and sealed up that cabinet with a strip of parchment, impressing the wax at each end with his own coat-of-arms. The seal he left by his will to Mr. Hargrave; so that it has never been in my possession, nor have I ever been at Milford Castle, since my father's death, till I came here with Mr. Hargrave. The key of the cabinet, sealed up in a letter directed to me, and explaining the nature of the papers I would find therein when I came of age, my father ordered to be given to me after his death. Mr. Hargrave witnessed my opening of that cabinet, the parchment being then uncut and the seals unbroken; and he wrote his name upon each of the papers found therein, to identify them in case of need. I mention these facts, Mr. Scriven, lest you should suspect me of fabricating these papers-- though what possible motive I could have for fabricating them it might be difficult to discover."

"Not so difficult as your ladyship supposes," replied Mr. Scriven, with a last spirit of disappointed spleen. "Love, we know, will make people do many strange things."

"Love!" cried Lady Anne, with a gay smile; "well, so be it. I do love him!" and she put her arm through that of Henry. "I do love him most dearly, most truly, most tenderly!"

"Then no wonder, madam, your ladyship tries hard to save a man you wish to marry," said Mr. Scriven.

"Marry!" exclaimed Lady Anne, laughing joyously. "Nay, nay, my good sir; not marry my own brother!"

Mr. Scriven looked confounded; and there was many a one in the room who was very much, though not equally, surprised. After a moment's silence, however, Lady Anne turned to Henry, placing the rest of the papers she had brought in his hands, and saying--

"There, Henry, my dear brother, I put you in possession of that which is yours. I am no longer mistress of this house, of this estate, or of any of the property of the Milford family. They go with the title to you. Harley Lodge and my mother's property are all that I can claim; and I do not think you will make me pay back rents for that which I have not kept willingly. One such brother is to me worth all the property in the world."

Henry threw his arms round her and kissed her tenderly; but, bursting away from him with her own wild grace, she cast herself upon the bosom of Maria Monkton and wept.

The magistrates rose from the table at which they had been sitting, and shook hands with and congratulated him who had been the object of so much interest and so much investigation. Charles Marston and Mr. Winkworth were not behind them; and poor Lady Fleetwood exclaimed with a sigh--

"Well, this is very extraordinary, and very fortunate!"

"Very extraordinary indeed," said Mr. Scriven, drily; "and not the least extraordinary part of the whole is a body of magistrates rising to shake hands with a person still under a charge of felony."

"I drop the charge entirely," said Mr. Stolterforth. "I am perfectly convinced, as any reasonable man must be, that there is not the slightest foundation for it whatever."

"Nevertheless," said Mr. Hargrave, who had heard Mr. Scriven's observation and the rejoinder, "Mr. Scriven is quite right. This is an unusual manner of expressing the unanimous decision at which I believe we have arrived. We must proceed more orderly--Sir Harry Henderson!--colonel!-- let me have your decision."

He spoke for a single moment apart with each of his brother magistrates; and then, resuming his seat with the rest, he said--

"It is the unanimous opinion of the justices present, that there is not the slightest ground for the accusation which has been made against the gentleman known here by the name of Colonel Middleton. Charge dismissed. Clerk, you will have the goodness to send all the papers to the proper quarter; and in case of any question as to our having acted out of our jurisdiction, I take the responsibility thereof upon myself. The prisoner, Samuel Nugent, must be sent to London, with a copy of the depositions by which he is affected."

"Then I am to consider that the case against Colonel Middleton, *alias* Hayley, *alias* Milford, is disposed of?" said Mr. Scriven.

"As far as we are concerned, this case is, sir," replied Mr. Hargrave. "There is another case, however, affecting subornation of perjury, which, not having any parallel case in remembrance, I do not know how to deal with. I will, however, when I get home, consult authorities on the subject, and confer with my brother magistrates. If you are still in the county, you shall hear from me on the matter." This delicate hint was not lost upon Mr. Scriven. Although he saw that the game was against him, indeed, he had a strong inclination to see if nothing could be done to retrieve it. But he was a man of calculation--hardy, persevering, it is true, in pursuit of an object, but yet unwilling to risk much upon a perilous speculation; and in the present instance he was quietly beating a retreat, as soon as Mr. Hargrave's eye was off him. He was interrupted, however, in his course, by a loud, clear, sharp voice exclaiming--

"Hey! Scriven, Scriven!" and turning round, as almost all the rest of the party did at this sudden exclamation, he saw the eyes of Mr. Winkworth fixed upon him through a pair of large spectacles. "Just let me remind you before you go, Scriven," said Mr. Winkworth, "that you owe the sum of twenty-one thousand two hundred and sixty-three pounds eleven shillings and fivepence to the heirs, executors, administrators, or assigns of the late Stephen Hayley, Esq. whose sole representative I take to be Miss Rebecca Hayley, now in confinement, by your orders, at Brooke Green."

If Mr. Scriven ever really felt fury, it was at that moment.

"What is that to you, sir?" he demanded fiercely. "Your assertion is false!"

"No, it is not," answered Mr. Winkworth. "It is quite true; and not only will I prove it so within the next three months, but I will prove that you have owed it for ten years, and denied the debt because you had got possession of the vouchers."

Mr. Scriven had waxed marvellously pale, and he gazed in Mr. Winkworth's face as if he had beheld a ghost.

"And who are you?" he demanded, in a dull, hollow tone; but those were the only words he seemed capable of uttering.

"I am one who have known you well," replied Mr. Winkworth, "for well-nigh thirty years; and if your memory of faces were as good as you pretend, methinks you might have remembered mine. There--go, go! We shall meet in London within a month; and pray you see that my accounts with your house are in somewhat better order than those of unhappy Stephen Hayley."

Mr. Scriven was very near the door; and a servant, opening it at that moment, gave him an opportunity of slipping out without any great bustle.

Henry was at that moment speaking a few words to Lady Anne Mellent and pale Maria Monkton--pale, I say, for agitation had blanched her cheek till it looked like the leaf of a lily.

"Shall I call him back and ask him to stay?" he said, in a low but eager tone, addressing Maria.

"No, Henry--no," she answered, laying her hand upon his arm: "it would only be a misery to himself and a restraint to us. You can never be friends, for you are nature's opposites; but you will endure him for my sake, and better at a distance."

At that moment Lady Fleetwood advanced towards them, her face beaming with every kindly purpose.

"My dear lord," she said, while Maria looked up in his face with a gentle smile, "I congratulate you most sincerely, and dear Maria too, upon the wonderful events that have happened. I don't understand it at all for my own part, though I see that it has all ended quite right and happily. You must indeed forgive my poor brother Scriven; for you know he is a dry, commonplace man of business, and I am sure did it all--with the best intentions."

Maria could hardly refrain from laughing; but Sir Harry Henderson, who was standing near, said, in a jocular sort of way--

"Indeed, Lady Fleetwood, few of us understand the matter completely, and should very much like to hear the whole explained, without waiting for a newspaper account of it."

"Such explanation, my dear sir, I shall be most happy to give you," said Henry, "but not now. I have my sister's directions to ask the whole party here assembled, and more especially yourself and Colonel Mandrake, to remain and dine with us. I would hold out the explanation of all mysteries as a temptation, did I not think that the bare request of Lady Anne would be quite sufficient for any gentleman here present."

"Assuredly, assuredly, my lord," replied Colonel Mandrake, who was a very gallant old gentleman, with bushy black and white eyebrows and an aquiline nose; "but, unfortunately, we are here in morning costume."

"That will be easily amended," said Lady Anne, with one of her gay looks. "Nobody indeed will remark Colonel Mandrake's costume when he is himself present; but, if he needs must attend to all those proprieties which so much distinguish him, a man and horse will be at liberty in a few minutes to bring whatever he requires. And now let us adjourn to another room, for this has been so full of agitating feelings that the air seems loaded with ill affections."

"Mingled with pure and noble ones, dear Anne," said Henry, laying his hand upon hers. "Now, kind Lady Fleetwood, let me give you my arm, and let none of us regret what has passed, as we have all acted--with the best intentions."

CHAPTER XXXIX

Sir Harry Henderson was very curious, and he longed to anticipate the explanation which he had promised for the evening; but he was disappointed, for the principal actors in the scene which had just passed had given up, they thought, enough time to facts, and were now disposed to afford a larger share to emotions.

For half-an-hour the whole party remained assembled in the drawing-room; but then one began to drop off after another, and the conversation, which had at first been of an eager yet gossiping kind, discussing all that had taken place, and the demeanour of several of those who had appeared upon the stage, languished for want of fresh materials.

Mr. Hargrave, though the oldest man of the party, was the one for whom a sensitive heart and intelligent mind had preserved, least impaired, that delicate perception--or rather, I should have said, intuition--of the feelings of others, which is so beautiful to see at a period of life when passions have become memories, and the emotions of life are stilled by the awful presence of the yawning grave.

He watched the face of Maria Monkton for a moment, as she sat with her cheek leaning on her hand, her eyes fixed upon the floor, and her mind evidently brooding over the scenes which had that morning taken place, her heart thrilling with sensations of joy and thankfulness. He saw the eyes of the young earl turn to her with a longing glance, as if he would fain have cast his arms round her and pressed her to his heart; and the old man said to himself--

"These young people would be better with fewer eyes upon them. Come, Sir Harry," he continued aloud; "you and the colonel must take a walk through the park with me, and see the improvements I was proposing to Lady Anne the other day. I do not know whether they may find favour with her brother; but I shall plead for them strongly, for there is no art so full of vanity as landscape gardening."

"Will you come and judge of them, my lord?" asked Colonel Mandrake; but Henry replied--

"I fear, my dear sir, my thoughts would be so busy with other things that I should not do them justice. In a short time, I think, I shall beg the advice of all three gentlemen upon many points, both of taste and business; but to-day I will not venture to do so."

Mr. Hargrave then, with his two companions, walked out into the park. Mr. Winkworth had quitted the drawing-room some time before. Lady Anne had disappeared: Charles Marston was not to be seen; and Lady Fleetwood, Maria, Mrs. Brice, and Henry, were the only persons remaining. Mrs. Brice slipped quietly away; and dear aunt Fleetwood sat for a minute or two, debating with herself what she should do. She knew that it would be very pleasant for Maria to be left alone for a time with her lover. She had not so much forgotten the lessons of youth as to doubt that; but she thought it would distress her niece if she brought the matter about too ostentatiously, and she puzzled herself for an excuse, finding none, till at length Henry laid his hand upon Maria's arm, saying--

"Dear Maria, I want to speak with you for a few moments."

Then Lady Fleetwood started up to go, without any excuse at all; first dropped her gloves, and then her handkerchief, and then the everlasting purse. Henry picked them up, with a smile, saying--

"Dear Lady Fleetwood, what I said need not banish you. We are going to the little breakfast-room."

"No, no; stay here," said Lady Fleetwood, hurrying away. But there was a fatality about her "best intentions;" and directing her steps to the library, she opened the door hurriedly, trying with one hand to keep fast hold of her gloves and handkerchief, and of the purse with the other, when, on the door flying back farther than she intended, she saw before her Charles Marston and Lady Anne Mellent, with his arm round her waist. Lady Fleetwood would fain have retreated instantly; but she had to shut the door, and in so doing she dropped the purse again, and as she stooped to pick it up, the door, coming to vehemently, hit her on the head, and nearly knocked her down. But while Charles was hurrying to her assistance, and Lady Anne stood half laughing, half crying, by the table, she contrived to pick up the purse and beat a retreat. Her next harbour of refuge was the little breakfast-room; but there again she found Henry and Maria, who had gone thither to avoid interruption; and at last she bethought her that it might be as well to try her own bed-room, which she had the happiness of finding vacant.

"Dear Lady Fleetwood!" said Anne Mellent, when Charles returned; "fate seems to lay traps for her. But now, Charles, remember our present compact, and keep it better than you did the last. Do you suppose that I did not see, while, under all your affectation of cool confidence and implicit trust, that your angry spirit was accusing me of every kind of coquetry, and grilling itself, like a London woman's head in a lace bonnet going out in August, in an open carriage, to a picnic at Shooter's Hill?" Charles Marston laughed.

"Well," he said, "it is true. I was uneasy, dearest Anne, but not with any doubt or mistrust, as you suppose, for of your love and truth I had no doubt; but it was impossible for me to divine such a cause as has now appeared for your conduct, and you yourself must confess that nothing else but such a cause could justify it."

"You might have been quite sure," replied Lady Anne, "that I had a sufficient cause. But I will own the trial was hard," she added, in a lighter tone; for her first words had been spoken gravely; "and therefore I forgive you. I took a sly, quiet look at your face, when the secret came out; and, I must say, I never saw a more remarkable look of foolish astonishment. However, perhaps I may surprise you still more before I have done to-day; and then I suppose it will be all over, and I shall sink down into a tame, quiet, every-day sort of wife, who, if ever she ventures upon one of her old vagaries, will be scolded heartily and will endure it with due submission."

"No, no, dear girl," he answered; "you must be ever, as far as possible, what you are now. I love you as you are, and could not love you better for any change. Depend upon it, dear Anne, it is the change after marriage from what people were, or seemed, before marriage, which is the source of nine-tenths of the unhappiness one sometimes hears of in married life."

"Then take care what you are about, Charles," said Lady Anne, with a look of surprise; "for you are actually changing already. You are talking like a reasonable man. Now you know quite well, if I had ever thought you pretended to such a character, I never would have consented to marry you. But I forgot one thing. You may very likely not wish to marry me now. Do you remember, sir, coming to me one morning, with a grave and serious face, and setting me free from all promises, because an alteration had taken place in your circumstances? Now a very great alteration has taken place in mine--I have lost more than thirty thousand a-year--and therefore I now set you free."

Charles Marston laughed.

"I won't be free," he answered: "I refuse emancipation: and, to tell you the truth, my love, I am very glad it is so. The marriage is not now so unequal as it was. The good world would only have said----"

"Never mind what the world would say, Charles," answered Lady Anne. "The world is a great fool, and says every day the most ridiculous things, which nobody should care about or think of. And now, to prove how little I care, I am going to sit with Mr. Winkworth, in his bed-room, for half-an-hour."

"Well, go," said Charles. "I do not wish to stop you; but come down again soon, for I am determined to have a long ramble in the park with you--all alone."

"We shall see," answered Lady Anne, and she left him.

While the conversation which I have just detailed was taking place in one part of the house, one of a very different tone went on in the little breakfast-room, between Maria and her lover. She had gone thither with her arm through his, but somehow, when seated on the sofa there, his arm had fallen round her and his hand clasped hers. We have heard of eloquent silence, and I am not very fond of the expression, nor indeed of any paradoxical figures. Still Maria and Henry were silent, quite silent, for a minute or two after they entered the room; and their silence might well indicate the presence of many powerful emotions in their hearts--too large, too powerful for words. The first which Henry uttered were, "Do you forgive me, Maria?"

"Forgive you for what, Henry?" she asked.

"For keeping you in suspense," he answered; "for withholding from you that full, entire, unclouded confidence which shall never be withheld again. The only cause was, dear Maria, that my dear, kind, generous sister, who rejoices as much to see herself deprived of a large property as others would rejoice to receive one, bound me to silence till everything was prepared, both to establish my claims and to meet any charges against me. She was fearful that the least hint escaping might precipitate matters, and place us for a time at least in a difficult, if not a dangerous situation. Perhaps, indeed, there might be a little of the spirit of adventure and romance in her desire for keeping everything secret to the last; but still you will own she has managed admirably for me."

"Admirably indeed," exclaimed Maria, with tears in her eyes; "and when at last she said, 'What! marry my brother!' I felt inclined to run forward and cast myself at her feet. But, oh, Henry! what can I say of my uncle's conduct? What must you feel towards him? And are you quite quite sure, that you will never let any of those feelings fall back upon me?"

"Can you believe it for a moment, my beloved?" he replied. "What! upon you, the dearest, the best, the earliest friend I have--you, whose noble heart judged mine rightly from the beginning--you, who never abandoned me, who never failed me, who received me on my return with the same affection, the same confidence, which had existed between us in childhood--you, who upon my simple assurance, unsupported, unconfirmed, believed the tale I told, and in the moment of danger and difficulty conferred upon me that blessed hope which gave me strength and courage to encounter every peril and triumph over every obstacle! Oh, no, Maria! no: I shall ever look upon you and your love as the crowning mercies of all those with which heaven has compensated for a short period of anguish and disgrace. So far from my feelings towards Mr. Scriven falling back upon you, I trust, and indeed am sure, that my feelings towards you will sensibly affect my sensations towards him. Angry and indignant I must feel; but I will try, as soon as possible, to banish all such emotions, and will never forget that he is the uncle of one who loved and supported me in adversity and sorrow."

Another silent pause succeeded, for Maria did not reply; but she thanked him in her heart, and then, looking up in his face, she said, "There is much, I suppose, still to be done to establish your rights."

"Not much," replied Henry. "The whole case, I think, is very clear. All the steps taken by Mr. Scriven to prove that I am Henry Hayley tend to establish the fact that I am the son of the late Earl of Milford; and my dear sister Anne had that in view, in suffering him to go on so long without bringing forward the proofs of my innocence which she possessed. Indeed, she managed the whole with a degree of skill and judgment quite extraordinary in one so young, and apparently so wild. The proofs of my own legitimacy I have myself obtained in an extraordinary manner; and two or three papers, which, luckily, were not in the pocket-book of which I was robbed, fill up every break in the chain of evidence. You will hear the whole fully detailed to-night, and will see that, though aristocratic by the father's side, I am plebeian by the mother's; but I do not think you will love or esteem me the less for that. Nor, to say the truth, do I myself regret it; for I believe that it is by the frequent mingling of plebeian with patrician blood that the aristocracy of this country is so different from, and so much superior to that of any other. My grandfather is still living--a fine specimen of the English yeoman; and I know that my Maria will join with me in making him forget his sorrows. Some prejudices, indeed, I know he has, especially against men of a higher rank and station than his own; but those I am sure will be removed when he finds that his daughter's son can be fully as proud of the upright honesty of one ancestor as of the rank and station of another."

"But what will you do with regard to the property you have inherited in Spain, and the family there which claims you as one of its members?" demanded Maria.

"That will be easily managed," answered Henry; "though it certainly is a curious situation in which to be--as Mrs. Malaprop calls it, 'three gentlemen in one'--Henry Hayley, Frank Middleton, and Lord Milford. However, Henry Hayley we shall soon dispose of; and Frank Middleton's conduct will be very clear--to renounce the name, to restore the whole property, to repay every dollar he has received from it. The family will be very well satisfied with the restitution, for it was left to me by will, not taken as succession; and I have a letter from Don Balthazar, at the time he made his will, stating that he knew me to be no relation, and that he was acquainted with my name and history, yet left me the property with that knowledge. The family, therefore, could establish no legal claim to that which I intended to restore. The letter will only be useful as justifying me in all eyes for having retained the property so long; but I would fain, in this as in other things, come out clear of any imputation."

"I am sure you will," replied Maria; "I always was sure of it, Henry; and I must do my aunt Fleetwood the justice to say, that she has never ceased to maintain your innocence."

"Dear aunt Fleetwood!" said Henry with a smile. "I know, Maria, she loved me when a boy, and would not easily believe any evil of me. We must not forget her in our own happiness, Maria, although ours will, I am sure, greatly contribute to hers. She must be with us as much as possible; and I trust and believe that her *good intentions* will no longer have any power of working in a contrary sense."

The conversation proceeded in the same course for some time, and then the whole party reassembled at luncheon. The afternoon was spent in rambles in the neighbourhood, and in those various ways of killing time which we usually see practised in a country-house. To Lady Fleetwood Henry was tender kindness itself; and he soon taught the excellent lady to imagine that her "good intentions," though they had taken a droll course, had operated for his benefit, and to congratulate herself upon the result. Joshua Brown was committed to the care of Carlini; and all the servants of the house, though they did not comprehend the matter clearly, addressed Lady Anne's acknowledged brother with infinite reverence, and at every other word called him "my lord."

CHAPTER XL

It was after dinner. The summer light had faded from the evening sky, yet there were roses in the west, and a bright star following, like a fair handmaid, upon Cynthia's footsteps through the sky. The curtains were not drawn, and the purple hue of the past day spread through the dining-room, mingling with the more powerful light of the lamps, like calm, sad memories tempering present joys.

The party at Milford Castle consisted, as the reader knows, of ten persons; and they were still seated round the table. Lady Anne was at one end; her brother had assumed the other. The dessert, such as it was at that season of the year, was still before them. The excellent wine had once gone round; the commonplace chat of the dinner-table had gradually subsided; and one of those fits of silence which very often indicate expectation had fallen upon the whole party. The one who was the most eager for the promised explanation was Sir Harry Henderson, who said, after the silence had continued for perhaps half-a-minute--

"You promised us a history, my lord--or perhaps even I might call it a romance, for certainly it savours of the romantic."

"It does, indeed," answered Henry; "but, like many another romantic thing, it is very true. I think, however, although with my dear sister and myself some painful memories may arise and some gloomy thoughts may be awakened, it will be better to read you the letter of him who knew the whole circumstances, from being the principal actor in them, rather than give you my own version of the details. I will only premise, that from this letter Lady Anne first learned that she had ever had a brother. The demonstrable proofs were found in the cabinet, which, as you have heard, was opened by her in the presence of Mr. Hargrave."

Thus saying, he rose and rang the bell, ordering, when the servant appeared, that a green box of papers should be brought him out of his room. When it had been procured, he opened it, and took out a letter from the top, containing several closely-written pages; and having looked at it for a moment, he said--

"After the death of my father, the late Earl of Milford, this letter was delivered by his executors to his daughter, Lady Anne, whom he then believed to be his only surviving child. It contained the key of the cabinet to which you have heard allusion made; and it bears, marked upon the back, 'To be opened by my daughter, Lady Anne, when she shall arrive at the age of one-and-twenty years--provided it should please heaven that she should survive me.' The letter then proceeds as follows:--

"'My dearest Child,--You must have remarked that my health has been gradually failing for some years. The medical men attribute this decay to an accident I met with, which you well remember. I myself connect it with a much more painful event, of which they know nothing. They cannot, therefore, by any drugs, remedy the disease. I am now about to unburden my whole heart, for the first time in my life, to you, for I feel that I am soon about to be called hence; and though most improbable events might occur, which would render the secret of my early life important both to yourself and others, I know you, my dearest child, well, thoroughly, entirely; and I can trust implicitly both to your heart and to your understanding. You are too dutiful and affectionate a child to blame your father severely, even if you find he has committed some errors, or to scorn his injunctions, even if you cannot always approve his conduct. Neither will I blame my own parent, although we did not live on those terms of tender confidence in which you and I have always dwelt together; but it is necessary that I should speak of his character, to account for, if not to justify, my own actions.

"'Let me tell you, then, my early history. I was my father's second son, and never was loved as my elder brother was. That brother was kind and good, and worthy of all affection; but even to him my father was usually stern, and often even violent. To me my father's demeanour was exceedingly harsh and imperious. Instant obedience to his lightest word was exacted in all things, as was perhaps right and due; but no command ever came unaccompanied by a threat, and no threat ever remained unfulfilled, if the command was, even by mistake, disobeyed. It seemed as if he wished to make fear supersede both affection and a sense of duty--and he succeeded but too well. I learned to dread him; and, even after my poor brother's death, that sad lesson was not forgotten. As his heir, I was furnished with ample means, and received a very good education; but before my brother's death I had been placed at a somewhat inferior school, where I formed a very close intimacy with a boy of the name of Hayley. You have often seen him as a man, and must recollect him. He was weak, timid, and somewhat cowardly; but I was in the custom of defending him from the attacks of older and stronger boys, and we naturally learn to love what we protect. When I afterwards went to Eton, Stephen Hayley followed me thither, and our friendship continued unabated. Even when I was sent on a tour through Europe, with a tutor, I regularly corresponded with Hayley, my new rank as Lord Mellent making not the least change in our intimacy, though he had now become a clerk in a great merchant's house. It was not long after my return, and while I was still a student at Oxford, that an event occurred, the consequences of which have chequered my golden fate with shades unalterably dark. One day, in a country village, where I had gone to study more quietly for my degree than I could do elsewhere, I saw a girl of the most surpassing beauty that can be conceived. The first meeting was merely accidental, but the second was designed; for I eagerly inquired who she was, and finding that her father was a wealthy and honest farmer, of the name of Graves, I contrived to introduce myself to him as a person wishing to purchase a horse. I soon made myself intimate in his family, and the admiration I had conceived for his daughter ripened into the warmest and truest love. She was as gentle and kind, as good and as graceful, as she was beautiful; and, even had such a thing been possible, my dearest Anne, which it was not, I would not have misled her for the world. But my position was very difficult. I knew my father's proud spirit and highly aristocratic feelings, and that his consent to my marriage with a farmer's daughter was quite out of all hope. But I loved her, and she loved me, and I told her all my difficulties. She, and she alone, knew who I was; for I had given myself out as a merchant, and the son of a merchant, to escape visits and civilities which might be burdensome. We hesitated, we doubted long; but at length passion triumphed over prudence, and she was persuaded to fly with me and unite her fate to mine. We were married in secret, and passed nearly a year in the fondest affection. All that she exacted was permission to write to her father to assure him that she was a wife. When the time approached, however, at which she was to give birth to a child, fears assailed her, and remorse for having left her parent's house. She made me promise that, if real danger occurred, I would send for him with all speed, that she might receive his pardon and his blessing before she died.

"'Danger did come, my child, and death; but she had the satisfaction she sought. Her father and her husband were with her at the last hour, and she died forgiven, leaving me with a poor, helpless infant. The old man fled from the cottage almost in a state of madness, and my own mind was so troubled that for three days I forgot all the dangers of my situation. Those dangers were many, as I will soon explain to you; and to avoid them I was obliged to leave that cottage with the child as soon as the funeral was over, to consign the poor infant to the charge of a nurse, and to appear in the gay world of London with a calm face, and none of the external signs of that mourning which was sincerely in my heart.

"'I must now go back to tell some other events which had occurred. Like most young men of my day, I had been somewhat extravagant, and had lived a good deal beyond the income which my father allowed me. My debts amounted to between nine and ten thousand pounds when I first met with poor Mary Graves. My creditors were importunate; I had not the means of paying them; and, about seven months after my marriage, one of them applied to my father. He sent for me, and sternly demanded that I should give him an account of everything I owed. I did so; and, to my surprise, I found him much less enraged than I could have imagined. But it soon appeared that he had a project in his head which would compel me to disobey and offend him. He asked me if I had ever seen a young lady whom he named--in short, your own dear mother. I told him I had not, but that I had always heard her highly spoken of. He then informed me that he was acquainted with her father, and that, as she was an only child and heiress of considerable wealth, he had proposed to him a marriage between her and me. Your maternal grandfather had consented, upon the condition that the marriage should be agreeable to ourselves; and my father now said, "On condition of your marrying this young lady, I will at once pay your debts and settle a larger income upon you." I cannot minutely describe the scene that ensued. Of course, I was obliged to refuse; and I did so decidedly and at once. That was sufficient to excite great wrath; but my father smothered it in a degree, and requested me at least to see the young lady before I decided. I endeavoured, as humbly as I could, to represent to him that, by pursuing such a course, and then refusing to marry her, especially after what had taken place between him and her father, I should be grossly wronging and insulting her. But now the storm broke forth. He told me that a rumour had reached him, that I was either keeping or had married some low woman; that he had refused to believe such an assertion; but that my conduct gave such strong confirmation to the report that he would take means to ascertain, the fact; and if he found I had been guilty of so base a dereliction of my duty to him, and of my rank and station in society, he would cast me off for ever; would bequeath every farthing of the property which he could alienate--and that was nearly the whole--to strangers, and leave me what he justly called that most miserable of wretches, a titled beggar. He would not hear me utter a word, but drove me forth from his presence to seek comfort with my poor wife, from whom I was obliged to conceal the sorrows which my marriage with her had brought upon me.

"'Thus matters continued till her death--knowing that I was watched, and obliged to have recourse to a thousand stratagems to conceal my movements. Even after the poor girl's death, I knew my father too well to doubt that, if he discovered I had a son by such a marriage, he would carry his threat into execution; and in my difficulty and distress I applied to my friend Hayley, made him my confidant, and induced him to promise that he would acknowledge the child as his own and superintend his education, till such time as I should be enabled publicly to declare my marriage.

"'Some months after, I accidentally met with your mother in society, found her beautiful, amiable, and in every respect agreeable to me, and I took means to make myself agreeable to her. She was quite unconscious of what had previously taken place, and gave such encouragement as no well-educated woman would afford to a man whom she would afterwards reject. Her father, however, who was well aware of the whole, at first treated me very coldly; but as soon as I had made up my mind to offer her my hand, I thought it right to have an explanation with him; and I pointed out to him that I had acted honourably towards his daughter, in refusing to be introduced to her with such views, unless I were positively determined to carry them out. I soon overcame all his prejudices. He became attached to me. His daughter accepted my offered hand; and I wrote to my father, whom I had not seen for some months, hoping that my obedience, tardy as it was, would be accepted. He was not fond of writing, and he sent for me to come to him. When I went, my treatment was that which might have been shown towards a very lowly dependant. He told me that, if I wished to show myself dutiful, my submission came too late; that now I might marry your mother or not, as I pleased; that he approved of the match, but did not require it; and that, although he would allow me an income equal to my station and expectations, he would settle nothing upon me. He added, in a low but very menacing tone, "I have my doubts, young man--I have my doubts; and if ever I find that you have degraded your name or rank, I will leave you without one penny of which I can deprive you."

"'I was obliged to bear these tidings to my future father-in-law; but, with a certain portion of ambition, he was a kind-hearted and affectionate man. He knew that his daughter loved me. He felt confident, from all he had seen, that I loved her, and his consent to our marriage was given-- unwillingly, indeed, for he was sufficiently wealthy to look high for a match for his daughter, and to desire a settlement proportionate to her fortune. However, all objections were waived, and we were married. My allowance from my father was liberal. Her fortune was large, and eight months after, it was trebled by the death of her father. All that I possessed, however, and all that I should ever possess, except a very small portion, depended upon the earl's never discovering that I had contracted a previous marriage, and had had a son by a plebeian wife. My dear boy therefore remained under the care of Mr. Hayley, was brought home by him while yet almost an infant, acknowledged as his son, educated with great care, and displayed in person and mind, in character and demeanour----'

"But I need not read all that," said Henry. "After a few commendations on my boyhood, the letter goes on thus:--

"'You have seen him often, my dear Anne. You know him well, for I brought him up with you almost as a brother, intending to tell you that he actually was so, before you reached the age of womanhood. I loved him-- oh, how dearly and how well! And you loved him too, I am sure, with that fraternal love which was exactly what I desired. No act, no thought, of his ever gave me a moment's pain; and without wishing for my own father's death, I longed to be able to tell you and your mother that this boy was my son.

"'At length I was suddenly summoned away to Belford, to attend upon my father, who had been seized with severe illness. I could have wished to remain in London or in its neighbourhood, for I knew that the affairs of Mr. Hayley were getting into sad disorder. I had already supplied him, more than once, with considerable sums of money, beyond the expenses of my dear boy's education and maintenance; and a new demand had been made upon my purse, accompanied by a vague and timid threat.

"'However, I was obliged to set out. My father died a week or two after; and I proceeded from Milford Castle to Caermarthen, to consign his remains to the family vault. On my way back, my carriage was overturned at the bridge at ----, and I was taken up insensible, with concussion of the brain. I remained ill for several weeks, and my recovery was slow and difficult. For a long time the medical men would not suffer me to read or write at all; but at length, one morning, after I had been permitted to go out once or twice, I took up the newspaper on the breakfast-table, and was struck with horror and dismay on reading a paragraph headed, "The Late Forgery." I cannot dwell on the particulars even now, my dear child. Suffice it to say, that that paragraph showed me that my son, your dear brother, had been accused of forgery to a large amount; that he had fled from the country, after having been traced down to Northumberland, and thence to Caermarthen, in search of me, it seems; and that the officer who had followed him to Ancona had there, by the monks, been shown a dead body which they solemnly declared to be his. My feelings were almost those of a madman. I knew my boy was not guilty. I saw it all in a moment: that Hayley, a bankrupt gambler as he had proved, had committed the forgery, and had induced the boy, who thought him his father, to fly, in order to screen his supposed parent. At the same time, a vague, wild hope--which haunts me yet--that my child might still be alive, that the officer might have been deceived by a pious fraud of the monks--took possession of my mind, and made me act upon the moment with a degree of fierceness and resolution which perhaps I might not have had the courage to display if I had paused to deliberate. I sent for the man Hayley, with a threat that if he did not come I would fetch him; and when he appeared before me, all pale and trembling, I accused him at once of what he had done, as if I had had a revelation of the whole facts. He was always a coward, and in his attempts to deny and equivocate he betrayed himself; but I wrung the whole from him, as if I had taken his false heart in my hand and crushed out the only drops of truth it contained. I told him that if he did not instantly, and at once, confess the whole, I would carry him from my house to the office of the magistrate; that I would prove, from his own letters to me, that he was a bankrupt and a beggar but a few days before that forgery was committed; that I would make him account for the possession of every penny which he had expended since, and leave the keen hounds of justice to follow out the scent. He did at length confess the whole, and put it down in writing, signing it in my presence and that of Alsager, the butler, upon the condition that I would not reveal the facts till after his death, unless my boy ever appeared in England again.

"'My hopes of such being the case have daily decreased, but they linger still. I have caused many inquiries to be made, and secret investigations to be carried on; but the only fact I have been able to discover, which keeps expectation alive, is that there were two lads, nearly of the same age, in the convent, at the time my poor boy was supposed to nave died at Ancona. In case he should appear again, before you arrive at the age of one-and-twenty, I have besought my dear old friend Charles Hargrave, of Detchton-Grieve, near Belford, to watch carefully the events that take place in London; and if Henry should come back, to desire you to open this letter at once. The confession of Hayley, with several other papers concerning my private marriage and the boy's birth and education, are in an ebony cabinet in my dressing-room at Milford Castle. It is sealed up, with an order written upon it, to the effect that it is only to be opened by yourself, after you have reached the age of one-and-twenty.

"'And now, my dear child, farewell. These lines will not meet your eyes till your father's are closed. I know I have no need to exhort you to do justice to your brother, if ever you should find him; and if you should not, to clear his memory, after Mr. Hayley's death. Your mother's ample fortune will be sufficient provision for you, and the estates of the family will descend to you, without being specially mentioned in my will; but remember that you hold them in trust for him, if ever he should reappear. Should such be the case, I trust that the affection which existed between you and him, as boy and girl, may be a blessing to you both in more mature years. And now, that heaven may protect you, and send you a happier fate than mine, is the sincerest prayer of

"'Your father,

"'Milford.'"

Henry's voice faltered as he read the latter sentences of his father's letter to his sister, and there were tears in Lady Anne's bright eyes; but those tears did not run over till old Mr. Hargrave laid his hand upon hers, saying--

"Well and nobly, my dear child, have you fulfilled your excellent father's last behest, and justified his judgment both of head and heart."

"And I am a proud man," said Mr. Winkworth, looking at her through his spectacles, which he had been wiping more than once, for some reason or another; "for I shall one day call her child who has so brightly performed her duty to a dead father and a living brother."

"Hush, hush, hush!" exclaimed Lady Anne, starting up: "you will drive me away. Did you not promise, most faithless of Indians? You are as bad as the man in the fairy tale."

"And as ugly," replied Mr. Winkworth, laughing; "but I fear, dear lady, I shall never find a kind girl to restore me to my pristine form again--though, if there be a sorceress upon earth who could do it, she were Anne Mellent. Pray use your interest with her for me, my dear lord, for I would fain have youth and beauty back, as they appeared before they had been taken away by that fell enchanter, Time; and here are two people in the room--my old acquaintance Hargrave and my dear sister Lady Fleetwood--who can tell you that I was a very good-looking fellow nine-and-twenty years ago, when I was called Charles Marston."

"Charles Marston!" exclaimed Lady Fleetwood, almost with a scream. "You Charles Marston!"

"Yes, my dear Meg," replied Mr. Winkworth; "even your poor brother-in-law."

"But, dear me!" cried Lady Fleetwood, "Scriven told me you were a bankrupt, and Charles says you are very rich."

"Both, Meg--both," replied Mr. Winkworth. "There Scriven told truth, and Charles too. Do you not know that I never did things like other men? and when I was coming from India, as there were some dear friends who owed me a couple of lacs, and were too gentlemanly to pay an old friend, I made myself a bankrupt, that the task of suing them might fall upon my assignees. I had the hint, by-the-way, from Grange, the pastry-cook, who made himself a bankrupt every year, just to call in his accounts; but I rather think I am capable of paying a hundred shillings in the pound; and now all I have to say is--and I say it deliberately before witnesses--if Lady Anne

Mellent will condescend to take up with a merchant, and does not object to old age, and is very fond of a yellowish skin and a lean person, I am ready to marry her as soon as this wound in my shoulder is quite well; and I will settle a quarter of a million upon her on her wedding-day, whether she marries me or----Well, well, my dear; I won't."

So complete was the surprise of all present, except Mr. Hargrave and Lady Anne, that there was a dead silence for half-a-minute; and then Lady Fleetwood, whose wit always fixed upon something collateral, asked aloud--

"What are lacs?"

A burst of laughter followed, and perhaps it was the best way of ending the explanation.

Lady Anne made good her retreat as fast as possible; and after the gentlemen were left together, Henry laid before Mr. Hargrave and the rest all the papers which went to prove his title--Lord Milford's account of his private marriage, in a more detailed form than he had given it to his daughter; the documents with which he had been furnished by the monks at Ancona, to prove that he was Henry Hayley, notwithstanding his long assumption of the name of Middleton; some letters upon the subject from Don Balthazar de Xamorça; and, last, the certificate of the marriage of Charles Mellent and Mary Graves, and that of his own birth.

"For these latter papers," he said, "I am indebted to the activity and intelligence of that worthy man, Joshua Brown; and by your permission, gentlemen, I will have him in, and thank him, in your presence, for all he has done for me."

The pedlar was soon introduced, and in graceful terms the young nobleman expressed his gratitude, making him sit down beside him.

"There is a lady," said Henry, "who longs much to thank you, Mr. Brown, and to-morrow, before breakfast, you must let me introduce you to her. Will you take a glass of wine to drink her health?"

"Willingly, my lord," replied the pedlar, "for *my lord* you are; but yet I think you will find a little hitch somewhere that will want making smooth."

"In good truth, my dear young friend, he is right," said Mr. Hargrave, who had been looking carefully over the papers. "Here is every proof that you passed as Henry Hayley; every proof that Milford was privately married and had a son; every proof that he believed you to be that son, and that Hayley told him so; but no legal proof whatever that the boy who was given to the care of the nurse by your poor father was the same that Mr. Hayley brought home and acknowledged as his own."

"I've got it here, sir," said the pedlar, producing an old pocket-book. "I told the young lord that he'd want more of my help; so, between the time when I last saw him and the day I went to listen at Lady Fleetwood's, I ran down to the part of the country where they were married; for I recollected quite well having seen a pretty babby, about that time, at Mrs. Goldie's, the grocer's widow's, with black ribbons upon its little white frock; and I knew it was a nurse-child, for she had none of her own--never had. She's alive to this day; and there is her certificate that the child she delivered to Stephen Hayley, Esq. was the child of Charles Mellent and Mary Graves. She has got, moreover, the order, in Charles Mellent's own hand, to deliver the child to Mr. Hayley, and Mr. Hayley's acknowledgment that he had received it. She says, too, that with the child she gave him a gold box, the top of which unscrews, and in it she put a paper, like a careful old body as she is, with all the marks the child had upon it, such as moles and spots, and such like, which most of us have more or less."

"I've got the box!" cried Mr. Winkworth, *alias* Marston, who had broken off a conversation with his son to listen: "I owe that to the care of my little man Jim. It was found in the goods and chattels of poor Miss Hayley; but there is amongst her papers a memorandum, written in one of her saner moods, stating that the box was brought with the clothes of her brother's son, Henry Hayley, when he first came home from the place where he was nursed, and that she always preserved it carefully, in the hope that she might some time hear news of the poor child's mother, who must have been of some rank, as there is a coronet engraved upon the box."

"Bravo! bravo!" said Mr. Hargrave: "the only link wanting in the chain seems to be supplied; and now I think we shall do, without any further question."

And so think I, dear reader, too.

FOOTNOTES

Footnote 1: It may be as well to state, that this story of Carlo Carlini was told to the author, word for word, as it is here written down, by Carlo Carlini himself, then the author's servant. I cannot forbear adding, that a more faithful, honest, intelligent man never lived; and that, after having left my service, on my return to England, he entered that of my friend, the late Mr. Scott, Consul-General at Bordeaux, where he gained the esteem of all, and died, I believe, in the arms of his young master, the present Mr. Scott.